THE HUNTED RISE

BROTHERS, VOLUME II
ELIZABETH STEPHENS

• A note to my readers •

Besides being a *long* book with a lot of characters and deep, *deep* emotions, for me 2018 was a wild year full of life that needed living. I moved from Johannesburg to Berlin, started a new job, got engaged, spent a short stint as a potter in Dakar and was thunked over the head with inspiration for a few new stories, which demanded more attention and time than The Hunted Rise could afford for me to give them.

All in all to say, this book took me a long time to finish. So for those of you who've been waiting, I offer my gratitude for hanging in there, and to everyone reading this now, thank you, *spasibo,* and *muchas gracias* for your support.

Enjoy the hunt ahead.

What Came Before

Mer takes a job in the fighting pits owned by five brothers. There, she draws the attention of Knox — the fighter. Brought together by the foster system, Knox never thought he would put anything before his brothers. But when Mer's life is threatened by Spade, a member of the Russian mafia on loan to the Mexican cartel, he intervenes, killing Spade. Left behind is a bag of drugs totaling nearly thirteen million.

Dixon — the leader — puts the drugs in a safety deposit box and together, the brothers and Mer wait for the Russians to recover them. Dixon suspects they'll come with violence and blames Mer. He wants her dead. He orders Aiden — the killer — to deal with her.

Aiden doesn't. His focus is on the Russians. One of them in particular. Alina is the most beautiful woman Aiden has ever seen. He feels connection to her that shouldn't exist because up to now he has felt connection to no one and nothing.

One day he visits the hospital where Alina's brother, Gavriil, receives care. Gavriil tells Aiden that Erik, the head of the Russian mob, distrusts him and as punishment, has taken Alina. Aiden doesn't hesitate to kill three Russians to get her back.

In the meantime, Dixon finds himself increasingly distracted by Sara, a single mom who takes a job in the strip club he owns and operates. The Russians know this, so Sara and her son are taken hostage as collateral. It's through sheer cunning that she escapes. But she wasn't the only one targeted. Charlie — the lover — was also taken. Dixon knows now that it's time for him and his brothers to act.

They confront the Russians in the fighting pits. Erik refuses to believe they have the drugs. Unhinged, all of his focus is on hurting Gavriil and Alina. Aiden won't let that happen and when the Mexicans ambush the lot of them, Aiden grabs Alina and takes her with him because it's the only move he can make that will save her life.

They get Charlie out as well, though Charlie was left disfigured. Now, the brothers hole up in their home with Mer and a frightened Alina and wait for the Russians' second strike. They wait to be hunted.

Contents

Part V
The Spy

Gavriil

The ceiling is cracking. Little veins run across its surface and each time it rains, they throb with a pulse. I watch water drip from the center of the orange ring on the sagging tiles to the foot of my bed where my feet are separated around a blackened stainless steel pot. Plip. *Derr`mo.* Plop. How can it end like this?

We grew up with every luxury imaginable, Timur and I, and then Alina. She came along when I was fifteen and I will never forget how I hated her at first, the brown five-year-old whose only resemblance to the family was her red hair. She was the product of our father's infidelities and still he'd loved her mother more than ours, whatever Moscow whorehouse he found her in.

It took me nearly a decade to understand why and by then it didn't matter. Whatever soft spot our father had developed for the girl rubbed off, and quickly, to the point that within two years I found myself treating her like a spoiled little princess. I know that no wife I take – if I live long enough to see the day – will ever mean more to me than that little girl.

Alina. *Moya sestra.* I turn in the bed, wincing as I tilt my hips in the wrong direction. There's a bullet lodged somewhere in my right side that no one bothered to remove because then I was still Erik's prisoner. Now I'm just the one he hunts.

I do not sleep well anymore. I have not for the past eight weeks, since the battle of the barn where I lost both my siblings. Three weeks ago, I made it out of Erik's dungeon with the help of a few men still loyal to me and Timur and the memory of our father before us. Of the three men in my family, I am the only one left.

I kick my legs over the edge of the bed as images of Timur flood my mind – not those from bars and beaches and from our childhood. Instead, all I see is Timur's body falling to the side while Erik lords over him, expression carnivorous and mad and so unlike his father.

I thought it might have meant something that Erik's father is my uncle. That Erik is my cousin. That his brother, before he committed suicide, was my friend. His brother's death sent Erik over the edge. But I suppose that is what happens when you lose family.

As it stands now, Alina is the only thing keeping me from plugging two bullets into my own skull. I must know that she is safe and I must ensure that she remains that way. Then I will revisit my Makarov and remove myself from this nightmare, this wasted country, this town of miserable creatures.

It takes me three short steps to get from the bed to the window. It's covered in flaps of molding cardboard. I peel down one corner and look out onto the street. It's still dark. Not yet five am. Beneath the streetlamp kitty corner to where I stand, a single prostitute shivers against the cold. She looks young. Too young. And I know that she is likely to die soon since she is here on this street corner away from the road where the other women wait. Those are cartel women. Here, this young one is alone.

A dusting of snow covers parked cars and the sidewalks, but does not cling to the road. It has been six years since I have been home to Moscow where the too-young whores are ubiquitous and where the snow comes up over the tops of cars, forcing us indoors. Then, the servants would go out and fetch us food and the maids would cook elaborate dishes – pagach, baked fish, kutya, bobal'ki, kidney beans, potatoes – suddenly I realize I'm thinking about Christmas. It is Alina's favorite holiday. I wonder who she spent Christmas with, if the ones who have her are treating her right.

I slam my palm against the murky brown pane as I think of who I put my trust in to care for her. The doctor with no medicine. The man with no name. He is one of the brothers that own Seventh Street.

I go to my computer and pull up the file I have on them. It has been difficult to amass information from this room with poor internet connection supplied by a fallible USB stick.

Across town from Seventh, I'm not even close enough to see them passing beneath the window of this derelict, second story dungeon. Nor can I go sleuthing. I have not left this room and I will not because the streets belong to Erik and he looks for me still. The notion that the brothers would willingly return his drugs does not even occur to him. And it will not until he catches and guts me.

So I wait for Anatoly to bring me news of the outside and I plot all the ways I will use my bare hands to tear Erik's skin from his flesh and his flesh from his bones and I pray. I never believed in God, but I pray because Alina does and she is the last family I have left in this world. I pray that the doctor with no medicine will keep her safe. She is the only thing that matters. The one thing I cannot lose.

"Alina Popov," I repeat, starting to get annoyed.

So is the cop seated behind the faded wooden desk. He gives me the same glare he did when I showed up unannounced in his office yesterday, and the day before that, and the week before that.

"Ifeoma," he growls.

"Robert," I say, knowing he likes the sound of his full name as much as I do mine. The crease between his eyes becomes a canyon and I force a quick smile. "Bob. A girl who looks like *this* doesn't just disappear. Somebody out there somewhere is keeping her and with her family's connections it probably isn't someone who's keeping her just to feed her gummy bears and give her back rubs, if you get what I mean. She isn't being kept to be protected. She's being kept to be used and broken and hurt."

"Ify..."

"I mean, you know who her family is as well as I do. It's public knowledge that they make up the vast majority of the mob. They've taken over our town. Don't you want it back?"

Bob leans back in his green leather seat and crosses his knees over one another. He's got a broad upper body and a lean stomach. He used to have a gut but he got rid of that what felt like overnight. The night his wife died. I start to feel sympathy for the guy, but I push it away.

"Were you in the military or not? Are you even a cop?" I point at the military patches and insignias lining the right side of his chest whose meaning I can only guess at. On his left breast hangs a detective shield.

He grumbles out a non-response, but I cut him off. "Look, Bob." I rifle through the short stack of papers in my arms and slam a printed photo of Alina, Gavriil, and Timur Popov onto his desk.

In it, they're eating at Alasha, a local Kazakh diner. They're smiling together, completely oblivious to the fact that across the street some paparazzi is taking their picture.

"What the…"

"This was taken six months ago. They haven't been spotted together since. I know that a mugging landed Timur and Gavriil in the hospital three months ago, but on November third of last year, Gavriil left the hospital unexpectedly. He wasn't meant to be discharged for another week. That was the last day anyone saw any of the Popovs. I've canvassed the city. It isn't just me. Nobody has seen them since and I mean *nobody*. Don't you want to know what happened to them?"

I stand back with my arms crossed and let Bob sigh at me this time, even if it makes me want to shake him. "How many times do we have to go through this, Ify?" I purse my lips and open my mouth, quick to counter, but for once Bob beats me to the beat.

"We leave the Russians alone. They leave us alone. So far the only people they seem to be disappearing are themselves. They don't mess with us so why get involved in their battle?"

"I can't believe these are the words of a police chief," I balk, "let alone a military man. Are you saying you don't care about justice?"

The edges of his mouth twist down towards his hard, square chin. "I'm saying we let them deal out their own justice. We worry about our own."

"And what about Alina? She's a member of the community. Clean as a gosh darn whistle and popular too. There are random fans out there doing more than you are."

I throw my arms out to either side and stomp my right foot on the ground, flinging my wild hair about wildly. The afro sits like a halo around my face, obscuring my vision of Bob for a second. When it — and I — settle back down, I look into Bob's face, which is now bright like a stop light, and I brace myself. I've been here before and I know this look.

This is the part where he gets angry.

Bob stands and I thrust out my small breasts, not intimidated even though he's just shy of six feet, built like a goddamn refrigerator, and I barely crest five. "You listen to me. You are a crime author…"

"True crime," I correct. "That makes me a detective with incentive, something you evidently don't know much about."

His teeth clench and he slams his knuckles on the table, but I just shoot him a bored look. I'm not afraid of him. Dad always says I only have one moment in life to be afraid because fear isn't worth spending any more time on than that. This isn't my moment, so if he's trying to freak me out, he's going to have to try a whole heck of a lot harder.

"Goddammit, Ify, if she hasn't been reported missing, then we have no reason to look for her, and I'm not mad about it." He comes around the desk, grabs my arm and leads me to the doorway. "If we go digging, you know what we're likely to find? Bodies. Maybe yours next. So don't you go down any dark alleys. You may be clever, but you're not that clever. You keep asking these kinds of questions and next thing you know, you'll find Alina at the bottom of a ditch because you'll be lying right there beside her. *Then* who will you get to buy your book?"

Ignoring that last quip, I rip out of his grip and shout loud enough for the bullpen to hear, "So that's what you think? You acknowledge that she might be dead and you're not going to do anything about it?"

The carmine in Bob's cheeks rolls up to his black hair and down to his blue shirt. He reaches past me and grabs the door handle. "Goodbye, Ify."

"She's a human being and so are you. This can't be the best you've got to offer her."

Laughter behind me brings my head around. Clifford is standing by the emergency exit door letting in cold air and bright white light. He holds out a pack of cigarettes, knowing that after a conversation like this, it's the only thing that'll draw me off the scent. I groan, roll my eyes and take the pack as I follow him outside.

We pick a park bench across the street facing the lake, but aren't yet seated when I start laying into him. "The facts are clear and still Bob and y'all's whole fudging department are determined to ignore them." I pause long enough for him to light my cigarette, then kick a piece of concrete down the gentle, sloping hill. It skates across the glass of Lake Marsha before sinking. Bloop. It's gone now. With no more grace or ceremony than the entire Popov clan.

"The Russians have been running guns and drugs up and down the coast for the past decade. Then four months ago – poof! All the drugs are gone. The market price of heroin in the past few weeks has skyrocketed. You know how many tweakers have walked through the doors of Westfield since then? Over sixty overdoses. Eleven of those didn't make it. That's almost three people a week, Cliff. Desperate people taking their heroin laced with painkillers and rat poison because that's all the dealers are selling and that's all they can afford. Doesn't that mean anything to you?"

Clifford leans his head against the back of the park bench and blows smoke up into the air. It takes the form of a wispy cloud and holds for a moment, then dissolves. "You know the Russians aren't running dope."

I groan. He's entirely missed the point. Just as dense as the rest of them. "Of course they are." I collapse onto the bench and Clifford edges right up against my hip. Ordinarily I wouldn't mind, but today I'm fed up and scoot away from him.

He sighs, "They don't run the dope. The Mexicans do. They partnered – dope in exchange for weapons and women."

"Shit. Really? But the Russians never dealt in women before."

"They do now." Clifford flicks his hazel eyes up at me, staring through the tips of his shaggy blonde hair, and I remember the moment we became friends back when we were sixteen, locked up together in the same holding cell. I'd chained myself to the front of the police station as a protest against legislation prohibiting gay marriage and he'd been caught underage drinking. He'd called me a pretentious bitch. I'd called him a fudge-brained moron. Then he'd asked me for my number. I don't know what compelled me then to give it to him.

That was the same night I met Bob too. He'd been a kid, green and trying to prove himself. Then he'd enlisted and I didn't see him again for almost a decade. When he came back, Clifford and I were sunk in the cement of a fast friendship and Bob wasn't a boy anymore.

"So they're working in partnership?"

"Shit, Ify. How'd you not know that?" Clifford rolls his eyes and touches my hand. I stare down at the contact.

"I didn't realize it was common knowledge," I grunt.

Lifting my hand to his mouth, Clifford brushes his lips across my knuckles, all sensual-like. I know he's only doing this to tease me — my body's quick to respond to stimuli, and I like sex. Sue me. But not with Clifford. Clifford's like my brother and I know he feels the same even though his teasing is borderline sometimes. Like now. I jerk away.

"Cut it out."

Cliff grins and pulls away from me with a half laugh. "You're so damn focused on Alina Popov, you're not asking any of the right questions." He puffs out smoke.

"What are you, some kind of oracle? What do you know about asking the right questions?" I stand and hoist my purse higher up onto my shoulder, push back my hair, make a face. "And why wouldn't I be focused on Alina? She's the subject of my new book. She's famous, has a huge fan base, is connected to the mob and is one of the most beautiful women in existence."

"You mean she'll sell when you shove her on the front cover of your next book. I can just see the title now. Murder in Paradise: Alina Popov dead at twenty-five. You'll make a killing." Clifford drops his cigarette butt so he can use both hands to gesture.

I narrow my eyes. "I don't like what you're insinuating."

Clifford shrugs, then pulls out a second cigarette. He doesn't bother offering me one, knowing I won't take it. Had an uncle who used to smoke once. It killed him. And I know what my folks would do to me if they ever caught me with a cigarette. It's just hard sometimes with Cliff, especially. The kid knows all my worst vices.

"I'm not insinuating anything, Ify," Cliff says. The breeze that rolls through feels like ice and tastes like snow. "You're a successful author. The kind people line up at bookstores to get an autograph from. To get where you are and stay there you have to do shitty things."

"That's not true." I frown.

Clifford adjusts his blue jacket adorned with a little silver nameplate and a badge number that I want to rip off and chuck at his big stupid head. "You're not a good guy, Ify. Stop pretending you are."

"You're right. I'm a woman. And you're just a junior detective who doesn't know diddly squat about anything."

"Ha!" Clifford laughs theatrically, and shakes his head. "At least I'm not pretending to hunt for Alina Popov when all I really want is to find her with a story written across her corpse."

"Go flip yourself." I stomp my right foot, toss my unfinished cigarette and start back up the hill.

"Come on Ify, you know I'm just yanking your chain," Cliff says and I can hear the smile on his tone. Oooh! He knows how to push my buttons. I've had enough.

"Yeah well I've had my chain yanked hard enough for one day. Plus, I've got a date."

"A date? With who?"

A junkie who, for the whopping sum of sixty bucks, has been tracking a member of the Russian mob for the past three days on my request. "None of your darn business."

"Aw, come on Ify. I've got something for you. About the Russian and the Mexican connection. It might help you with Alina!" He's shouting after me now, voice chasing me to my car parked beneath a spindly cherry tree whose limbs are bare and crooked, like broken bones.

I'm not interested – at least not at the moment. I've got too many other leads for me to consider before groveling at Cliff's feet. So rather than wait for him to jog across the park towards me, I roll my eyes and rev my Jeep's engine. With or without his help, I'm going to find her, dagnabbit, even if trying kills me.

Gavriil

Anatoly sits perched on the edge of my desk while I pace the length of the room. It is no bigger than the closet of my home – a house which Anatoly tells me is under surveillance twenty-four hours a day, every day.

"He keeps watch, but all he cares about are his shipments."

I nod, knowing but only because Anatoly is the one who has been my eyes, watching Erik and the brothers and the bank. The only eyes I have outside of this room. "He is moving many shipments these days."

"More and more. We met with the Mexicans Tuesday and they requested the product in double to recover the drugs that were lost."

"Drugs that the brothers will give back. The brothers do not want either – drugs or money."

"They haven't retrieved it from the safety deposit box and Erik still doesn't believe they have it. That's why he doesn't attack the brothers' house."

"*Da*, I know this," I say to him, before switching to our mother tongue. It is uncomfortable for me to speak to him in English, but he has been here much longer than I have. Since he was a boy. Now, even though his accent carries little inflection in English, the same cannot be said for his Russian. I used to tease him about his American lilt, back before when

I used to tease and laugh and make jokes. It is only fair, for he jokes all the time about my English, which, like Alina's, is piecemeal at best.

In this slightly accented Russian, Anatoly says, "He cares only to recover the money from the drugs that were lost so as to appease his father. We are getting questions from Roman. Questions that Erik cannot answer."

Roman leads the *Bratva's* operations worldwide. Patriarch of all patriarchs, he has sat with the title since my father died. My father led the *Bratva* before him. I was meant to take over after he was shot, but I didn't want it so the title passed to his brother. Roman gave the US operations to his son Erik and now I am here, Timur is dead, Alina is taken, and shipments of women continue to arrive every day in a desecration of the empire my father lived and died to build.

My chest is heavy. I can hear it scream though I do not give voice to the sound. "I can imagine he would want to know why his only son's operations have taken such a turn in his absence. We never dealt in women before."

"Jordan," Anatoly sneers.

"Jordan," I growl. Jordan is the lawyer who helps Erik. He plays Erik like the pawn that he is while Erik only thinks he has the upper hand. It is because of Jordan that we were able to set up operations importing women into the States so quickly, and it is because of Jordan that Erik rushes to import so many more — because for all the suffering it causes, Jordan takes most of the profit.

"Bastards, the both of them." Anatoly runs both hands back through his hair as he exhales deeply. The room is so small, when I pass in front of him we are separated by a nose.

A caged bird has more freedom. "And Erik is a man who sees the path to light and turns only to the dark. It will not be long before he breaks."

"Even if he does, he will always have support from Jordan and from his father. He may ask questions, but Roman will always support Erik. He always has. His allegiance to family is the one thing that will never break."

"It didn't used to be this way."

"I know," I answer.

Anatoly watches me pace the room with his jaw clenched. "You should be our leader."

I don't respond, though I feel Anatoly's gaze on my face.

"You should lead the *Bratva* as you were meant to."

"But I don't."

"You can still negotiate your freedom. You just need to speak with Roman."

"Roman is not likely to leave Russia." I click my tongue against the backs of my teeth.

"He will. Eventually. When Erik's fuck ups get too big to ignore."

"But you don't know that," I snap. "Do you know anything? What do you come here for? To bait me?"

Anatoly's eyebrows draw together. "You will be free of this place. We just need to wait…"

I throw my fist into the bathroom door, carving out a small depression in its face. "Wait for when?"

Anatoly frowns with his mouth that has always been too large and his eyes that have always been too slight. He is full Russian, but could just as easily have been Greek. His mother is Yakut, so his skin is darker than mine and the hair on his head and the stubble on his face is black. His eyes are dark as well, but he got his bone structure from his father.

I knew the man before cancer took him and he was as Russian as they come. Hard jaw and cheek bones, head shaped like a sledgehammer and about as dense as one, but anyone that knew Anatoly's father, knew that he loved that Yakut woman. Erik had always taunted Anatoly for it. Yakut people looked too Asian. Too far from what he considered pure.

In the end, what Erik thought never mattered much to the rest of us until the death of his brother and then my father. But now everything is in ruin, while Erik lords gleefully over the desolation.

This is my fault. *Pashol nahui*, this is my fault. In English, I say, "Leave, Anatoly. *Bajalsta.*"

"*Prosti*, boss. You know I respect you. I am your man on the inside."

"And right now, I want you outside. Go." I turn from him, swiping the bag on the table that he brings me. I show no gratitude even though the meager contents of this bag – filled with things that prevent starvation – are worth more than Anatoly's, life in Erik's eyes. "Next time send Ivan."

"Ivan?"

"Ivan."

"Ivan can't be trusted."

"No one is trusted."

Another long pause fills the gap before Anatoly speaks. "You can trust me. I would never lie to you. You are *moy brat* and you have always been my *Avtorityet*," he says, using the *Bratva's* term for leader.

"This is no *Bratva*. This is *mafiozi*. We are not brothers. Just criminals."

Anatoly does not delay long. He knows that this is the end of the conversation. It is only at the door that he turns to me. In English, he says firmly, "The pressure is building. More and more of the men speak of you in hushed whispers when they know Erik isn't around. The shipments to Elmer aren't turning profits quickly enough and most of the men still working lived under your father. They're also disgusted dealing in women."

He goes on, "There will be a meeting soon, and Roman will have to come from Russia. That will be the time. It won't be tomorrow or the next day, but it won't be long. You won't be here forever and you won't be alone. I am with you, brother."

He waits for my reply, but I don't give it. I stare down at the single pillow on my mattress. Sleeping on that mattress sends flares of pain shooting up in all the places I bear shrapnel and the pillow is no help. I stare down at its grotesque and lumpy form until eventually the door closes and I am alone. Anatoly says I am not. He may not be lying, but I know the truth: here, in this cell, alone with only my thoughts and darkness, I will not last months.

Charlie

I'm with a woman, laughing like a lunatic – no, laughing like I used to – her long, tan legs are wrapped around my hips and we're just having a fucking ball now, aren't we? My dick is hot and hard and this bitch knows what she's doing. I want to flip her over but I can't move my arms. Maybe she's got them tied down. Anyways, it doesn't really matter.

I buck my hips and she laughs some more, moaning deep when I hit that spot I know she likes. I want to use my hands, but they're stuck somewhere above me and that's alright. This is all alright. Ain't nothin' wrong with a bitch riding my cock, hair so long and blonde it tickles my chest when she bends over to kiss me. I don't like kissing and that other girly shit, so I move my face and let her suck on my neck. I tell her how much I like it in words and moans, but she doesn't seem to hear me because she asks me how she's doing.

She's doing, I tell her, but she asks me again. And then a third time. And her voice darkens and I want to push her off me, but my hands are still fucking tied down and my whole body feels like its sinking. It is sinking. I'm sinking into the mattress like Johnny Depp in Nightmare on Elm Street. The thought gives me panic.

I remember watching that movie in the first foster home I ever stayed in. The terror I felt then seeing Johnny Depp explode in a fountain of blood starts to surface but this fucking hoe is still whispering and her pussy's still clenched around my dick, and it's hot but no longer wet and it feels like it's burning. She is burning, and so am I.

She pulls away from my face so that I can see hers and I scream, but there's no sound. There's only falling as she tilts her head to the side. Don't I like it? She asks me as her pussy ignites and we both go down in a ring of fire. Isn't she pretty? She says, while the cut that slashes across her face weeps thick blood all the way past her chin and down her neck. Her fake tits are oozing crimson too from too many stab wounds to count.

Jesus baby, you're bleeding, I want to tell her, but she's crying now and then she's laughing and her blonde hair is red and its caught fire and so has the bed and I remember that everything burns if the flame is hot enough, the world is nothing but a crucible.

I open my eyes.

It's dark and even though the window is open, letting in frost-laced air, I'm soaking wet. The tee shirt and boxers I've got on are toast and so are the sheets on this shitty twin mattress. I kick them off. I kick everything off and I just lay there, letting the wind from the fan dry my eyeballs until they're like her pussy in my dream. Hot and dry and craving moisture.

I want to cry but I've done that already and it's fucking old now. So I just lay there and glance at the gun on the bedside table. The barrel's pointed right at me and I stare it down, daring it. Sometimes I imagine that the neighbors I've got in this shitty fucking building – the ones who fuck like banshees – will fuck so hard it knocks some of the ceiling free.

That hunk of plaster'll land on the lampshade and when the lamp falls over, it'll knock against the gun and the gun will fire and end me. I'll never even wake up. Never even know it's coming.

I don't keep the safety on so it's possible. Possible, but unlikely. And not a guaranteed death. Maybe it would just hit me in the shoulder and then I'd have to go to the hospital where Mer and Clifton and the whole fucking motley crew would coalesce around me and ask me stupid questions like what was I thinking keeping a loaded gun that close to my bed, or was I trying to kill myself. Course I wasn't, I'd reassure them. Because if I were trying to kill myself I'd reach over there, put the gun against my temple and pull the trigger.

I'm not that brave. No, I'm a fucking coward. Always have been the weakest of my brothers. Aiden damn sure wouldn't have indecision like this. If the bastard cared enough about himself to end his suffering, he'd have done it a long time back. No, he likes the suffering. I don't. I don't like the suffering. But I don't like the alternative either. It's too bleak to imagine. Too empty. Too unknown.

So instead I lay awake, staring at the gun and hoping that some divine entity or freak accident or horny upstairs neighbors will knock loose a piece of ceiling and that I never wake up.

I get up and head out of the bedroom. It's smaller than the one I'm used to. The first few nights I walked right into the door or the wall, because at home the door's two feet to the left. Home. I catch myself on the doorframe as the thought brings me up short. There's no such thing as home anymore. There's just prying eyes. They see everything but understand nothing.

Mer thinks I want to die. My brothers probably do too. Sara and Knox think I'm salvageable. But they don't know, because they didn't see…

Her face. Her breasts. The blood.

I didn't love her but that didn't matter either.

The pain.

I find my way to the living room and go to the punching bags in the corner. I've got two set up side-by-side. One's thirty pounds heavier than the other. I go to the lighter one first and jab, hit, upper cut, body shot, kick. When I've worked up a sweat, I go to the heavier bag and try to replicate the moves I always saw Aiden use in the ring, back at the barn when it still stood. I'm no Aiden though. I'm no Knox. I'm no Mer. I'm not even a Dixon and he hates fighting. I'm just hitting the bag because I want to feel something but I don't know what it is I want to feel. What am I after?

I don't know. I don't know anything but that one memory. The one that is crystallized out of time. So I hit the bag and resist it as I do the images dripping in scarlet. Because once it starts, I am no longer Charlie. I am no longer a man. I am no longer anything.

Maybe I never was.

Ify

"You said you were tracking him. I gave you sixty bucks!"

Lenard scratches his neck and dances from foot-to-foot like he's got to pee. He's only eighteen but he looks like he's at least forty with thin, pasty skin I can see all his veins through. They dance like severed snakes in the wells of his eye sockets each time his eyes flick back and forth, like he's struggling to focus on me.

"Sixty bucks to track him. It'll be another sixty if you want me to tell you where he went." He licks his lips, clenches his jaw, sniffles.

"You cheeky bastard." I give him my best impression of a Catholic nun scolding her least favorite pupil, but it has no effect. He's not looking at my face, but at the black leather fanny pack slung around my hips.

"What's it worth to you?" He smiles, revealing a row of blackened upper teeth. Most on the bottom are missing completely. He's rotting from the inside out and as I reach into the belt at my waist, I know he's got just a few years left, and that's only if he doesn't OD first. But I'm desperate, and if not from me, he'd be getting the money from somewhere else, right?

"Not much for a big shot author like you," he says, bringing the cash to his lips and inhaling deeply. Probably the only thing in the alley that doesn't smell like piss or feces aside from me is that money – and it doesn't smell good.

"Alright, you got your cash. Where'd he go?"

"Fifty-Fourth and Eighth."

"Fifty-Fourth and Eighth," I repeat and I can feel my face scrunch up. "Fifty-Fourth and Eighth? You're messing with me. That's past the projects. Nobody goes out there."

Lenard smirks. "Nobody but the cartel and their pros." Lenard takes a step back into a pitch black shadow. The light from the fire raging in the oil barrel two blocks up doesn't reach him. Neither does its warmth.

It's freezing out here yet the Ternary is lousy with homeless. I wonder how many of the bodies lining these three square blocks will freeze to death by morning. The hypothermia trucks don't come this far out of town. Too dangerous. If my friends – or my parents, heaven forbid – ever knew I came out this far, they'd throw a collective conniption.

"You think he's dealing with the Mexicans?" My spidey senses are tingling and I begrudgingly admit to myself that I might need Clifford's help on this after all. If there is a connection between the mafia and the cartel and something went wrong, that could be very clear and very compelling evidence as to who's responsible for Alina's disappearance. And if the cartel has her, then it's unlikely she'll last very long.

My fans are going to love it, and I'm feverish as I jot down just a few more chicken scratch notes. With as dark as it is, I hope only that they'll be legible enough when I type them up at home.

Lenard makes a face and glances down at my notebook. "Maybe. But seems unlikely Mexicans would deal with a Russian after what happened at the barn."

"The barn?"

"You don't know about the barn?"

"What barn?"

Lenard laughs. "You asked for information on the tail. Not on the barn."

I groan and reach beneath my down coat again for my fanny pack. This time I only pull out a twenty. "That's all you're milking me for today, hustler."

He crushes the twenty in his fist. His eyes are glossy and glimmering. "The barn out on the 401 South. Doesn't have an address but it's the exit after Glenrock. Dirt road leads to a gravel pit. Used to be a fighting pit. Some shit went down there. I'm not sure what exactly, but talk is that some Russians got plugged that side and Mexicans are the ones who done it. Ain't nothing left now but ash."

"How long ago was this?"

Lenard pauses to consider. I know his estimate of time is poor to nonexistent, so I don't expect much in the way of accuracy. "I don't know. Not that long ago. Maybe three months. Actually, two. Yeah, two. There was a raid on the Ternary the night before. I remember that." He's nodding to himself, and speaking under his breath in a half-hearted whisper.

My interest is piqued, pen flitting across the page like a subway rat across the tracks. "Are you serious?" Two months ago. If he's right, that's the same time the streets went quiet and not too long after Alina and the Popovs disappeared.

Lenard shrugs. "That's what they're saying."

"Who's they?"

"The streets." He shrugs again.

I'll take it. "This is good. So umm," I race back through my notebook, trying to remember what it was I came here for. "So Anatoly. If not one of the cartel men, you think he's seeing a prostitute?"

Lenard's hand is twitching and though his body is slouched in boredom, his eyes are wild and eager, like he's late for an appointment. I look at my crumpled cash in his hand. He probably is. "Dunno. He goes in with a full gym bag, leaves without it."

"Maybe he found one he likes," I speculate, "one the other Russians don't know about, or aren't trading. Maybe she's even in the cartel so he has to see her off the main strip so he doesn't get caught if there's beef between them. Maybe he told her something. You know what time she gets there?" This is great news. Great flipping news. Pros are excellent to harvest information from. Like Lenard, they're willing to do a lot for a little and don't ask questions in return.

Lenard shakes his head. "Nah. You paid me to trail Anatoly, not the chick. Sixty bucks and I'll tag her for you though."

"No, I wouldn't ask you to do that. She's not important."

He shrugs. "I don't know what you'd ask. You're crazy."

I laugh. "Coming from the guy who's eaten deep fried rat before."

"Can't be picky when you live on a budget."

I roll my eyes though I'm sure he can't see much of my expression in the shadow of my hair. "Any reason you think it might be dangerous?"

Lenard shakes his head. "Nah. Goes in for about twenty minutes every time. Sometimes more. He's packing but they're always packing." I'm pretty sure he means the Mafiosos, but he could just as well mean everyone in the whole damn city with one notable exception – me.

My folks always tried to get me to carry 'in my line of work.' But I'm pretty sure I'd just as likely shoot myself as I would a robber. I'm terrible with guns, much to my uncle's shame. He's a sniper in the Marines and bleeds red, white, and blue. Oohrah, baby…

"Anything else you got for me?" Squinting, I write down what he's said. Every word and nuance. What's that expression again? The diamonds are in the details?

"The place is in the apartment above an old Chinese restaurant."

"Old Chinese restaurant. Got it." I glance at my watch, though I can't see the time in the darkness.

"You leaving?" he calls. I didn't even realize that I'd already turned away from him.

"Damn straight. You're a goddamn saint, you know that right?"

He shuffles, making a ton of sound in all of his clothes, which are lined in the newspapers I bring him. "Where you going?"

"For Chinese food."

"Now?"

"Girl's gotta eat!"

"Alone?"

I shrug. "I'm here aren't I?"

"You a crazy bitch." He laughs and I wave at him over my shoulder, watching as his frail form disappears into the shadow of the next building. Bodies line the block, but most are passed out or comatose from whatever they're on. As such, nobody tries to bother me as I reach the main road leading out of the labyrinthine squatter town of Ternary.

I hang a left and then another, moving fast until I reach streetlights and beyond that, the sounds of cars. I parked about a mile away – any closer and my Jeep would've been stripped the second I stopped it.

Once I'm behind the wheel, I look up the address. Pros all work nights and it's not even nine yet, so she probably just started. If I hurry I may just be able to book her next slot. I bite my bottom lip, hoping that the girl will talk or better yet, that Anatoly left something behind.

Fifteen minutes later and I'm throwing the car into park some place far enough from the cartel's prime strip to avoid getting car jacked. I shove all my valuables into the locked safe I had custom installed behind the gear shift, between the driver and passenger seats so that the only things I keep on me are my Nokia, cash, my license, my library card, and my notepad.

The Nokia is a brick that, in the past, has made a call to only one individual – Clifford. He's always been there in case I get into a jam. That one time I was writing about the unsolved murder of a thirteen-year-old girl, I snuck into a backwoods slaughterhouse. I thought the slaughterhouse might have been where they buried the body. Turns out, it was where the family was keeping her – alive. I helped her escape, but was caught by the family who tried to use me in a satanic séance. By the time Clifford got there, I had already been tied to a wooden post the family was trying to set on fire. Thank the lord I still had my Nokia in my pocket.

As far as cash goes, I keep two grand on me in case I get robbed. I like to keep enough on me that they're satisfied when they realize I didn't bring any of my cards. And I learned the hard way that one grand isn't enough.

My license I stash in my pocket whenever I'm investigating anything – not to prove who I am, but to prove who I'm not. It might have helped me in proving I wasn't a demon in the slaughterhouse scenario if I'd had it on me – and if they'd been interested in anything more than my skin color. I learned that night the hard way that backwater psychos tend to think the devil is black.

Lastly, my library card. At first, I thought it would help convince muggers and the crazies I encounter that I am who it says I am on my ID, but the last couple times I was mugged I realized it served a tertiary aim: it confuses the heck out of people. I don't know if it's because it comes across as innocent or awkward next to all of the other stuff, but twice I've been mugged with it in my pocket and the muggers gave the cash back. One said that he went to the same library when he was a kid. The other gave no explanation. Just shrugged and scrunched up his face, then meandered away.

The notepad, I keep on me for obvious reasons.

My hair bounces along as I jog and I make sure to keep up the pace too because the pimps glare at me from their parked cars and the pros eye me up and down like I'm either a threat or fresh meat. If I stop for too long, I know I'll be in a world of shit. Not that I think I'm pretty enough to be any sort of a threat, but ugly never stopped a pimp from whoring a woman out either – or a John from picking one up.

I round the next right corner and start down the block. The number of pros here dwindles. Only the ones without pimps and who aren't affiliated with the cartel come this far. Away from the heavily trafficked roads, they're lucky to get any pickups – or unlucky. I guess it depends on your perspective.

A younger girl wearing a pair of underwear, fishnet stockings, and a short down vest shivers on the corner. I think to give her my coat, but I can't know if she's with a pimp for *sure* and I don't want to get into any sort of situation before I meet with Anatoly's lady. Plus, it's cold out. Smiling at her slightly, I cross the street onto Fifty-Fourth. She smiles meekly back.

The first building on my right has open holes for windows and a door barred by caution tape and big red signs I don't stop to read. I cross the street when I see a sign for Mr. Chang's. The paint is faded and the brick building abutting it has totally collapsed in the center, spilling so much wreckage and rubble into Mr. Chang's that I can see through the front entrance. It's wide open.

I nudge the door open with my foot and am greeted by the sound of a rusting hinge groaning, and wood scraping over tile. Even though I expect her to be up on the second floor, I still would have expected a warmer reception than this. The whole ground floor is abandoned and the only thing that gives it away as a restaurant is the counter in the back.

Vertical bars cover the shelves behind it, but all the alcohol is gone and all the locks swing freely, like prisoners escaped.

Debris litters the space where tables and chairs used to be. Now the whole place just smells like dry concrete, piss and dead animal. Long dead. I don't linger to investigate which kind. Heck, I'm not even sure it isn't of the human variety.

There are stairs to the left so I take them, sure to keep to the outsides of each slat because their centers look slightly caved, and wet. I'm not scared as I reach the landing, but I am uncomfortable. It's dark – I mean, really dark – and though my hand reaches into my pocket for the flashlight on my Nokia, I don't pull it out.

Some instinct in the back of my head tells me to be quiet, to be still, to leave but I know that's ridiculous. Prostitutes, as a general rule of thumb, don't tend to be the belligerent types unless they're doped up but if she were doped up, then she'd probably make more noise than this. No. I think back to the smell of decay downstairs. If she's doped up and making this little noise, she's more likely passed out or ODed.

I approach the door in front of me – the only door at the end of a long, windowless hall – and I stretch out my hand. The grey wood is damp to the touch and there's no knob so when the wind howls against the outside of the building, the whole door sways. It hits the lintel in uneven thumps that remind me of feet on stairs. I glance over my shoulder, but the darkened stairwell I've come up from is just as it was – a dark and lonely obsidian.

But still. I'm not afraid. This isn't my moment.

I reach past the doorframe and ease myself inside the room. It takes my eyes a second to adjust to the hazy light.

Fuzzy orange beams from the street lamps outside filter in between the cardboard patches taped over the window. Similarly, there are slats in the wooden walls, through which I can see rotting insulation.

A twin bed sits to the left and across from it is a desk. Straight ahead is a chest of drawers and just beside that is a bathroom with no door to prevent me from looking in on the smallest shower and toilet combo I've ever seen. The room is empty but somehow still feels lived-in and I am relieved. She's just out for a minute. Maybe this room belongs to the girl on the corner, or maybe I passed her on my way here.

In her absence, I go right for the drawers since there's nowhere else in this room to hide anything. The top drawer is full of men's stuff and I know I've hit the jackpot. Maybe Anatoly likes her enough to keep some things here. Not common, but not unheard of. I don't find anything but boxers, undershirts, and socks so I move to the next drawer, filled with tee shirts, sweatpants and jeans. The next and final drawer contains only boots and sneakers. Wait a second…

I go through the drawers again and a tornado takes off in the back of my skull, then sweeps the rest of my body. I can hear the ocean raging in my temples as it occurs to me that these are men's things. *All* of them.

Turning around, I notice the silver gleam of a Macbook lying shut on the desk – something most pros hustling in this neighborhood can't afford, and those that can don't leave lying around – before frowning. Because the second thing I notice is that the door I've just walked through is shut and dead-bolted and in the blackness of the shadows behind it, there is a man watching me.

Gavriil

I am prone on my bed, but I am not asleep when I hear the door downstairs creak. It is a subtle sound, followed by muffled footsteps. They do not bend the floorboards of the stairs as Anatoly's boots do, but rather tread with calculated caution. My pulse is slow and measured even though I cannot help but wonder how they found me. I refuse to think it could have been Anatoly's betrayal but I know that there are few other options.

The cops do not come here, the brothers would not search for me and even if Alina wanted to, the one I entrusted her life to would never have allowed it. If, by chance, she managed to escape, she would not have made it this far. I am well into cartel territory now. Even Erik would know better than to look here unless he was explicitly instructed and then he would have had to broker a deal with the right men – cartel men and *my* men.

A savage disappointment rivals the anger in me as I remove the twin Makarovs from beneath my pillow, unlock the door and move against the wall beside it. The footsteps are terribly quiet and I almost resent the man for being clever enough to fool this building into believing he's lighter than he is. Who is he, this one who moves like a ghost? Who did Erik find worthy of the task of killing me?

I click off the safety just as the body comes up against the other side of the door. I can feel heat radiating from the man standing there, so close, and my bloated but underused muscles are starved for a fight to the point that I have half a mind to put my guns away. *Pizda rulyu.* I remember that I am not yet to join Timur because I first must take care of Erik in order to care for Alina. My stillness echoes through me and I am stone as the door opens and a smudge of black passes through it and into my room. *I hooly?*

As I shut and lock the door, moving with a silence that is not breached, the room grows, expanding rapidly in size around her slight, petite frame. For a moment I think that I am looking at a child until she walks to the far wall, heading straight for the chest of drawers, and I recognize that no child is built this way. Though her shoulders are narrow and her waist − even in a coat − is big enough that I could fit both hands around it, her hips, thighs and ass are all woman. Perfectly round and deliciously thick.

I've had porn to keep me company these sleepless nights, but I never liked watching it and seeing her here now, I don't react as I should. Instead of plugging a bullet in the center of her back, I watch her for a moment as she moves from the first drawer down to the second. She seems to be whispering to herself. I can't make out the words and I wonder if she's even aware of it.

Something in the bottom drawer must startle her because her rapidly flitting fingers freeze and she stands up. She turns and I watch her small face, shrouded by so much hair, as she sees me. Women in Russia do not have hair like this. Like an African princess. Or an African warlord. Which is she? Both?

Is the contradiction why Erik sent her? Did he know I would hesitate to kill one with her face?

It is not a beautiful face to be sure – at least not in the traditional sense – with a nose that is too small and a mouth that is too large and slanted eyes atop high cheeks. Then there is the issue of her body which, like her face, is also wildly out of proportion. Her tiny upper body does not complement the full, tight curves below her waist.

Put together the way she is, she looks like a sex doll. Something you'd buy in a store if you had all the parts to choose from and could put them together yourself.

Every inch of my skin stretches and tingles. I do not allow myself the breath I am so eager for, but wait. There are two moves for her to make and she knows it: run for the window and hope the fall does not kill her, or do what she came here to do and pull the gun out of the pack at her waist.

She lifts up her hands and her mouth opens, lips so large they look drawn on. "Oh wow. Hi. You must be Joe. You told me to come to Fifty-Third and Eighth for my audition. I'm ready to go whenever you are. Really eager to hit the streets. I could use the cash."

I don't say anything, but she must not have expected me to because she continues speaking without taking a breath. "Oh dagnabbit. Are you not Joe? I must be in the wrong building then. I didn't see any street numbers but the door downstairs was open so I just assumed. This is Fifty-Third Street, right?"

She laughs and shakes her head, playing the silly little girl role poorly. This is an unconvincing performance, and in its theater, utterly confusing. No assassin hired by the *Russkiy mafiozi* would behave like this. So unprofessional. Is this all that Erik thinks of me? And yet…I haven't killed her. Perhaps he is smarter than I give him credit for, because there is something that stays my hand.

"I'm so dumb. I better get going. Joe will be waiting for me and I can't miss my chance…"

She walks confidently towards the door. I take two steps to the left to block it. Now she is directly in front of me, a rough gap of about three strides between us. She stands in the center of the room and a triangular swatch of orange light from one of the street lamps outside cuts across the bridge of her nose, illuminating the brightness of her eyes and the darkness swimming within them. Her skin is nearly as black, with just a hint of an amber glow, while her hair in contrast, shines pure midnight. Only her lips are pink on the inside when they part. So is her tongue when she licks them.

She glances at the window with intent so obvious that I reach the window before she lifts a foot off of the floor. I grab her arm, take her little body by the waist and throw her onto the bed. She doesn't make a sound, just tosses her bushy hair back and edges across the mattress, tipping the pot of water in the process. I don't make a sound, but internally, I groan. It looks as if I'm sleeping on wet sheets tonight.

"I'm a building inspector," she says. The girl's voice is low, but I still find it grating that she can speak so incessantly.

Why say three words when one will do? This is the mantra under which I was raised – a notion that she spits at as ribbons of speech flow from her lips. Which is why it vexes me that my cock doesn't seem to feel the same sense of irritation. It is at attention for this girl. Hard as a tire iron. I would reach down to shift its length in my jeans, but at this point it would cause me physical pain even to touch it.

"I'm hired by the city to canvas these blocks for a new development. You weren't supposed to be here. This place was supposed to be empty except for a prostitute I heard was squatting here. I was supposed to convince her to move out. Then the developers could come in and do what they do to all neighborhoods. Gentrify — am I right?" She chuckles awkwardly.

My voice is flat when I respond. "Do I look like prostitute?"

"No," she says, holding up one hand. She licks her lips and I notice that the upper is a darker brown than the lower and between them her teeth are bright white. "Not exactly." She shakes her head fiercely, closes her eyes and swallows hard. But it isn't in fear. I don't understand it. "I mean, you don't look like a prostitute."

She wears no jewelry and no makeup and from where I stand, a cool, clean scent rolls off of her like a fresh breeze. Lily and coconut and something softer, something subtle. It pulls at a childhood memory.

A day trip from Moscow, our father had taken us to swim in Lake Oka in Polonova. It had been freezing, but the family had been together and I can recall the exact moment the sensation had come over me – wedged between Timur and Nikoli while Alina tried to splash water over us and Erik complained that he was not being included while our father and Erik's laughed and Erik and Nikoli's mother tried to take a photo.

I still have those attempts somewhere. Or I did. And I treasured them because in that moment I felt the pure and unadulterated blast of raw love. I can count on one hand the times I have felt such a way. And to be reminded of it here, now, when the idea of scratching love's surface seems so distant…it moves me.

I inhale deeper as I stand up straight, hand reaching for the memory when it slips away. I pull myself back into the present. It has been a long time since I have smelled a woman. That is all.

"What do I look like?" I finally grunt. As I speak, I lower my arms and reveal the guns I've got in each hand.

She sees them, grabs the pot and clutches the flimsy thing to her chest. I might have been angry that she has poured water all over my bed if this were my old house. There, Alina was constantly tripping and falling and destroying things and it drove me mad. But this is not a home. This is a cardboard coffin.

"I don't know."

"I am a dead man. Are you ready to join me?"

"I'm an anthropology student!" She shouts and the sound echoes when she lifts the pot to cover her face. There is still only a breathlessness in her tone that is closer to exertion than it is to fear and I understand then that this little sex goddess still doesn't realize she will die here.

She speaks like one who still believes that this is a game, or a joke and that a pot may stop me from plugging all twelve rounds into her tiny frame. "I'm doing a research project on the prostitutes in the area…"

"You are liar and I hate liars." I point the gun in my left hand at the pot against her face.

"I'm not lying," she says, and her voice echoes in the pot. My lips twitch. It is kind of funny. There is something overall kind of humorous about this woman. But it will not change her fate. It should not...

"You lie more."

I click back the hammer and she lowers the pot, flinging it aside. It clatters noisily as it hits the leg of the desk nearest me, then the floor. "No!" Her voice is strong. Surprisingly so. I wonder if she has had many guns pointed at her in the past, or if she is really unafraid. The former irks me more than the latter for reasons I can't pinpoint.

"Don't do that! Stop it. Put it down. I have cash. You look like you could use it. Just take it and I'll walk out of here. No harm, no foul. No one will ever know I was here and no one will know where you are either. I'll keep my lips shut."

I steel myself against the pain of her accusation, which cuts through my pride like a saber through skin. I am a millionaire and I have worked hard for my earnings and done many bad things, and yet it is because of that work and those things that I am reduced to nothing.

She touches the purse at her belt and I whistle. The whites of her eyes gleam as I walk to the edge of the bed. Our knees brush as I press the barrel of my weapon between her small breasts and shove her flat against the mattress.

She doesn't beg and she doesn't apologize. That is what most do who are going to die. They plead for life and when that fails, seek forgiveness to guide them into the after, yet this woman does nothing but inhale and exhale air that smells like lilies and peppermint.

For one so reluctant for death, I am made more reluctant to deal it.

Buying myself some time, I reach to the ugly sack she wears around her hips. It's lighter than I thought it would be and when I rummage through it, I find no gun. No weapons of any kind. Instead, I withdraw car keys and a wad of cash which I throw to the ground, along with an ID and a library card. The latter stalls me. A library card?

In her picture, her hair is in many small braids that frame her angular face. The look pulls her closer to pretty along the spectrum than how she appears now. Now, she is pure sex. I prefer it, this mane of dense curls, and I find myself suddenly distracted again. What was the purpose of this card? What did she intend to use it for? Cracking a lock like in some spy thriller?

Frustrated, I toss it onto the ground with the cash and turn to her ID – the one thing on her person she should certainly not be carrying. I hold it up to the orange light. Ifeoma Smith. Twenty-eight years old. One hundred and three pounds. Five foot one. On Venus and Eleventh Street, she lives in the expensive part of town, not far from where Alina used to live on townhouse row.

Her license expires next year and in the photo, her hair is much shorter than it is now. Like one of those cloud-like candy sticks American children eat at carnivals. I am compelled to touch this hair and as I toss her ID card down, I stow the weapon in my right hand and reach for the fluff, but she hits my hand away.

I grunt, but she speaks first, despite the barrel of my Makarov still trained on her sternum. Makarov or no, I gather that this is a regular pattern with most of the people she interacts with.

"Don't touch my hair." No begging. Not even a please, but a strict command. "Don't you know not to touch a black woman's hair?" I did not know that, nor do I understand why it matters here. "What are you...what are you doing?" she huffs.

I pull the cell phone out of her pocket and the belt from around her waist and toss them behind me onto the floor. I pull her sneakers off of her feet next and when I shake them out, there is nothing in them. Where are theater things the assassin brought with her to murder me?

Her mouth is moving and she is talking still, but I ignore her as I move back up to her face. Shoving both guns into the back of my pants, I begin the process of patting her down again, but this time I work meticulously so that I am sure there is nothing I do not miss.

My fingers skim her neck. They move beneath the collar of her coat and pull her arms free. I crush her jacket in my fists to make sure there isn't anything buried in the lining. Finding only feathers, I toss it with her other things. Then I lay both hands on her chest, covered by a thin layer of black cotton. There is little she could conceal beneath the long-sleeve tee shirt, but I cup her breasts anyways, squeezing hard to ensure she hasn't hidden anything in her bra.

She releases a soft murmur, and it occurs to me only now that sometime in the past few seconds, she has shut up. Lies no longer coat her tongue, which flashes when she licks her lips. She wears an expression I do not understand, but that strikes me as odd. It's also an expression my body, more than my mind, seems to want to respond to.

My thighs are suddenly rock and I can feel the pulse jumping around in my neck as I massage my hands down the length of her arms to her wrists. She grips the sheets fiercely and when I slide my palms over hers, she laces her fingers through mine for a moment before clenching them. Her eyelids flutter as I push her hands away from her body and move to her stomach.

I lift the hem of her shirt, revealing smooth skin and the tight and straining muscles of her abdomen. My face is much closer than it needs to be, because I am not using sight or smell to identify the weapons on her body. I don't pull back, but exhale against the small sliver of flesh between her hips. She shudders. At the same time I slip my fingers inside of the waist of her jeans, checking for knives…or something…

My fingertips brush over the top of her panties. I want to know what kind she wears because I feel strands of elastic where more fabric should be. Her ass presses down into the mattress then and when I glance at her face, her eyes are closed.

I drop one knee between her thighs as my hands circle the small of her back, then work their way down, carefully memorizing her ass's every curve. When I stand back away from her, she's breathing harder than she has all evening and I'm dumbfounded, not even sure what I was looking for anymore.

She licks her lips and when I step away from the bed, she winces. "Please," she says, slightly out of breath.

My stomach kicks and all the blood in my body rushes to my cock. Somehow in the minutes that it took for me to touch her, her body has become primed for me. My body is ready to answer her call.

My cock is a cruel pressure in my jeans and muscles across my body are flinching uncontrollably. Despite them, I keep my hips rigged to the spot because every synapse in my mind is telling me to move away from her before I do something damaging and disgusting to her tiny, sexy body.

The bullet lodged in my right hip sings like a metal tine against a great gong, but I do not feel the pain. I am numb to everything but lust. Her watery charcoal gaze is pinned to mine and her chest is moving up and down in great waves. Her fingers clench and unclench and her knees, which were pressed together fiercely, peel open when I glance at them as if I've ordered her to do so out loud.

I entertain the notion that it is fear that compels her. It is not impossible to presume that she thinks her body is the only item she has to barter for her freedom. Or perhaps she is truly the most ingenious assassin I have ever come across and she knows that if she gets me disrobed and disarmed she stands a better chance of completing her assignment. Funny, because as I look at her tiny, doll-like frame and that mouth made for sucking, I am willing to take that risk.

I move across the room and set my guns down on the desk, showing them both to her as I do. Then I step away from the desk and away from her as far as the small confines of the room will allow. "You are free to leave now," I say.

This is a gamble because my mind wants answers, but the desire of my flesh is greater than that of my reason and I know that if she turns and runs now – as any sensible woman would – pain wouldn't even begin to describe the state in which she'd be leaving me.

It is the way she watches me. There is something in her darkness and her deceit that rings with a power I want to own and a truth I want to dismantle. When I do not say more, she swings her legs over the side of the bed and stands shakily. Her gaze flashes to the door.

"But," I tell her just as she begins to move, "if you stay, you will take off your shirt."

"What?"

"You do not speak. You listen now." She sucks in air and sweeps a hand back into her curls, pushing their mass out of her face. Her gaze is intense as it holds mine without looking away and yet, this girl who does not stop talking quietly obeys.

"If you choose to stay, you will take off your shirt."

The pause lasts only a fraction of a second before her hands move to the hem of her tight-fitting tee, which she lifts. Her bra is pale blue and vibrant against her flesh. The clasp is in the front and she flicks it free when I tell her to. The bra floats down her arms, yet the two soft swells on her chest remain fixed as they are, tiny black nipples hard already.

"Touch your breasts."

She swallows as her hands travel up the length of her body and, finding her tits, squeeze. The inadvertent, animal sound that slips from between her teeth is what finally breaks me. I grab my cock through my jeans and massage its length, a similar bark tearing out of my chest. With my other hand, I release my belt.

"Trousers," I grunt. She reaches to her waist, but I stop her. "Turn to the side." I want to watch them come down and as they do, I don't manage to restrain the even deeper growl creeping up my throat. She is wearing a thong that is the same pale blue color as the bra she'd just shed as if knowing just what I wanted from her before I did. Assassin or victim? I still do not know, yet it matters less and less.

"Take off your panties, and the rest."

Her fingers are sure as she slides her panties down to her feet, then removes her socks. She steps away from her clothes with her legs slightly parted and *suka blyad*, the insides of her thighs and the top of her hairless pussy gleam. She's wet for me already.

I reach up and grab the back of my shirt by the collar, ripping it off over my head. I take a step towards her and then another, then another until we are chest to breast. I can feel the tips of her nipples against my skin and shit. *Derr`mo*. I could come now just looking at her, but other plans race through my mind. I have thousands of them.

She looks up at me, head tilted all the way back to meet my gaze. I run my finger down the length of her throat. "This is your last chance, *printsessa*."

She catches my hand as it slides over her chin and instead brings it to her mouth. She licks her tongue up my middle finger, then traps it between her teeth and pulls it into her tight, wet, heat. I don't need more of an invitation than this. Ripping my hand free, I bend her head back and I take her mouth without further consideration.

There was no way to have known that my day would end like this.

The moment my hard lips crush against the softness of her mouth, she gasps, ripping air right out of my mouth along with my sanity. This woman could be here to kill me, but as her hands snake around my neck, I grab her ass and lift her halfway up my body. In that instant, I am ready for any death she might deliver.

When she wraps her legs around my core, her wet pussy drags across my abs. She's soaking and we haven't even begun. I bite her throat lightly and she combs her fingers through my hair. Her inner thighs are trembling. I cup her ass cheeks, feeling that tight, puckered hole that I plan to claim before this evening's end.

As I set her down, I slide her body slowly against my hardened length. The pressure of her wet pussy lips against my shaft makes us both moan in the same instant. I wonder if she too feels the pain. If she doesn't yet, she will.

I set her down and turn her around. I aim my cock for her ass hole and she tightens her ass cheeks around it. Heaven hits me like a cinderblock to the skull. Her skin is softer than butter. Wanting to touch all of it, I slide my hand over her front, from her neck, between her breasts, down past her belly button.

"Oh god," she says, but I know that God is not with us right now because nothing I am about to do to this woman is anything He would approve of.

I grab her by the throat with my left hand and with my right, cup the beautiful brown lips of her femininity. She's a submissive and in the power I have over her, a renewed rush of liquid flowers from her pussy over my hand. "You are to come when I allow."

My tongue slides into her mouth and she moans, gasps and writhes against my palm, desperately seeking salvation like she is some sort of sinner and I am her penance. I am filthy and she is the cleanest thing that's ever set foot in this entire building. Mint and rosewater, her hair is like feathers against my chest. Her hands grip my thighs and I slide a finger into her while my palm massages her clit. She reaches behind me for my cock but her legs are shaking so violently that she can hardly stand and I want her full attention. I kiss her cheek, the side of her head, suckle on her ear.

"Come for me, *printsessa*. Now." I feel power in ways I have not in weeks as her whole body tenses, then bucks. A weak shout falls from her lips as the product of her orgasm drips through my fingers. I spread the sticky nectar across her thighs, stomach, and breasts because I like the way the small mounds gleam. Then I hold her against me, effectively distributing her weight over my right arm. She clings to it with both hands and rubs her face against my shoulder and I catch myself smiling after a moment. My need dulls for a second as it too, waits for her to recover.

"Are you ready for more?" I say.

"Yes." She kisses the inside of my arm, then works her way to my chest, catching my nipple between her teeth.

I push her away from me. "Good. On your knees."

She drops down the length of my legs and when I take a seat on the edge of the bed, she wedges herself in the space between them. Her body is warm against the chill of the room, which is so cold I can see my hot breath. It doesn't matter.

"Kiss it," I command.

Her hands slide against my inner thighs and she edges herself closer and closer. Then she lifts up and eyes the erection before her with an appreciation that makes me feel like I've just won a pissing contest against every man in existence. Her tongue strokes the bead of precum budding along the head of my dick and the sensation is like lightning.

I fall back onto my elbows and watch her lips close around my hardened length in rapture. Her cheeks concave and the violent pressure is enough to pull every thought out of my body. There is nothing but the present. I urge her on and she moves down, my cock hitting the back of her throat, her nose still not meeting the thatch of my pubic hair. She chokes and I hold her still, then wrench her back and kiss her so hard I wonder if I'll bruise her perfect lips.

"Balls," I say.

She nods and I fall back on the crumbling mattress, gone. Her lips are soft and warm and wet as I let her work me over for what may be hours. She pulls each of my balls into her mouth, alternating squeezing and flicking with her tongue. The suction and pressure of her mouth is an indescribable euphoria.

"Down," I grunt, and she does not hesitate, but moves to my ass, licking and sucking while her hand continues to pump my cock. I want to come on her chest, on her face, on her ass most of all. I want her to sit on my face and shower me in return. A thousand visions roll through my mind as my eyes roll back into my skull. I pull away from her and grab her by the waist, then wrench her tight, pliable body onto the bed. I press her chest against the mattress and pop her hips up.

"My turn," I tell her, and I bury my face between the smooth lines of her ass. I taste her raw flavor, lick every inch of her crude shape. I live out every fantasy I've ever had, waging a war against myself over her body. I am not a man anymore, but an animal. She is screaming into the pillow and when I roll her onto her back, her teeth tear the lining apart and tufts of cotton spill over everything.

I grin again and hold the sides of her face and I am caught by the sight of her face, eyes glazed and unseeing. Perhaps, trapped. I want to stare at her some more, so I grab her knees and pin them over her head. I curl her into a tight ball and lower my mouth to her clit. She meets my gaze, but only for seconds at a time, while her hands reach above her head. She comes when I slide a pinky into her tight, puckered asshole, whole body shuddering as a series of screams rip out of her into the night air.

"Did I say you could come?"

"Oh god." For the girl of many words, these two are all she says anymore.

I chuckle as I flip her bottom up to the air and spank her hard. I spank her again and again, then I work two fingers into her pussy and another into her ass and she comes at the contact almost immediately as the pain excites her and fuels my own need. How I've managed to hold on to this point is beyond me. I roll a condom on, cover her body with my own and tilt her face to the side. My mouth is on hers as I push deep inside of her body in one single thrust.

The lips of her pussy catch my cock in a vice and I bite down hard enough on her shoulder I know it will leave a mark. As it should. I want to mark her. At the same time she shouts, "Gavriil," to the rooftops, and when she does I do not worry that she knows my name even though it is not a name I have given her, because I am no longer Gavriil, or a stranger, or a man on the run, or a man left wanting. I am complete.

My fingers drag through the curls I was at first forbidden from, and I am completely convinced that assassin or not, she is the last person that I want to kill. I pound into her. Fronts of my thighs slapping against the backs of hers. I can't think. I am at Lake Opa. I am drowning in it.

And then a heart-stopping, gut-wrenching, ball-busting, orgasm wrecks its way through every inch of my body, tearing me apart. I am lost to the euphoria and when I resurface to the sensation of her kiss, I cannot remember where, for the past several months, I have been. There is only now. Only this.

Only... again.

Ify

Pulling my pants on is hard, and it's not just because I'm sticky everywhere below the waist. My pussy is throbbing, my ass hole is on fire, my thighs are rubber, and I'm pretty sure I popped something in my hip and snapped something else in my neck.

I slide my jeans up over my ass with my right hand while my left clings to the knobby footboard that's disintegrating in places. Soft wood flakes off on my fingers when I stand, lock my knees and wait a second or two to make sure they hold. When they do, I brush my hair out of my face and search the floor for my jacket in the dark.

He's standing by the bathroom door with his arms crossed over his chest and a towel slung around his waist. It's a good look for him and I do my best to ignore the fact that I'm still wet – a wetness that has nothing to do with the pot of water I threw across the bed.

I can't believe I just did that. All of that. Like what the heck? I seriously can't. believe. I. just. did. that. I boinked a guy who had a gun pointed at my chest and almost looked like he meant to use it. I had sex with Gavriil Popov, a guy who's supposed to be dead.

"You can speak now," he tells me. His accent is thick and low and even as serious as he seems, I can sense somewhere beneath the brooding surface that he's teasing me. At least that's what I hope I'm hearing.

I shake out my hair and hope to high hell it's still shaped in some kind of circle and that I don't look like a crazy maniac. "I tend to talk a lot."

"*Da.*"

"I mean I don't talk all the time, I just talk when I have something to say. Not that I have something to say all the time. I just…" I expect him to cut me off but he doesn't. He just watches me with eyes that are the color of winter and all things cold, even though his hair is a fire's outer shimmer. I mean, I'd seen his picture a thousand times before but whatever I thought I saw in film was wrong. Like trying to take a picture of the sun. I feel like I only really saw him for the first time when he was on top of me, cupping my chin and forcing me to meet his gaze as he impaled me from behind. I took every inch of him hungrily.

I tug down on my shirt, feeling downright ugly standing in front of him, but I don't let it show. I never do. Mama always taught me that confidence comes first and that is how I stare at him now, even as my voice falters. "I just…like talking," I say lamely.

"*Da.* I see this."

Pulling on my coat, I cross my arms over my chest, noticing the cold in the room for the first time since I arrived. Didn't feel so cold in his bed surrounded by his huge body. And he is *huge*. I don't remember him looking so buff in the photos either. I start to wonder if, for the past few weeks, I haven't just been hunting for someone else entirely.

"How I will pay for this?" he says.

"You know I'm not a prostitute right?" I chuckle awkwardly. He doesn't smile back. I clear my throat and try again. "I won't say anything."

"You know much."

"Not really…"

"How you know my name?" He readjusts his towel and in the process, fans it open so that I get a full picture of his dick. It's still hard as bone and like the dog that I am, I salivate for it.

I lick my lips and clench my knees even tighter together. I can't decide whether to tell the truth or lie. "I'm a…"

"I do not need to hear your truth, if you are not want to share it."

"Oh. Okay. Well I umm…I won't tell anybody that you're here."

"If you do, I will be dead."

I gulp, wishing for the life of me I had a glass of water and perhaps a set of crutches so I could limp the heck on out of here. "Like I said, my lips are sealed. I won't tell anyone."

"You may not have choice." He walks past me to the door, which he unlocks and opens. I don't blame him for wanting me gone.

He probably thinks I'm a nutter, stalking him, lying to him, banging him and never shutting up. And lying to him. Can't forget about that. Lying has always been my best defense mechanism, but weirdly here with him calling me out for it, I feel bad about it.

He says, "They catch you, you will talk before they kill you."

"Then why are you letting me go?" I move to stand beneath him, just outside of his apartment. All I can smell is cum. I want to lick it off of him and find myself leaning forward onto the balls of my feet. He edges back and stares down his nose at me with confusion, so I rock onto my heels and ignore the embarrassment that hits me as hard as his hand against my bottom. I'll have bruises by tomorrow. I want more of them. All of them. To do whatever he says.

He clears his throat and glances past me into the darkness of the hallway. Then he says something in Russian that sounds like a curse and goes to the window. He flips up a piece of cardboard and orange light turns the hard edge of his face to gold. He curses again.

"Is something wrong?" I say.

"How did you get here?"

"I drove."

"Where you park your car?"

"Over on Thirty-Seventh and Seventh."

He rips off his towel and throws it onto the ground, like I've just insulted his mother in the foulest possible terms. Russian flows from his lips a lot smoother than the English does — not that I mind — and he heads to his chest of drawers. He pulls on boxers, black pants, a long sleeve shirt, a white baseball cap and a hoodie. He draws up the hood and his face is almost entirely obscured by shadow, then he follows me out into the hall.

"What are you…what are you doing?"

He has me by the upper arm and is mostly dragging me across the rickety floorboards. When we reach the stairs, he pounds down them, unconcerned with the ruckus he's making. He also manages to avoid every piece of overturned furniture and the stacks of concrete and rubble that take up most of the ground floor. The way he moves is like chaos and grace made a baby. It's intriguing and so is he. I'm still staring when he pushes me out into the cold. I struggle to zip up my jacket with his hand on my arm and when I glance up at the intersection, I notice the young pro is gone.

I pause for a moment, digging my heels into the sidewalk until he either has to let me go or literally drag me like a dummy. He elects for the former, for which I'm grateful. "Wait, I forgot my ID." And my cell phone and my car keys.

He fishes into his own pocket and hands me back my phone, my keys, and the cash. Everything but the one thing I asked for. "You will not carry this on you in places like these again." He holds my ID and my library card inches away from my face. Their plastic sheen flashes in the light and I'm annoyed.

"This isn't my first rodeo," I say, reaching for the cards. He transfers them to his other hand and I trip over his feet when I try to steal them back. He catches my elbow in one hand and with the other, continues to keep the cards out of my reach. "Give them back."

"You do not carry these again at night when looking for trouble." He narrows his eyes.

"I don't go looking for trouble. Besides, having my ID has gotten me out of trouble."

Gavriil stops dead in his tracks. He glares at me hard with his jaw clenched and his arms hanging off his broad shoulders like he's about to hit something. Me. I take a step away from him and the back of my foot slides through something slippery. Plastic bags on the sidewalk cover something soft that smells like feces. Probably human. Then the scent of shit greets me and I groan and try to skip away from it.

When I look up, Gavriil is still staring. "You do not bring ID at night when looking for trouble." His voice is severe and a shudder rips through my whole body. I'm reminded again that this guy is one of the head honchos of the Russian mafia. This is how men who are in that position speak. I'm just not used to men speaking like this to me – at least, outside of the bedroom.

I'm nervous but I want him to know that I'm not affected by him. Even if I am. "Fine," I say, rolling my eyes and holding out my hand.

He bites the inside of his cheek. I can identify the action by the way his hollow cheeks suck in even further. His nose twitches and so does his mouth. I glance at his hand, still unsure if he's going to hit me or what. Finally, he edges close enough to slip the ID and library cards against my palm. The plastic is warm. I curl my fingers around the cards, but he grabs my wrist before I can stash them away in my coat.

"You do not bring this when looking for trouble. They catch you, they know your name, they find your house, kill everyone you love. No identity and you are safer." He exhales heavily through his nose.

I inhale deeply through my mouth. "Who is they?"

He rolls his eyes and adjusts his cap. For a moment, I get a glimpse beneath it and see that his orange hair stands up in every direction. I like it long. I also like the unshaved scruff on his face. I imagine that if he totally let it go, he could grow one heck of a beard.

Releasing a frustrated grunt, he comes to me and shoves me in the center of my back. "Come. We go." As he drags me along, I stuff my things back into my pockets. Glancing at my phone, I have to smirk. "What?" he barks.

"I didn't think you'd let me keep my phone."

"Why take it away? Only three numbers on it, and not any one that I know." We cross the next street and head in the opposite direction, away from my car. I understand why only when I hear the sound of gunshots echoing behind us. "You are not assassin."

That makes me laugh outright, though I immediately regret it. He stares down at me, face hauntingly stern in the shadow of his hat. He steps closer to my side and reels me in by the arm when I try to put distance between us. At all times, we are flush and the closeness does nothing to ease the stirring of my libido.

"Is that what you thought I was?" I balk.

"What else?"

"I could be an old building connoisseur, or a Chinese food fanatic paying homage to one of my favorite dives. Or I might be a homeless runaway looking for a spot to crash. I could have a bad habit of late night sleep walking or I might be a detective investigating a case."

"Then again," I go on, "I could also be exactly what I said I was. A girl looking to change careers. My best friend Clifford once told me that I'd probably do pretty well as a corner girl. Or the reverse. Maybe I really was looking for a good lay." Realizing what I've said, I laugh. The sound disrupts the sinister silence that blankets the block. "Then again, I guess I succeeded in that regard."

One edge of his mouth twitches and I wonder if he might not be nearing something like a smile. "Detective," he says honing in on the one thing I wished he would overlook. Ears like a bat this one…He makes a purring sound and guides me to the other side of the road. It takes me a minute to realize that there had been two guys hanging out behind some empty dumpsters.

They shout my second least favorite name for a woman when we walk past. Gavriil twitches, pauses, then continues without looking back. "Detective looking for what?"

The next corner takes us in sight of my car. I shrug. "Clues on a couple local disappearances."

"Who?"

I want to say his sister's name, but my throat chokes. I mean, I was so excited to get laid that I kind of forgot that I scored a huge win tonight – better than Anatoly, I found Gavriil Popov — alive! I should ask him about his sister – I'm sure he knows what happened to her – but one look at his steely expression and my brain-to-mouth filter throws up a safeguard just in time.

He's not a talker. And he's not into talking about his current situation. After all, my speculation on his lifespan must not be too far off if there are assassins after him. And if there are assassins after him and he's here alone, I can rest assured that his little sister is dead. Someone like her doesn't survive long on their own on these streets. I frown, feeling momentarily guilty for the direction my thoughts have turned and in that guilt, sorry for him.

"Who?" He repeats.

I shake my head, clear my throat, and look away from his glare. "This guy called Oliver Tremblay. Mostly people called him Ollie. He went to my high school and we sometimes hung out, but I haven't seen him in weeks."

True. Sort of. Ollie did go to my high school, but we never hung out. He was the grade below me and part of the stoner crowd. When I left for college and came back, I saw him a few times hanging out on Seventh. He was just the same. When I found out about his disappearance a couple weeks back, it didn't surprise me, but I don't think he's connected to this investigation. He was an idiot – not a Mafioso, or a junkie.

Gavriil doesn't say anything, but it's more what he doesn't say that irks me. He drags his feet and watches me with an intensity that leads me to say, "Do you know him, by chance?"

"*Nyet.*" His voice is a whole octave higher.

"Ha!" I clap my hands, stop in my tracks and point at him. "You're lying!" And that fascinates me. What could he possibly know about Ollie?

He grunts, but doesn't speak.

I laugh and my breath puffs up in the dark concrete world around us like gusts of smoke. "That's why you hate liars! You suck at it." He doesn't smile back or seem to find it in the least way funny. Instead he grabs my hair and pushes me against the concrete wall. His face is close to mine – dangerously so – because it looks like he's about to tear a chunk out of me with his teeth.

"Stop it!" I bat at his hand with both of mine until he releases me, a look of surprise slashing through the anger on his face. "I told you I don't like that."

He narrows his eyes and puts a body's breadth of space between us. "You did not seem to mind before."

The gust of wind that lifts my hair away from my neck turns the sweat there to ice. I'm fiery hot underneath all my clothes. Still, I cock my chin up. "I'm not the same person all the time. That other girl – the other me – she likes different stuff. Bedroom stuff. This me is professional and curious."

He leans in close to me, moving swiftly enough that I fall back against the brick. "I see." He pulls gently on the ends of my curls then snarls, "I like bedroom version better."

He starts off without me, and I try not to feel butt hurt as I follow. "I appreciate you walking me to my car, but it's really unnecessary." The car bleeps twice when I push the button. It's only as I climb into the driver's seat that I realize he actually left his apartment to walk me to my car. I haven't met a guy yet on Tinder who'll put in half that effort.

"Of course. Not necessary at all for you who walk fifteen blocks with no weapon," he mutters facetiously.

In the light of my car, everything looks harsh and unfriendly. His skin looks pale and his eyes look bloodshot. I can't imagine that I look any better. There's still cum caked along the insides of my thighs – both his and mine – and I shuffle uncomfortably against the seat.

"What's that supposed to mean?"

"You understand little."

"Thanks," I sneer. "Do you want a ride home or not?"

"*Nyet*. I do not need attention of big car." He turns from me and starts off and there's a hollow ringing in my gut where the lust just was. Crap.

I roll down my window. "Hey!" He hisses and comes back up against the door. He and I are at eye level now but I don't find his expression any less alarming. "Sorry. Sorry, I'll keep it down," I say, holding up both hands before he rips off the car door and clocks me good.

"What you want?"

Caught off guard by his rage, I stutter, "I just...can I come back?"

"What?"

"Can I come back? Like, to see you?"

"You want to come back?"

I nod.

He shakes his head, looking downright flabbergasted, and rubs his face. The man looks exhausted and I feel simultaneously guilty and vindicated that at least part of that might be my fault. "*Da*," he says, turning away again.

"I'll take that as a yes?"

"*Da*," he echoes.

"Okay then maybe I'll see you on Friday?"

He doesn't respond and I watch the back of his black jacket blend in with an even darker night. By the time I get home, I'm jittery again. I sit down at the massive desk that occupies the center of my loft apartment where a dining table should theoretically be. It's covered in a gajillion papers and my laptop, leaving me to either eat on the couch or at the kitchen bar, and if I have people over, they know they're welcome to eat and chill out anywhere – but on the table.

I gather up all of the documents I have on Gavriil and throw open my computer. I type the first words that come to me: *Gavriil Popov, found on Fifty-Fourth and Eighth streets in apartment above Mr. Chang's.* And then latently, *Not missing. Hiding. But from ~~who whom what~~ which baddie?*

I throw myself back in my chair, feeling the sticky sweat of my clothes against my flesh and hating them, but loving the memories they induce. Flipping open my notebook, the sight of the chicken scratch notes I jotted down when I last saw Lenard makes me want to kiss the man on the mouth. Fifty-Fourth and Eighth was where I found Gavriil.

Time to go back to Lenard and pay him double his rate to get me the next address. Maybe that's where I'll finally find some of the answers I've been looking for – Timur and Alina too. Alina, I think to myself as I bend over my computer and start typing up some of what I remember from crossing paths with her brother, I'm coming for you.

Gavriil

I stare at the bed. *Suka blyad.* What in the hell happened last night? The woman. She'd come in and now there are feathers on the floor and my thoughts are blank and my body is sore, but I can no longer feel the pain I once did in my hip. I feel my muscles, primed and eager, and I hear the distant sound of my balls slapping against her pussy as I rode her from behind.

She had been wet as rain and just as sweet. My mouth dries and I palm my cock through my sweatpants. She left and I have been hard ever since. It was only an hour that she was with me, if she had even been with me at all. I feel myself frown as the creeping doubt washes over me. Perhaps this is the beginning of my madness. Perhaps she was just a Fata Morgana on the horizon.

I turn and exhale the air in my lungs, then go to the window and lift the flap. The young prostitute is still there, shivering in her stockings, looking so very lost. At another point in my life I might have helped her, but I fare no better in this moment. Or well…I don't know how I fare anymore.

I look to the bed. The sheets are ruffled and they smell like coconut and rose and rainwater. I've tried to tape the pillow back together. Seeing the grey tape zigzagging across it is how I know that I did not just imagine her. She really was here. She came from the darkness wreathed in flame. And she incinerated everything she touched.

I press my fingertips to the center of my chest where I bear a cruel and unusual pain. I am too tense, too tightly wound. That is all. And I do not need to be thinking of this sex doll when there are many other pressing things.

I sit at the desk, which is too small for my body, the chair too small for my frame. I open the laptop and scroll through the inventory lists and transport schedules Anatoly has shared with me. The records bother me because while they show shipments coming in from the ports to our warehouses in Elmer, they also show shipments veering away from Elmer heading to another location. What is Erik scheming and with whom?

I rub my eyes. Erik is all over the place. Paranoid, the shipments operate on a random schedule which makes it difficult to know when Erik will and will not be in the building. This is why Anatoly does not want me there. Without enough men on my side, any confrontation that took place between Erik and I in Elmer would only end in bloodshed. Likely mine.

Still, I fantasize about the idea of walking right in through the front doors of one warehouse, as I have done so many times. The men would shoot me clandestine smiles, signaling their support. And I would walk right up the stairs to Erik's office, shoot out both of his knees, rip out his tongue through his throat and force-feed him his own kidneys.

We are a family of murderers, surrounded by death. Timur, my father, Erik's brother, both of our mothers. My mind flips momentarily to Timur and his blood cascading over Alina's screaming face. Then to Nikoli, parked in his garage. At the ripe age of ten, Alina had been there to see his corpse, jaundiced and bloated after he died of carbon monoxide poisoning. She never spoke of it though. She'd been traumatized, but not as much as Roman.

He moved out of that house immediately, leaving his living son behind to fester in grief and madness. If I am being true, then Roman is as much to blame for Erik's insanity as Erik's own biology. He abandoned one son after the death of another, leaving for the motherland never to return. It is for that return that I wait. Roman will come to the US and when he is here, I will be able to speak to him. He is a reasonable man.

And until then — I glance at the bed — until then, I will wait for Friday with dangerous anticipation. I pray that for each day that passes, Alina is able to find some grain of hope that will keep the world in motion and keep desperation from winning out, as I have. Brought in the form of a woman with big soft hair and a large lying mouth and a body made for endless adoration.

Part VI
The Monster

Alina

Vy v bezopasnosti s nim. Vy v bezopasnosti s nim. Vy v bezopasnosti s nim. That's what Gavriil told me. That's what he said. He would not lie to me. *Moy brat* would not lie to me. He would protect me with his own life, but now he's probably dead. Do I trust the words of a dead man?

I try to think of Gavriil hatefully for deserting me, because if not hate, then I will cry and I have spent the past weeks crying alone in this strange bed. Timur and Gavriil made this town home for me. And now that they are gone I am stranded in a sea of sharks, kept adrift only by those words. Gavriil told me I could trust him – the one with the pale eyes and the tortured expression – but how can I when he is the shark that I fear the most?

I stare at the door. I find I am always staring at this door. I keep it locked, but I do not know why. No one has tried to come in unannounced or unexpected. In fact, everyone has been very polite and very good to me. It doesn't help.

Mer is the one I prefer. She is an open book, easy to read. They never send Mer though. They always send Sara without understanding that her niceness reminds me of the false charisma of the women the *Vainakhs* employed when trafficking girls in and out of Chechen. My father shut the operation down. It angered Erik's father, Roman, for we always suspected that he was in league with them. But my father won. And then he died.

I never knew if the Chechen's had picked back up the practice, but I am sure one of them killed my father. Even so, the day we buried his body in Polonova, I was proud. He did something good even though it might have cost him his life. The memory seems so distant when I look at where we are now. Our family is about to be erased and I am the last one of them. How long can I cower like this?

Forcing myself to move, I roll slowly off of the bed. It takes me an hour to shower and dress and when I finish, I stare at the brushed bronze doorknob, as if waiting for something to happen. It doesn't. I exhale and finally fit my fingers to the knob. It's cold under my skin. The sound of the lock clicking back gives me shivers. Carefully, I inch the door open and glance out into the hall. There, I wait.

Moments pass until I hear feet on the floor. Someone walks by, and his steps come to an abrupt stop. He turns to face me with a friendly smile. "Oh hello."

I don't smile back. Not because I don't want to but because...I don't know why. Maybe it has to do with the fact that I can't shake this dream I had. It came to me right after Gavriil saved me from being kidnapped by Ivan, Aleks, and Maksim and I woke up in my own bed. The dream had been so lucid and in it, I had seen his face. This face that I look at now.

He meets my gaze but the eyes are wrong, different from the ones I saw in my dream. This is Clifton. The other brother. I look down. "*Zdravstvuyte,*" I say formally.

He grins and there's a pink hue to his cheeks that I'm sure must rival the red in my own. "Whatever you said, I'm glad you're out of your room today."

I open the door a little wider and he looks me over from head to toe, then seems uncomfortable he's done it. He clears his throat, edges back a bit farther and glances away. Then he laughs quite abruptly.

I would say I'm surprised by his reaction, but I'm not. I am aware of how I look and I am used to men responding to me in this way, even when I'm only wearing a tanktop on loan from Mer and a pair of Sara's leggings. They're too short and so is Mer's shirt so both the bottom portion of my stomach and ankles are visible. I would grab a jacket but I've selected this outfit specifically to make a point.

I close the door behind me. Clifton licks his lips and gestures with his hands warmly. "So are you hungry?"

I am because I haven't eaten yet today, but that's not why I'm here now. I run my hand through my thick hair. It's fluffed out today, unrestrained and rampant. "I hope to…" It takes me a long time to get the words out. English isn't coming easily to me these days. Even though I'm surrounded by it, I haven't spoken it. I haven't uttered a word to anyone in three days.

"I am…" *Nu naher,* I curse to myself. "The brother called Aiden. Is he in the house?"

Clifton's eyebrows raise and he smiles, but without meaning it. There is hesitation in his expression. I have met Aiden before, so I understand why. Aiden is violence. "You want to see Aiden?"

"*Da.*"

"Really?"

I'm not used to being denied a request and I feel momentarily irritated. "Is he here?"

"Yeah." Clifton nods slowly. "Do you want me to..." He shakes his head. "I'll take you to him."

I could have guessed he would be in the gym, and that is where Clifton leads me now. Music blasts up the stairs, some sort of opera, which might have been lovely had it not been so loud. It frightens me now and does nothing to ease the tension I feel here alone with two men in some strange house.

I clutch my opposite arms as Clifton pushes open the basement door and guides me down the stairs and to the right. The doorway opens up onto a concrete gym – one that I've only been brave enough to venture into once. I'd only been running on the treadmill for a few minutes before Aiden walked in and gawked at me with the same horror he has on his face now.

He sees me in the mirror and trips, catches himself on the arms of the treadmill, pushes the emergency stop and jumps off. His grey tank top is lighter grey in patches. The rest is sweat-soaked and clings to his body so that I can see the definition of every muscle lining his torso and abdomen, including the lump of a small pendant hanging between his pecs.

His enormous frame must be cut out of some kind of rock because there is no fat on him anywhere. His shoulders are wide and his arms are thick, so are his legs and so is his neck. He pulls his basketball shorts up and I wonder if it's because he noticed me staring at the V-shaped muscle carved between the waist of his tank top and his hips. It disappears beneath the elastic. I swallow hard, but it is difficult to look away from him. He is...not an ugly man.

And suddenly I wonder — is this how Clifton felt just moments ago looking at me? The urge to laugh at the thought is only curbed by the immediate realization that even if that's true, I do not see Clifton in the same way I do Aiden, and Aiden must not feel that way about me. He hardly looks at me at all.

Without speaking, Aiden snatches a towel from the rack on the wall and punches whatever button on the remote that ends the music. The sound of silence shocks me and I feel strangely cold and alone. My lips part and I look to Clifton for assistance. As if sensing what I need from him, he takes a step closer and slips his hand between my shoulder blades.

The gesture is comforting and I don't mean to, but I lean into the pressure of his palm and out loud, I thank him. "*Spasibo.*"

He gives me an encouraging smile and I am embarrassed when Aiden severs the connection between Clifton and I by clearing his throat. "Why the fuck is she here?"

I am equal parts amused and terrified by the fact that Aiden uses Clifton as a crutch in the same way I do. With Clifton here, we never have to interact with each other. We haven't at all. Well, almost. Erik shoved me into that black bag himself, but then when the bullets were raining and the fire was at its hottest and I was sure I would follow Timur into the afterlife, I saw his face. This face. The same face of the man who haunts my dreams.

I remember what Gavriil had shouted when he'd been taken from the building seconds before Aiden saved me. *Vy v bezopasnosti s nim.* You are safe with him. I try to remember that, and hope more than anything that Gavriil was right.

Clifton seems to gain more confidence and takes a half step closer to me. "Alina was looking for you. We thought we might find you down here." He keeps his voice pleasant and light. I don't know how because there's nothing pleasant or light about his brother.

"What did you *both* want?" There's something nasty about his tone, and I am still trying to decipher it when I realize that the two brothers are watching me and are expecting that I answer.

"*Da...ya...*I mean yes." My hands have become fascinating and I watch them with intensity. "I would like to leave the house."

"Not an option," Aiden says curtly.

"*Yobannye passatizhi,*" I curse. "You must allow me to leave the house."

"No. You don't go anywhere alone..."

"I did not mean alone. I mean with you. I need to shop. I cannot live here like this. I cannot even read books you give me without glasses. Mine are lost and I need to get new phone. I need to buy computer. I need clothing." He does not look at my body, even as I gesture at my second hand clothes. He looks at me like I am anyone and that both irritates and comforts me.

"Listen to an audiobook. You're wearing clothes. You don't need a phone."

"You miss the point," I huff. "I...just would like..." What do I need with a phone? I have no one to call. Audiobooks are a good idea for when my eyes hurt. And I have no one to

• 72 •

impress, so why bother with new clothes? "I have bank accounts," I blurt out. "I will not need money from you."

"You can't get to your cash. Erik will have eyes on the Russian bank."

"No, my money is clean. I have account at Bank of America."

Aiden frowns. "How?"

"I am model."

"I know."

His statement leaves me nowhere to go so I stammer, "I earn more than *dvesti*...more than two hundred and fifty thousand dollars a year. I need to leave the house."

A long silence fills the space and I wonder if Aiden hears my unasked plea at all. I am desperate to leave the four walls that keep me safe and that keep me prisoner simultaneously. Clifton clears his throat. "I can take her quickly before dinner. Alina, we were hoping you would join us tonight..."

Aiden stalks by Clifton's opposite shoulder and shoves him hard enough that he loses his balance. "Not on your fucking life." The contact is severed between Clifton and I, and I am left cold.

Aiden is halfway up the stairs before I find the courage to follow. "You can't..." I fall and the hard edge of the wood clacks against my forearms. Clifton is behind me, lifting me up like a gentleman. I thank him and as I find my footing again, I glance up to see Aiden standing a few stairs closer, fist clenched around the rail.

"Be more careful," he rasps.

Ignoring him, I stutter, "You must let me out of here. I don't have any things and I am bored." I trip again as I reach the top stair and tumble out into the hall. He watches until I regain my footing, then quickly races away. "I want to call my friends. I need to speak Russian to someone I know. I want my food. Food that I know. I want computer to watch Russian movies. I want to buy clothes that fit me. I want to buy watch. I do not know what time or even what day it is!"

"February ninth," he shouts over his shoulder, missing the point again and at the same time, crippling me. The words hit me in my empty stomach and I lurch at the memory of Ana's honeyed bread. I missed Christmas. I missed it by over a month.

Every Christmas Eve we would break the fast with *pagach*, though only I ever fasted the day before. Gavriil and Timur never believed in the tradition, and goodness how they ate. They'd eat everything to the point that Ana would serve me separately just so there would be something left. Now Christmas is long gone and there is no Ana and there is no Gavriil and Timur and there is nothing but hunger. Hunger and desperation.

Clifton is trying to mediate between the two of us. He is saying something about possibilities and compromise and is busy listing other options. I don't want to hear anything from the nicer brother – the one I wish had opened the black duffel bag and had come after me in the barn despite the fact that he was shot twice for doing what he did. Why did the cruel brother do those things then and why now does he speak to me like this?

I run to the room they keep me in, lock the door and dive onto the bed. There is a light rapping and several times, the cooing of gentle voices – Clifton's mostly and Sara's. It has been days since they invited me to join them for a meal because they know I will refuse.

I am not wanted here and yet I am kept here, trapped in a prison that will likely be my tomb while Gavriil lies six feet beneath the earth alongside Timur and our father and Erik eats Ana's leftover *pagach* from the Christmas Eve *velija*.

Anger fills me, along with hate and sadness. And it's as I wonder what Erik ate for this *velija*, if he thought of us – his family – or if he laughed at the thought of all of our deaths that I cry, just as I said I wouldn't.

I cannot stay here. I cannot. I must leave and find Gavriil or die trying. Glancing around this cell, I feel some distant strength rise up in my body. My tears begin to dry. A plan begins to form. I cannot stay here. I *will* not.

Charlie

I'm not used to this and though I feel nervous jitters in my legs and wrists mostly, I tell myself I'm imagining them as I step into the cage and the bitch with the dyed blonde hair locks the door behind me. Not so much a door as it is two ends of a roll of chain link fence held together with zip ties. Still, it does the job of keeping fighters in admirably. I've seen losing men claw at those ties with all their strength and still not make it out. Two of those guys ended up dead.

I wonder if that won't be me.

The cage cunt squeezes my cock as I slide past her, but I shove her off hard enough that she falls back onto the dry concrete floor. Everything in this basement is concrete – the walls, the ceiling, even the few concrete blocks holding up unoccupied bench seats. Ain't nobody sitting here though. Everybody's standing, sweating, screaming, pressed as close to the cage as possible – the fuckers here to fight, the others here to bet, the bitches that want to trade body parts for cash, and the others who just come for dick.

When the cage cunt stands and dusts off the thong she wears in place of pants, some of the guys standing at the fence's perimeter boo. Others laugh. She flips me the bird, but I don't give a shit about cage cunts. I used to. I used to love it when they showed up at the barn – the way they'd grovel on their knees when I won, or the way they'd straddle my lap and shove my face between their tits to console me when I lost.

I've always been prettier than all the other ugly, beat up fuckers so cage cunts would do anything that I asked. But now — even if I had any desire to shove my cock into one of those disease-infested snatches — I'm not pretty, and they don't look at me like they used to anymore.

Ants rush over my skin and I shake out my neck, twist my torso from side to side and jab a couple times into the air. My hands are wrapped in tape because the last time a guy wore wraps, he had small hooks buried inside of them that completely shredded the other guy's skin. That guy's almost as ugly as me now.

I look up at my opponent and watch the way he watches me. There's no announcer. No name calling. No amping up the crowd because it's already amped. Just the cage cunts opening and closing the cages, the money man collecting bets, and the guy holding a list of names who tells you when it's your turn.

This fucker across from me decided he wants to stay in the ring until he gets beat and I wonder as I size him up, who or what he lost along the way to bring him to this point. Everybody that ends up in this ring has suffered loss in some way.

His shirt is off and so is mine. He's got tattoos covering most of his left rib cage. The largest one is of the Virgin Mary, head bowed in prayer, tears in her eyes. He's bigger than I am. A lot bigger. This fucker's bigger than Aiden and Clifton, but I don't think of them now. They're not here. Aiden hasn't shown up once even though I told Mer and

Knox I wanted to see him. I still want to see him. I need his help if I'm going to take this guy down. I know already that Aiden would step into this ring, see the bigger guy and think nothing of him. Aiden would take him down in a couple strokes. Maybe play with the guy for fun. Aiden should be in here right now. Not me. What am I doing?

Fuck. I need to get my head in the game. He's coming towards me now, wearing a smile, like he knows what the fuck I'm thinking. He knows that I know that I'm smaller than he is by a good two inches though what matters more is the meat – I'm up from one sixty to one seventy five since I started packing on muscle, but this guy looks like he's nearing two ten. Maybe more. I've got longer arms though. Longer arms… What the fuck am I thinking? I can't beat this guy. I can't beat this guy.

I get in three clean hits – enough to bloody the guy's mouth – before he throws my ass to the floor. He kicks and punches and hits and slaps. He taunts me until I'm just the dregs of a person and only then, when I'm incapable of getting up, does the cage cunt come back and open the door. Two of the spectators drag me out. They send another guy in and the crowd roars.

Out on the street, I walk home. Well, I stagger. He did something fucked to my right leg so I can't put too much weight on it. I think he might have busted one of my ribs. Maybe two. My mouth is full of blood and there are wounds on my chest that I don't understand. Fists don't tear skin do they? Must have, because the blood over my left nipple is seeping through my tee shirt. It was green once, but now it's brown and hangs stiff in places. It smells like metal and bile. Did I throw up? I can't remember.

I stumble over the curb and glance up at the people on the other side of the street. Just a couple walking towards their car. The man's got his arm around the woman's shoulders protectively and both of them are watching me. She's got red hair. He drives some sort of fancy car and helps her into the passenger's seat, like a real gentleman.

I know they can't see my wounds, or the blood on my shirt, or my face beneath my hood in this darkness, but they still have sense enough to steer clear of me. There ain't nobody on my side of the road and I laugh at that fact while the fancy couple pulls away from the fancy stores in their fancy car.

The woman's pale face is like a light on the other side of the glass. She looks up and our eyes meet, or maybe they don't. I don't know what of me she can see. But she's watching me with such detached pity it gives me the impression that she knows exactly what's going on in my head, even when I don't. I fucking hate the way her judgmental gaze roams over me, so just before she slips too far out of my sight — or I slip from hers — I lift my left hand and force my battered fists to unfurl. I toss her the middle finger. Her mouth opens in horror.

I laugh. I laugh for the first time in weeks and the sound is manic and terrifying, even to me. Especially to me, here, alone on this empty street. I quiet and pull my jacket tighter around my shoulders and in the darkness I see a few flurries begin to fall. They look like ash from some horrible fire, and cast a sinister pall over everything. Or maybe that's just how I see the world.

I trudge on through the cold, as the snow turns to a violent breeze and the pain I couldn't feel courtesy of my adrenaline finally greets me. I trudge all the way to my apartment, wondering what's up at the house right now, wondering why I pushed them away, why they let me.

And as my feet hit the stairs of the shitty building I live in now, I'm not a big enough man not to feel the acute sting of abandonment. But hey. I'm a foster kid. I'm used to it.

Aiden

"I'm sorry, Sara, but what do you mean, she won't eat?"
Clifton is trying to reason with Sara as if she's the problem.

Sara shoots Clifton a frosty glance and tugs on the hem of
her shirt. "I mean we're nearing seventy-two hours and she
refuses to do anything besides lay in the bed or the bath. She
won't talk to anyone."

Sara doesn't try to hold my gaze for more than a few
seconds. That's why I stand behind my brother. He says what
I'm thinking in the way I wish I could say it. I was never
meant to take care of the girl, I was only ever tasked to keep
her alive. Now my only task – the only thing I've done right in
my entire existence – is being put at risk. By Alina. Unlike
me, she can do no wrong and yet, I could kill her for this.

"Have you tried…" Clifton starts. My fist meeting the
wall cuts him off. The drywall buckles and paint flakes off
around my hand. "Fuck Aiden, another goddamn wall? You
know Dixon's going to make you pay for that."

I don't give a fuck about the wall. I glare hard at Sara.
"How am I supposed to know what's wrong when she won't
speak?"

Sara and Clifton share a glance. There's something I
don't understand passing between them and I feel stupid. I
am stupid. I'm dense as a goddamn wall and I have no
business taking care of perfection with a face. I hit the wall

again while the heat in my stomach works its way up through my torso and down through my thighs. I want to kick the shit out of something. "Fucking say it."

Sara jumps. Clifton holds up both hands and turns to face me. People around me are constantly making this gesture. I wish I knew what it meant. "Easy, brother."

"How many times do I have to tell you not to call me that?" I surge towards him and he plants his feet, preparing to take the full weight of my body.

"Sh… Stop! Just stop it! Stop it, stop it, stop," Sara huffs. "I can't deal with you two flying off the handle every time we talk about Alina. I need you to calm down and try to be helpful. Both of you," she adds as an afterthought. Always the lady and it pisses me off. I want to stab her and for the tenth time in the past three minutes, my hand twitches for the butterfly knife in my back pocket.

"And if we're going to keep talking about this, may I suggest we do so outside? Just our luck, she'll choose this moment to wake up and hear everything we're saying," Sara says.

Clifton glances over his shoulder, like he's being stalked, and we both follow Sara outside.

"Then tell me," I rasp as I walk, "why the fuck is she doing this?"

"Because she's bored. She's lonely, she's scared. She wants to go buy things to make herself feel better staying here, but you have her confined to the house. She's a prisoner." Sara bites her bottom lip, wrenches open the glass patio door and takes a step into the breeze. It's cold outside, but it's sunny so

I don't bother with a coat. Shrugging on a heavy flannel, Clifton tells me I'm crazy. I tell him to fuck himself.

"I'm not supposed to keep her happy. Just safe."

"Well that's one approach," Sara mutters. Her sarcasm and her condescension don't go unnoticed and when I stand taller she takes another step back. Clifton licks his lips and shoves his hand through his hair. It's longer than it should be. He's also growing a beard. I wonder if it's so people have an easier time telling us apart. I'd want to distance myself from me too if I were him.

"I think what Sara's trying to say is that this isn't working," Clifton grunts.

"I may be stupid but I'm not deaf." I kick a stone and watch it skate over the grass. It needs to be mowed. Normally, that's a me task but I've been too busy ignoring and neglecting Alina. I frown so hard I feel it in my bones. The sudden urge to kill something sweeps me. It's accompanied by an equally strong desire to collapse. My legs feel funny. I wonder if I'm getting sick. I never get sick.

"Sara," I bark.

She flinches again and bundles her sweater more snugly around her arms. "If this is you asking me to do something, then I think you could strike a different tone."

"Sara." Clifton's voice is gentle, but firm. "Please."

She blinks at him quickly, then looks at me, then back at the house, thirty meters away now. Dixon's just appeared behind the glass carrying Brant. I can see him pretending not to watch us, but even his presence must ease Sara because she releases her arms and relaxes her shoulders. Not that his presence from this far away would do her any good. She doesn't answer soon and I could snap her neck before Dixon ever drops the babe and gets the glass door open.

She sucks in a breath. "For starters, I would take her to whatever stores she wants to buy whatever she needs to feel comfortable and safe in the house. Stick to her like white on rice, for sure, but you need to get her out doing stuff that is normal for her, otherwise she'll never be okay staying here."

"Fuck if she's comfortable staying here," I roar. A flight of birds takes off from the Crabapple behind me. They squawk up into the clouds and disappear. Birds are the animal I hate most. They are the only ones that I envy. "She's not supposed to be comfortable. She's supposed to be in her room, safe, where no one can touch her."

"Brother," Clifton tries. The sun catches the greys of his eyes, eyes that are much darker than mine. The only physical difference between us. "Listen to her. She knows what to do to help Alina."

"No," I spit.

Sara groans and shrugs her shoulders, like her bones can no longer support their weight. They sag down her back and she looks defeated. "She's not going to stick around. She'll either try to run and someone will find her and murder her, or she'll die right here in this house with you lording over her. How will you feel knowing that you helped kill her?"

"Aiden!" I hear my name shouted in Clifton's voice at the same time that I hear the gunshot. It whizzes past my ear and when Clifton throws me back, I look up to see Dixon cradling a sleeping baby in one hand. In his other, he holds a long-range pistol with a booster and silencer attachment. That's one way to keep me from killing his girl.

His girl. The sound echoes through my skull, forcing me to imagine for one harrowing moment what it would be like to use that term to describe the woman I'm killing. The one that I can't imagine a world without. I'd die happily in her place knowing she'd never die, and would always be safe.

A roar rips out of me. "Fuck it. Are you happy now? I'll take her fucking shopping." I storm towards the house, dead twigs cracking under my boots. They do little to fulfill my desire to break something.

Sara tries to edge in front of me. Clifton holds her back by the arm. "Before you can take her anywhere, you need to get her some food she likes. Russian food. I already looked up the best places in the city. Three of them deliver, and the rest all do takeout."

She digs in her back pocket, then hands over a slip of paper. I rip it from her grasp and read down the list of names. Vizir, Kishlak, Mari Vanna, Alasha, Madeni…There are ten names on this list. She's circled some and I place an order at Alasha. It's the first call I can remember placing to anyone but Dixon in the past decade and a half. The woman on the other end of the line asks me what I want. I tell her one of everything, read her my credit card number and hang up. I'm standing outside of Alina's room.

"Alina." I bang on the door. "Let me in."

There's no answer.

"You're going to have to eat." I keep myself from cursing. It isn't easy. I want to tear through the wood and hurl myself at the girl with every intention of violence, but I know what will happen when she does open the door and I do see her – the same thing that happens every time: I fall the fuck apart.

"Alina, open the door. You will eat." Statements don't work, neither do threats, so I try pleas. "Goddammit, Alina. Do you want to die? I told your brother I'd keep you safe." Then coercion. "I'll take you shopping, alright? Just eat something. Alasha delivery will be here in half an hour. Sara says to try to eat bread or soup beforehand so your stomach doesn't hurt. Alina? Alina."

She still hasn't said anything and I'm hot. The hallway is shrinking around me and I can hear other people in the house, but they don't come into the hall. They've learned from their past mistakes, which is a fucking pity because I could use someone right about now to be my punching bag.

"Alina! Open the door, or I will." My hand closes around the knob and twists. Bloody hell. It's unlocked. My mouth dries up. Sweat beads along the back of my shaved head. I lick my lips and step inside her room without her permission.

The bed is empty. The bathroom is empty. She's not hiding in the closets or beneath any of the furniture. But the window in the bathroom – barely bigger than an air vent – is open. I reach for my phone and pull up the security app Clifton had installed on all of our devices, hoping that it will prove something that my eyes cannot. But no, there's a blinking red notification from seven minutes ago – left unread – telling me that someone exited the house. Alina is gone. My blood turns to slush and for a moment, the world ceases to turn.

Alina

I'm not breathing well and my muscles aren't working as muscles should. They are soupy and slow. I'm hungry and the water I've drunk is sloshing around my empty stomach. It's all I can hear next to the sound of cars tearing down the Interstate.

I am cold and all I have is a hoodie zipped up over a tank top and tights that are too short for my legs. I don't have any shoes. They only gave me house slippers. I didn't realize what they'd done at first because they are clever jailers, but without shoes, I know I won't make it very far. Today is sunny though, so even with the wind bleeding in through my clothes like it's trying to stop me from moving forward, I push back. I fight.

I have been running – jogging, walking, falling, swaying – for the past hour and so far I've managed to make it through the forests surrounding the brothers' house to the main road. For a while I thought I was lost. Then the blare of sirens heading to and from town echoed through the trees and their long, skeletal arms pointed me in the right direction. I wonder if I look any better than those dead trees do right now. I wonder if this is what Gavriil had in mind. Is this what Timur would have wanted? If only our father could see me now.

A huge eighteen wheeler slows down the minute I step onto the asphalt and I don't even have to hail it. A white guy with a big belly that is only mostly covered by a heavy yellow coat flings open the passenger door. "You're looking a little lost there, sweetheart."

"Do you go into town?"

He makes a face when I speak and I pull my hood up and shove my hands into my pockets. His small eyes glance down to the grey slippers on my bare feet. "You in some kind of trouble?"

"No trouble."

He shrugs. "Alright then. Climb on in. I'm headed South through town, but I can drop you wherever you need to go."

"Thank you." I climb up into the red cab and the trucker reaches across my body to close the door. His elbow brushes my breasts but I don't comment on it. Neither does he. I hold my hands towards the vents then stretch my face towards them too, letting the heat fan down my zipped jacket in a blast of dry warmth. The man watches me more than the road and after some time – ten minutes, maybe twenty? – he asks for my name.

"Ana," I say after a slight pause. "And you are?"

"I'm Garth." He holds out his hand and it's covered in some dark smudges, but I take it anyways. He smells like oil and so do the seats. "You got a weak grip there, little lady. Anybody ever teach you how to shake a man's hand?"

"No," I answer him honestly. "I'm from Russia. This is how women shake hands there."

He slaps his knee at that. "All the way from Russia? You a commie?"

I don't understand what he means, so he elaborates for a while, going into a detailed history of Russian and American affairs that is mostly wrong. When he finishes, I shake my head. "I am not a communist. I am an American."

"A Russian American?" He whistles. "Well I'll say. Don't come across your like very often. You come for work or for pleasure?" He flicks a little card dangling from his rearview mirror. The words Happy New Year are small beneath a portrait of a nude woman.

I shake my head. "Neither. My family is here."

"Aww, now ain't you an angel?" He laughs and I am not able to force a smile. He does not seem to mind and continues to hum some inane tune that I do not know as we drive in the slow lane. The journey seems to last eternities. A sign indicating that town is nine miles away passes by the window but I glance beyond it up at the sky, surprised by how quickly it has turned from bright blue to grey. It reminds me of a set of eyes I saw once in my dreams.

"Maybe it will rain soon," I offer.

"Sure looks like it. You got a place to stay?"

Empty places that I once called home. I wonder if my flat is still there, knowing that even if the men who were my family did not burn it to the ground and all my things are exactly as they were the day I was attacked, I still cannot go there. I am barred from it.

I shake my head. "No."

"What about that family you mentioned?"

"They are dead."

He doesn't even pause. "Any friends?"

I shake my head again. My heart is a hollow stone. "None."

"Such a crying shame." He watches me, but his gaze is low, settled somewhere between the seat and my waist. "You must have quite the story to tell."

I do, but I don't elaborate. We drive on for some ways before a car on the other side of the highway starts swerving and honking crazily. It causes a bit of a traffic jam and as I lean closer to the trucker man to try to glance out of the window, I notice the signs directing cars into town.

"Wait!" I point at the freeway exit we need to take, but it just zooms past until I'm left pointing at nothing. "You missed it."

He reaches for the radio and turns it on. Some country song starts playing and he winks, like he hasn't heard what I've said. I repeat myself twice before he slows down, pulling off at a sign on the left. It's brown and decorated with a white table and benches. Buildings vaguely resembling the drawing sit nestled between a dusting of tall evergreen trees. I almost imagine this place would be serene if there weren't so much trash on the ground.

"Where do we go now?" I say.

"This is a rest stop. We're going for a quick rest."

"A rest?" I wonder if I haven't heard him incorrectly, or if the American uses an expression I do not recognize. He drives to the far end of the parking lot – past the families running through the cold and the wind to get to the toilets before piling back into their RVs and their mini vans – and parks underneath a low-hanging tree. He turns to face me the minute the engine clicks off and unzips his coat.

"We rest in here?"

"Sure do sweetheart." He takes off his cap and I see he is mostly bald. The top of his head is red and veiny, like his eyes and the crisscross pattern swimming over his bulbous nose. "Why don't you make yourself more comfortable?"

I shake my head, long strands of my hair clinging to my hoodie in the static. "I do not understand."

He laughs. "Course you don't, sugar." The man unbuttons the top of his pants in a gesture I find unsettling. Understanding tickles the back of my thoughts like an itch I can't scratch.

I reach for the door. "Why it is locked?" The silver handle is cold to the touch and clacks uselessly when I pull.

The fat man pushes the stick shift into the reverse position and I think he will start the truck again, but he only scoots closer to it. Closer to me. "Not often a man like me gets to meet a pretty little Russian lady like you." He touches my knee and his meaty fingers are big and chapped. Their weight is not much, but their intent is clear. Panic and fear fill me.

"No, thank you." I push him away. He grabs my leg harder, squeezing the pressure points. "Please do not."

"I think I will. You know rides into town aren't free."

"I am innocent," I tell him, giving his shoulders a hard shove that probably hurts me more than him. "God will punish you for this." All of the spit in my mouth turns to molasses. This is why Gavriil and Timur always took such good care of me, and my father before them. I miss them all desperately as the man grabs my wrists and tears bubble to my eyes for so many reasons. I think of Aiden, only looking to protect me. But they are not here now. None of them are. Now I am helpless and alone.

The fat man laughs and I smell beer and tobacco and rot on his teeth. He presses his belly close to my side so that I am fully wedged against the door and the window. It's fogging up and covered in shadows. Soon no one will be able to see inside.

"Seems to me like God's sending me a pretty fat reward for all my good deeds. Little orphaned Russian girl who looks like some sorta mulatto angel stumbles out of the woods and into my truck. Seems to me like God's a big fan of mine, darling." He laughs into my throat and grabs the front of my hoodie. He pulls and the pressure throws my whole body into the dashboard. I am a rag doll in his arms. I am so weak.

The panic and fear in my chest begin to turn to rage and a small realization clicks as my head cracks against the glass windshield and blood trickles idly into my right eye. It is *me* who is about to be defiled and tortured, not my brothers or my father or Aiden. So why do I depend on them to save me now? I am a person. I am a person who escaped a prison. I can escape this monster now.

The rage in my chest turns to froth and foam and I shout at the top of my lungs, "I do not give you permission to touch me."

"I don't need your permission, sweetheart." He finds the too small shirt underneath and buries his fist in the fabric. My fists are much smaller and I don't know how to use them as he does, but I do have something he doesn't: nails. I curl my hands into claws and I swipe at his cheek. The first strike only surprises him, but the second, with my left hand, scores his face from temple to chin.

"What the…" He dabs at the blood with his fingers and when it comes back red, balls his hand into a fist. If he strikes me, it's over. It will hurt me too badly to be able to fight through and I am not used to pain. I need to escape now.

I strike him again, with both hands at once, sending twin rivers of blood rolling down either side of his face. My knee is wedged near my chest, but I roll forward, bringing me closer to him. I manage to shove my legs beneath me and use my knee to crush his testicles. He swings his fist, but the momentum is lost the moment I feel the crunch of his genitals beneath me. He whacks the dashboard instead and as he howls into the ceiling, I scramble off of him and to the driver's side door.

My hands are shaking, but I find the button that unlocks the doors and I tumble out of the truck without looking at the drop beneath me. I fall and hit the ground and pain radiates up through my knees. There is blood on the heels of my palms when I lift them from the concrete, but I don't stop to examine them or any of my other injuries. I run.

The parking lot passes by in a blur and I am again on the highway. This time, I run back the way I came. I don't know what I'm running towards, but it doesn't matter. Minutes are all it takes for a car in the fast lane to swerve wildly onto the curb, blocking my path. The car is black and one I recognize from the garage at the brothers' house. Relief blisters through the panic and the anger that had consumed my body.

The driver's side door opens and Aiden steps into the wind. His face is even paler than usual and his eyes are wide and round. The veins in his neck are jumping and he's in only a tee shirt, so I can see the muscles ticking in his forearms as well. He doesn't come towards me. He doesn't speak. He looks so afraid. He looks so empty. He's not going to come towards me any further so I will have to do the work. And I can do the work.

As I start forward, my gait staggered, I hear him inhale shallowly once and then stop breathing entirely. I'm within arm's reach of him now and when I close the space between us, I throw my arms around his neck. I am shaking and I am shocked, but I am proud that I rebelled — against the brothers, against the man in the truck, against him.

Aiden's fingers fumble through my thick hair and press firmly against the nape of my neck while his arms wrench me hard into his chest. Here, with his body wrapped around mine so completely, I feel hurt and battered and bruised but also more human than I have ever been. I exist without my brothers. I can exist without a savior. I can save myself.

"You're hurt," Aiden chokes.

I shake my head. "I am okay. I will be okay."

"Mer and Knox were driving and they saw you...in the cab of some fucker's truck. Was he the one that hurt you?" His voice breaks.

"He tried. But I do not let him. Did not," I correct, burying my face in the darkness of his tee shirt, through which I can feel the outline of a pendant hanging on a long chain.

Aiden curses and jerks back but I hold him firm when I feel him start to release me. "I'm going to kill him," he snarls.

"*Nyet*," I whimper, tightening my grip around his neck even more and inhaling deeply. "Hold me. *Bajalsta*. Stay with me."

"What did he do to you?" Aiden's voice is a menace and I can feel how his body shakes, compelled by a desire to hurt something. Someone. But pain is not what I want.

"It does not matter now. I got away."

"Did he…" He chokes, unable to complete the sentence.

I shake my head. "*Nyet*. I fought back. I saved myself."

"I was supposed to be there," he whispers, "*Bajalsta, prosti menya*." Please, he's just said in my own language, forgive me.

I hold him tighter and look up at him, pressing my chin against his chest. He looks down and though he's got fear in his eyes and pain chiseled into all the hard lines of his expression, I'm not scared when he touches my cheek. Not this time.

"You are forgiven," I say in English, "So long as you stay with me. Will you stay?"

The darkness of his gaze breaks for just a moment and in that moment, I imagine that I'm falling. I am falling. His fingers slide through my hair and with his other hand, he catches me when my knees give out and I slump against him. Now I have started to shake and I do not know why.

"I'll stay with you," he breathes into my hair. "And I'll never leave you again."

Ify

"So wait, you're telling me that two cargo containers from Russia just went missing?"

"Mmm hmm." Clifford lifts an eyebrow and runs his tongue over his bottom lip. "Yes ma'am." His gaze glides from my face down to my ass as I lean against his desk.

I slap him on the shoulder with the back of my hand. "Focus."

"Yes ma'am." He laughs and drums out a pattern over his desk.

I glance over my shoulder, keeping a weather-eye open for Bob, but things are so crazy with the murder of some trucker yesterday that nobody's giving me a second glance. "You didn't answer my question."

"The containers shipped to Port Emery and after, nada until we received these just an hour ago. You were the first person I called. I knew only you'd be crazy enough to find this interesting." He clicks away from the PDF copy of the port entry list, which had two container items highlighted, to a folder of JPEGs.

"They were sent to us by the port authority. Somehow there isn't a single soul on site who can corroborate what the cameras are telling us even though the two shifts overlapped by half an hour and nobody was off that night."

Taking the mouse from him, I scroll down the list of photos. How much were those men bribed to conveniently overlook two massive shipping containers being wheeled away on the back of two separate eighteen wheelers?

"They didn't go the same way?" I lean in and squint at the photo, as if somehow that will make it less pixelated. Despite the blurry quality, I can still make out one truck taking the road to the left, while the other's right blinker shines bright.

Clifford shrugs and lifts his coffee to his lips. He takes a long sip before answering. "Nah. Who knows though. Probably were going to the same location, just thought to divide the risk. Or set up a diversion. Maybe one was empty. This one though…" He points at the truck headed left. "… was headed towards the Ternary. Found it stripped deep in the heart of the slum with about ten thousand different fingerprints covering it. We haven't got a clue where the other one is. Wanna know something crazier?"

"What?"

"This isn't the first week it's happened." He clicks through a file of folders, each marked with different dates. He picks one at random and I see two identical trucks carrying identical containers away. "Pretty crazy, huh?" He swivels in his seat so that I stand between his legs. Setting down his mug, he leans forward and cups the backs of my thighs, pulling me closer to his crotch.

I roll my eyes and slide my knee along the chair, right up against the lump of his dick, which bulges against the underside of his tight blue uniform. "You get any friskier and I'll crush those little raisins to nubs."

He laughs but doesn't drop his hands. "Don't I get any perks for bringing you the juicy dirt?"

"What dirt? I can't do anything with this. Here I am trying to track down the Popov family and you're getting me all riled up about some container beds, probably carrying a million *pirozhki*."

"But I like getting you riled up." He winks and I extract myself from his grip.

I snap a few pics of the photos and manifest in front of me, irritation flaring when I feel his hand creeping over the curve of my ass. This playful behavior used to be kind of fun but recently he's been playing at this too much. I know he's not into me and he knows I'm not into him. He needs to quit it.

"I gotta go," I snap.

"Drinks tonight at Cactus?"

"No, I can't. Got plans."

"Tomorrow?"

"Tomorrow's the big barbeque at my folks house, remember? You said you were coming," I remind him.

He nods, managing to look boyish and sheepish in the same go. There he is, my Cliff. "Yeah sorry. Forgot."

"Of course you did." I roll my eyes.

"How about next weekend?"

I stop to consider and point at his chest. "Sure. But you better take me dancing."

He grins and his hazel eyes glitter like diamonds. The smell of coffee and cigarettes rolling off of him is strangely comforting. "Sure thing, Ify."

"Oh! And the gang is coming." His smile falls and he groans. I laugh and toss back the mane of my fro. "You think there's a chance in hell I would go dancing without Lara?"

He waves me off when his telephone rings and I snake though the bullpen, keeping low in the hopes that Bob doesn't see me. My eyes are pinned to the gleam of Bob's office door. The gold plated letters read: Police Chief, but should read Poop Chief or Police Liar or Bad-at-my-job-poop-head. Okay, so I'm not a gifted trash talker. Still, his apathy surrounding the Popovs...

Oh god. Gavriil... I've been looking forward to it all week, but somehow I lost track of time. I'm going to be late. He doesn't seem like the kind of guy who likes girls that show up late. Part of me wants very much to be the kind of girl that he likes, but another part of me – a much bigger part – wants to be punished.

"Ooph!" The force of a body knocks me to the floor. I land hard on my hands and stare up at the suit-clad giant above me.

"Watch where you're going," the suit sneers.

"What the heck, guy. You ran into me."

The suit might have been dressed like a male escort but he looked like a cage fighter, one with a stick shoved so far up his ass that a spelunking team wouldn't have had a chance at retrieving it. "Who do you think you're talking to, girl?"

Oh, to hell with that. "Who do you think you're talking to, boy?"

He opens his mouth, but it's Bob's gruff brogue that cuts between us. "Ify. What the hell are you doing here? I thought I ran you off Monday morning."

I hold the suit's gaze a moment longer before flashing Bob my best contrite look. "I was just making friends with this jagweed."

Bob's face tenses and he clamps a hand down on my shoulder, looking like he's helping me up – which he does – but also using the opportunity to wrench me back behind him. I can no longer see his face as he speaks even though he's talking to me.

"Ify. This here's Mr. Monroe. Mr. Monroe, I apologize on behalf of my foul-mouthed friend. She's just a nosy author with a Napoleon complex. Didn't mean anything by the slight."

Mr. Monroe takes a moment to respond. In that time, he watches me around Bob's frame and reaches into his pocket to produce a packet of disinfectant swabs, like so much as the thought of touching me grosses him out so much he's got to disinfect immediately.

I open my mouth to protest the obvious insult, but Mr. Monroe speaks first. "I should hope not. I don't want to have to alert one of my clients to the fact that the police station is being mismanaged by its chief. He's the governor. I believe you might have met at last year's military ball."

From the side, I see Bob's face turn blood red. His broad arms jerk up against his sides, so tight that I doubt a brush of air could pass between them and his abdomen. "No need for that now, Mr. Monroe."

"Good," he says. His gaze searches mine around Bob's body, but Bob shifts in a way that almost seems casual. Almost. Something isn't right.

"Mr. Monroe, shall we get started?" He holds out his arm and Mr. Monroe waits a beat, gaze hovering over a faraway point in the bullpen, before he walks past Bob into his office.

Bob doesn't look back at me, but I know I'm in trouble when he glares at me through the window of his office door as he shuts it. He bares all of his teeth. And if I don't get a move on, Bob won't be the only one looking to take a chunk out of me today.

Gavriil

It is Friday, it is late, and I am angry. Why does she come in the dark? Does she know the risk she takes when she walks those many blocks without any protection but her library card? The thought of that stupid library card makes me stand up from where I had been seated in front of my computer, a picture of her on the screen. She had not been difficult to track down, even if she does write under a pen name.

I.R. Smith. Ifeoma Roberta Smith. Roberta.

I am angry but I am smiling. Roberta is a silly name, but somehow in its comedy it suits her. There is something overall funny about her. *Smeshnoy,* as we would call her in Russia. The divine shape of her body coupled with that insatiable and incessant mouth, vocal chords that would put the world's finest battery to shame, hair wider than her hips and soft like the inside fluff of a pillow. I want to press my face against it. Have dreamed of burying my fists in those curls. I want to lick the sweat off of her body. I want to roll her in my cum.

I bite my fist and stamp my foot on the floorboards just to hear them rattle. The hope of seeing her is a comfort in this hell on earth, a soothing balm on the wound that is my soul. The realization that she might not come – will not come – has begun to dawn on me and I attempt to tear my thoughts away from such an eventuality before the little world around me implodes.

I look again at my computer. She is a real crime author. In my spare time I read one of her books online. She is good, writing with a sharp precision that I wouldn't have expected from someone who says everything that they think. Her first book followed the murders of a series of young boys, but the killer had already been discovered by the time her book was published. Her second book, the one that I read, was the one that garnered her fame.

Here, she tracked the unsolved case of a murdered thirteen-year-old who, in the end, had not been killed, but had been held captive in some perverted monster's basement. It had been Ifeoma who'd broken into the right room of the house, unchained the girl and helped her to safety. Along the way, Ifeoma was abducted by a cult who tried to burn her alive as part of some devil ritual.

The book had made my blood thicken and my heart race from the first chapter to the last. Though she writes in the past tense, the first person telling of the story makes me feel as if I'm there, with her yet powerless to protect her from being put in harm's way. It is not unlike the way I feel now and I glance at the door, hating it and all that it represents as it protects me while I cannot even pass it to head out into the night to protect myself, my sister or the little spyauthor-assassinsirenseductress for whom I wait.

I am staring at the door still when there is an abrupt knock against it. Clack, clack, clack. She is here. My mouth salivates and my palms grow clammy. I could have sworn a moment ago they were dry. The anger in my body is displaced by something treacherous and feral and barbaric in its masculine simplicity: a lust of the most possessive kind.

I know she can hear the sound my boots make on the floor, so I try to marshal them into something less manic. I want to appear relaxed and at ease even though every muscle in my body is charged and my cock is as stiff as a bat. The knob is cool and misshapen under my palm, but I grip it firmly in my right hand as my left clicks back the many locks.

I twist and fail to control my expression. I am excited. I feel like a boy again swimming through the crystalline waters of Lake Opa. So much as the thought of her takes me to Polonova and I am biting down hard on the insides of my cheeks to hold at bay the fierce riptide of a smile that I cannot mask with anger. I am not used to this. Anger comes easily but now, I feel delirious. *Derr`mo.* Delirious.

I tell myself it is because I am starved for human contact, but that is not true. Because when I open the door and see Anatoly standing where Ifeoma should be, all of the blood in my body sinks to my feet. Disappointment does not touch the man that I am. Shame does though. A cutting humiliation.

I run my hand down the front of my tee shirt, to regain control even though it is because of the tee shirt that a chill vibrates through my bones. It is too cold for a tee shirt, but it is one I look good in and I selected it because I wanted to appeal to her.

Anatoly grins and steps past me into the room. "What are you looking at me like that for?" he says to me in English.

I swallow hard and stare out at the blackened hallway longer than I should. The staircase is empty. Why would she come back? She has no reason to. I frightened her half to death and threatened to shoot her. It's a miracle she hasn't called the police.

But then I wonder, why hasn't she called the police? And why did she ask if she could return to me? I had not offered or suggested I wanted that in any way. Maybe I should have. Because now, knowing that she lied to me and will not come at all makes my teeth ache. My cock is a shriveled thing and I am cold everywhere but on the inside, which desiccates.

"Gavriil," Anatoly barks.

"*Shto?*" I spit acerbically.

A slow, surreptitious smile slides across his face that makes me want to blacken both of his black eyes. "You're wearing pants," he says, head cocked to one side.

I look down. "I always wear pants."

"You always wear sweatpants. Today you're in jeans."

I shrug, shut and lock the door. Then I throw myself down onto the edge of the bed, hoping he won't notice that it's been made.

"You made the bed." His grin grows wider.

Fuck him. "*Suka blyad.* Who cares?"

"You cut your hair and you trimmed that disgusting beard." He goes to the window and lifts a cardboard square and I bear down onto the flimsy mattress with my whole body as if that might help me cage the splinters shooting up my legs. "You're expecting someone and judging by the look on your face, it isn't me."

"Anatoly, that is enough."

He leans against the window, turning to face me, and sets the bag he's carrying on the table beside my laptop. It's still open. *Blyad,* if he nudges it in any way, the black face of the lock screen will dissolve and her picture is the first thing he'll see.

"Who is she? Is it that young pro? Standing there on the corner of the street?" Panic. For a moment, I believe the *shopa* has seen Ifeoma outside, on her way to me. But then I remember the young professional who lurks on my corner, hoping to catch a fare. I feel guilt and pity.

"That is what she said she was," I answer cryptically. It is not a lie. Because she said she was many things.

I stand and shut the laptop, grab the bag and throw it onto the bed. I begin emptying its contents. Materials for American-style sandwiches – peanut butter, bread, jelly, tuna, lettuce, tomatoes, mustard, deli meat – plus some fruit and raw vegetables, cookies, chips, dried meat and other snacks, topped off with about two gallons of vodka. Enough to last me another week. Perhaps less now that I know she is not coming. That skin, smooth like the outside of the clear bottle in my hand. Skin I will never feel again.

A momentary pang guts me like a hook through a fish as the desire to leave this hovel builds in me with such intensity I wonder how I do not fall. I inhale, and remember who I am. I am *Russkiy Mafiozi*. Longing has no place in this world. In a decision that comes at great cost, I close my eyes and raze away all thoughts I ever had of the woman.

"Gavriil."

I feel Anatoly watching me in a disconcerting way I am unaccustomed to. "What is it, Anatoly?" I bark, when I meant to thank him for the food. Putting the last of it away, I slam the cabinet shut and turn to face him. I doubt it will come as a surprise to him. I am never grateful. It is not the first time I have made such a realization but it stings all the same.

He doesn't answer right away, but watches the cabinet beneath my hand. He uncrosses his arms. "I am sorry that I cannot do more."

He is sorry, and my shame spreads. "You do what is needed. As do I. As you said, it will not be this way forever." My words are uttered in half a growl, half a sigh.

Anatoly nods and seems to gather strength on his next inhale. "I cannot stay long. Erik is moving shipments from Beijing. Apparently there have been requests for more *exotic* product," he spits and his fists clench and his entire body twitches as his gaze grows distant, seeing something that I cannot.

"What is it?"

"*Nichego,*" he barks, before repeating the word in English. "Nothing. I will need to meet him and the other men at Elmer in half an hour."

I want to pry, but if it were important, Anatoly would not keep the information from me. And as of now, I am still distracted by treacherous thoughts I can't seem to shake. Her sweet pussy clamping around my dick. Her fat ass. The nasty, degenerate things I want to do with those lips...

"*Da.* Go." My whole body is tense, muscles rippling in longing – for a body, for blood. I need to slake my thirst and yet I'm trapped here, fucking impotent.

"We all want Roman and Erik gone. We want you to lead us. We always have."

I close my eyes and nod, but say nothing. I fail Anatoly. I fail our brothers. I fail my father. I fail my family. I fail myself. Every single day.

"There is something else I must tell you, Gavriil. Something important."

"What is it?"

He inhales. "I had not wanted to get your hopes up in case something goes wrong, but I can't keep this from you another day. Another hour. It's happening."

"*Shto?*"

"Roman." Anatoly licks his lips, looking wary as if the walls may very well be listening to our conversation. If they could, Anatoly would have been dead weeks ago. Erik would have killed him for the simple act of bringing me tuna fish. "He…"

We both hear the creaking of the door downstairs as someone opens it. Blood explodes in my ears with the violence of rocket fuel and dynamite, a trigger on the igniter. Anatoly places his body directly in front of mine and rips an M1911 out of the holster on his hip.

It's his lucky gun, one given to him by his father and his grandfather before that. The story is that he was shot by an American in World War II seven times with the gun, but the American stepped on an IED before he could finish him off. The gun remained intact and Anatoly's grandfather took it, and never missed another shot. And within the past twenty years that I have known Anatoly to use a gun to torture, kill, and maim, neither has he.

My hand goes to the Makarov beneath my pillow, but it trembles just a little bit because the hardening of my cock hits me hard and fast when I hear a curse echo down the length of the short hallway, followed by the sound of a girl whispering to herself. I cannot hear what she says over Anatoly's gun's hammer clicking back.

Anatoly has his finger on the trigger and I lurch forward, wrapping both arms beneath his and wrenching his hands behind his head. Anatoly bites out my name as I slam him face-first against the window. It cracks, but does not break. His slick black hair, tied back into a pony tail, tickles my chin as I lean into him – my brother, and my only lifeline – and threaten him.

"Do not shoot, or I'll break both your arms. Stay here." I shove his back with my knee and while he absorbs the pain with a grunt, I arrive at the door.

As I rip it open, Ifeoma jumps, yelps, and drops the flat white box and blue oversized bag she carries. Ignoring the items, I wrench her to my chest, slap my hand over her eyes and whisper English words into her small, rounded ear. "You do not speak. You do not make a sound. You do not open your eyes."

"What in the heck, Gavriil?"

"Ifeoma," I rasp low enough that I hope to hell Anatoly will not be able to hear.

"Don't call me that. And don't touch my hair!" She tries to bat my hands back and I could just about strangle her. Just about. But not quite.

"Do not…"

"It's Ify."

"What?"

"Ify. My friends call me Ify."

Friends. Ify. I hate myself for being distracted and find myself gripping her closer to me. The hard shaft of my dick presses against her lower back the whole time. "Ifeoma," I repeat again, "you will quiet yourself or I will punish you." I don't know what I mean by that but Ifeoma – Ify – opens her mouth. Air comes out soundlessly and she licks her lips. In the light glowing from the room before us, they shimmer.

"Good." I press my lips to her temple because I can't go another second without tasting her supple, lavender scented skin, and drag her forward. Her feet trip over themselves and she holds onto my arms to keep herself standing. I drag her past Anatoly to the bathroom, shove her in, and throw a towel over her head. "Don't move."

I press her to face the wall in the darkest corner before lumbering back into the bedroom to find Anatoly gaping at me, eyes large and black and round. I grab his arm and drag him in the opposite direction, out of the room. I kick the box and the bag inside and I slam the door.

"You saw nothing," I say in Russian.

Anatoly's surprise is muddled by his amusement. He answers in our mother tongue. "That is no prostitute. Who is she?"

"You saw nothing." My voice is dark and dangerous and as unsteady as I feel and there are too many emotions circling my mind to process words in any language. Shock, desire, longing, lust, pleasure, rage, anger, wrath, need, fear, panic, heat, cold. My adrenaline keeps my focus on the man before me and not on the bulge beneath my belt.

Anatoly turns towards the door, but shakes his head. He clicks on the gun's safety in his hand and tucks it back into the holster on his hip. "You're right. I saw nothing. I wasn't even here today and I certainly didn't come to tell you that Roman is coming to America, and he's coming in six weeks."

Ify

What the jiminy cricket is going on? I got here as fast as I could, thought he was expecting me, and now I'm in his gross bathroom under a dirty dish rag. Well, not for long. I peek beneath the rough cotton and, sure that the coast is clear, quickly cross the room.

At the door, I press my ear to its surface. It's dewy and smells a little like mold, but through it, I can hear words whispered between Gavriil and another man. Crap on a spatula. They're speaking in Russian. The conversation sounds somewhere near an argument, or maybe that's just Gavriil. Maybe he's just naturally stern. The thought makes me stifle a giggle. Stern doesn't even begin to describe our last encounter. He was a lot more than stern with me and I loved every second of it.

I remember the way he pulled my hair as he slid into me from behind, his length filling me up in a way I can't ever remember being filled before. He was uncircumcised and I had knelt between his thighs, watching the head of his dick strain for me as all the skin tightened over his cock. It had been red and veiny. Angry in its own right. I hadn't been able to fit all of it in my mouth though I'd tried. I'd like to try again.

He'd ordered me lower and I'd juggled his balls in my mouth. His precum had dripped over my hands as I worked him over, tasting his dick, his balls, his ass. I felt powerful when his head dropped back against the pillows, narrowly missing the wall even though he's three times my size and was the one making all the demands.

Lordamercy. I straighten up and clench my thighs together, trying to forget momentarily what it had been like to be ordered around like that. Thrilling more than terrifying, though certainly a bit of the two. I would have done anything he'd asked. Any sick thing that came to his mind because the truth is that I'm a bit of a sick puppy too.

I wonder if he even thought I would come back, because he certainly didn't seem to want me to and I hadn't been invited. Maybe he'll punish me for it… Immediately, I start to regret having worn white panties because I know they're going to be dark with desire by the time he returns. Focus, Ify, focus.

I've only got a few seconds before he comes back, and I don't want to waste them so I leave the door and quickly take inventory of the room. His computer is locked, so I scan the dresser drawers instead – nothing I haven't seen before – and then the cupboards. They're full of food, each shelf ripe with dried and slow-to-expire ingredients. It looks recently stocked.

My gaze flashes to an open duffel bag on the bed and my mind spins, wondering what had been in it and what the man on the other side of the door brought him. My hand is on the duffel's zipper when the doorknob at the other end of the small room turns. By the time he cracks the door, I'm back in the bathroom, positioned against the wall like he'd left me.

My heart is beating hard for a whole plethora of reasons, not least of which is the wetness soaking through the crotch of my pants. How embarrassing. He hasn't even touched me yet, but the sex we shared was better than any I've had before. So is the fantasy.

The door opens and shuts. I hear the click of many locks and say, "So can I turn around now or am I going to be stuck here all night?" I try to sound annoyed, but I'm just excited. I really want to turn around and not because of any puzzle pieces, though I try to remember that's what I'm here for. My next book. Alina Popov. Not the sex. Definitely not the sex.

"If I'm going to be here all night the least you could do is let me eat some of the pizza I brought." As I speak, I hear him behind me, kicking things across the floor. I turn.

"Hey! There's a computer in that bag and a pizza in the box. Don't be a dick." I start towards him but he takes an even larger step to meet me. It's full of warning. I look up. "Woah. Hey. You don't have to…" Have to what? What is he doing besides liquefying my knees?

He stares down at me with fire in his powder blue eyes. His red hair is messy up top but shorter on the sides than I remember it. Am I losing my mind? Because his once-scraggly beard also looks neater now, and trimmed. It makes the sculpture of his face stand out even more and draws attention to his straight nose and high cheeks.

I mean, I knew he was attractive before, but right now he looks hot. Crazy hot. Too hot to be backing me up against the wall, planting one hand on either side of my head, and kissing me.

His lips catch mine as I try to speak. He has to bend way down to do it. I'm in flat shoes and he's in boots. He's over six feet tall and completely dwarfs me. His mouth is fire and a moan rips out of me that seems to propel him into motion. He grabs the front of my thin, black underarmor jacket and dang near tears the zipper off. My whole body shakes with the violence of his touch as he rips through the thing, then moves to my shirt. He lifts it over my head, his wide hands cup my breasts and he pushes my bra beneath my small tits so that they form perky mounds below my chin. He suckles both of them, taking equal turns that make me crazy. I moan.

His hands slide around my ass in the same way Clifford's did earlier, only this time a wave of heat – rather than irritation – rushes through me. I'm breathing so hard I feel lightheaded. My fingers are in his hair and his face is pressed between my tits, lips and nose teasing my areolas. But it's not enough.

"Gavriil," I hiss.

"Do not speak," he orders me, but when his teeth bite down hard on my perky black nipple, I can't help but say his name again.

He pitches my body forward, grabbing both my arms behind my back at the wrist. My body is at a sixty degree angle to the ground and his grip is the only thing keeping me from face-planting. The sockets of my shoulders burn and the breath that rips out of my throat is ragged. My stomach tenses, taut and fleetingly afraid before desire blossoms through me and beats all my other senses to death.

"What did I say about speaking?" His tone is dark but his hands are gentle as he lowers me to the floorboards. They are uneven and I'm sure I'll get splinters – not that I care – until he fans a flannel blanket over the ground. It's hard but warm as I press my right cheek against it. He unbuckles my bra –

white to match the panties – and slides my arms through the straps.

The tender way he moves makes me shake. He says nothing, but I know he notices by the soothing way he rubs my back. Then fabric comes around my wrists. My whole body lifts from the ground when he ties a tight knot, then a second. I can't see what he's used, but it feels like part of a tee shirt. Tight, but against my skin still bearable because it's a soft cotton.

"You are here to please me, yes?"

Oh god yes. I nod.

"I wish to enter you in each hole," he says. "Do you want this?"

Oh fuck yes. I nod again.

I gasp as he wrenches my jeans free of my legs in one single tug. His fingers trail over the soles of my feet, up the length of my calves and tickle the backs of my knees. I shudder as he continues across my skin. His thumbs sweep the moisture that's formed along the curve of my ass and the sticky that's coating the insides of my thighs. Then his tongue.

His flat, hot, wet tongue takes a full sweep of my right ass cheek. I make a sound I can't ever remember making as my hips jerk up. I'm so close to creaming my panties right here and he hasn't even done anything. I can't think straight. I just want release. I moan.

"Does it hurt? Your wanting?" His Russian accent is nearly what sends me over.

A dry sob guts me. I bow my head into the floor and try to squeeze my thighs together to relieve some of the tension coiled inside of me, but he holds them apart with his hands. "Yes."

His palm hits my backside with bruising force. Then very gently, he traces a path against the outside of my undies from my ass hole to my clit. He presses, but not hard enough to save me.

"Please." Now I beg. I have tears in my eyes and I wonder if this is what the CIA does to prisoners to extract information. If not, they should. I'd have given him anything he asked for – the nuclear codes – without caring what he needed them for.

I bite down hard enough on my bottom lip to draw blood when he spanks me a second time. The tingling, painful pleasure is so intense I could pass out and I'm definitely going to pass out if he doesn't touch me some more.

"I say not to speak. I say it many times. I say not to move in the bathroom, but you take off the towel and run around like I cannot hear the sound of your feet. Did you find anything?" He hits me again and as I lay there, trying to recover from the sting of his palm, he shoves two fingers past the cotton barrier of my panties and into my pussy. My legs spasm and I gasp.

"Shh," he barks, "you will make no sounds. Keep your legs apart. Wider." He slaps the inside of my thigh until I'm splayed before him like a starfish with no arms.

I thought I'd been in pain before, but now the true torture begins. He licks the underside of my ass, tasting it before moving lower. He slides his tongue all the way into my body, but when I start to pant, he withdraws. He does this half a dozen times until I'm so dizzy I start to see stars.

"You want to come?"

I nod vigorously, biting my lips between my teeth to keep from screaming.

"What will you do, to come?"

Anything, I mouth.

"*Khorosho*. Sit up."

I struggle to complete the task with the way my mind reels and the way my hands are bound. Eventually, he grows impatient and jerks me upright by the arms. He stands in front of me with his pants around his ankles and slides his fingers through my hair. I nearly unhinge my jaw as I struggle to capture his entire length. The salty musk of his precum makes me whimper. He moans in response. His mouth falls open and he caresses my cheek with his thumb as he looks down at me.

"Good girl. Tighter." I suck him harder, my mouth forming a vacuum around his cock. "Very good. *Khorosho*," he says, and though his voice is even I can still see how his chest heaves beneath his tee shirt. He removes it and I stare up at his face between his pecs, each decorated with a different tattoo. Last time, I was too dazed to focus on them. I'm too dazed this time too.

He drops to his knees in front of me and he kisses my mouth. My lips are swollen from the size and pressure around his nine-inch shaft, but his skin is so soft. I kiss him hard and he clutches my body to his chest. I'm shaking badly and his surety embarrasses me. He must feel how badly I want him. If he were to stop now, it would ruin me but he might be able to walk away from this.

"I will fuck your ass now. Do you want this?" he says, breaking the kiss. I nod, panting so hard I nearly suffocate myself. He doesn't smile and there is a sort of haunting emptiness in his eyes that frightens me. "Would you tell me if I hurt you?"

I'm not sure how to answer that. I want him to do everything to me that he wants just so long as he gives me the release I know he knows how to give.

"You can answer," he says when I do not.

I nod. "You won't hurt me."

The darkness that had been clouding his expression lifts and when he leans in towards me it's to kiss me softly on each cheek. I've never been kissed like that before and my eyes are closed for a long time after the pressure of his mouth fades. Cool air brushes every place his lips travel, sending fireworks exploding across my skin.

He lowers me to the blanket and the head of his cock strokes the crease of my ass for many moments before gently probing, seeking entry. At the same time, his body contours to my back. Hand slithers across my stomach and snakes between my hips, first finding my clit and then my pussy. He slides into both of my holes at the same time and when my mouth opens, two fingers of his free hand coat my tongue. I close my lips around them and pain and pleasure roll over me in alternating strokes as he begins moving slowly in and out of my body. He has me entirely pinned to the ground beneath him and his breath is hard in my ear.

"Ify," he whispers.

I moan around his hand, trying to relax while he captures me entirely, penetrating me at the same time and in any and every way possible. He glides forward again, stretching my tightest hole with his length and his width. Then it comes. The orgasm I so desperately needed. I can't hold it back and it hurts like hell as my ass pulses around his dick.

I bite down on his hand and he pulls his fingers out of my mouth with a grunt. Spit drips onto the blanket but his mouth finds mine regardless. He kisses me long and deep, absorbing the sound of my scream into his mouth. My pussy clenches around his hand and something enormous fills my ass, like a balloon blown. When my fluttering eyelids open for a second, it's to see his face contorted in a mask of lust.

"Ify," he moans and as his hips jerk forward, pushing his dick as deep inside of me as anything has ever been before, his fingers pick up their pace, this time focusing on my clit. The second orgasm builds up in me too quickly and I gather a swatch of fabric in my mouth to keep myself from biting off my tongue as it roars over me like a locomotive on the run. The pleasure is so overwhelming it hurts and the pain serves only to intensify it. I'm sweating and his sweaty chest is against my skin as each of my muscles chooses that moment to give in and give up.

The orgasm cracks like an egg over my head and I am sucked into the pleasure for so long, I don't remember resurfacing. Maybe I don't. Because the last thing I feel is his cock slowly pulling out of my ass and the last thing I smell is his cool, minty breath and his hot, salty cum. Then I float away and it's high tide.

Gavriil

Suka blyad. My body is pulsing and raw, like one exposed heart, as I roll off of her. *Derr'mo.* I wait a moment for the world to settle around me – until I no longer see double – and I rub my eyes, then glance over at her. Her ass is what I see first and despite how she has wrung me out, a surge of blood rushes south, out of my chest and head, at the sight of her semen-covered ass hole.

I sit up and spread her cheeks, just so I can see it better. The little gaping hole full with my seed. It covers her ass like a glaze. I wonder if I haven't been too hard with her. She said it was alright and she seemed to enjoy it, but she is not an honest girl. Perhaps she was not ready and I took advantage.

"Ify?" I say. I hate that my voice is no longer strong. What I hate more is the fact that she's not moving.

Panic climbs up the backs of my thighs, much like the orgasm had, but I now feel fear where I had felt pure, unadulterated pleasure seconds previous. I grab her by the shoulders and roll her onto her back, push her hair out of her face with my hands.

"Ify!"

Her eyelids flutter and her large, moist mouth curves up in a smile. "What time is it?" she says.

I bark out a laugh that I have never heard before. It is one of relief. "Do you feel pain? Are you injured? Did I bring you harm?"

"Holy shit," she whispers. She shakes her head. "No. I... that was...I need to sleep now."

I laugh again, the sound rattling through my core. "Stay awake with me."

"I can't."

"At least tell me how you feel."

"I feel wiped." Her voice is a cracked whine. She needs something to drink, but I'm loathe to leave her side.

"But the pleasure. Did you feel it too?" Not knowing if I used her still vexes me. I should have been more careful, but when I walked into the room and came upon her fidgeting there in the corner all I had seen was myself inside of her. I did not care that she ran around, disobeying me, because I had lied to myself earlier. I care that she is here. I care more about that than anything Anatoly has said to me tonight. I have never met a woman like her before. One who I wanted and wanted to gag simultaneously.

She smiles. "Pleasure must be your middle name. Gavriil pleasuretown..." Her eyes close and her slurred speech fades. Her light breathing is all that exists between us and I carefully rub my thumb across her face. Leaning over, I kiss her forehead and sigh.

I cannot say I'm not pleased that what I gave her was enough to knock her out. But I can say that I had wanted to give her more. Gathering her in my arms, I kiss her neck. It tastes of salt and rose, a little like lavender. Clean and fresh and also like come. My come. Mine.

I don't like the weight of the word as it rolls through me or the possessiveness that warps my speech and thoughts and steps, so I shrug it off and stagger with Ify unevenly towards the bathroom.

I turn on the water and wait until it is warm – or as warm as it ever gets – and I attempt to use my body to block the direct rays so she is comfortable. I still don't expect her to sleep through it. She does. As I soap up her body and carefully clean each crack and crevice of her skin, the girl even starts to snore. I laugh at that, and I'm laughing still as I dry her off and lower her onto the bed.

I wish I had more to give her, but as I lie beside her, I feel like I have enough with her here. It is an uncomfortable and uncommon feeling, for I know that this is only an interlude. That she is only here out of boredom or the thrill. She does not know what her coming does for me. I find myself nodding off as I lie beside her, but I am afraid to sleep in a way that I have never been. The faster I sleep, the faster she is gone from me, so I force myself to stay lucid.

My eyes are closed despite my best efforts when I feel soft patterns being traced over my skin. I wake and there is sunlight threatening the horizon and peeking in through the foul edges of the stained cardboard shutters. I scowl, disappointed.

"Did I wake you up?" she asks.

I shake my head, then nod, deciding that I will not lie to her. She lies enough for two. "*Da*, you did."

"Sorry."

"No need for sorry. You should have woken me sooner. Have you been awake many hours?"

She pauses to consider and I look over at her and see that she's wrapped a brightly colored piece of fabric around her hair but other than that, is still unclothed. That pleases me to no end. I had thought she would be gone by now, or at least, dressed and ready for the day ahead. After all, she got what she came for.

"No. Like thirty minutes."

"Why you not wake me?" I grab her hand and bring it to my mouth.

She smiles and I see she has small, straight teeth. "I don't know." She shrugs. Her shoulders are so narrow, her bones all so small. She could break if I just looked at her wrong. "I like watching you sleep. You look like a boy. Your face is so calm, you don't have any of these lines." She skims her pinky across a space between my eyes, then around my lips. "You look about nineteen."

She giggles and she is teasing me and I love the way she teases. It makes me want to spank her again. I roll onto my side and wrench her beneath me, but she holds up both hands. "No, no, no. If you punish me again I might just fall apart." She laughs and winces in the same breath.

I settle to the side of her, rather than on top, which is where I want to be. On top of her, hips between her legs, pumping into her mercilessly. "Are you hurting?"

She smiles and wrinkles her nose. "Well, I'm not *not* hurting."

"What do you mean?"

"I mean, if I could move my arms, then I would totally fuck you again."

I grin and pull the clean blanket at the end of the bed back up to her chest. "I like to fuck you."

"I like to fuck you too." She laughs and reaches up to touch my hair. "Did you cut it?"

I am embarrassed that she notices, but pleased that she has. "*Da.*"

"You do that for me?" She sticks out her tongue.

I lean in and nibble on it. "*Nyet,*" I say, remembering that I just told myself I would not lie to her. I have broken this promise to her that she does not know I have made. I will not do it again.

"Well whoever you did it for, it looks good on you."

"*Spasibo.*" I kiss the underside of her chin and the lean line of her throat, over her collar bones before she gasps and I wrench away. "I do not mean to get you excited." And suddenly I have lied to her a second time.

"I'm easy to excite."

I do not like that answer, but try to maintain my easy expression as I ask, "Do you have husband?"

"What?" She laughs. "Get out of here." She flips back the blanket and hesitantly places her feet on the floor. She shivers and though my skin is warm, I am cold on the inside. "What happened to that box I brought?"

"Your things are on desk."

She pads over to them and I close my eyes, unwilling to watch as she puts back on her clothes. While she shuffles around, I lie down, stare up at the ceiling, and wait to hear the door open and shut. Then there is a depression next to me on the mattress and I look over, shocked to see her sliding back under the covers. Her warmth settles against mine with confidence.

She hisses when her ass meets the sheets, and I feel a rivaling guilt war with my irrevocable need. I have never wanted any woman more. I do not know what it is about her. Her lies, that massive mouth, or the need that shines in her eyes when I bend low to kiss her lips. I had not found her beautiful at first glance. Now when I think of beauty, I cannot think of anything else.

She props the box of pizza on my stomach and pulls open the blue bag she'd brought with her. From it, she produces a 15-inch Macbook Air and when she opens it up, she selects a movie from her iTunes. "Wanna watch the last Avengers?" She presses play before she waits for my answer and I roll my eyes.

"You are only child, yes?"

"Shut up." She shoots me a sideways glance, but as she flips open the box top and the movie title flashes across the screen, I see the way her bullet-proof pride is denuded a little bit. "Maybe."

The pizza is scattered across the cardboard, toppings in disarray, but we sit up together and begin in on the slices. I had not realized how hungry I was until it occurs to me that the box is empty and she has only eaten two pieces.

"You're an animal," she says with a laugh as I glance around, searching for more to consume. I go to the cupboard and fish out a two liter of coke and we share it, drinking directly from the bottle.

The movie is on, but we don't watch. Instead, she asks me what other kinds of foods I like to eat and the next thing I know the movie has ended and we are still speaking about Russian food and drink and customs both modern and old. I tell her about Lake Opa. I tell her many things. And I ask her questions in return, not because I feel obligated, but because I want to know.

By the time I can feel the sun on the windowpane, I have learned that she broke her arm three times. She hates avocados but guacamole is her favorite food – because of the texture, she says. She had a pet ferret growing up and it bit her many times and this is why she does not like pets now. She is not married but she has had many lovers. Over thirty. I ask her for their names but she does not relinquish them and I wonder if it is because she knows I would store them and wait until I am out of this hell hole to hunt down each man one-by-one.

She tells me of her parents. Her mother, who is a retired university dean and her father who is a retired detective. She maintains that she is a perfect amalgamation of the two though she looks like neither. I ask her to see photos and she pulls them up on her laptop. I laugh. Of course she does not look like her parents – they are both white. She was adopted.

She tells me how it was for her being dark skinned in this town and again, my list of people to kill grows longer as she recounts the taunts she experienced at the hands of the football quarterback and his cheerleader girlfriend. She had a difficult time in high school making friends, but a boy called Clifford was there for her as well as a small group of girls who she says she loves and who love her back. How could they not? She is pure, selfish affection. So callously herself and in that raw honesty, even her lies become something endearing.

As she speaks of her parents, her entire face lights up. She cannot lie about such things, as I'm sure I cannot when I speak of Russia and Lake Opa. I want to tell her about Alina and Timur and my family, but I know better than that. We may be bonding now, but she still has an agenda. I want to trust her and hate that I cannot. She cannot trust me either. Even when I was living in luxury on First Street, I was still a man of the shadows. It is only just that to the shadows I return. I do not want to bring her with me, or rather – I want her with me always, but that is not what I want for her.

I learn that she loves her laptop more than any other thing she owns – not because of its value but because it is home to all of the books she writes, published or just for her. I ask her to read the unpublished ones and she struggles with my request. When she finally consents after many rounds of pleading and bargaining and threatening, I tell her that she must read them to me – after all, my English is not so good. I feel guilt when her embarrassment grows for that is lie number three.

She reads me a fictional story of a recluse woman who lives in a house on a hill. The story is steeped in superstition and the principle character suffers from mental illness, making her unreliable. The story, at just twenty pages, is riddled with imaginative details and though very little happens, I find myself compelled to fill in all of the silences with sinister things. The dark pall of her storytelling adds to the experience and I find that when she is finished, the hairs on my arms are standing on end.

I tell her she is good. She smiles, then frowns and looks towards the door and tells me she must leave for a barbecue at her parents house. It cripples me that I cannot accompany her. Too soon to meet her parents? *Da.* But do I want to? *Da.* Without question.

I see her to her car and give her my phone number, making her one of two people that have such a thing. I do not ask her not to call and I do not ask her not to share it. I understand the risk I take, and I am willing to take it.

She kisses me from her car and asks when she can see me next before I am forced to debase myself and ask her first. Pride perhaps, or cowardice. I do not tell her what I want, but that it is up to her. She asks me if she may come Sunday and I feel crazed not knowing why she cannot return to me after her barbecue that night. I tell her that is fine. As if I could suffer any longer a break than the one day.

She tells me she will bring more food and things for us to do and I tell her all the things I will do to her if she does not remain safe. She smiles at me and waves out of her window as she drives off. I stand there and stare after her with a grin on my face, wondering abruptly where my desire to leave this Earth has gone. Perhaps with her, in that car.

No, I will not leave. I will make a stand. Because I have found happiness, no matter how brief and ephemeral, and I am too selfish a man to give it up. If what Anatoly says is true, Roman will come soon and I will negotiate a truce, one that allows me to leave this darkness and live with Ify in the light.

I watch the computer screen with my eyes squinted. It doesn't make sense. "It doesn't make sense."

Dixon nods in agreement. "He's been standing there for twenty minutes."

Staring at the bank. The man with the jet black hair tied back into a ponytail doesn't even wait in his car. He just stands on the sidewalk staring at the front entrance of the bank with his head cocked to one side and his arms crossed over his chest. We wouldn't have even known he was with the Russians if he hadn't shrugged out of his jacket and exchanged it for a heavier one in his trunk.

When he did, that gave us a glimpse of the eight-pointed star on the back of his hand and a two-headed eagle perched on a sickle on the back of each of his elbows. The former likely denotes that he's a trigger man, the latter, a member of the mob.

The moment I'd seen all that, I'd pulled my coat on and strapped up to the nines. I was ready to go into battle over the bank. But then Dixon had told me to wait. I'd waited. Minutes passed. No one else showed up to lay siege to the property. Even if they were prepared to, Dixon had asked me, why was I prepared to stop them?

We didn't want the drugs. We didn't need the money.

In fact, letting them raid the bank for the drugs we'd offered up willingly would be the best possible solution for us. Would save us from having to transport it and from the need to confront the Russians directly. A disappointment for me, but only one I'd be willing to stomach because leaving the house to kill them meant leaving Alina behind where anything could happen. Where it already has. That trucker fucker deserved worse than the quick death I gave him.

So I'd stayed with Dixon and watched the screens, which showed the live feed from a series of cameras covering all possible bank entrances. For twenty minutes we've been waiting for him to do something, but all he does is stare at the bank front, fixed like a gargoyle.

"Can you ID him?" Dixon says.

"No." I'd been trying, but with only a profile to go on and the back of his head, I'd been unable to, despite having names and IDs associated with nearly every member of the *Bratva's* operations in the States.

Dixon pauses a long time before he says the words I predict he's going to. "We could ask Alina…"

"No."

"Ask me what?"

I jerk upright as her tiny, sultry tone hits me in the back, threatening to take out both my knees. I turn. She's half visible behind the doorframe. Her hair is braided back behind both ears giving me a full view of her perfect face. The muscles across my stomach tighten like I've just swallowed dynamite while my cock and thighs stiffen. It's like this every time and I feel like a goddamn pervert. Still, I don't look away.

It's been over a week since she ran and since then, I still can't believe how much time we've spent together. Hours out of the day. Hours into the night. She reads and I watch her. We gym together. She insists on making me breakfast every damn day. We go on walks together around the property. She speaks to me now with increased regularity, half the time not seeming to care whether or not I give her a response.

I wonder how much she knows.

Does she know what I did to that trucker? I found him three days ago. It hadn't been too hard. She'd been sleeping and I'd stolen out in the middle of the night. He runs the same route every week. Or at least, he ran it. Not anymore though. Now they'll be finding pieces of him scattered around town for weeks. He'd been alive when I dismembered him.

I open my mouth to tell her to leave, but I can't get the words out. I can't say no to her like I could before. Before I knew the risks. If she runs again, it'll slaughter me.

Even now, I can still see the fresh scar along her right temple that disappears into her hairline. *And I did that.* I can't believe she fought the fucker. That she had to fight him. Seeing the scratches on his face had made me proud and afraid. They were the reasons I was able to take my time. Knowing she got away. Imagining what could have happened if she hadn't escaped or if I hadn't found her haunts me anytime she isn't in the same room. Because seeing her is the only thing that lets me know for sure that she's okay. The only thing that makes breathing okay. Seeing her. And also touching her. I want to touch her.

I wonder how much she knows.

She's in my bones. Does she know that?

My mouth dries up as her brows furrow and I wonder if I haven't spoken out loud. Panic consumes me until she comes into the room, looking past me at the computer screen. What the hell did Dixon just say?

"*Da.* I know him. That is Anatoly."

Anatoly Zherdev. Not high in the global hierarchy, but one of the more established presences in the US. From what info I'd gathered on him, he'd been this side since he was sixteen. Damn near fully assimilated, I wonder how he knows Alina, who'd only been in the US on a permanent basis for the past five years.

A lethal emotion – brought on by a dangerous thought – cuts me in half like a sabre through a sheet. And it isn't a thought I should have. There are more important things. But I can't shake it. I need to know how she knows him. Because I'll have to kill him if I find out they dated.

I wonder if Alina can feel the heat rolling off of me because her mismatched gaze flashes once in my direction. She leans in towards the computer, standing on Dixon's other side and her full breasts push against the barrier of her black tank top. It's Mer's and far too small for her, so I can see her stomach, above the waist of her tight pants. For fuck's sake, she's distracting. I can't think. I can't breathe. I can't be near her but I can't be anywhere else. I made a promise.

"Can you tell us anything about him?" Dixon tilts the monitor in her direction.

She nods. "*Da,* of course. I have known Anatoly since I was girl. He has always been close friend of Gavriil and Timur and my family."

"How close?" The words are mine, spit through clenched teeth. My self-hatred blossoms like a bloody rose as soon as I say the words. I wish I could take them back. They aren't fucking relevant.

She blinks at me the first time with rounded eyes. Then the next time, she grins. She tries to hide it behind her hand, but it's too late. I've already hallucinated heaven. Embarrassment and shame and a hunger more powerful than both leave me paralyzed. I'm ready for death.

"Very close," she says and I turn to ash inside, "but to my brothers only. I do not know him that well." She smiles with her eyes and turns back to the computer while relief harpoons me. My body shatters around it, and disperses in the wind.

"My father and brothers keep me out of the operations, so I do not know his position except that he is body man. Now I think he also helps with shipments to Elmer."

"What's Elmer?" Dixon speaks at the same time I ask, "What would bring him out of Elmer now?"

Alina answers Dixon first, despite the fact that it irritates me. This is old information. I know about Elmer and what happens in that hell hole. It's disgusting and if Anatoly has anything to do with what happens there, it doesn't matter that Alina doesn't know him very well. I'll kill him all the same. Ordinarily I wouldn't give a fuck what cartel and *Bratva* men were dealing in, only now that I know it's women I imagine Alina among them. It gives me nightmares so that I can't sleep unless she's in the room with me. I sneak in at night and sleep in the chair in the corner of her room.

I wonder how much she knows.

Does she know I sleep in her room? Does she know she's the only thing that makes sleep possible for me? In her room, I can even sleep in the dark.

Alina says, "Elmer is place not far from town. It is where shipments go before distribution to US buyers."

"What are they dealing in?"

"Drugs."

"They were dealing in drugs," I correct. "Now it's women."

Alina shakes her head. "*Nyet*. You are wrong. My father never allowed sex trade. Gavriil would have shut it down."

I see pain flash in her eyes as I shake my head slowly. "They started dealing in women right after shit went down at the barn. Not all of it goes to Elmer though. Some of it is going somewhere else. I think somewhere in the Ternary."

Alina's eyes are huge. She doesn't answer me.

"Are they trying to cover the deficit from the drug loss through prostitution?" Dixon asks.

"Elmer isn't a brothel, it's a way-station. They bring the women from the port to Elmer, small vans and cars take women out of Elmer. My guess is to take them to brothels or to be sold individually."

Alina's got both hands clamped around the edge of the table. Her face is white as a sheet. I'm worried. What if she collapses?

"How much money can they possibly make doing that?"

I shrug. "I guess not enough. More women are coming in all the time."

Dixon curses and takes his hands back through his thick hair, shoving his mohawk off-center. My eyes are pinned to

Alina. "That's gotta be hundreds of women then every month. Fuck."

Alina clutches her chest with one hand. I catch her just as she starts to fall. The long lines of her shape feel like water in my arms. I carry her to the leather sofa against the wall, the one flanked on all sides by books I've never read. There's an empty bottle and a blanket with railroad tracks printed on it on the ground in front of the couch. I kick it aside and kneel in its place. There's baby shit everywhere in the house now.

Alina plants her elbows on her knees and holds her face in her hands. I say her name repeatedly and she shakes her head. "So many women…" Her watery eyes meet mine. "Are you sure Gavriil didn't know?"

I'm not sure, and I go to tell her that, but looking deep into her eyes and seeing her pain so unruly and raw, I can't tell her that. So I do something I've never done before. I lie to her. I lie to her because I want all of the agony she experiences now and forever to be mine. "I'm sure. Erik didn't trust him. He would have kept his operations close."

"But Roman did. Roman trusted him and how could Roman not have known?" Alina's hands find mine and she squeezes. I don't know what to do. I let her hold me. Feeling like an idiot. I want to know what to do. What would Clifton do in this situation? He'd probably put his arm around her, cradle her like a kid and whisper nice things softly into her ear.

If I put my arm around her I'll probably crush her. If I cradle her, she'll feel how perverted I am to still be hard at the sight of her, even like this. And I don't know nice things. I know nothing but violence and cruelty. I see the pain on her face now. *And I did this.*

"Who is Roman?" I speak through my teeth.

"Erik's father. My uncle. He took over after my father died."

This comes as news to me and I feel stymied by it. "Erik isn't in charge?"

"*Nyet.* Not even US operations. Roman does not trust Erik to do things alone. Our father wanted Gavriil to take over. Gavriil would have stopped them from selling women. He would have stopped them if only he'd taken control…"

She's going to cry and if she does I'm not going to survive it. "Don't cry," I snap at her.

She bites her lips between her teeth and opens her eyes. Seeing me, she inhales once, and then again. I realize she's mimicking my breathing. I slow it down even more and watch as eventually the glass glaze coating her gaze subsides. And I did this.

"He still might," I say quietly, "If Erik has enough support on the inside to run women without Roman's approval, then Gavriil could have enough support to overthrow him."

"He is dead." Her voice cracks.

I shake my head. "He's a tough guy. He'll come back for you."

A few moments pass. The sight of color returning to her cheeks feels like a goddamn miracle. Something in my chest explodes. It's big and sifts through my ribcage like sludge. My core feels hollow and full at the same time. And that's when I realize what my hands are doing.

They are gripping her hands and bringing them to my lips. I kiss her knuckles and then turn her hands over so I can taste the insides of her palms. The taste of her isn't like anything I've ever had before. I want to smoke her. Swallow her up one piece at a time. My arms are moving in patterns they never have before, patterns I can't control. I just want to keep touching her, but I know she's going to recoil from me any second. Move away. Move the fuck away. Finally, my mind succeeds in battering my muscles into submission. I lurch back towards the computer monitor and Dixon, still seated in front of it. As I do, Alina stares after me with large, moon eyes.

"Your brother is a good man," I grunt.

She blinks rapidly, then nods after a moment. "But only if he is alive."

"We're sure he's still alive," Dixon says. "We think that the reason that Erik hasn't come after us or the bank is because he believes Gavriil has the drugs. If Gavriil were dead, we think he'd be more likely to come looking for us. As it stands now, we don't even seem to be on his radar."

Alina nods, and the grief finally clears from her expression. She rubs her legs rapidly with her hands as if trying to warm them. I want to help her do that. Badly. "It is good. You must keep your family safe. That is most important."

And then my own voice, though it doesn't even sound like mine. It sounds like Clifton's. "You're family too."

A blush unlike anything I've ever seen consumes both of Alina's cheeks. She looks away from me quickly.

"That you are," Dixon confirms.

The blush only grows simultaneously brighter and deeper, rolling down her neck to touch her freckled chest. *"Spasibo,"* she says, "You do not know how your words..." She chews on her lower lip, as if searching for the correct English. "Here." She touches her heart and meets Dixon's gaze first before holding mine in a way that will keep me rooted to the spot until she chooses to release me. "I feel it here."

Me too. I nod at her. She moves towards the door. "I came to look for you because you said you will train me now, *da?"*

Oh fuck. One-on-one time with Alina is not something I'm prepared for right now. But I made a promise. "Dixon, call me if anything changes."

He nods, and the fucker can't keep the smile off his lips. "Sure thing. But I'm sure it won't." As soon as Alina safely clears the room, Dixon winks at me. I trip as I follow her. I don't think the bastard's ever smiled at me before and I can be damn sure that no one – *no one* – has ever winked at me. Because winking at me means that they're treating me like something I'm not: like I'm human.

Alina

He corrects my stance by kicking my feet first closer together and then wider apart. He keeps his hands clasped behind his back and is looking down his nose at me, frowning, but not in the way he did before. No, now he frowns less. Now he meets my gaze and sneaks stolen glances at me when he thinks I am not looking, more and more.

"Use the power from your back leg to push your torso forward. Swivel your hips. No. Don't ball your fists like that, you'll break your thumbs. Cross your thumbs over the front of your fingers. Yes, like that. Now jab."

I try to follow all of his instructions at the same time as I throw my weight forward into the punching bag. My hands are wrapped but my knuckles are still aching and I sweat from every pore. I wonder if he can see it. There's no way he can't. It makes me feel even more self-conscious than I already am because I know I'm doing it wrong.

He hisses. "You're not pivoting, you're falling. Plant your feet. Don't drop your arms."

It is difficult for me to remember why I asked him to train me now. He had rejected when I'd first asked, but I'd insisted and now I'm wondering if maybe I haven't really lost my sanity after all.

"No. Don't sink into your stance. Keep your feet rooted when you swing, but you should still be light on the balls of your feet in between jabs," he says, and then when I start bouncing between the balls of each foot, he snarls at me, "Faster. Faster!"

My bones are all rattling and so is the breath in my lungs. I want him to be proud of me and when I dare a glance up at him, I miss my next step. He catches me around the waist so I do not fall. He's wearing a tee shirt and jeans, though I wonder if he is not too hot in them because they are stiff and unyielding when he demonstrates the poses for me.

I imagine him in the basketball shorts that I have seen him in before and my thoughts come up short. My breathing hitches and he is looking down at me now, expression unreadable, like I hope mine is. Because I am picturing how he might look in basketball shorts, with the outline of his thighs visible. I want to see this. I want to see him in less.

"I think it's time for a break," he says, releasing me and flexing his hands. He does this every time we touch and I do not know why. The small, very insecure part of me fears that I do something to disgust him though the larger part of me knows that is not the case. I see how he watches me. Not like other men. But more.

He hands me a bottle of water and I take it in shaking arms, then drain almost all of it. "*Spasibo.*"

"*Pozhaluysta.*"

"Your accent is very good," I say and watch him redden. I laugh.

"*Spasibo,*" he mumbles, turning away.

We sit for a little while more in silence. It is not unpleasant. It is nice. At least for me. I watch him openly, enjoying the way his shoulders are broad and his arms are muscular and strong. His tee shirt flutters over his stomach in a breeze I cannot feel. I want to see his stomach and the ribbing of his abdomen. His face is hardened lines, but he no longer looks so starved – not of food, but of affection. He is starting to look more approachable now, or maybe it is just the way I see him. Either way, something changed after the man in the truck, after Aiden brought me home.

He'd taken me to his room, carrying me the whole way. He hadn't put me down. Like he was afraid to. He'd closed the door behind him and the lights had been on, bright as ever with no possibility for reprieve because they'd been taped that way. He'd taken me to the chair in the corner and had sat down with me on his lap. He'd been shaking as he told me he would never let me get hurt again. And then he'd short circuited completely when I told him I wouldn't let anything hurt him either.

Maybe it was just the adrenaline, because after I'd fallen asleep in his arms and woken up in my bed, stitched and mended, we'd never been back to the conversation. But even if it had just been nerves, there is something different now between us – scary in its own right, but scary good.

"Aiden?" My throat catches when his too grey eyes pass over mine. They are so light, like an overcast day. I smile down at my water bottle. "Never mind."

"What is it?" He insists.

I divert, both my gaze and my question. "I hear others say that Charlie asks for your training. Do you help him?"

"No," he says after a slight pause.

"*Pochemu by i net?*" Why not?

"Because." And then Aiden does something very small. Because though he has all but ended the conversation, something greater presses him on. His voice catches and in the brokenness that is left, I make out a few words. "Because I don't want to see myself in him." And I have never heard a greater truth or a greater sadness.

I open my mouth to say something and am nearly grateful he beats me to it. "Are you ready?"

My gut drops and my shoulders sag involuntarily. "We are not finished?"

"Did you want to be?"

"*Nyet.* No," I lie.

"Good. Then come here." He points to a stack of mats on the floor behind the boxing bags. Starting towards them, he shoves one with his foot so that it skates out into the middle of the empty gym. The gym is grey walls and a grey ceiling and a grey floor. There are no windows anywhere, and only the one door. It's cool in here too, and quiet now that Aiden is no longer playing such violent music.

"Come here," he says and I feel that I am compelled forward, like a hook is buried in my chest and bound to his will. He pulls and I go. I follow him and when I am close enough, he takes my elbow in his wrist and positions me on the mat across from him. Electricity fires between us at just the brush of his palm over my skin and when he looks at me with his grey, hooded eyes, I know he feels it too.

"Hands up. Good. Like that. We spar now."

"*Shto?*" He can't mean...

"*Da.* Against me."

"But I..." I shake my head. "You are too strong."

He inhales quickly and I wonder what I have said to get this reaction from him now. He shakes his head, like he's shaking himself out of a stupor. "My size doesn't matter. There are tricks against a bigger opponent. You've seen Mer fight, and if you haven't, you will. Once you get the basics down, I want Mer to join our practice sessions. She is a disciplined fighter and goes up against men three times her size and wins."

I nod, understanding that Mer is a bull in the ring though I have not yet had the privilege of seeing it. For a moment I feel guilt and something ugly at the thought of Mer. Maybe… would Aiden like me more if I were stronger like her? My back jaw clenches and when I stand in the center of the mat and form my hands into fists, it is with renewed determination.

"Good," he says. He adjusts the angle of my wrists and I memorize the hold, then he steps back. "The body shot we practiced. Aim here." He pats his left side, just below the sternum. "The solar plexus. If you get close enough to a man as big as me, it'll be your easiest shot. You'll have to hit him hard though…" His voice trails off, as if he has not completed his sentence. I realize after a moment, that he is waiting for me to act.

"You…want me to…"

"*Da.*" His voice is hard, unyielding. He smacks his own chest hard enough the sound echoes against the concrete surrounding us. "Hit me."

Hit him. Hit him? "I practice against the bag. How can I hit you?"

"Hit me!" I jump. He hisses. "Don't you dare flinch. Now do it. Hit me, Alina."

I strike the place he shows me, hitting him as hard as I can.

"You couldn't hurt anyone with that. Now hit me. Hit me like I'm the fucker from that truck," his own voice catches, and when he speaks again, his pitch is gravel. "Hit me like he's here, and you want to show him you're not afraid."

I rotate my arm so that my wrist is facing up and then I hit him in the space he showed me. He blinks longer than he had the last time and nods once. Then barks, "Good. Again." I hit him again and can feel the clenching of his muscles through his tee shirt. "Don't ease up. Again." I strike. "Again!"

I'm breathing harder and harder with every punch to his solar plexus until finally... "Oomph." I win that sound from him. Just the one, but it's enough for me to turn my face up and smile.

"Did that really hurt you?"

His mouth twitches and I see, not a full smile, but the ghost of one. He tilts his head to the side. "Maybe." And suddenly his leg sweeps my feet and I am falling.

I hit the mat on my back and gasp – both because I am winded, but also because he is on top of me as men are known to be on top of women. My heart is in my mouth. There is a fire all across my abdomen that I have felt only a few times before. His shoulders eclipse my frame and my first thought is not to push them away, but to hold onto them.

"Now if a man is ever able to get you down on the ground, you hit the same spot on his stomach, but with your knee." His left hand is on my hip, sliding down my thigh. I am wearing leggings and a tank top, but I feel as if I am in nothing.

I gasp as he jerks up on my left leg, gripping it underneath the knee. "This motion. Try it."

"I don't want to hurt you."

He meets my gaze, and it softens, just as it did when he held me in that chair in his arms. "You can't hurt me," he whispers. And then he clears his throat and looks away. "Try it," he says, but his voice is gruffer than it was before. He does not look at me in the eyes. It seems he struggles not to look at me at all.

Carefully, I jerk my knee up. "Like this?"

"Almost. You need to aim a little bit higher." His hand is on my thigh again, repositioning my leg. "Try now."

I try once more.

"Good. Harder now."

I practice the move a few more times to his encouragement until finally I bring my knee up – hard – and he emits a light grunt. The motion causes his hand to slip from my thigh even lower. His palm cups the curve of my ass. And lingers. *Moi boch…*

My eyes close and my fingers dig into the cotton covering his shoulders. His body is so warm and I'm absorbed in his heat. The tension in my body releases and my head drops back. I wrap up his tee shirt in my fists and I try to pull him down, closer towards me but in the next instant he is gone.

I blink my eyes open and Aiden is standing off of the mat, staring down at me with a strange expression I can't interpret. He backs away, clears his throat, looks at the mirror that lines one wall and, seeing me in it, begins gathering the water bottles and towels he brought up off of the floor.

"I think that's enough for our first lesson."

"But I was just getting it," I say, and I wonder if he can hear the longing coloring my tone because he trips.

Carmine colors his cheeks, which glow brighter than his full lips. They look soft, those lips. I lick my own as I think of his. "We're done here."

He's halfway to the door before I amble up onto my knees. "Will you…" I can't remember what I want to ask. Other than for him to come back to where he was on top of me. "Tomorrow?" I blurt.

He nods. "*Da*. Tomorrow," he barks, and just before he leaves the room he turns back to me. "You did well today."

I grin and a little fire kindles in my chest. I did well today. Yes. I think I did. And so does he. "*Spasibo*, Aiden. And Aiden?"

"Alina?"

My chest sizzles at the sound of my name in his voice. I nod at him. "You are good teacher. You should help Charlie."

He waits a moment before quietly disappearing, leaving me thinking about a blush the color of blood, and eyes the color of water. Something in each of us and between us is changing, and I no longer feel so much like the hunted. I feel almost as if I'm beginning down a path, one in which I am no longer the princess, but the one who hunts.

Charlie

The crowd is pitching like the sea and sounds like thunder. I'm sweating so much the tape has started to peel back from my wrists. I'm bleeding from a wound in my forehead and another one along my right rib cage, but I'm still here. I've already gone one round and I'm still standing.

Aiden came by for the first time yesterday. It was completely unannounced and he'd scared the piss out of me when he'd barreled into my shitty apartment and started barking orders. I tried asking him what was up, and why he changed his mind, but he hadn't responded to that either. Instead, he'd come and filled my head with so much stuff that I feel like I should have known for years and just as quickly, left. Like a ghost, it would be easy to imagine having hallucinated the fucker, but the evidence is here. I'm still here. Still standing.

The bear across from me roars and beats his fists together, but he's not half as intimidating as Aiden or even that Jesus, Mary, n' Joseph mother fucker I'd fought weeks before, and I'm not half as intimidated as my muscles recall some of the new tricks and techniques Aiden ran me through yesterday. I'm nervous, yeah, but I'm not afraid. I can do this.

The cage cunt comes into the ring and the guys pressed against the chainlink fence shake fistfuls of money and light up the underground parking garage in howls and hollers. She takes a turn around the ring, sweeping first in front of me and trailing her fingers across my scarred chest, before mimicking the gesture for my opponent.

It's a signal I understand, and once would have riled me up as it has this idiot across from me. He tracks her with his gaze as she saunters around the center of the blood-spattered space, massaging her big, fake titties, and spanking her round, fake ass. Most of the time the cage cunts stay outside of the cage, but when they come inside it's to offer themselves up. Ring winner gets an added bonus. I never understood what the cage cunts get out of it and I still don't. The idiot across from me is an ugly fuck and he's still twice as pretty as I am.

She leaves the cage, zips it up with ties and loiters near the entrance with the four other cunts eyeing the men holding the fattest wads of cash. I attack first, while he's still glancing around at the women and the crowd cheering him on.

Aiden told me to use any opportunity I have to surprise my opponent. Don't show fear. Don't hesitate to strike first. I always did before – wanting to understand the fighting style of my opponent so I can learn how to defend to survive. But Aiden says I'm not here to survive the ring. I'm here to win. And in the blunt way that bastard speaks, I'm inclined to believe him.

The crowd screams louder behind my opponent. He's the favorite and I haven't proven myself in the way some of the others have. Like Aiden. Last time I saw him fight in here, the crowd lost its goddamn mind. He hasn't been back in a while though, since he brought home that pretty girl in a black duffel bag.

My fist collides with my opponent's rib cage. I nail him once before switching under his arm and swiveling to the right. My knuckles find the tender space above his kidney and I manage to get three shots off before he retaliates. His elbow meets my abdomen and I jump back as he kicks. He connects with my left thigh the first time. The second time he misses. I don't. In a new move Aiden taught me, I kick him in the chest so hard that it throws me back. I almost fall – shit, I need to practice that – but at least I don't lose my balance altogether. I'm able to recover faster and find him before he ambles up off the dusty, sweat and blood-soaked floor.

I kick him once, but he trips me up in a move I don't know. He drags me to the concrete and we grapple over it. He manages to bloody my mouth, but I regain the upper hand when I twist his arm behind his back. He won't cede, so I dislocate his shoulder and when I stand back, the crowd lets loose a cheer, though most of the men around me are booing. They lost money tonight, but the next time, they'll think twice about betting against me.

I don't try my luck with the next guy. I'm winded and my muscles are juiced, but soupy. Another lesson from Aiden. When your muscles are screaming for the next fight, deny them. Don't get greedy. It's advice he gives, but not advice I'm sure he follows.

I exit the ring and some men move in to drag my opponent out. He's bleeding from his nose and eyes and mouth and I watch a trail of crimson follow him until it disappears into the crowd and so does he. The whole place smells like metal and salt and concrete after a storm. My fingertips feel like all of those things too as I rub them together. The cage cunt has her hands on my bare chest but all I feel is that blood, that sweat, that rain.

She's telling me things I would have wanted to hear in another lifetime but all I hear is the sound of bare feet thudding over the floor as two new men take the ring. She shoves her tits in my face, but all I see is that trail of crimson and when I blink, a set of breasts shredded and weeping. I did that.

I shrug off the cage cunt and am prepared to leave until I notice the next contenders taking the ring. The guy who beat the shit out of me last time. The Virgin Mary. He grins at me as he shoves past me past the cage cunt and I hesitate, lingering in the folds of the crowd as it screams his name.

"Gor-ge, Gor-ge, Gor-ge!" He's the favorite. Unbeatable through the first few rounds.

He breaks the ribs of the first man he fights, the arm of the second, and both legs of the third. The fourth... The man lies beneath him on the concrete floor, defeated and spent, but the Virgin Mary pounds his fists into the man's face again and again. He kicks and hits until the man is limp. No, not limp. Dead.

The crowd is screaming, frothing and wild like the sea around rocks. Violent memories squeeze into my thoughts. They are brutal and impenetrable. And this is my fault.

The bastard lifts both fists into the air and, with blood streaking his chest and his fists hardened to blocks, he glances around, waiting. There is no one left. No one but the screaming crowd and the cage cunts throwing their bodies at the chainlink fence, eager to be brutalized in whatever way he'll take them.

What is wrong with them? What is wrong with him? What is wrong with everyone here? I know what's wrong with me, but what did the world do to the rest of these fucks to make them like this? Pain clutches at my chest, and it's not of the physical kind. And as I turn around in the crowd, Virgin Mary meets my gaze and winks.

Out in the darkness of the night, I take a left at the corner of Sixty-Ninth and Starlight. Low brick buildings span to my left and right. The black night hovers above, but can't touch one brightly lit building two blocks down.

Making my way towards it, I flex my fists and jab them in the air, keeping my body temperature up to fight against the winter. I dive, duck, and flex against imaginary opponents. I try to relive my fight from the night without dwelling on the injuries I sustained or caused. I don't picture the bodies leaking crimson across the floor. I don't hear the sound of flesh cracking through flesh. I definitely don't see the cage cunt's fake tits or the knife... I definitely don't see the knife.

"Augh!" I slam my fist forward and my whole body clenches. I feel the foe I'm fighting, but I can't hit him and I'm left broken and wanting. The wind rips and my mind wanders. I'm not strong enough. I have to keep fighting. I need to go back to the ring. Maybe if I can kill like Aiden can I'll be able to kill the ghosts that haunt me ceaselessly.

"Are you alright?"

I open my eyes. It's two am and the typically empty sidewalk is broken up by a woman wrapped in baggy black clothes. Her face is pale, but familiar. She looks like the moon in the bright light of the storefront across the street. A vet clinic. Wonder what sort of overpriced poodle she needed to take in at this hour. It's as I imagine what brought this rich bitch out here tonight that I realize, I recognize her. She's definitely the same woman who stared at me, so aghast and appalled, all those nights ago. She'd been with a man. I wonder where he is now that he lets his poorly dressed wife walk in the dark at two am all alone on the streets with thugs like me.

"Are you alright?" she says again. She tucks her hair behind her ear even though it's already tied back into a ponytail at the base of her skull. She's got car keys in her hand and when I glance up the length of her body, gaze finally settling on her face, she turns and presses the button.

Beep beep. Car lights flash behind her and she edges back towards it – same car I saw her in before. I scoff, amazed by her arrogance, and move forward. She's scrambling back now, and falls against the side of her car as I brush past and as I brush past, I spit, "Don't flatter yourself. Fuck if I'd be bothered."

The words are terse and clipped and I hate myself for saying them because I speak with every intention of wanting to hurt this rich bitch in the way I've been wounded by her fear. At the same time, I still pull my hood down as I pass her and turn my face away so she can't see the carnage.

Aiden

My feet pound on the treadmill completely out of contrast with the classical music – Bach, I think – that's playing. Clunk, clunk, clunk, clunk, clunk. Crick. My ears flex back and my gaze searches the mirror in front of me for the grey paneled door at my back. It swings open and Alina is there, hair full and wild like I like it, though slightly damp in places like she's just come from the shower. Her cheeks are red and pretty and her eyes are bright. She sees me in the mirror and smiles and I almost let the treadmill just take me now.

Alina points to her ears and then to the stereo system on the far wall. I mute the random Reggaeton that's overtaken Bach and climb off the treadmill while she steps fully into the room. "*Prosti*, Aiden. I hope I do not disturb you."

I curse under my breath, grab my towel and rub my face with it hard, hoping that the pressure will distract from the sudden bulge along the front of my shorts. Seeing her down here, I can't help but think about having her pinned under me. Sweat shimmering along her hairline. Grunting as she thrusts up with her knee, aiming for my solar plexus. Jesus fucking Christ had I imagined it, or did she moan when I touched her? Since then, our practice sessions have been completely fucking hands off. No more sparring. Shadow-boxing only.

As it is now, I do everything I can not to look at her. "No. It's fine."

I'm conscious of my blood boiling and my pulse racing, but I manage to remain composed even as I take in the sight of her there in nothing but a pair of baggy jeans that don't fit her – Sara's I'm guessing, because they're both too baggy around the thighs and too short – and a crop top with the words "El Camino Boxing" printed on the front of it – Mer's for sure.

Her belly button is visible and there are freckles covering her stomach. For fuck's sake. There are freckles covering her entire body. I've known that for a while. But knowing doesn't curb my desire to count and name each and every one.

She opens her mouth, but doesn't speak. Instead her eyes have widened as her gaze takes me in. What does she see? Does she like it? My mind wants answers that my body doesn't seem to care about, because she's taking inventory and damn if that doesn't perk my dick right up. Fuck.

"What do you want, Alina?" I grunt into my fist.

"Aiden, *kak dela?*" She shakes her head and smiles. I love when she speaks Russian, even when she's reprimanding me. I love my name on her lips. I want more of me on her tongue and the sudden swift and painful image of Alina's perfect mouth wrapped around my cock hits me with enough force to make me see stars for a minute. I need to get out of here. Need to get *her* out of here. Need to get her alone. Fuck. No. What I need is a whore. I haven't had one in weeks. And the thought of going back to one of those women is suddenly exactly what I need. My hard on dissolves to a wilted thing and I'm able to focus on her face with renewed clarity.

"*Khorosho*," I respond, though it's a lie. She's asking me how I'm doing. Good, I tell her, even though the truth would be harrowing if only she could read my mind. "Do you need something?"

"Only your company."

"What?"

"I make...made dinner for you," she stammers, and I feel renewed empathy for her as I do every time she stutters over a word or bit of English grammar. She has lived in the US for almost five years now, but still sometimes speaks as if she's a beginner. It's not as if she can't – I saw some of her essays printed when going through her room and sorting through her things those many months ago before she was hunted and before her safety was my top priority – she just doesn't like to.

That's why in the dark hours of the night when most people sleep, I stay awake trying to learn Russian online. I want to speak to her in the language she likes most. I want to take on the burden of her struggles. At least, I study the nights I'm not sleeping in her room. Like a goddamn pervert.

"You did what?" I say on an inhale.

She nods. "I made *khaliniki* and *pierogi*. All dumplings with different things. The *pierogi* I make are sweet and the *khaliniki* has meat and spices. I make with lamb. And then I make... made *soleniya*, which has cabbage and some vegetables. I don't like it very much but my brothers love...loved it," the word tumbles brutally out of her mouth in the past tense. She blushes and looks like a rising sun, even in the heat of her pain. "I made enough for everyone but the dinner is for you, in your honor."

"Why?"

She shrugs. "To thank you for helping me."

"I haven't done anything."

"You saved me at the barn and I never thank you for that. You came for me after the man in the truck. And now you teach me how to fight." She shrugs. "Plus, I like to cook. So will you eat?"

"When?" I hack out because it's the only thing I can think of to stall. She wants me to eat with her and with my *family*. In my honor. Fuck. How did this happen? Maybe this is still leftover trauma. Maybe she's starting to get that Stockholm thing.

"The food is ready, but I keep it in the oven to stay warm. So take however long you need. I know I interrupt you here." She wrings her hands together, and suddenly it occurs to me: this was difficult for her, and she's wary of my rejection. She doesn't want me to reject her. I choke on my own thoughts and immediately break her gaze.

"Fine. Okay," I choke, and my voice has all the texture of broken glass or gravel.

"So you will eat with me? With us?"

Us. Fuck. Everything. "*Da*. I said okay."

Her subsequent smile is a punch to the gut. She looks striking, and radiantly happy. "*Bolshoy.*" She clasps her hands together underneath her chin and I'm surprised that she doesn't start clapping. She's on the balls of her feet. She turns towards the door, then turns back. "What time do I expect you?" Her hair whips around her shoulders. I want to feel it in my hand, those thick crimson strands, softer than velvet.

Never, I want to tell her, I can't be around you. All I see is the hope in your eyes. All I see is my capacity to destroy it. "I'll shower then come."

"To the kitchen, *da*? That is where I have set up."

"Fine."

"*Spasibo*, Aiden. I'll see you soon." She darts up the stairs and I lumber slowly after, wondering what the hell happened and what I've just agreed to.

I jack off in the shower, head bowed, fisting my cock, hoping it'll be enough to keep me from springing a woody around the chick because I don't need her or any of the brothers seeing that. The brothers. It's only as I pull on a pair of faded jeans and a light grey shirt that it finally occurs to me that I'll be doing something I've never done in this house: I'll be eating with these people that call themselves my family. The thought gives me pause. Not enough however, not to continue.

A chill rips through me as I exit my room and take a left down the hall. I pass through the living room, pass the stairs leading up to the second floor, and finally round the corner into the kitchen. The voices that had been speaking stop. There they are. Seated around the table looking like a Norman Rockwell painting, whoever the fuck that is. The tiles beneath them are black and white checkered and all the appliances are stainless steel.

Mer's standing at the fridge, juggling too many beers in her hands. My doppelganger is laughing at something Knox is saying. Sara's sitting on Dixon's lap, smiling at baby Brant in the kid's seat beside her. Alina is standing at the oven, bent over at the waist, concentrated on something behind the glass.

Everyone stops what they are doing when I walk into the room and looks up at me.

"Hey, you made it. We were waiting for you to eat," Dixon says, glancing up at me with a grin I find unsettling. "Take a seat, brother." I find the moniker even more unsettling.

"Alina was just explaining what we were eating," Mer says, lifting a knee to balance the sixth beer in her arms. The position is precarious and without thought, I find myself moving towards her.

"Here," I grutn.

She freezes when I approach and I can hear the whole room behind me start when I take a few beers from her and pass them out. Jesus, this is fucking tense. I feel a bundle of nerves take root in between my shoulders. This was a mistake. I start to turn, prepared to make a run for it, but then there's Alina, holding a plate.

"*Da*, but I already tell Aiden this," she says, passing me and setting the plate on the table. It's full of little balls of something I can't name. Maybe one of the dumpling things she mentioned.

"Aiden, for you." She pulls out the seat at the head of the kitchen table. It scrapes across the floor and she makes a face. A blush rises in her cheeks. She looks so nervous it discomfits me even more than I already am. Mainly because her reaction would suggest the impossible – that I was right, and that she is the one trying to impress me. "Please have seat."

The one to the left of the seat she stands behind is empty. Presumably hers. Dixon sits at the table's foot, Sara on his right with a giggling Brant between them. Clifton sits across from her on my right while Mer and Knox take the two spaces on the other side of Alina. The table is silent except for the crunching of my chair as I fall into it. I don't make eye contact with the people, but rather wait for Alina to come out from behind me. I don't like people behind me and turn so that I can see her in my peripheries. She's gone to fetch something off of the granite island and when she returns, she holds the bottle of clear vodka towards me. It's frosted on the outside except for the places where her fingers have touched it.

"This is homemade from Russia House. Knox was nice and went to pick it up for me. Can I pour for you?"

I nod and watch her slender wrists as she fills the small bourbon glass on the edge of my placemat, then fills glasses for everyone else. Arriving at her own glass last, she sets down the bottle and speaks. "I want to thank you all for everything you have done for me so far. I would be dead if it weren't for you."

Hearing her say the words out loud makes me shudder. I do so visibly, and I know that these people see it, but Alina keeps smiling and nobody interrupts her. "I know these past weeks have not been easy for anyone, and that my family matters are complicated." She wins a few chuckles at that. "But you all have been brave and kind and I was not...am not easy to take care of. But you all treat me like I am part of the family and I will never forget it. I am grateful. Deeply."

She raises her glass. "So to hospitality and to family."

She glances around at everyone and meets each and every set of eyes with warmth. Something I haven't been able to do and may never be able to do. I don't try now, but look at my glass instead and drink when my family echoes the words back to her.

"To family," they chime in unison.

"How do you say cheers in Russian?" Mer asks.

"Nozdo…dorina? That's it right?" Sara tries. Dixon, Mer, and Knox all laugh. "Hey! I don't hear you guys giving Russian a go. Do you want to try, Dixon?"

Dixon opens his mouth, but laughs. It's Knox who says, "Molorindya!"

"Nozdoroyina, she said," Clifton adds, "Or something…"

The group devolves to laughter again and when it dies, I hear my own voice whisper, "*Nozdorovya.*"

"Damn, Aiden. How'd you know that?" Knox asks. The innocent way he pitches the question doesn't help me feel any less mortified.

I shrug and say nothing. Alina speaks for me. "Aiden speaks very good Russian."

Mer balks and Knox claps her on the back theatrically, as if anyone might have believed that that was a cough. Sara clears her throat, all calm diplomacy, as she brings her vodka to her lips. I'm not sure she's actually drinking any of it though. I've already finished my glass. No sooner than I've set it on the table does Alina rise and refill my cup.

"That's impressive," Sara says, "Have you been taking classes on the down low?"

"No," I lie.

Alina spares me the grief of a follow up. "But you must know that only foreigners say *nozdorovya*. We don't use. More vodka?" Alina asks Knox when he sets down his cup. She doesn't miss a beat and after refilling everyone's glass for a second – and in my case, a third time – she rises and heads to the two ovens stacked one on top of the other. "Are you all ready to eat?"

Unanimous agreement is followed by a serving of dishes. Sara offers to help, but Alina won't hear of it. She serves the dishes one-by-one, rather than setting the trays on the table – not that they would have fit. Even though Knox and I can pack food away, she still cooked for three times our number.

"This one is the *khaliniki*," she says, pointing to a mound on my plate. It's tan in color but when I cut it open it's brown beneath – some type of ground meat mixed in with vegetables.

"Damn. This shit is good," Mer moans. Agreement rises up from everyone at the table. "Beef?"

"Lamb. And this is the *soleniya*." Alina doles out a heaping of vegetables and by the time we've finished the vegetables, it's time for more *khaliniki* and more vodka. "*Pierogi* for when you are ready. They are traditional Russian pie, but they are sweet. I use the recipe from my grandmother."

"I'm ready mamasita," Mer crows. Her eyes are already glazed and Sara is laughing at something Dixon's whispered to her.

"What about you, Alina?" Clifton prods. "You've hardly eaten anything."

I rise to stand and reach for the dish she's holding, shocked at the fact that Clifton's noticed this before I have, but Alina keeps it from me. "*Nyet, nyet*," she laughs, "I must serve. I am the host."

Dixon laughs, "As much as I love to hear it, that's not exactly the way things have worked out in this house." He winks at Mer at the same time he slides his arm over the back of Sara's chair.

"Well, I am still Russian and hospitality is very important. It pleases me to see you eat." She sets another sweet *pierogi* on my plate and I am locked in the way she watches me with such delicate severity. Her gaze does not flinch from mine, not even as she says, "I like to please you."

My throat dries and my cock forgets where it is and who's surrounding us. I want to touch her. I need to touch her. In a poor presence of helping her lower the serving tray of *khaliniki* back to the table, I let my fingers move over her hand and touch her wrist. Soft as satin.

Alina's eyes round and the whole room is suddenly immaterial. She licks her lips. "Do you like?" she asks, and I've got no fucking clue what she's talking about.

"*Da,*" I answer swiftly.

She opens her mouth, then something must catch her gaze because she glances to the left at the table and a beautiful scarlet rises in her tawny cheeks. "*Da,* yes. Here you go," she stutters and serves Clifton more *khaliniki* even though I hadn't even heard him ask for it.

"It's delicious," he says and his grin is wide and knowing. He meets my gaze and I look around at the table. They are all watching me and Alina, all of them with the same knowing Clifton does.

"More vodka?" Alina asks, and her voice hitches just enough for me to know that she feels it too. This blooming awkwardness between us – or maybe, between us and everyone else in the room.

She serves the next round and no one but Sara abstains. When Alina serves me, I hold her hand in place, forcing her to make my single a double, but mostly so I have another excuse to feel her touch. Everything is a little easier as the vodka loosens my muscles and the food helps me sink into my seat. I listen as the people around me make conversation and let Alina put whatever she wants onto my plate.

In between the talk and chatter I've heard a thousand times before between my brothers and their women, Alina participates. She participates with increasing regularity and confidence, asking them questions and answering the questions they ask her in return. She makes jokes and they laugh and she laughs at the jokes they make too. It's a careless laughter. Head thrown back on her neck, red hair cascading over the wooden chair. The alcohol brings out a pink in her cheeks that I stare at in silence. I don't look anywhere else between the plate in front of me and the girl to my left.

"So." Sara says in a moment of silence. She's nervous as she speaks and drops her tone so that it's quiet, as if trying to communicate a secret. "How is he?"

Mer's grin becomes a grimace and in the severity of her face, she looks about five years older. She opens her mouth, makes a couple unintelligible sounds and shakes her head. Knox rubs Mer's shoulder and answers in her place. "He's recovering – physically and emotionally – but it's a slow process."

"And his face? Is it healing?"

"Healing, but it ain't pretty." Knox winces. Mer does too. I remember pulling Charlie out of that barn, that den of human corpses. It hadn't been pretty and the damage wrought over his face had compounded it. He'd stayed in the basement for days, refusing to go up to his room. And then one night he just left. He didn't take anything with him but his car and his wallet.

I watched him pull out of the driveway in the dead of night when the rest of the house had been quiet and sleeping. His souped up engine had purred in the same way it always had, but now he was different. Instead of the smiling kid with the perfect face that had seduced hundreds of women, he was a mutilated warrior come home from a lost battle and his scars had been deep, but what had crippled me more than seeing his wounds was the dark pall in his gaze. It reminded me of me.

Sara glances down at her empty plate, face full of remorse. Knox barks, "Don't you dare, Sara. You did the most. Charlie's face was beautiful before. You weren't the one who took the knife to it and if you hadn't been there, it would have been a fucking disaster. Now, it's just a scar. It'll fade and he'll get over it. Nobody stays beautiful forever."

Sara nods. "Is he…where is he staying? Does he need me to come look at him?"

"No, definitely not." Mer tips her glass back, finishing it. She doesn't stop Alina from giving her a refill and tosses that back too. "He doesn't want any help. He doesn't want to see anybody. He doesn't want to go anywhere except to the pits."

"The pits? But the barn is closed," Sara says with a frown. She doesn't understand what everyone else does and none of them understand what I do. Charlie is going to the pits because after being tortured, torturing others is the only thing left.

"The pits in town," Mer says. "*Puta* is going to get himself killed."

No. He's trying to lose himself.

Sara shakes her head and Dixon leans over Brant to kiss her below the ear. Brant's soft face turns up at Dixon and shrieks with shrill delight. The sound bursts through my stomach and I look at Brant, really look at him, for maybe the first time. He's a little baby. A little human being with a brain and emotions and a heart.

Dixon hands Brant a piece of *pierogi* off of his plate and the little human spends a while gnawing and slobbering over it. I feel guilty because when I should be thinking about Charlie, all I can suddenly think about is whether Alina wants one just like him. She does, surely. And I can't be the father. I can't...I mean, I would never have considered it. Am I considering it now? To have a kid? To see Alina pregnant with my child?

Dear fucking shit. The thought makes my cock hungrier, but the feeling that builds up in my stomach like a balloon is even more ravenous. It wants more than just her pussy. It wants to be wanted by her too. And I can't give into it. It's too painful. Too unstable. Too unknown. So if I can't give into it, and I can't give her what she wants, she'll find someone else. And then my time on this earth will be done. Maybe I'll go join Charlie in the pits then, and let the other broken monsters of the world drag me into hell where I belong.

"He's grieving in his own way," Dixon says softly, "He'll come back in his own time."

He will. But he won't be the same.

"And it's not as if he wants to cut ties with all of us." Knox gives me a funny look then, one eyebrow arched higher than the other. "He wants to see you." I don't answer. Knox takes no offense. "He wants you to help him train. The only thing he's been doing these days is training. You should see the kid. Our little brother's really stacking up." His lips turn up as if to smile, but he doesn't. "So. You keen to go see him?"

I don't answer. Alina interjects, "Aiden already has. He is a very good teacher."

I grimace, and still don't answer. Silence reigns.

Mer grins at me across the table. "Why didn't you say anything? I've been asking you to go see him for weeks."

I shrug and wring out my neck. I have an answer for her, and it has everything to do with the redhead seated beside me. She told me I should so I went.

"Good work, man," Knox says, "Thanks. He needs some guidance and since he's planning on hitting the pits anyways, it needs to come from the best and nobody's better than Aiden."

"You...fight often?" Alina asks.

I shake my head. "Not anymore."

She exhales like she's...relieved. "Good. And it is good you help Charlie. I...he..." She starts, stops, and clears her throat. "I was there already when they captured him. They keep us...kept us in the basement of some house. I do not know where. They took me and my brothers and put bags on our heads and did not remove them for many days. When they finally did, Charlie was there."

Her embarrassment and the sadness in her tone make my whole body hurt and hunger for pain — both to receive and to deliver it. I should have taken her before, the first time when her brother asked me. She'd have been spared then from her kidnapping, from ending up in a duffel back in a shallow pool of water back in that barn. Because she'd have been safe. I'd have protected her.

"Did you see what they did to him?" Mer asks.

Alina nods and shivers. "Some. But when they bring him in he already had blood on him and he was so angry. So much blood." She looks down at the ground between her chair and Clifton's. He slides his hand beneath the curtain of her hair and kneads the space between her shoulder blades. Rage hits hard and fast. Mostly at him for having the audacity to touch what doesn't belong to him. But also at myself. Why can't I do that? Why can't I show her comfort?

"You don't have to talk about it if you don't want," Clifton says softly.

"*Spasibo*," Alina exhales and glances at Clifton. Her eyes widen and she gives him a very soft smile as she does something else. Something important. In a way that is almost casual, she shifts in her seat and swivels her neck, using her hand to push his away. She doesn't want him. Why not? Why did she do that? Is it the act of being touched or is it the one touching her? How would she have reacted had it been someone else? A woman? Me?

A thousand questions fire through my mind, but I have no answers to any of them, least of all the latter. And I will never know the answer to it because I lack the courage that Clifton does not. He tried. I wouldn't dare, because I'd rather have my skin flayed off my cock before watching her do what she did to him, to me.

"I am ashamed to say," Alina picks up, "but I am grateful that your brother was there. I owe him a debt." I remember when Gavriil said the same to me, and I tense up. She is the debt that he paid. No matter what words come out of her mouth, I will not pay the same price. "Erik ordered Yefim to beat me, but Charlie lose his mind. Just as angry as my brothers, he attacked Yefim. That is when Erik cut his face. It is my fault."

And suddenly my world tilts on its axis. Alina would have been beaten if it hadn't been for Charlie. Dixon is busy rebuffing her claim that it is her fault but I cut him off. "Charlie won't lose a fight again." He will get a lot more than one training from me. He will get whatever he needs. "The debt is mine."

"*Spasibo*, Aiden, you are kind but you cannot assume all of my debts. Some are still my own." She sets down her fork and inhales deeply. "And that is another reason why I gather you here. I did not just bring you to eat. I bring you here also to tell you that no matter where Gavriil is, if he is dead or alive, he is not able to act. If he could, he would have made move already. Maybe he is hurt, maybe he is still taken by them. Maybe they torture him each day. Whatever it means, he is gone, and with Gavriil out of the picture, it is up to me to make things right in the *Bratva*."

The fuck is she saying? The booze rages inside of me, making things cloudy. Did she want me this way? Fat and happy and docile so I'd listen to her spew some crazy shit? Not fucking happening.

"The hell it is," I snarl, a sudden vicious anger rising in my chest.

She looks at me and her eyes are harder, two mismatched flints, one steely blue, one the brown of petrified wood. There is a small smile set between her cheeks and her hand reaches for mine. I pull away quickly, but her smile remains as it is, as if she'd anticipated it. "I am the only one that can. The only Popov left. And the only one who knows the truth about Erik. I can crush him, but only if you let me do it."

Alina

Aiden is watching me with fury in his expression. No, not fury. Fear. It isn't a good look for him and when my fingers reach to stroke the hardened skin on the back of his hand, he twitches and jerks away from me just as I'd known he would. He opens his mouth to speak, but Dixon speaks first.

"Alina, what are you thinking?" Dixon meets Aiden's gaze and Aiden sits up higher in his chair, as if challenged.

I raise my hand and the room stills. Aiden listens. I glance first to him, and then to all the others who have taken me in and protected me and each another at the expense of the whole. It's a beautiful thing. And something that I know my own brothers would have done for me. It is only right that I assume this role too.

"*Spasibo*, Dixon." I nod, stealing my breath. The family is a little tipsy, but not drunk, and I am dead sober. It is exactly the right moment to approach them with my ask, when they may be the most malleable, but the words are still hard. Not just the words, but the fact that I mean them.

"I think that Erik is madman who does not see truth. The drugs you all put in the bank are useless if Erik does not accept they are there. We need to act. *I* need to act, or else I will live the rest of my life in fear and so will you. The former I could tolerate, but the latter I cannot. My old family does... cannot terrorize my new family."

Aiden does not speak, yet his silence says enough. Mer looks at me from across the table, face drawn in severity. She's holding Knox's hand under the table, I can tell by the way his face twists at the same time the muscles jump in her arms. Like she's squeezing so hard it hurts him.

"What are you saying, Alina?" Mer asks, "You want to go after Erik on your own?"

"The fuck she does," Aiden grumbles again.

I swallow and look to him, directly. "What I say is that many of the men will not...are not...they cannot be happy with Erik's new mission, to trade in women. Many of the men will be loyal to my family still. And I am the only Popov left, so it is up to me to take back control of the *Bratva*."

Knox balks. "You want to take control of the entire Russian mafia?"

The disbelief in his tone makes me flinch. I stand up from the table, my chair scraping over the tiled floor like nails over glass. I cross my arms over my chest. "*Da.* I do."

"That's not a small task, Alina," Clifton says gently at the same time Knox rebuts, "What the fuck are you planning?"

"Give her a fucking minute." Mer shoves an elbow into Knox's ribs. "She wouldn't be here telling us this if she didn't have a plan."

Aiden exhales heavily through his nose, as if acknowledging that Mer is right. That makes me hopeful. At least two of them here think I am smart enough to have started this conversation knowing how it will end. Knowing how Erik will end.

"I know where Erik lives," I say once the dust has settled, "If I can bypass cameras, there is woman that works there who will let me into Erik's house."

Aiden slams his palms flat onto the table. He stands so quickly his chair falls, clattering loudly over the floor. I don't flinch, and I still don't flinch when he looks down at me, but instead stand to my full height. I am not so short and am able to meet his gaze without shrinking beneath it. The fighting lessons have made me more confident too. Maybe too confident. Knowing how to punch does not mean I am strong enough to kill Erik. But it might be good enough to get me close.

Or killed.

He seethes, "Then what the fuck will you do? He's a madman, not capable of negotiating."

"I will not negotiate. I will kill Erik. I will go in alone and I will do it myself. I cannot have you help me or it will not…it will…" I struggle for the word and quickly curse when the English evades me. Eventually I settle on, "delegitimize me. I need his blood on my hands. I will return drugs to Roman and stop operations of importing and exporting women."

"Fuck you, Alina. It isn't that simple. Roman wouldn't let you kill his only remaining son and live."

The horror steals into my chest on the heels of a memory I had long tried to shake. I close my eyes and stop resisting, but fall back into the moment. I was ten. My brothers had gone with my father and uncle to shooting practice. Nikoli was home with a cold, because usually he would have gone with them. He was teasing Erik because Erik was never invited. Looking back, I think Roman knew Erik was unstable even then.

"You're just a mistake," Nikoli said. He was not a nice older brother, and had told Erik much worse, and much more often. Erik closed his eyes and his hand around the toy truck he carried. "Are you going to hit me?" Nikoli asked him in Russian. Erik was only a few years younger, but he had taken to English much faster than his older brother. Nikoli laughed. "You wouldn't dare. I'm going to be next in line to take over the Bratva. Dad would never let you lead it because you're a coward."

Erik dropped the toy and launched himself at his brother. His fingers closed around Nikoli's neck. Nikoli laughed and so I did too. I thought it was funny. A joke among brothers. I'd seen my brothers wrestle before. But never so long that their faces turned blue. Nikoli was purple. He was clawing at Erik, but he was weak from his sickness and Erik's eyes were not like I had ever seen them. So wild. Feverish. Something had swept over him and I'd sat there, stunned and silent as my eleven year old cousin killed his older brother.

I tell this story to Aiden and his family sitting around the table. It is the first time the truth has ever left my lips.

"So you see? When Roman knows the truth, he will have to release Erik and choose a new successor. That is if he does not kill him. Roman loved Nikoli more and everyone knew it. That is why he had to die. Why Erik killed him."

The room is silent. Even Aiden's eyes are wide. Sara says softly, "Alina, why didn't you ever tell anyone?"

"Because after he drags Nikoli's body to garage and turns on the car, letting exhaust fill the space, he came back upstairs to me. He said to lie or he would make the same thing happen to both my brothers. He said that he would never hurt them so long as I keep his secret."

I inhale the rich scents of the food I baked through my nose. It reminds me of home. Of my brothers. I'm doing this for them. "He broke that promise. So now I must too. Roman found Nikoli in the garage, suffocated, and left for Russia the next day. He thought he did something wrong. He still blames himself. Once he knows, Erik will be ruined forever."

The silence that follows is not breached for many moments, until all at once Sara stands. Brant has started to cry and I wonder if her little baby can feel the tension in the room as I do, radiating up my arms and shooting like splinters up into my brain. Sara excuses herself with a flushed face and hand pressed to her forehead. She gathers Brant in her arms and leaves the room.

Mer leans forward onto her elbows. "How can we help you?"

"You're out of line, Mer," Aiden hisses. His hands are clenched so hard I worry his nails will cut into his palms.

"Aiden," Knox hisses, rising too. His chair jolts back and the two brothers approach one another around the table. Mer tries to push Knox back and then Clifton is trying to reason with his brother and as the room dissolves to chaos for a few frightening moments, I begin to feel my plan, and this entire orchestrated moment, slip away from me.

Dixon raps his knuckles on the table then and barks loud enough to calm and settle the masses. "Aiden's been entrusted with Alina's safety. But Alina is a grown woman and I tend to think she's right in her assessment of the situation. If we don't act and wait for Gavriil, then we'll be waiting – potentially for years – in fear. I've got a kid now and I can't have him caught in the crossfires, or inheriting this legacy. So I'm speaking now to both of you on behalf of Brant. We need to work together to engineer a plan that's bearable enough for everyone, and will keep the whole family safe. That includes you, Alina. That includes everyone in this house and Charlie."

He glances at Mer as he says that and a blush rises in her cheeks. She mouths back to him, "Thank you." Knox returns to her side and wraps his meaty arm around her shoulders, then plants a sloppy kiss along the side of her face.

"Aiden," Dixon says, looking deep into his brother's eyes. His brother, my protector. "What do we need to do first to prepare for this kind of a plan?"

Aiden does not speak. I can see his jaw clenching and unclenching, the flinching muscles in his shoulders itching to jump out of his skin. He opens his mouth several times. He looks at Dixon. He looks at all of his brothers and Mer around the table. Then he finally looks at me. He jerks forward and I hear Clifton shift closer though I don't move. Clifton still does not understand what I have begun to. Aiden will not ever hurt me.

"We need…" I wonder what he will say. Building plans? Guns? More training? Knives? A man on the inside? Erik's schedule? "Shopping," he grunts.

"*Shto?*" I whisper.

"If I'm going to make you into a killer, you're going to need to look the part. I'm taking you to the fucking mall."

I grin and some of the tension in the house starts to break apart, like loosening stone before the dam breaks. "Finally."

Aiden

I can't believe I'm doing this. We're so far off track. After hitting up two sporting goods stores, Alina convinced me she needed a sports bra. I still don't see anything that fits that description as Alina rifles through bras in lace hanging off of silk hangers.

I stand like an oaf just behind her, trying to keep the bottom half of my jaw from falling off as she turns to me, a fluorescent pink lace bra and matching underwear set in hand. She holds the hanger up against her body and I stroke for about a minute and a half.

"It is good?" she asks, prompting me for a response. Past the hanger, she's got leggings on and over that, one of my massively baggy sweatshirts. I also forced her to pin her hair up under one of Knox's baseball hats and put sunglasses on, as if suddenly in specs she isn't still the most beautiful woman in the world.

I nod, grunt and look away. "Yeah. It's good."

She smiles, looking very pleased with herself. She should be. Can't remember the last time I was in a mall and I've never been shopping before for women's things. But this was step one and I remind myself of that. Without the basics – clothes, sneakers, a new pair of reading glasses, contacts, underwear for fuck's sakes – she can't go on any kind of mission. And without the reassurance that she can function in the real world without getting killed – and that I can function for a few moments without her – I can't let her go on any kind of mission. All in all, this is a needed test. And even in its fucking simplicity, it might kill me nonetheless.

Alina turns towards the rack and my eyes track the long line of her body. The red sweatshirt brings out the red in her hair. Her thighs, wrapped in skin tight black fabric peeking out from beneath the sweatshirt make me want to rip the damn thing off. My fists clench. I exhale the breath I'm holding, grateful for the counter of clothes in between us. Easy, Aiden. Easy.

"Good. I'll take one in pink, black, white, teal, this grey for every day." Her fingers pause over a little red number. When she lifts it from the rack, saliva pools in my mouth. "Does red go with my hair or not?"

She drapes the hanger over her head and sets down her overfull basket so she can use both hands to capture the bra against her chest. The sound comes from deep in the back of my throat and there is nothing I can do to prevent it. I try to mask it by coughing into my fist, but the edge of her mouth still curls up.

"It goes," I grunt, moving towards her in a rush. I pull the bra off the hanger, shove it into her basket, grab the basket and head to the front counter. I can hear her protesting behind me and ignore her.

The woman with the overly made-up face behind the counter laughs at me in a forced way that I imagine makes others feel at ease. "You've got quite a shopper on your hands, there. Maybe I'll wait to give her a few more seconds." I pull out my black credit card and the woman's eyes widen.

"Then again, if you're paying," she whispers. She rings up the total just as Alina comes up behind me and throws another dozen items down. I pay for them all, grab the bags and try not to look at Alina as we head out.

"You should not pay for all of my things. I have plenty of money." She struggles to keep up with me, though I'd bet the girl's legs are just as long as mine. And in a single move I'm thinking about her legs spread into a perfect upside down V as I slam her torso down onto a table and penetrate her from behind. "I make over *dvesti pyat'desyat tysyach* dollars when I'm working…"

"Well you aren't working." I bark over my shoulder. She grabs my arm and plants her feet into the ground, bringing me around.

"But this is thousands of dollars," she says, gesturing around at the four bags hanging off of my arms. "You cannot pay…"

"Alina," I exhale, and my shoulders bunch when I meet her gaze. It is wide and round and lovely. Perfect. She's fucking perfect. "You aren't working. I don't need your money. And we should keep going. We don't need to start a scene." We've entered the food court and I glance meaningfully at the Sbarro across the glossy, beige-colored space.

She looks where I do and touches her mouth as she registers the mall cops loitering there. "*Prosti.*" She nods. "*Spasibo,* Aiden."

I shake my head. "For what?"

"For this." She shrugs. "I know it is not easy for you, but it is very important for me. I appreciate how you help me, even though I know you are afraid."

I narrow my gaze. No one has ever, ever accused me of being afraid before. "Afraid? Of what?"

"Not of," she says softly, "for. You are afraid for me, but you help me anyways. Thank you." She reaches up to the bill of her hat and swivels it around. Then she comes very close to me. I can't pull away because if I do, I'll crush some toddler on a plastic toy bike peddling away behind me. So I stand there, stiff in every way imaginable as she slides her hand over my shoulder and brushes her lips across my cheek. I didn't remember that they could be so soft. I didn't think I'd be this weak.

I drop one of the bags I'm holding and it sounds like a bomb going off despite the kids shrieking and people talking all around us. I'm frozen under the pressure of her long, slender fingers. They are ice against the outside of my black hoodie. I want to bring them to my lips to warm them. But her fingers move too fast, all the way down to my belt. My hips twitch as she narrowly misses the bulge forming along the front of my pants, but she isn't looking at that. I can't decide if I want her to be.

She bends down and picks up the bag I dropped. She makes it a few steps before my senses return. Then the damn girl winks at me over the upper rim of her sunglasses. In her backwards hat with tufts of red hair sticking out of the sides, she's the cutest fucking thing. I wonder if she's teasing me. Would she if she knew how badly I lust after her? How insane I feel when I'm around her? How murderous I am when I'm not? I'm sure she does. She isn't an idiot. And she seems to know everything I'm thinking. Maybe even the things I don't know myself.

We skip through two other stores and among the clothes Alina picks out, she buys black leather gloves, a black beanie, and black stockings. Are these normal items of clothing for her? Somehow I don't think so, and by the time we reach my car, my blood is boiling. I picture her slender, perfect body in all black, climbing in through the window of some generic house. Erik is there waiting for her. Pop pop. Two bullets is all it takes to take her from me forever. And then I'm lost.

And I wouldn't have even been there to stop it. What am I doing letting her do this? That's the question I've been asking myself the past three days, since our dinner. I know the answer though.

I love her. I love her too much to lose her. But I also love her too much to stop her.

"What are you thinking?" she says, breaking me from my stupor as I pay the ticket and pull out of the parking garage.

"Nothing," I say.

She shrugs and turns on the radio. Classical music moves gently through the speakers. She rolls down her window and comments on the fact that it's getting warmer, even as cold air claims the space, sliding into the openings of my leather coat. I chide her when she takes her sunglasses off.

"You think from here my eyes will make difference in being noticed?"

"Yes."

She frowns and flips down the visor above her. "Maybe you are right. My eyes are ugly."

I bark out a laugh, but one that's scathing and causes her to jump. "Don't say shit like that to me."

"Why not?"

"Because your eyes are the most beautiful thing I've ever seen. You're fucking perfect and I won't hear anything else." I lean back and glance over at her in time to see her plump lips curve up. She breaks my gaze first and pink rises in her cheeks in a way that jacks up my pulse.

"When we go dancing?" she says abruptly.

"Dancing?"

"*Da.*" She's serious.

"You're fucking out of your mind."

"You say many bad words."

"Do they offend you?" I adjust the rearview mirror as I glide to a stop at the next red light. There aren't many cars on the street, so I notice right away that the Jeep behind me is maintaining an unusual amount of space between his car and mine. His windows are tinted and the windshield reflects too much sunlight for me to be able to see his face. The car is huge and when a red Prius glides between us, I lose sight of the license plate. Damn.

"*Nyet*, it reminds me of my brothers." She unbuckles her seatbelt so she can turn to face me. I can feel her eyes wandering over my skin and I fight to control my body's response, which is demanding. But whether or not she's provoking me intentionally, is no longer the question on my mind.

"Hey. What are you doing?" She says when I reach across her body and click the strap into place. I take the next right turn and when I see the Jeep following us, I curse.

"*Shto*, Aiden? What is it?"

"We're being followed."

"We are?" She shoves on her sunglasses and glances back over the seat. I grab her shoulder roughly, keeping her where she is.

"Don't look at them. Look forward. They don't need to know we're onto them yet."

She nods and swallows and reaches under her sweatshirt for the gun she wears flush against her skin. Another reason the sweatshirt was a good choice for today. She doesn't have a permit to carry a gun, and barely knows how to use the Ruger I've given her. Three rounds of practice at best doesn't feel anywhere near sufficient, but even a lucky shot could mean the difference between death and survival.

"Don't let them know you have the gun either, Alina," I tell her. "Not until the end. They won't be expecting it and surprise is your greatest advantage." That and me and the fact that I'd die for her, no questions asked. The red light in front of us gears up to turn green and I glance at Alina once. "You ready?"

She nods, removing her hand from beneath her sweatshirt and gripping the seat beneath her with one hand, and the passenger's side door with her other. "*Da.*"

I tuck my chin and stare between the road and the rearview and the second the light goes green, I peel away from the pavement. Alina chirps and behind her lenses, I can see her close her eyes.

"Don't worry, baby. Nothing can hurt you," I think, without realizing that I've said the words out loud.

The Jeep is barreling after us down the road and as it chases us from one block to the next, struggling to make sharp turns in the way my smaller vehicle can, I think about closing the distance between us, pulling over, taking the Ruger from underneath my jacket and making a stand.

"Nothing can hurt you either, Aiden," Alina says in a voice that's soft and scared. I glance over at her and she's biting her bottom lip and clenching her hands. "I won't let it."

My chest implodes and explodes in a hundred small bursts, each one more devastating than the next. I don't answer her as I take the next left.

"The parking," Alina blurts, "can we lose them in there?"

The entrance is well hidden, carved into the side of a concrete building with no signs. I turn hard and speed down the short ramp, punch the button to collect my ticket, then stop.

"What are you doing?" Alina says.

"Waiting to make sure he sees me."

"Why?" I glance at Alina and she inhales sharply. "Not to lose him. To corner him."

I nod and the moment the nose of the Jeep edges into my mirror's view, I burn rubber and drive up the first ramp, then the second, then the third. There's another floor above us, but only one. I stop at the top of the ramp and carefully crack my window. It takes me a few seconds to locate and shoot out the half dozen cameras in each of the four corners of the place.

That taken care of, I yank up on the brake, quickly unbuckle Alina from her seatbelt, and throw open her door. In the time it takes her to get out, I'm already on her side of the car, dragging her back down the ramp towards the third level as we abandon my Ford in the center of the ramp. I've got her arm in a vice grip and pull her behind me beside a parked SUV that is wedged in close enough to the car beside it to conceal us both. There, we wait.

Alina is silent as the grave. Her bottom lip is trapped between her teeth and her eyes are large. She's not wearing her sunglasses anymore and I wonder where they've gone. Hopefully she didn't drop them. We don't need anyone noticing where we are. Then I see them in her hand, clutched fiercely. She is shaking. I want to comfort her, but I don't know how.

In an effort, I shrug off my jacket, throw it over her shoulders and reach for the guns safely strapped to each of my shoulder blades. I click off the safeties and clear the chambers. They are both fitted with silencer attachments and I rise, angling them towards the back of the Jeep as it finally crawls past us up the ramp.

The car slows as it reaches my Ford, whose doors are thrown open wide in abandon. The Jeep idles, but the driver doesn't get out. I couldn't have orchestrated the scene more beautifully. I'll cross behind the car, duck behind the safety of a support beam and fire – first to take out the tires, second to take out the rearview mirrors. Then if the passengers don't unload from the vehicle, I'll shoot for the windows and hope they aren't bullet proof. Either way, the fucker'll have to get out of the car or roll down their windows if they want to fire back.

I lift my Ruger shoulder-level and rise up into a crouch. I move in a burst, one foot forward then the other, but Alina snatches up the back of my tee shirt and pulls, hard.

"*Nyet.* This isn't Erik. This is not one of his."

"It doesn't fucking matter."

"It does! You cannot hurt someone innocent!"

"They aren't innocent! They're fucking following…" And then the sound of tires screeching on concrete fills the pause between her silence and mine. Without looking back at her face, full of fear and frustration, I tear out of her grip and as I do, it feels like I just ripped a part of my heart free of the rest and handed it to her.

"Don't you dare fucking move," is the last thing I tell her before I surge forward, prepared to kill even if she is watching. She should watch. She should know I am and have always been a monster.

The Jeep is trying to get around my Ford and escape to the upper level. I give chase, keeping one row of cars between myself and the Jeep at all times. I fire for the driver's window. It cracks. The second shot shatters it. The Jeep lurches towards a white Volkswagen that, if it were black, would look just like a hearse.

I fire for the Jeep's tires this time and with little effort take out all four. Narrowly missing the back of the VW, the Jeep slams into a concrete support beam. Though the airbags deploy with violence, the car was moving so slowly, the concrete barely puts a dent in the grill or the front bumper.

It concerns me then that no one gets out of the car right away. I'm positioned behind the hearse – not a great spot for me, granted, as it provides little in the way of cover – but I've got my sight trained on the driver's side door. Anyone comes out, they'll be dead instantly.

Still, nothing moves. The air is chilly against my skin. Inside I'm a goddamn torch. I can't stop thinking about Alina hiding behind that SUV half a dozen cars below. Six badass motherfuckers get out of that car, I might not make it and she could be hurt – or worse. Any less than that, they won't.

I lick my lips as the driver's side door shudders. It opens a crack and I aim for the darkness. I fire once, shattering the windshield or maybe the dashboard or both. Then there's a squeal – a woman's squeal – that cleanly cuts through my plans to commit murder.

"Don't shoot," the steady, female voice orders. "I'm so sorry! I'm a huge fan and I thought I saw Alina Popov. I shouldn't have followed but I just wanted her autograph so bad. She's like the older sister I never had. I saw her in the magazines when I was a kid and thought that if a girl that looks like her can make it, maybe I can too. I mean…not to say I look anything like her. I just, you know…she's not white and she's got red hair. I mean Christmas on a cracker, she is way prettier than I could…"

The woman doesn't shut up.

I fire again, this time aiming carefully for the side mirror. I don't need her seeing anything she shouldn't. My bullet shatters it cleanly. The woman stifles a quiet gasp, but I'm unsettled that she hasn't begun to scream if she is truly who she says she is. Anyone would be frightened of a gun, but this fan doesn't seem to be. A gun nut perhaps? The guess doesn't seem right and I don't move from my position, refusing to let

Alina's pleas for compassion sway me, or this woman's lies deceive me.

"Get out of the car with your hands on your head." The order is quickly obeyed. Two dark brown hands stretch through the shattered window and carefully jostle the door open. Then I see a black-clad leg.

The woman gets out of the car and trips over the glass shards. With windmilling arms, she manages to catch herself and jerk upright and when she does, I am startled by how tiny she is. Her hair is the biggest thing about her. Like a black halo, it sits around a small face and neck and nose and chest and feet and hands. She can't be more than five feet – in boots.

She smiles tentatively even though her whole face is twisted up in an uncertain, but not yet afraid, expression. It's like she hasn't realized I'm going to kill her yet.

"Hey, like I said. I'm so sorry. I didn't know you were… well, I don't know who you are but I thought you were with Alina Popov and I've always wanted to meet her in person and I…"

"Where did you follow us from?" I bark through clenched teeth.

"The mall. I was at the food court and I thought I saw her and I wanted her autograph…"

"Are you alone?"

"What?"

"Are you alone," I roar.

She jumps and glances back at her car. "Yeah! Of course. I mean, yes. Like, that's not to say that no one would miss me if you shot me." She laughs and the sound, echoing off of the walls, is so out of place I flinch.

"Empty your pockets." She lifts up her shirt and unbuckles some hideous pack from around her waist. "Kick it over here." She does and I slowly rise, one Ruger trained on the vehicle and the other on her simultaneously.

Her eyes widen. "I swear I'm not armed or anything. I don't even have a camera phone. I was just planning on getting her autograph on a piece of paper. Call me simple or old school or traditional or whatever. I don't even have any of that social media crap or use a computer. I still read books on paper, not on a Kindle or Nook Book or Sony eReader. Actually, I think Sony went out of business or maybe they sold their e-readers. Maybe Kobo books bought them. That's a thing, right? Do you read books on e-readers?"

Unable to stand the sound of her talking anymore, I bypass her shit and go to her first. I grab the front of her black hoodie and wrench her into my fist. She chokes on a grunt and reaches for her cheek as she goes down, but she doesn't cry and she doesn't cry out for help.

She should be crying. With a body that size? I hit her with my gun as much as my hand so I know it hurts like a bitch. Strange that watching her writhe in a near silent pain on the concrete, I feel a flurry of respect for her. That, and a satisfaction that I got her to shut up.

I check the car and find it empty – more than that – conspicuously clean except for whatever's in the locked box behind the gearshift. It's a custom job, which raises my concerns. I return to her fanny pack for now. Inside, I find a wad of cash, a Nokia that looks like it might be the close relative of the first cell phone ever made, an ID and a library card. Ifeoma Smith. She's twenty something, five one and weighs a hundred three pounds. That doesn't give me shit on her, which pisses me off.

"You're a fucking spy." Either that or a killer. I grab her by the back of her hoodie and wrench her up to standing. It takes one hand. Very little effort at all. I wonder if the little murdering bitch is working for the Mexicans or the Russians. I wonder which of them was stupid enough to hire a girl who didn't even rock up to cross swords with me, with a sword on her.

Damned bitch chuckles when I force her up against the concrete support beam hard enough I hear something in her body crack. "You're the second person who's called me that," she whispers, entire face clenching in pain.

I roar and throw her into the center of the lot hard enough her sweater tears over the right shoulder. I point my gun at her body. She doesn't scream or cry, but covers her head with her arms. I cock the hammer. Three...two...

"*Bajalsta*, Aiden! *Nyet!*" Alina rushes up the ramp, moving right out into open space. All the blood drains out of my body as I imagine how easy it would be to shoot her from any angle.

"Alina, no! Get on the ground."

She doesn't fucking listen to me, but keeps coming forward. She's almost on me now and the fuck? The fucking princess thinks she's going to move *between* me and the spy sent to tail her? I lose it and grab her arm, shoving her back. I point my gun at the spy and chamber the next round.

"Aiden!" Alina reaches beneath her sweatshirt. She produces a gun. Her hand shakes as she points it at my left leg.

The sight of her holding a weapon pisses me off more than the fact that she's pointing it at me. "You're not strong enough to shoot me, Alina. You're not strong enough to shoot anyone. Now go back and get to safety and wait for me to come to you."

"Only if you promise not to hurt her."

"I'm going to shoot her, Alina. And there's nothing you can do to stop me."

And then Alina fires. She angles the gun away from me, firing absently into the space. Surprise hits me with the same force of the bullet hitting some random car's windshield. Her hands aren't sure, but her gaze is. The look she levels at me is pure carnage and in that look I see something I wish I never had: Alina's capacity for violence. She is capable of going to Erik's house and she is capable of killing him — or at least she's capable of trying. And if she can do all that on her own, then what does she need me for? I was only ever her killer. But if the princess is a killer in her own right, then she needs me for nothing.

I hear the sirens at the same time the assassin behind me speaks. "I called the cops when I was in the car. Alina, if you need help, they'll be here in just a few minutes – maybe less. You have a gun. While he's focused on me, run..."

"Are you fucking kidding me?" I roar, "Who the fuck are you telling Alina to go to the cops? The cops that have done shit to try to find her, and are in league with the mob. I'm the one protecting her!"

My fury climbs towards its apex and then passes it, reaching a dangerous world of instability. An instability I can only ever remember having felt once — the moment that the brothers and I walked up onto the barn and I looked through a gap in the walls to see Erik's men lowering a black bag into a tub of water. The realization, based on Timur and Gavriil Popov's furious and fiery reactions, that Alina was in the bag had been my life's lowest point. But now, I feel that moment revisit me as Alina puts her life at risk by protecting a woman spy potentially sent here to kill her. And now that woman spy is *daring* to suggest that *I'm* the threat even though I plan to kill her for jeopardizing Alina's life. I'd kill anyone for her. I'd die anywhere for her.

In the past seconds, I've closed in on the small, big-haired spy. My gun is pressed to her temple and as she looks up at me, it's without fear. I hate her for it because it doesn't help me understand who she is or what she's after. Her dark gaze flashes to Alina. She holds up both hands in the same way people always do around me and makes me feel like a mad man.

"Alina, run," she says.

I chamber a round and press the metal so hard against the spy's forehead it will leave an indent. But I still don't kill her. Because it occurs to me that she's trying to help Alina too, even if it is to take her away from me, and this knowledge is loud enough in my mind to stay my hand. It's shaking. My hand is fucking shaking. I can't remember ever wanting to kill someone so badly. But this little spy is trying to help Alina. Even if she's wrong.

"*Lyubimiy* come. Come!" Alina tackles me from behind, her weight crashing into me — not with enough force to knock me off balance, but the word she called me does. *Lyubimiy*. I know this word. I looked it up the other day when I was thinking that if I were brave enough, I might call her it once.

Lyubimiy means my love.

She grabs my arm and as the sirens grow louder, we race back to my car. Then we fly. It takes longer than I want to maneuver my car around the Jeep and the spy writhing and shaking in the glass scattered across parking lot floor. Once on the street, I fight every ounce of rage in my body for the strength needed to drive at controlled speed. Any faster raises suspicion, and at the speed I want, my car would end up wrapped around a telephone pole, Alina dead beside me.

Cops pass us, heading towards the garage and I know I've only got minutes after they arrive before the spy describes our car to them and, if she's smart, gives them the plates. Depending on their levels of competence, the fumbling coppers should be able to make the connection. No doubt, they'll also find security tapes of us entering and exiting the garage. We'll need to be long gone by then so I can keep Alina safe.

Renewed anger tunnels through my bones and I distantly become aware that Alina is silent. Silent, but fuming. Doesn't matter how pissed she is though, because I know my rage runs much hotter. It was a mistake to let the spy live. She has seen my face. She has seen Alina's face. She knows that Alina's alive and worse, that she's in town. She will share this information with the Russians and I will fail the only person who's ever meant anything to me in this world, in my life.

Alina

He pays the man at the front desk while I wait in the car. The car is the fourth I've been in today. He lit the first one on fire in a deserted place. We walked about a mile along the highway until finding a rest station at which point Aiden stole some family's Subaru. I'd protested — there was a baby seat in the back, *derr'mo* — but the stubborn man wouldn't listen to me then either.

We drove the stolen Subaru around for a while before stealing a third car, and then replacing its plates with those of a fourth car. I don't know what kind of car it is that we ride in except that it stinks of something foul. Cheese and body odor. Maybe anger too. Aiden's and mine both.

I stare straight ahead at the weather beaten motel doors in front of me. They sit in a row, one after the other and they are orange layered atop grey, but most of the grey still shows. Motel Regent, is the name of this place. I have never stayed in a motel. I do not know where we are except that we are not in town. Where we are is smaller than town, perhaps built for commuters because there are a lot of motels and places to sleep though the parking lot of this place is mostly empty.

Knox would probably call this place a shit hole. Mer would call it worse. Sara would say that it's perfectly adequate and they would all be correct. Anywhere remote without many people around so I can unleash some of the rage that has built like a dam in my chest, one about to burst.

The door to the reception swings open and Aiden walks down the long row of doors towards me. He motions for me to get out of the car. I have trouble unbuckling my seat belt, and when I finally get the thing undone, he is standing in front of the car with all of my things.

"Move," he spits acerbically when I step out into the breeze. It smells like car exhaust. The sky is grey overhead and I can sense a storm coming.

I follow him into the room marked thirty-four and after he closes and locks the door behind me, he throws the many bags from our trip to the mall down onto the first of two beds covered in a sickly green bedspread. There are flowers on it that are grey and faded pink and the threads tying the cloth together are all fraying. The fabric is pilling and when I glance up, I see that the yellow wallpaper boxing us in fares no better, but is also peeling in many places.

Aiden punches his fingers back through his short, blonde hair. His cheeks are no longer blotchy with color because his face is a single shade of red. "Do you even understand the risk you took today?"

The sensation of vomiting builds up in my throat and when I speak, it hurts. "You disgust me." My crossed arms uncross and my hands ball into fists. I take a step towards him so that we are separated by less than the width of the bed. "You are a selfish, cruel bastard and I hate you! I hate being trapped with you! You are a barbarian. You almost kill that woman. You would kill if I have not intervened. You do not care to protect me, you just want to kill because you are nothing but a killer. You don't deserve the life you lead when all that you live for is to take the lives of others. You are a bad man…"

"I don't fucking care what you think," Aiden roars, and the sheer volume of his voice is enough to throttle me. I fall back half a step and catch myself on the edge of the dresser. Its faded surface is covered in a thick layer of dust that comes off on my fingers and feels like sand when I clench them into fists.

I go to speak, but Aiden shouts over me. He throws out his arms. "I have never cared what you think. You are a selfish, spoiled princess who has no understanding of the way things work. The world is a murdering bitch, Alina, and what you did today put both of our lives at risk."

His chest is heaving and immediately, I feel guilt. I did not think. So focused on the woman's life, I did not think how *she* could have hurt *him*. I am ashamed, and in the tumult of my shame and anger, tears begin to sting the backs of my eyes.

I rush on him and shove both of his shoulders, knocking him back only half a step. "I hate you," I say again and again. I slap his cheek and he growls, reaching out to catch my wrist when I aim for him a second time.

I remember the moves he taught me and am able to free my arm. He blocks when I try to punch him in the gut, and his abdomen clenches when my knee meets his solar plexus. To arrive there, I have hooked both of my hands onto his shoulders and pulled our bodies flush. When he grunts, his warm breath mingles with mine and when he meets my gaze, it is with only a few inches separating us.

"I hate you," I breathe. Tears creep more viciously into my vision. Aiden's hand holds my leg up now at the knee before sweeping back and cupping my ass, much in the same way he'd done when we fought for the very first time on the gym floor. Only then it had been an accident, and now there is nothing innocent about his touch. There's intent in mine too as my fingers find his neck and chest and I feel the pulse of his heart beating with ferocity.

His other hand is inching up from my lower back to my shoulder blades. He cups the outside of my arm, squeezing it hard enough to leave bruises. "I know," he says.

"You're nothing but a killer." I snatch up his tee shirt and yank him forward though there's nowhere left for him to go. Now we are belly to belly. I can feel his belt pressing into my abdomen, and below that the thick shaft of his manhood. *Suka blyad.* How did we get here to this moment?

My heart is pounding out of control. I can't feel my skin. It's on fire. Everything is on fire. "You're nothing but a killer...you're my killer. Aiden, you're mine..."

My arms are moving with a zeal I did not know I possessed. They circle his neck and his hooded eyes watch me with rapture at the same time that his hand on my ass shifts so that his fingertips brush the space between my legs. He reaches around my body and cups my vagina through my thin leggings using his whole hand. I could scream. I have never been so hot before for a man. I have to have him, this killer, this madman, and I gasp. He moans. And as I gasp his name, I wonder if I am not just as mad as he is.

"Aiden." I rise up onto my tip toes and go to kiss him. He turns his head at the last moment so I kiss his cheek. He tastes like heat and clean soap and sweat and earth and fabric softener. It's only as my lips trace the path of his chin and his ear that I realize how long I have wanted to kiss him.

"I hate you," I tell him and when my tongue tastes the line of his throat, I can feel the muscles jumping in his neck beneath it. The heel of his palm is massaging my core in a way no man ever has before. The heat of my anger only amplifies it. I'm going to orgasm and we are both still fully clothed.

"*Derr'mo*, Aiden," I gasp as he turns me around roughly so that my back is to his chest and I can feel his erection pressing into my behind. I swivel my hips, hoping to ignite a reaction in him similar to the one he is winning in me. It must work, because he growls into my neck before biting it.

He whispers my name and his voice is so hoarse I can barely understand it. It doesn't matter though. His hand rises up and he uses all four fingers to rub my clitoris through my pants. His other arm is draped across my chest, holding me to him and I bark out a plea as I fall against it. He holds me upright and his fingers increase their speed and pressure. He presses it like a button. I'm right on the cusp.

And then I scream.

I scream his name and a Russian curse as the orgasm hits me like a slap to the face. The arm that Aiden uses to hold me is shaking and when I gasp his name in pure ecstasy, he tries to pull back. I don't let him.

"You are not free of this," I say in Russian or English or some combination of the two. My mind is a haze and I am panting, but as crippled as I am, I still manage to turn around and face him.

I want to kiss him, but when I stand up on my tip toes, he pulls away. I grab his tee shirt at the collar and wrap it up in both of my fists. I wrench him around and he moves with me, and there is surprise in his eyes when I push him onto the edge of the bed. I straddle his waist and his cock is still hard – harder than stone. It is pressing against his jeans and I grind my hips against it, titillating my most sensitive part, which has not yet recovered from its previous shock. It's almost painful how sensitive it is, but I want more. All I can think is that I want more of him. I go to kiss him again, grabbing either side of his face, but he pulls away from me even as his hands massage my ass and his hips pulsate against me.

"What is it? What's wrong?" I say breathlessly. My high has started to part. I am worried. Did I do something wrong?

"Fuck. Nothing. This is heaven." His eyes are closed and his face is tilted up towards the ceiling. His jaw is clenched.

I brush that severe line with my palm and whisper his name until he looks at me. His eyes have never been so deep a grey. Like I'm looking directly into a storm cloud. Into the world of the gods. "Why do you not kiss me?"

Panic. It's the first emotion I see etched across his forehead. He chokes and quickly looks away from me. "I…I don't want to…disappoint you." He is so timid. I do not understand this man and where the one went who was just holding a gun, prepared to murder.

"How could you disappoint me?" I palm his chin and plant very small kisses between each of his cheeks, across the bridge of his nose.

"Oh god." He squeezes my hips. "Oh fuck. I…" And then he spanks me. The feeling in my right butt cheek is so unexpected and the pain, so sharp and sudden, that afterwards, I can't help but laugh. The laughter in my chest breaks up all other emotions and sounds and feelings.

Aiden still has his teeth clenched, but his eyes are searching mine and they are desperate with wanting. "I've never kissed anyone before."

It takes me a moment to process what he says, and in that moment I can feel him withdrawing from me. I catch him quickly before he can withdraw all the way, and though I yearn to know why and how this is possible, I don't ask. I clasp his neck and I press my mouth to his and I hold him there as he fights me for the first few seconds, but only for the first few seconds.

He gasps when I pull back and his torso strains forward as I lean away from him. His eyes are closed. He licks his lips. He smells like fabric softener and rich, fragrant soap and when I watch his face, as it is, I capture the moment forever. He looks twenty years younger. Like the boy he once was before the world broke him so completely. His lips are parted and his eyes are wet and watery and so very pure.

"Alina…" His voice catches and he tucks his chin so I can't see his face. Oh god oh god oh god. Oh no. Is he…

"No, Aiden, please…" If he cries, I will not be able to handle it. "I'm not strong enough."

He surges up to meet my mouth with his. He kisses me like someone kissing someone for the very first time and I hold onto it and I hold onto him as he takes me by the waist and flips me over. He moves us further up onto the bed and holds either side of my face, angling my chin so that he can kiss me more deeply. His tongue meets mine in quick bursts before growing more sure.

We kiss for hours. We kiss for eternities. His mouth is warm and his lips are softer than they have a right to be for someone whose hands are so hard. They paw over me hesitantly until I take his wrist and move his palms to touch my breast. A moan chokes his throat and mine simultaneously as his fingers move over the outside of this stupid sweatshirt, squeezing now on their own accord.

"Take it off. Please undress me."

Aiden doesn't hesitate for the first time all day. He rips his sweatshirt off of me and then rips off my shirt and bra. He takes his own shirt off next, and while I watch him work his belt and pants, I kick off my leggings and underwear. When he covers my body next he's fully bare and so am I and the feeling of his bare skin on mine frightens and elates me.

"*Moy boch*, Aiden."

His hips ride against mine and as his fingers work my nipples, twisting so hard that it hurts, but only just, the head of his cock slides meaningfully over my most private crease. His dick finds the lips of my pussy. It seeks entry, probing once, twice...

"Aiden!" I push on his chest.

He freezes. "What is it? What's wrong?"

I laugh and hook my elbow around his neck. I kiss him hard. "Nothing is wrong. Everything is perfect. But I...I don't want to disappoint you."

"What?" He makes a face that makes me smile even more.

"I've never done this before."

His eyes close. He turns to stone. "I thought…Erik and his men…"

I shake my head. "No one touched me. You are the first. I want it to be you."

"I can't… Not for your first time."

He starts to pull away from me, but I hold him where he is. "Don't, Aiden."

His fingers drag through my hair. He cups the back of my neck. "You deserve so much better…"

I cut him off and blurt out, utterly without ceremony, "I love you."

He waits a moment, eyes as round as quarters as he searches my face for some contradiction that will not come. "No, no…You can't…"

"*Ya lyublyu tebya*, Aiden. I have for some time." My chest hurts as I say the words and at the same time, the rest of my body feels lighter. I have said what has been on my mind for the past many days, but he has not said it back.

He just stares at me expressionlessly while his body settles onto mine further and further. His weight is hard to absorb because there is so much of him, but I wrap my legs around him nonetheless, wanting more. "You do?"

"*Da*, Aiden."

He bows his head over mine. Our noses meet. His warm breath smells like peppermint. He kisses my lips hard. He kisses my cheek, and then my chin and then my forehead next. He kisses my nose last and when he does, his breathing hitches. He repositions himself between my thighs. His manhood tickles my clitoris first, before sweeping lower. He parts my lips. I am dripping wet, but I have seen the size of him and I am still nervous.

"I love you, Alina," he whispers, and when he draws away from me there are tears dotting his high cheeks. "I've loved you since the beginning." He pushes forward. The pressure is surreal. My fingernails dig into his biceps. He cages my cry with his lips.

He draws back enough for me to be able to look down at the space between our bodies. "Oh Aiden." He is only inside of me up to the head. No further. "You can come."

"I'm not going to hurt you. We'll take it as slow as we need to, for as long as it takes." He moves another centimeter deeper.

I cry out. He withdraws. We repeat the movement a dozen times or more before finally our bodies come together at the hip. I can't deny that it hurts. It does. There is a stinging pain as my body adjusts to the size of him, but he does not move. He just remains inside of me as he is while our lips fuse together and our hands explore each others' bodies. I love to touch him. He is carved of wood and I love the way he touches me, as if I am not some delicate flower, but am something just as tough as he is.

And then he starts to move. I can feel every place he touches, each imprint left in fire. It feels like no other type of euphoria. He spreads my legs very wide and wraps himself around me. He pushes in and out and there is some space inside of me on the roof of my vagina that his dick touches and another separate place at the base of my labia that he presses against as he moves and there is a train barreling off of its tracks inside of me. I can't think of anything. There is no longer pain. There is no longer anything but this.

"Alina, I'm sorry, but I can't hold on much longer. I've wanted this for too long."

My response comes out in between gasps. "I am not on birth control."

"I'll pull out." He speaks also in between heavy breaths.

"Please don't. Just this once, I desire everything."

"Oh fuck, Alina."

"Aiden!" My voice comes out as a scream. The orgasm pulls me under as Aiden curses above me. His mouth finds mine once more and he is kissing me as he fills me up to the core, all the way down to my most fragile center. With him, here and now I am warm. With him, here and now I am whole.

As the world settles again around us, his head drops forward so that his forehead touches mine. I lift up, pushing on his cheeks and sweeping my thumbs beneath his eyelids, smoothing away the moisture.

"You are safe now," I whisper.

He nods, mute.

"You are safe."

And then Aiden's whole body shudders. He wraps me up in his arms and when I draw the itchy blankets up over us both, blocking out all light, I hold him to me as tightly as he holds me. "It's okay, Aiden. It's alright."

He doesn't answer, but a sob, poorly stifled, racks his body and I am there and I am proud to hold his heart as well as his tears. For the first time, I am the strength he leeches as he grips me in the darkness.

"Aiden," I whisper, "Nothing can hurt you here."

"You are late. You are always late. And I stand out here waiting for you for half hour. Where are you?" It is ten pm and she was supposed to come at four. She has come every night but one for the past two weeks and she is always late, though never by six hours. It matters little that she texted me three times, delaying her arrival, because I still find myself standing outside in the shadow of a crack den waiting for her. For half an hour? No. It's been nearly two.

"Hold onto your britches, cowboy." Her voice is fuzzy as it greets me through the phone. That phone...a ridiculous thing. Just like Ify. Yet even for as annoyed as I am, my excitement is still as palpable as a child's incapable of sleeping the night before Christmas. The only reason to sleep these days is to visit her in my dreams.

"I told you I had to go to the police station and I had some problems with my car so I had to take that to the garage too. Everything took a bit longer than I thought, not least of all because your cranky ass still wants food."

I frown. A pile of garbage skitters past me, followed by the clicking heels of two pros. They scan me up and down as they pass, slowing but not stopping when they finally read my expression in the shadows: Get fucking lost. "I do not need food. I have food."

"PB&J doesn't count as food. Not when you have it for every meal and not when you get as much exercise as we do."

My frown becomes a poorly restrained grin and my balls grow heavy in my jeans. My cock stretches. I will never forget the way she had shown up yesterday, wearing a police outfit consisting of tight blue shorts and a tight blue half-shirt, beneath her regular clothes. The costume had even come complete with a leather baton and handcuffs. I'd put both to good use – lady cop punished by her criminal.

Speaking of cops… "Why you go again to police station? You said you met with Clifford yesterday for your book."

She pauses, says something to someone else in the car, before answering. "Yeah, this was for something different."

"Who is with you?" I snarl.

"Just a cabbie. Now could you please quit it with the Q&A. I'll be there in two minutes. Because I'm in an Uber, I'm going to ask him to drop me a little further away."

"How far? I do not want you walking alone at night anywhere." I glance left and right. There is a row of cars parked in front of this town's best version of a Red Light District. Other cars stop at the corner and pick up prostitutes to do their business elsewhere.

Across the street, Mexican men in puffy coats loiter beneath two sparsely lit street lamps. They wear their guns conspicuously and I know that their pockets are full. At first, I thought I might go to them to buy something to take my mind off of the pain of my loss. I don't think about doing that anymore. In fact, the thought of Ify seeing me high puts a sour taste in my mouth. The thought of seeing Ify high?

Derr'mo, it makes me want to shatter teeth. She is perfect the way she is. No substances needed.

"Here's good. Thanks again," she says to the driver before speaking to me. "I'm on Forty-Fourth and Tenth."

"Forty-Fourth and Tenth?" That is four blocks from where I stand. Four dangerous blocks. "Do not dare stop walking. I come to you now. Walk down Tenth."

She doesn't say anything and that bothers me. I have never known the girl to be silent unless we're fucking. "Ify," I growl, "what is wrong?"

"Sorry. I was just thinking."

"About what?"

"I…I think you might be mad."

"Mad at what?" Now I grow impatient. I jog across the street, and keep jogging. "Mad at what?" I repeat.

"Oh shit, I see you," she says nearly the exact moment I turn onto Tenth. I look up and see a shadowy figure in the distance. There aren't any street lights so it's either Ify or a hooker. I don't see a wild rush of hair, so I can't be sure.

"That you?" I say.

The figure in the distance lifts a hand and waves. "It's me."

"Your hair."

She laughs. "Yeah I went home before coming through. Needed a shower and just didn't feel like dealing with my fro so I had Mandy French braid it for me." She speaks of everyone in her life as if I am as good a friend with them as she is. Ordinarily I would have asked her about this Mandy for I like to know about all of the people in her life, but I am too eager to reach her. I've never seen her with braids before and that excites me. Everything about her excites me.

"Just promise me you won't be mad, okay?" she says. There is only one more block between us.

"Do you give me reason to be?"

"I mean…no. But…"

"Then why but?"

"Just nevermind," she groans and hangs up. Half a block separates us and she's begun to slow. Something is off with her and I don't like it. I don't like it at all. My long strides eat up the cracking concrete and as I land at her feet, she leans back against the defunct lamppost behind her and tilts her face up to look at me.

The moon may be the only light I have to guide me but it might as well be a spotlight. My blood runs cold. All warmth and excitement and happiness is snuffed, and I do what I can not to lash out and hit something. That won't help either of us.

Instead, I lift my hand to sweep her cheek, but she twists away from my touch and speaks before I do. "It's really not as bad as it looks. 'Tis a flesh wound,'" she says in a British accent, a light chuckle on her tongue. I don't understand the reference and I despise her jokes in that moment.

She rolls her eyes. "Anyways, I know I probably shouldn't have come at all and you probably want me to go home. For some weird reason after the crazy day I had I just…" She holds in a breath and looks away with a distracted, dreamy smile on her lips. It's also a sad smile, and I want to kiss her to make it right.

"You just?"

She smiles a little more fully and meets my gaze. Her eyes are so watery and beautiful. Like coals before a flame. "I just really wanted to see you."

She was hurt so she wants to see me. She wants to see me. My mouth dries as my mind turns over her words.

"That said, I still am not really up for a good ole' romp in the hay. And I know you're pissed because, well, you probably wanted to but…"

I guffaw unattractively as my whole body shivers. "You think I am angry because of no sex?"

She glances from side to side with her one good eye. The other is swollen shut, along with the entire right side of her face. Entirely swollen shut. Like she was beaten over the head with a cinderblock. "Well yeah. I mean, that's kind of what I come over for."

The good feeling in my chest telling me she wants to see me desiccates, like my cock in that moment. I wonder how it doesn't just fall right off. "The only reason." I mean to ask her a question, but my inflection is that of confirmation, if anything.

She winces and I hollow out. My empty stomach pitches. She hands me the plastic bags she carries. "It's Pho." She shrugs. "I don't know if you eat it or whatever, but here."

She pulls out her phone – an actual phone this time, not that plastic block I usually text her on. Seeing her actual phone, the plastic bags she carries, the swelling on her face makes me choke because it reminds me that regardless of what we have together, she lives another life.

"What are you doing?" I say, taking the bags from her as cold wind crashes against me from behind.

She tucks her chin into her puffy black coat and the face of her phone further illuminates her skin, the color of eggplant on the right side. Pus or ointment or both weep from her eyelashes. "Calling an Uber so I can get out of your hair." I rip the device from her hand before she's finished speaking and shove it into my own pocket. "Hey…" But she doesn't finish speaking either. Not when I press my lips to her mouth.

Being so near to those curves makes me juiced. My dick that, moments ago was near to giving up the ghost, throbs with life. The willful beast is on its worst behavior and even as I gingerly tuck her against my chest, I make sure to keep my hips away from her. I don't want any confirmation of the lies she was preaching. Want her just for sex? If only. Because if it were that simple, the sight of her face wouldn't pain me like my heart is being pulled out through my rib cage.

She sucks in a sharp breath. "Ouch," she whispers as my kiss deepens and my hand slides over her back.

I withdraw, tasting the cut on her bottom lip and the metallic tang of blood on it. "Where are you hurt?"

She winces as her hand touches her face first, then reaches around to her back and finally to her shoulder. "I'm pretty banged up all over. The doc says I've got a pretty bad muscle bruise on my back. I'm not supposed to do any heavy lifting for the next week or so. My face and my shoulder are the bloody bits. He really wasn't holding back."

Her mouth turns up in a grin, as if trying to make light of it, but she sniffles in the same moment. I have never seen her anything but confident and sure and here she is, vulnerable before me. I am not the same man I was.

I touch the sides of her face and my fingers skim her arms. I hold her small hands in my much larger ones. "Who did this to you? Was it that policeman who is in love with you?"

That startles her and she shakes her head quickly, good eye widening with a truly innocent surprise. "Clifford? No way. Clifford isn't in love with me either. We're just friends. He would never hurt me."

I don't believe her, but I don't think she is lying either. The perniciousness with which he tries to steal her time from me bothers me. But perhaps I am just jealous. "Then who?"

She chuckles and stares up at me, allowing some of her weight to release against my chest. "This guy. Big like you, but blonde. He had a gun – a couple of them – and after he hit me he was going to shoot me dead." Her statement, issued so blandly, pierces like a bullet. What would the world be like without her? Quieter. Quiet like the grave.

"*Shto?*" I rasp, clutching the back of her head. It is so small. Like all of her. The braids drape over her shoulders and are beautiful. I appreciate them because, for once, they allow me to see her whole face and I also hate them for that same reason. The sight of her pain is pain in itself.

"Do you know who he was?" The moment she gives me a name, I will call Anatoly and tomorrow I will leave this wretched part of town on an assignment for her. She could tell me any name right now and that person would die. Any name...but the one she does.

"I don't know who the man was, but I do know the woman who stopped him."

"Who?"

Her left eye blinks. Her right, puffy eyelid twitches. "Alina Popov. Your sister saved my life."

"You saw Alina?" I ask before I can retract the words, or try to shrug them off. This little girl, in so many ways, has put a jump start on my heart. I feel rabid seeing her injured and hearing her words. Totally crazed.

She nods. "Yeah. In this parking garage near townhouse row. I followed them from the mall."

"They were at the mall?"

"Eastgate. Alina was all dressed up incognito, but I could recognize that girl anywhere." Ify chews on her bottom lip until, seemingly remembering that she's got a cut there, winces and stops. She tries to pull her arms away from me, but I don't let her. She stares up at me in an unusual silence before all the words come tumbling out.

"You've got to know, I'm an author. A true crime author. And the book I've been writing isn't about my missing friend Ollie. It's about Alina, and you. Your family and the Russian mafia. I was with Clifford today at the mall because he said he might have something for me. He called at the last minute to cancel because something came up. Then I ran into some friends from high school and we had lunch – pizza from this shitty takeaway spot in the food court where there were some of Clifford's other cop buddies I was trying to extort a bit of info from. It didn't really work. They don't know anything about y'all's case or if they do, they aren't willing to share. Maybe they're corrupt. Have you ever been to a Sbarro? I mean, nevermind. I…"

She pauses, but only long enough to draw in air. "I saw the two of them at the mall and I tailed them in my car though they spotted me almost right away and gave me the runaround. Now that I think about it, I wonder if they hadn't been leading me to the garage because when I arrived, their car was parked and they weren't in it and then someone started shooting at me and I panicked and crashed into this stupid pole. The guy made me get out of the car and he took apart all my stuff and I think you might be right, this stuff keeps getting me into trouble." She sniffles and laughs and gestures to the fanny pack at her waist.

"What did he do?" I say and her eyes linger over my fingers, distracted perhaps by the way my hands flinch in pulses.

"He thought I was a spy, just like you did. He hit me when I wouldn't shut up and was going to shoot me, but Alina stopped him. She begged him – threatened to shoot him – and he did what she asked. This is all why I was late today and why I found you in the first place and I'm kind of fucked up from the drugs they gave me at the hospital. Clifford insisted on taking my statement but I swear, I didn't tell them about Alina or you or the man. I would have but it was clear that she was with him and that he was trying to protect her and when they left, it was her pulling him away and not the other way around. I just said it was some thug and gave them a generic description of a white guy with brown hair. I told them he robbed me but I…"

I cradle her injuries, lean in and brush my lips over her temple. "Shh."

"Are you pissed at me for lying to you?"

"*Da*," I say, though I could have guessed most of what she has told me. That she found me when she was searching for me is alarming. And that she found Alina when she was searching for her surprises me equally. But in this moment, I find it impossible to want to frighten or reprimand her. Because in this moment, she is trembling just a little bit and I am nearly brought to my knees by the sudden honest vulnerability of this spyauthorassassinsirenseductress.

"You going to punish me?" There's just a lilt of wanting on her tongue, but it makes me smile, despite everything. I'm not sure how that is possible.

Against her injured cheek, I whisper, "You will be punished. Absolutely. But like the man who gave you this, it will not be today. Today you will come with me and I will care for you and tomorrow, you will stop this hunt for trouble because I promise you, the man you met who guards my sister is not the most dangerous man you will meet if you continue hunting."

Sniffling, she nods and crosses her arms between us.

"You will stop looking, Ify?"

"Yeah." She nods again, glancing meekly down at her feet. "*Da.*"

"Is that a promise you will break to me?"

She shakes her head, and it makes her look about ten years younger. Far too young to be here now with me. "*Nyet.*"

I smile and kiss the center of her forehead. She tastes like soap and is smooth like cream. "Good. Because I do not know what it would do to me if I lost you."

"What?"

"Let us go now."

Ify's mouth falls open, but she does not speak. She does not move either so I press my hand to the small of her back and inhale the clean scent of rose on her hair as we walk down the sidewalk that smells of piss and feces. I take her under my arm and under my protection as we near my apartment – the prison to which I am bound.

Being with Ify is not unlike a prison itself. One in which I am happy to be shackled. Because I am starting to care for this girl just as much as my own flesh and blood – and I do mean Alina. Because I already care for Ify far more than I care for myself. In her little hands, she holds my whole heart.

Part VII
The Traitor

Charlie

I push my way through the crowd and head out into the night, wondering if I like the new way people watch me – with two parts fear, one part uncertainty I'm not one of the losers anymore. Now I've got three wins under my belt in as many weeks.

But why don't I feel any fucking better?

Frustrated, I walk out of the underground garage and cold air cracks against all of the exposed bloody bits of my skin. I wipe my face with my hand. It comes back dripping in red.

The sky is black overhead and speckled with stars. It's a clear night. The wind sobs through the streets, hitting the brick faces of the buildings and ricocheting back at me. I'm caught in a vortex and the temperature is so cold, it feels like fire against my hands. I don't have gloves and my pockets offer little resistance. Maybe I will die out here. I laugh a little at the thought and my breath is bright white. Death on a night where I won in the pits? And here I thought, I'd get stacked against the Virgin Mary dickhead and that's when death would come for me...

Somewhere in the distance a dog barks. I don't stop until it barks again and keeps barking, over and over. And then it squeals. And then there's laughter. More squeals. More laughter. I see a flash of bloodied breasts and hear Russians joking and laughing in words I don't understand. Rape. Violence. Impotence — mine, not theirs.

Grief makes my knees lock, but anger helps me focus. I pick up my pace and duck into the next alley, where the sound finally finds its provenance. Halfway down the dead-end street, two twenty somethings wearing suits three sizes too big for them pass a bottle between one another and hover over a brown animal. It's a dog and it looks scared, cowering against the concrete. It's not very big and even from where I stand I can see its ribs. A skinny street runt. I was one of those once until the foster system caught back up with me.

Then one of the boys kicks it. The other grabs its tail and yanks when it tries to run and my feet are propelling me down the alley as the dog shrinks down even farther when one of the kids pours whatever its holding over the animal. That same boy pulls a lighter out of his pocket. I reach him in the next moment.

I hear Aiden's voice in my ears: plant your feet shoulder-width apart, lead with the left foot, swivel your hips and let your core do the work for you, keep your elbows locked at your sides, jab-jab-uppercut, jab-jab-hook, straight punches. The boy carrying the lighter screams when I hit him, and then starts to curse. His friend backs away and makes no effort to help. That doesn't mean I go easy on him.

I bloody both kids to the point they'll never be able to wear those suits again. I've never been a natural fighter, but this has never felt more effortless. I think about Aiden. He's a better fighter than me hands down, but I don't think he ever fights like this. Not with incentive. I think he just fights because he wants the world to bleed.

"Get the fuck out of here," I growl, grabbing one kid by the scruff of his neck and tossing him towards the mouth of the alley. It takes the other half a dozen tries to stand, but eventually both of these piss-brained sociopaths manage to haul ass down the block, shouting curses about who they know and how much trouble I'm going to be in when they call the cops.

I roll my shoulders back and I'm not so cold anymore. Inside or out. There's a warmth blazing across my chest and the lightness has spread to my stomach. Almost feels like the sensation before you throw up. Makes me smile, though the expression doesn't come easily. It hurts. Not because of any physical pain, but because it's a cruel reminder that my face isn't one I recognize anymore.

Whimpering draws my attention down. The dog is still there, lying in a puddle of booze. Its head turns to the left and right and it sniffs a whole bunch, but it doesn't move.

"What are you still doing here?" I nudge its bottom with my shoe, and it charges a few inches forward, then stops. It's shaking bad. "Jesus, you look about as shit as I feel." Tentatively, it lifts its head in my direction and sniffs a little. Its nose is black and its fur is light brown and white in patches and its eyes are a very human amberish brown. "Go on. Go back to wherever you came from." But I know it came from nowhere and it has nowhere to go.

We're not totally different, after all. Marguerite picked me up when I was seven, three years after she adopted Clifton. She was as close to a mom as I ever got and I know that if she were here, she'd have taken this little dog home and nursed it back to health at any expense it took.

I groan as the dog continues to shake and shiver and cower. Now it's started to breathe weird and I know if I leave it like it is, it'll be dead by morning. "Alright, get your lazy ass up." I bend down and scoop up the mangy mutt, trying to keep it as far away from my body as possible – no easy task — as I try to decide what to do with it. The solution hits me all at once. The uptight bitch I ran into the other day. She'd been coming out of a vet clinic. Maybe it's still open.

The dog whimpers and whines as I jog down the street. It's wet and I don't know if it's the booze that the kids poured over it, or if the mangy thing pissed on me. Either way, the chill has seeped through both sleeves of my hoodie and even though the dog has stopped shaking, now I've started to shiver. I look left, look right, and cross the street, near blinded by the fluorescent light that shines a spot over the awning.

The store is a burst of brightness against a bleak black block. The storefront is all glass and I bang the flat of my fist on it. A bell inside jangles angrily, but inside there's just an empty waiting room, complete with sterile grey countertop, white tiled floor, and plastic chairs.

"Fucking hell, why keep the goddamn lights on if you're not open?" I mutter.

I kick the silver bit at the bottom of the door and the dog I carry yelps. At the same time, my ears cock forward. I think I hear movement. A door inside the shop definitely opens, but when no one appears I wonder if I'm not losing my mind. A second later, my rational side is rewarded.

I'm surprised by the sight of the woman who appears behind the counter. It's the redhead. I thought she'd been here to get her seven thousand dollar designer poodle pampered. I didn't expect that she was actually *the* vet. She looks up at me and the surprise that flashes across her face mirrors the one that I feel. I wonder if she can see me through the glass, past the reflection, given how dark it is out here and the way I'm dressed. I hope to hell she can't. The dog getting any treatment at all depends on it.

"Shut up. Stay still," I tell it as it starts to fidget, but it doesn't listen to me. It barks in a raspy, pitiful wail and I'm so focused on keeping it in my grip – and still keeping it away from me – that I don't immediately notice the door in front of me swing open.

"Sorry sir, we're closed," she says in that same polite ass voice she'd used the last time.

My first instinct is to look at her, but right now my hood conceals most of my face. I'd like to keep it that way. "Yeah well I didn't make an appointment."

"I'm sorry?"

"It means I found this thing and I don't want it."

"I'm a vet clinic, not an animal shelter, sir." Is that sarcasm I hear in her tone? Is this politeness really just a veneer? If the answer to both questions is yes, I might be inclined to hate this rich bitch a little bit less. But only if it's a yes.

I grin at the thought and the scarring on my face twists painfully. Tickled by her, but frustrated by the knots of my skin and the dog and the cold lying thick on my arms, I thrust the creature towards her. "I was walking home and saw a couple kids about to light it on fire. I stopped them and brought it here. Thought it might be injured. That's a *you* problem then, isn't it?"

"You were…walking…on fire?" she huffs and suddenly I see her hands stretch forward and mold around the dog's ears. It shrinks back and I feel strangely compelled to protect it.

"I guess that whole experience didn't make it a big people fan," I grunt.

"I can see that." She runs her short fingers through the dogs disgusting fur, pressing in places that seem arbitrary to me. The dog whimpers. "Poor baby." Deep emotion cuts through the woman's voice, opening it up like a canyon at the bottom of the sea, and I'm so damned disturbed by it, I nearly forget about my face and look at her. Before I can, she's pulling back and letting me inside the building.

"Come in," she says, holding the door open. She closes and locks it behind me and I wonder if she's stupid, or if she really is this trusting. I'm a dark villain and she's a nice white veterinarian of the female variety. It's dark and we're completely alone. She doesn't know that I'd take a cut to the face a thousand times over before I hurt her or any woman.

"You can bring him straight through." She walks in front of me, leading me around the counter. The white door we pass through opens onto a white hallway. Her shoes are just as white – plain Keds – and they're all of her I can see with my face tilted straight down. Just the little dog in my arms with its too human eyes can see me and even though it looks up at me with cloudy eyes, they watch me without judgment. Dogs don't care about your scars.

Somewhere past the end of the hall, which dead ends in a right turn, I can hear birds chirping, a cat's meow, dogs grunting and claws scratching on metal. We don't go that way though, and instead head straight into a small room with a cabinet full of medical supplies and a sink against the far wall, a small bench against the near wall, and a metal table between them.

"You can put him here. It would help if you stayed close to give him moral support. He's not going to like what comes next."

"What comes next?" I set the dog down, grateful not to be carrying it anymore. My arms are stiff and angry with me when I do, but when I pull back, the dog tilts its face up in my direction and sniffs a whole bunch. It whimpers and I frown, and my stupid hands stay where they are along the dog's back, gently patting its damp, matted fur.

I spare a glance up when I hear the water running. Distracted, the woman doesn't see me as I watch her tie her hair into a low ponytail, turn off the water and pull on a pair of gloves. Her hair is bright red. Nearly orange. And straight as a toothpick, even if the rest of her couldn't be farther from it. She's packing a lot of extra curve – a good thirty pounds over the heaviest woman I've ever been with.

Her hips are wide even though her ass is a little flat, but her tits... Woah. Just woah. Not sure how I didn't notice those cans first. The kind of tits a twelve inch dick could get lost between. I wonder absently how big her nipples are. Are they pale pancakes? Or bright pink and cut like diamonds? She might be wearing a turtleneck, but a goddamn parka couldn't camouflage those canons.

"Why don't you take a picture? It'll last longer," she says coolly and without looking up at me. There's that sarcasm. That veneer must be paper thin. Thin enough to see through.

"Bah," I laugh remorselessly for a second before it occurs to me that I'm fucking laughing. I haven't laughed since… since… I swallow the breath and shake my head, rubbing the back of my neck as I look away. "Kind of hard not to notice."

She sets down the long plastic stick she's holding and the clattering of plastic on metal jerks my attention up. Her eyes lock with mine and her mouth opens but she doesn't speak, all of those retaliatory words knocked back down her throat like a pin ball.

Her chocolatey brown gaze flits rapidly over my face and her lips part. But where others look down as quickly as they can, she just stares harder. Her auburn eyelashes reach for her eyebrows and her nostrils flare ever so slightly.

I lean forward, one fist knuckle-down on the table, one hand still on the dog. Irritation tickles my spine though I know it shouldn't. I'd stand out in a dermatologist's office. Fuck that. A burn ward. "Why don't you take a picture? It'll last longer."

One edge of my mouth is cocked up in a snarl that I don't even fully mean. It's just like that now, held there permanently by slick, stretched skin that glistens in the light like water under moonlight.

She swallows and finally looks away. Quietly, she mutters, "Kind of hard not to notice."

My grimace turns to a grin that I can't help, though I want to, because I know it only succeeds in making me look more terrifying. "You're kind of a bitch."

She looks appropriately shocked and for a few muted seconds, her jaw works away. "You…you are very rude."

"I'm not the one insulting an invalid."

When she lifts the plastic wand from the table in a gloved hand to wave it at me absently, I can tell that the gesture is as perfunctory as it is accusatory. "A scar doesn't make you an invalid. You're a healthy young man. This is just superficial."

Well then. Fuck me. I'm speechless. Who does this bitch think she is? "You don't know shit about me or what I've been through."

"I..." Her cheeks redden. Her gaze flicks to the dog. She pats its head and it stretches up to her, as if seeking more. "I'm sorry," she whispers then, though I don't think she means it. This woman is a stone cold cunt. I hate her, I decide then. But what I hate more is the fact that she isn't wrong.

She starts looking the dog over then, working diligently and in silence. I get the impression that she's good at her job and she cares a lot about animals. She's gentle, but works with purpose, not doing anything unnecessary, but giving herself the opportunity to do more if one test or another doesn't yield a conclusive result.

There's still a healthy heaping of tension between us as she finally wraps up with the tests and leads me and the pup to the back room for a bath in a room much bigger than the exam room. She gestures for me to place the dog in the second of three large tubs in the center of the space. Each has a hose roped up above it as well as a flat table beside it. The metal table has hooks on each end from which hang shearing and grooming tools.

I set the dog down and it lifts its face and inhales deeply as warm water splashes over it. I ruffle its hair and massage its ears and its black lips stretch back towards my hand in a stupid kind of grin. The woman is smiling at the dog, hands steeped in soapy suds up to the wrists as she carefully lathers it.

I shift around uncomfortably. "Can I help?" I offer.

She flicks her brown eyes up at me and nods. "Of course. Do you want to take the hose? I'll get some more shampoo."

Her fingers brush mine as they pass over the nozzle. I notice that she has short nails, bitten down to nubs. Looks painful. I open my mouth to comment on them, but as the Doc turns around and lathers more shampoo in between her hands, I say instead, "You're right about my face."

She shakes her head, her ponytail whipping around, soft strands slipping free and framing her slightly rounded face. "No, I shouldn't have said anything. It was dumb."

"No, you were right."

"Even if I was right." We finish together. Our eyes meet. She's biting the inside of her cheek to try to stop herself from smiling.

I narrow my eyes, but I can't stop myself from smiling too. "You've got some kind of lip on you, kid. You know that?"

She bites her bottom lip and her pale cheeks turn rubicund. She doesn't answer, which is fine. Question was rhetorical. Instead, she reaches to the temperature dials to my left and adjusts them so that the water runs a little bit hotter. The minute I pass the nozzle over the dog's head it starts doing some sort of erratic twitching dance. Doc laughs and the sound throws me so off guard that I laugh too.

"What?" She says.

"Is that a real laugh?"

The splotchy color in her cheeks becomes a solid sheet of carmine. "Yes it is," she harrumphs.

"Hey, don't be embarrassed about it. It's cute." Cute. Cute? What am I saying? Her laugh is insane. This high pitched breathy thing that makes it sound like she's dying. It also makes me, and I imagine anyone who hears it, want to laugh too. But I tell her it sounds cute because I want to take away the sudden expression that's crossed her face. I can't fully define it, but it's some relative of embarrassment and hurt, and more importantly, it's incompatible with that laugh. A laugh that makes my primitive male instinct want to do other things so I can have the pleasure of hearing it again.

"No, it isn't. But thank you for saying so."

"It is cute. On you it is anyways." What the fuck am I saying now? Am I fucking flirting? Jesus. Maybe some of the old Charlie isn't entirely dead after all. The thought makes me nervous, so nervous that I don't hear her response.

"What?"

"I said I'm married." She lifts a necklace out from under the collar of her sweater. On the end dangles a ring fitted with the biggest damn rock I've ever seen.

I whistle. "Damn. Your husband compensating for something?"

Her blush burns brighter. Her lips flop open again and her pointy little chin bobs. "I...no. I just didn't want you to get the wrong idea."

I click my tongue against the backs of my teeth and finish rinsing off the dog. "Don't worry, lady, you're not my type." No woman is. Not anymore. But I think back to the old Charlie...would she have been his type?

Probably not then either. She's got a little extra around the waist, and her tits are almost too big. I can't tell what her legs look like, but her face is pretty. Real pretty. Or at least interesting to look at. Fuck, I don't know. All I do know is that face is getting redder and redder. I didn't think she could get any redder, but now the woman's one solid sheet of color that matches her hair. It rolls down her neck and even her damn hands get splotchy.

I make a sound, half-laugh half-grunt and shake my head. "So what's next?"

"I…" She shakes her head, like she's clearing her mind. "Let's get him out front and I'll run you through everything you need to know. You are taking him, right?"

I open my mouth to tell her she's lost her damn mind, but the expression on her face isn't up for debate. She's a little fierce, this vet, but it seems only when an animal's life is on the line. I grin again at her and she doesn't wince or look away. She presses her mouth together in that way she seems to be doing so often, like at one point in her life someone convinced her that smiling was a bad thing.

"I guess so."

We towel dry the dog and when I set it back onto the floor, it's no longer shaking and no longer cowering, but tilting its head up at me expectantly.

"What are you going to call him?" Doc asks when she walks me to the front door with the pup, a blue-and-white checkered bandana tied around its neck. The tests she ran came back positive for dog flu and fleas and negative for everything else. Doc gives me medicine for all of it along with two huge bags of dry dog food and a case of wet food. She also gives me a garbage bag full of dog toys and a dog bed.

"I don't know," I say, actually looking down at the rascal and giving it some thought. Never thought I'd ever get a dog. I say the first thing that pops into my head. "Checkers, maybe."

"Very clever." She laughs, adjusting the bandana so that it sticks out more prominently. "I like it."

I smile back and shrug, then tilt my head to the side. "So you ask for the dog's name before mine?"

"Sorry," she says, biting her cheek again.

"Charlie." It feels awkward, but I hold out my hand.

She takes it and grips it firmly. "Molly. It was nice to meet you Charlie."

I nod at her and flex my fingers when her grip releases. Weirdly, I agree with her. "So what's the damage?"

"Sorry?"

"What do I owe you?"

"Oh no, it's fine. I'm just happy to help."

"Jesus. You think I'm homeless don't you?" I laugh long and hard. I laugh so hard my stomach starts to hurt. I clutch my injured ribs and when I wince, she lifts a hand but doesn't touch me.

"I don't like to pass judgement."

"You really are a bitch." I reach over in a move I'd only do to one of my brothers or Mer and I ruffle her hair. What the fuck is wrong with me?

I muss her ponytail and she stares after me, shocked as I pick up the dog in one hand and the bag full of stuff in my other. Without giving her a chance to retaliate — and I know she would have because she's got a fire trapped in there she tries way too hard to harness — I head for the door.

I cock my chin at her over my shoulder. "Thanks for the free shit, Molly." I let myself out and head into the cold night, feeling strangely warm. The door clangs shut behind me and I laugh when I see Molly's shocked expression tracking me through the glass, on which is printed in gold and green, Monroe Vet Clinic.

I turn then as the next gust of wind hits and the dog in my arms looks up at me, as if expecting that I've got some sort of plan.

"Well, Checkers," I tell it with a soft shake of my head, "you can thank Mrs. Monroe for this, but it looks like it's you and me from now on."

Aiden

I don't know who I am. And I can't say I don't know who I am anymore because I never knew. But the person that existed within this skin is gone. I can't find him anywhere. Because he never wanted to exist, and now I do. Now, I want to exist with violence. Because the thought of being anywhere – in this world or the one that comes after – without her is suddenly worth existing for. Violently.

I watch her with a smile on my face. I even manage to lean back where I sit. Relaxed. Sort of. The thought of her getting hit still hurts, but I remind myself again and again that that's what she's here for.

"*Puta*, you're worrying too much about what I'm doing and not enough about what you're doing. Stop looking at my feet and focus on my fists." Mer is barking orders in the impromptu ring and Alina is trying to follow them. She's too nervous.

"Hell, I'd be nervous too," Clifton says.

I glance over at him with a start. "What?"

"You said she's too nervous. I'm agreeing with you."

"Didn't realize I said that out loud."

Clifton grins. He's sitting on one of the folding chairs to my right, near the gym wall. Close enough to watch, but still far enough away that if Mer hits Alina and if Alina gets hurt and if I choose to react to kill Mer that he'll be able to cut me off before Knox does. Knox is standing much closer to the girls.

"Well, all I'm saying is that Alina's got a right to be nervous. I'd be nervous too boxing that crazy girl," he says affectionately.

I can't remember the last time we had a conversation, or that I had a conversation with anyone but Alina. It feels strange to want to try, but stranger still that answering him has become my body's most natural response.

"You're right. She wouldn't be my first pick in the ring either."

Clifton barks out a laugh. I don't know what to do. My face feels funny. Like it's searching for a complementary expression. A smile? Is that what he wants from me? Or maybe he wants nothing at all.

I nod, but Clifton's already turned his gaze back to the two women sparring on top of the mats laid out in the middle of the floor. "You've done great work with her though," he says when Alina successfully blocks Mer's next upper cut with her forearm. "It's hard to believe this is the girl you fished out of that bodybag so many weeks ago."

It is. But it also isn't. That girl was terrified. This one no longer lets that fear rule her.

"And she's clearly done great work on you." Clifton's grin is blinding and I have to admit that he's an attractive man. I wonder...would I look like him if I could master that expression? Would Alina like that? I want to be for her, everything.

"I..." I try to answer. My throat chokes. Clifton sits there with a smile on his face, waiting patiently. He reminds me of that woman, Marguerite, who raised him and tried to help me. She would leave little notes for me around the house that said stuff like "You're a gift from God" or "Hope" or "You are loved" — stupid shit that I couldn't understand and had no desire to.

But now I wonder if I shouldn't leave those kinds of messages around for Alina. And even for this idiot sitting next to me, the one with the misfortune to share my face, but who was blessed enough to be nothing like me. Do I love him? Who is he? Who am I? I'm a new thing wearing that old bastard's body, experiencing everything for the first time.

"I love her."

His eyes widen and his lips peel back from his teeth. Not to bite or hurt or maim or defend himself, but to continue smiling. He laughs and reaches out to touch me. He claps my shoulder in one big hand. "I know man, I know."

"Alina, for fuck's sake! *Hijo de tu puta madre*, if you don't hit me I'm going to bloody your goddamn face!" Mer is getting pissed, and so I stand. Clifton's hand tenses on my arm, though if I had more words I'd tell him not to worry. I didn't kill her when I was ordered to — and that was the old me. I'm not about to change my mind now.

That said, I might incapacitate her if she screams at Alina again like that. If I can get close enough. I don't miss Knox standing up from where he'd been lounging on one of the bench presses. The two women don't notice, and are still focused on each other.

Mer swings for Alina's face and Alina lets out a chirp as she blocks shakily. She doesn't return the punch and Mer lets out a groan, then stops going easy on Alina. She steps back and kicks. Alina is able to ward away the blow aimed at her thigh, but she uses both hands, which leaves Mer free to knock her in the side of the head. She hits her hard. So hard that Alina loses her balance and hits the ground. Ice ripples across my chest and becomes my bones, but when the tension tries to work its way up my throat, I swallow. The bloodlust burns all the way down.

I approach Alina on the floor and ignore the fact that Knox is closing in on me, Mer is backing away, and Clifton is leaning forward onto his elbows with his eyebrows drawn together. His beard twitches, but our gazes meet in the mirror and I wonder what he sees because another small smile curves his lips up at the corner.

"Alina, *pochemu vy ne atakuyete?*" I ask her why she didn't fight back. Alina has been supplementing my Russian night classes. I'm getting better.

She blushes as she lets me pull her up to standing by her gloves. I hold her closer than necessary. My dick is hard and pulsing. It has been for the past hour. I wonder if she can feel it against her. The slight widening of her eyes and the blush in her face tells me she can. She licks her lips – either an inadvertent gesture or to bait me. Either way, it's painful not to kiss her.

"I do not attack because I do not like to attack when you watch me." She thrusts her lower lip out in a pout. "I am nervous."

"I'm not going anywhere." I speak with finality. "Not now and not if you get close enough to Erik to kill him, so you're going to have to get over it."

"*When* I get close to Erik," she insists, shaking her head and backing away from me. "No if. When."

Ignoring the supposition – because I am still determined to make sure she never gets close enough to Erik to be injured by him – I glance at Mer, who's watching me with one eyebrow cocked.

"Don't hold back," I tell Alina, "Hurt her like you hurt me once."

Alina blushes again, and the dick in my shorts damn near sings. I can feel precum budding along the angry, pulsating head just at the memory of our last training. She'd managed to sneak a jab in to catch my jaw and my adrenaline had been too amped and I'd been too proud not to coil my arms around her in a move she'd never be able to free herself from, and kiss her long and hard.

We'd forgotten about training after that, which is one of the reasons Mer stands in my place now. No chance of Alina and Mer letting sexual tension distract them from a fight. And even if there were, no chance of anyone kissing Alina but me while I'm around.

So much as the thought of someone else kissing her makes me want to interrogate Alina to find out every man she's ever kissed and eviscerate them all. She's damn lucky that she'd never let anybody else but me enter the heaven that is her pussy or I would have had to resort to extreme forms of torture that I could only hope she never found out about.

Alina and Mer refocus on one another and Knox stares me down with a frown that fills my chest with that strange bubbling sensation that I know comes before laughter. I choke it down, still made uncomfortable by it. But I do let myself smile.

Knox looks away quickly, like he's been caught doing something he shouldn't. Or maybe the sight of me smiling freaks him out. I don't blame him. The feeling of my mouth in that position is alien and I probably look equally as alien every time I do it. I try to stop, but around Alina, restraint in all forms is difficult.

Mer and Alina bounce around each other, Mer throwing jabs and Alina blocking. I've seen Mer fight a few times, and my respect for her grows greater each time I see her skill in action. It's clear she's holding back, but only in some instances. She doesn't give a shit that I'm there and could kill her if she so much as looked at Alina wrong. She's genuinely trying to help Alina. I like that. So she pushes Alina as hard as her limits will go without breaking them, punching her hard enough to give her bruises but no fractures, straining her stamina but not collapsing her.

"*Hermana*, if you don't hit me now, I'm going to..." Mer pauses slightly. Her eyes flash to me standing a few feet away from the edge of the mat. "I'm going to kick in Aiden's knee. It might not be now, but when he's got you pushed up against a wall and y'all are fucking each other to pieces, I'll come right in and kick in his knee so he can't walk right for six weeks."

Odd. I don't feel threatened in any way, but I grow cold when I see the sudden red that claims Alina's face. She's upset. She shouldn't be upset. I look to Mer, targeting the source of the problem. Clifton says my name, but I don't move.

Mer doesn't notice the fact that I'm about to hurt her. Badly. She's still speaking and dancing around Alina, who I notice is suddenly holding her gloves more stiffly and is moving more rapidly as she swings her torso out of the way of Mer's next body shot.

"Or better yet, maybe I'll just ask Aiden to spar with me. He's good practice and I know what happens after you do a good job. He throws you down on the mat and gives you the D, but maybe I'm just the thing he's missing. Maybe he wants a girl that really knows how to fight, or just one with a little more Latin flavor."

Fucking shit. What the hell is happening?

Knox's frown is cutting lines from the corner of his mouth to his jaw. Even Clifton is sitting bolt upright in his chair, eyebrows high enough to touch his hairline. Alina releases a grunt as she ducks again and blocks Mer's next jab. She pushes Mer's arm out of the way and circles it with her own. Did I teach her that? I can't remember, but I'm surprised as hell and I think Mer is too, which is why she doesn't react in time to stop Alina's gloved fist from crashing into her.

Alina punches Mer square in the face and when she releases Mer's arm, Mer stumbles back. She loses her footing and damn near crashes through the fucking gym equipment – would have, if Knox hadn't been there to catch her.

Alina gasps. The whole world is quiet. All I can hear is my pulse hammering. Fuck. I'm more turned on than ever. Still confused as shit. But the pride coursing through my veins feels like dynamite and smoke and is there to replace every frozen relic of my tortured personality that remained.

I grin. Clifton is laughing. Mer is too. Knox is still grumbling about something and when our eyes meet, I can see he wants to fight me. It clicks as to why, and for the first time in maybe forever, I suddenly understand what a human person is feeling because I can imagine myself in their position. He wants to kill me because of the things Mer said. And I know this because if I heard Alina speak that way about some other man, they would already be dead.

"*Hermana*, that is what I'm talking about! Well fucking done, *penocha*." Mer advances on her, lifts up to reach around Alina's neck and drags her into her side. She grinds her glove onto the top of Alina's hair and Alina laughs as she lets herself be pulled around. "And to think. All it took was an image in your head of Aiden fucking me. Hold onto that." She looks at me, sticks out her tongue and winks provocatively. "But don't get any ideas."

Alina lets out a short grunt as she does something she hasn't done before – this training session or any other – she attacks first. I stand back and don't realize my mouth hangs open stupidly until the fight breaks up fifteen minutes later. In that time, Alina's managed to get in one more hit – this one a bodyshot hard enough to throw Mer off balance – and only gets taken to the ground twice more.

I'm irritated by the end of the session because I don't fully understand what's happened and how Mer managed to get Alina to this place, but when Mer finally takes off her gloves and heads for the stairs, I reach out and touch her shoulder.

"Thank you," I say.

She looks at the contact of my skin on hers, then meets my gaze. She winks again and pouts her full lips. "Like I said, don't get any ideas." I think she's making fun of me. I think, but I'm not sure. And I don't get a chance to wonder, because Alina is suddenly charging her. Mer squeals and sprints towards the stairs, a laugh on her tongue. Knox is hustling after her and when he passes me, he jabs an elbow into my back and I can't retaliate because I've caught Alina around the waist to stop her from chasing Mer out of the gym.

I can hear Knox grumbling at Mer in the stairwell. "You're a fucking ass hole."

"Yeah?" Comes the husky response. "What are you going to do about it?"

"Fucking punish you. And kill Aiden if he ever fucking touches you." Mer laughs again, but then I hear the pounding of feet, Mer screams. Knox roars, "You're mine."

And then the hushed reply, whispered in rapture without any of its hardness, "I fucking love you, you dummy."

Another grunt, and then a screamed laugh before the door at the top of the stairwell slams shut. The minute it does, Alina shoves her elbow into my ribs and then punches my chest with her gloved hand. She takes a few steps away from me and a chill swirls through my chest, and is exacerbated by the fact that my stupid fucking ass doesn't understand anything that's happening.

Knox's anger makes sense, but Alina's? I don't understand her reaction at all, and it pisses me off. Nothing is supposed to bother her, because I'm supposed to be there to stop it.

Alina shakes her shoulders, as if trying to calm herself, but the color of blood still sits high in her cheeks. Her gaze flashes to the room's only door.

"You did well," I grunt.

She doesn't acknowledge me. Just keeps biting her bottom lip in a way that makes me worried for it. I like that lip. I want her to leave it alone so I can have at it.

"You need help with your gloves?" I grunt.

Words explode out of her, some in Russian before she catches herself and repeats, "You like her?"

The words have no meaning. I shake my head. "*Shto?*"

"You hear me." Her voice is deep. She's upset. With me. What the fuck? Who has to die? Is it Mer? Because fuck what I said before. If she costs me Alina, it will cost Mer her life.

"I don't understand."

"You like Mer. You like that she is better fighter than me. And she is sexy. You like it…" Her voice tapers off as she searches for more words.

At the same time, reality slaps me. A reality I was utterly unprepared for. Knox was jealous. That's why he was mad at me. And so Alina is mad at me for the same reason. She is jealous. "You're jealous?"

"*Pashol nahui,*" she curses. She rubs her forehead with her glove. Her lips are pursed tightly together. "*Da,*" she says finally. "I am jealous."

"You don't want me to be with anyone else but you?"

"*Nyet.* I kill them." And in the look that glazes her eyes, I know she's telling the truth.

My blood rushes with emotions, all of which are foreign to me. All I can do is move forward. Alina pulls back, but I don't let her. For once, I don't hesitate to touch because she is mine and more importantly, I am hers. I have been from that first moment we locked eyes in the hospital. Back when I'd been sent to murder her.

Instead, I take her by the arm and by the back of the neck. I pull her underneath me and I lower my mouth to hers. I expect resistance. Desire is what I get. She surges forward, biting at my mouth, needing with desperation, but I keep my kiss gentle and slow. She starts to moan. My cock screams and I have both of her hands pinned and she cannot break away from me. Her body is flush with mine. I feel each of her curves. Her breasts pressed against my chest. Her hip bones vying with mine, fighting to be closer.

I keep her at a distance. Feel her frustration mount. She starts to writhe and wrestle, body wanting mine. She wants me. And the thought of me with Mer, as unimaginably ridiculous as it is, is enough to piss her off.

"Aiden," she cries and she's rubbing herself against my body now in a way that's going to bring me to my knees. But right now, I can't. I have to hold this moment. Bask in her wanting. Bask in her heat. And then she kisses my throat very tenderly, and like a tether pulled, I release.

I step away from her and remove my shirt. The pendant thuds against my chest and her gaze moves to it. Time pauses. She hesitates. Her gaze flashes to it, not for the first time, but for the first time, I acknowledge it. I catch her hand, kiss her palm, and place it over the pendant. Her skin is so soft. So warm.

"You ask if I like Mer? You if anyone should know. I have only ever loved one thing in this lifetime, in this world. And it isn't me."

Her pupils grow even larger, the one on the right nearly obscuring all of the blue. I love the way she looks at me then. It is part of the reason that I love her. Because she doesn't look at me like everyone else does — pity or fear. Instead, she is a princess and a princess has expectations so she only ever looks at me in the light of someone who wants something more. Who sees more, even in a beast.

"Do you understand, Alina?"

She nods.

"Tell me you understand. Tell me you know what this means," I grunt. I press her fingers more firmly against my chest, against the orthodox cross.

"*Da,* I understand." She licks her lips and when she approaches me this time, it's with delicacy. Her lips are tender as they move between my pectorals before finally kissing the pendant that hangs between them. "It was belonging to my grandfather. He would be proud that it is now yours."

Her warm, soft lips trail down my body now, caressing each rung of my abs with her tongue. Her fingernails on my ribs tickle and I twitch. She laughs against my navel before working her way lower still.

My eyes close. My face lifts to the ceiling. I am in heaven or somewhere near it. I wonder if Clifton is watching this, mesmerized or if somewhere along the way he's had the decency to leave the room. I suddenly don't care if he watches. Because if I'm not inside Alina in the next few minutes, I'm going to explode through my skin and that's all that matters. Just her and us here, alive and living.

"But why you saved my life? You did not even know me then," she whispers between feathery kisses.

And maybe it's because I'm in a state of pure ecstasy that tastes like lilies and rain and rapture, but I growl out the truth, "I loved you. I think from the first second I saw you."

She freezes, her fingers on my hips, her mouth below my naval, her tongue…dear fuck, that tongue. So warm as she tastes me, lathes me with it. I want her lower.

"How?" She says.

"I don't know."

She smiles and drops into a crouch while her fingers pull my belt free in the same motion. She yanks down on my pants, freeing my erection from my boxers. I hold my breath as she traces the line of her lips with my cock.

"Alina, you don't have to," I growl, shaky as my fists find her hair and my fingers tangle with her locks.

"I have not done this before," she says, and her whispered words fan cool air over my dick. It roars and twitches on its own accord, fighting an invisible opponent. "But I want to do this for you."

"Fuck." I'll be the first dick in that pretty mouth and I can't help the surge of desire that throttles me. I can't wait. Being her first in every way imaginable is the greatest gift I have ever known after so many years of degrading sex with women who deserved so much better than the soulless shell I'd given them.

"Please, Alina," I hiss, begging now. I can't remember begging anyone for anything before this. At least not in this way. Begging them to stop, maybe, but never because it was something I wanted. I might not have been a virgin, but I was a virgin to pleasure. Every sensation I feel with her is a first. Damning. Damn her. I'm fucking *ready*.

"Alina," I growl. And when her mouth finally opens and she slides her tongue against the bottom of my dick, unable to capture its width but using her hand to make up the difference, I curse again and a hundred times more.

Her tongue is so smooth against my shaft. She licks me like a candy at first. Tasting every curve and edge. The head of my dick thrusts forward angrily, preparing to come on her face, and soon, and she hasn't even put all of me inside of her yet.

I angle my cock for her lips and hold her head steady by in my shaking hands. Her mouth opens wide, and then wider. I move in slowly, and then slower. I feel every inch of her tongue and cheeks as they tighten around me, and I whisper soft words of encouragement as she tries to take me all the way into the back of her mouth. I withdraw when she gags around my cock, but she digs her fingers into my thighs and urges me forward again.

Fuck. Dear fuck. God. Dear god. Her tongue sweeps my cock and I can feel the back of her throat work against my dick's head as she swallows. And by the time she finally finds a rhythm and falls into it, sucking, breathing, licking, swallowing, I'm in nirvana. Nothing can touch me here. Nothing but euphoria.

I plan to take her for everything she has and, after this, return the favor in full, a hundred times over. But for now, I just want this gift, and I never want it to end.

She chokes and I start to pull back, but her eyes flick up at me and are full of a watery desire and a ferocious confidence and that's it for me. *Fuck me* is all I think as the cannon of my dick unloads into her mouth. I empty into her for what might be seconds or hours, feeling the back of her throat gag and clench and tighten each time I jerk forward. She doesn't pull away and she swallows it all. Every last drop.

And when I finally pull back and look down at her, wavering where I stand, I can't believe I've got a princess on her knees looking up at me like I'm everything. Who knew a monster like me could deserve a heaven like that.

Ify

I hiccup and Anne Marie laughs, slapping me hard on the ass. She ropes me into a sandwich between her and Nikita while the other girls grind on guys they've found on the dance floor. I'm dizzy and for a minute, I can't remember where I am.

The night wasn't supposed to end up like this. I was supposed to drop by Clifford's after leaving Gavriil. Cliff was meant to take me to check up on my car and pass by the police station – Bob was still unconvinced by my story in the garage and wanted a follow up – but instead, Cliff took me out for drinks.

I'm not sure I'm even supposed to drink on my pain meds because even though it's been four days and the swelling's gone down, the fractured bone in my cheek still hurts like a muffinfudger. Cliff told me it was okay though, that he'd done it loads of times. But I don't feel so good. I only had two drinks. Why did I believe him?

Drunk as a skunk, I stumble as I fight my way out of the club and through the packed throngs on Seventh Street. I need some water and am starting to feel claustrophobic. Not even my Napoleon complex can compensate for the fact that everyone on the road is half a head taller than me – whether naturally or because of the talons they've got strapped to their feet.

My face is hot but the wind is cold. Do I have a jacket on? Whatever it is doesn't seem like a jacket. I don't recognize any of my clothes. My mind is full of murky thoughts, all pointing in one direction. I want to be back at Gavriil's. He'd been so unexpectedly gentle, taking care of me the past few days. Talking to me, making me laugh, watching all my cruddy movies, only having sex once, and so slowly it opened up a whole new world of tortures, all by him and for me alone.

I've got a smile on my face and I'm smiling still when a hand clamps down on my shoulder. "Hey, where'd you go?" Clifford's grin matches mine and when he puts his hands on my face, I try to pull away, but they're so warm and the only anchor I've got against all the people and the cutting wind.

The night air swirls around us and is frigid. My breath fogs up in thick, white clouds that pulsate between Clifford and I like a heartbeat. Thumpthump. Thumpthump. Thumpthump. Mine is beating so quickly. I'm lightheaded. The world is all flashing lights and sounds and a momentary spear of euphoria washes through me at the fact that I gave Gavriil my word and even though Lenard texted earlier with some news for me, I didn't respond. I'm off the clock. Indefinitely.

"Need to catch a cab."

"Nah. Stay a little. Take a much needed night off," Clifford says.

"I'm always off the clock now." I beam up into the night sky. There aren't any stars I can see, but I can see Mars. It flames just as red as Gavriil's hair. I miss him even though I just left him. It's a strange and uncomfortable feeling. "I don't feel so good."

"Here, let me help you." Clifford runs his right hand back through his hair and slides the other down my back. He pulls my body flush to his and for a second, I frown. "Your slur is so bad," he chuckles.

"I know," I say slowly, further proving his point.

His hands around my body keep me upright as I get less and less stable. Eventually, I feel myself being lowered into the back of his cop car. "Are you arresting me?" I say, hooking my fingers into the grate that separates the front and back seats to keep myself upright and focused.

Clifford tilts the rearview mirror so he can see me and winks. "Have you been a bad girl?"

I roll my eyes and try to think of something sarcastic to say, but for once I'm out of words. I think about the time I showed up at Gavriil's in my last year's halloween costume. That costume had been Cliff's idea then too. Kind of weird that he picked it out for me. Weirder still that I wore it. But at least it came in handy. Gavriil had damn near salivated when I took off my coat and he saw me in it. I love the way he looks at me. Not like I'm some black girl, but like I'm *his* and I'm the sexiest piece of ass he's ever seen. It feels dirty and hot and all the right kinds of fudged up. Like he really, actually likes me. Which is good, because I like him too.

I love him, maybe.

A burning below my rib cage and between my thighs makes my stomach clench. I need to think of something else, but when I try to roll down the window to cool off, it doesn't budge.

"Can't have the criminals escaping, can I?" Cliff says, that same edge on his tongue. I still can't think of anything to respond to it, which is why I'm grateful that soon I start to see the familiar outline of townhouse row pass by on the other side of the glass. I press my fingers against it, wondering when I'll be able to show Gavriil where I live. I want him to come over. But he can't. Who's he hiding from? I never found out. Maybe Lenard can help me… But I promised. Maybe — and this is a crazy thought — but maybe I should just ask.

"Home sweet home," Cliff says as we pull up in front of my house. The short walkway leading to the front stoops looks ominous and arduous with how my head is spinning. I reach for the handle, only to realize there isn't one.

I'm still looking around dumbly for it when the door swings open in front of me. "How many times do I have to tell you, Ify – it's a cop car?"

Cliff smiles down at me, but instead of reaching for my hand, which I stretch out to him, he reaches into the car and grabs my ankle. With one swift tug, I go sprawling over the seat and I can't help but laugh at the sudden sensation.

"Cliff!" I laugh. The movement accidentally yanks my dress up and when I glance down at my body, spread over the seat, I see that my hem is up to my bellybutton. My sheer tights, and the black panties beneath them, are now both visible.

I try to cover myself, but Cliff grabs my wrist. His eyes meet mine, and the words I was about to say die when I catch his expression and read it. Actually read it. He isn't joking. This isn't a joke. And maybe…it never was.

His lips sweep the side of my hand. He pulls my middle finger into his mouth, and then works his way over all of my fingers to my palm. He draws figure eights over it with his tongue. Oh my goodness. What is he doing? My jaw works but no words come because I'm looking into his eyes, and I suddenly get the impression that this is the first time I've ever seen him.

"Cliff, stop."

He pauses and looks like he just might pull back, but then he shakes his head. He pushes my hand up over my head while his other hand reaches between my legs. A soft tearing sound fills the silence between us as he rips my tights, and then slips two of his fingers past the barrier of my panties and inside my heat.

"Oh my god. Fuck, Cliff, what is the matter with you?" My drunk parts like a curtain and I surge up into a seated position. My body doesn't respond the way I wish it would because I'm horny and turned on. Cliff knows better than anyone what I like. That I like being manhandled, but this is too much.

He takes my throat in his hand and plants a sloppy kiss on my mouth. I turn my head and even though my body is heating up, my head is in a fog and I don't like this. I know I don't. So I shove him off, hard.

"What the fuck is your problem, Ify!" He stumbles back and shouts at me from outside the car. I'm quick to edge out after him and even quicker to put distance between us. "You know how much I want you."

I'm rattled and confused and I start away from him, rendered speechless for maybe the first time I can think of. There's so much I want to say to him, but I can't. He's my best friend and he just put his fingers in me when I told him not to.

"Ify, come back! You are being such an ass hole. I've been your friend for ten years and watched you go home with hundreds of guys. You fuck everyone but me? How the fuck does that make any sense? Those guys, they just use you. You're just an exotic plaything. Not anything to keep. And if they get a chance they'll just leave and move on to the pretty, tall white chicks that they can actually show off to their parents."

I'm running now, and when I reach the end of the street, I fall. Clifford's words only reach me at a distance now and I've got tears in my eyes and my head is all messed up and I can't think because if I try too hard to think about what he's said and done, the more it sounds like he's telling the truth. He's right. Gavriil only likes me because I am the only thing available. But I'm just a short black girl and nobody ever told me I was beautiful or anything, so I know he could do better. Aren't Russians racist anyways? Maybe I should be with Cliff. But Cliff? What? He's my best friend? No. Not anymore.

Where am I?

"Is this where you want me to drop you off?" The car I'm in slows and the driver looks over the seat at me with skepticism scrawled across his face. I don't remember calling him, but my phone is clenched in my hand. I don't have my purse or a jacket or anything but I'm still gripping my phone angrily. The destination that it shows matches the sign on the building outside of the window. Mr. Chang's, in faded yellow.

Oh no. I forgot to have him drop me off somewhere else. And I didn't tell Gavriil I was coming. He won't expect me until tomorrow, and I was supposed to come with food, and now look at me. "You want me to let you out here?" the guy says again.

"Um, yeah." Because I'm too selfish to have him drop me off somewhere else, or better yet, drive me to my parents' house three counties over. They would understand. They would be kind. They're good people. They would tell me that it's possible for a hot white guy to like me and that color doesn't matter even though I know it does. We're not evolved. People don't change. I'm still the ugly one. The ugliest one. Oh my gosh. My chest shudders. How, with just a few words, did Cliff make me feel this way?

I open the door and stumble out of the cab, which doesn't bother waiting for me to even clear the entrance of the building. So much for chivalry. I struggle with the door and the debris, using the light of my cell phone to try to find the path Gavriil made for me. My heart is beating hard, but I tell it that I'm not scared. But I'm suddenly not so sure. Is this it? Is this my moment?

There's a creaking on the landing above me and I freeze. "Gavriil?"

I glance up and the creaking grows louder, then becomes a pounding as he charges down the stairs and emerges from the darkness. There is wind in the wake of his movements and the clean scent of his skin carries. "Ify," he says on a breath.

"I..." I want him to invite me upstairs, ease himself against me and help me unwind the night that's led up to this. I want him to tell me he cares about me, without me having to say it first. I want him to tell me that he likes me. That he thinks I'm pretty and that in a line of beautiful women, he'd still want me first. I feel like crying. I clutch my chest.

"I'm sorry," I blurt out, but I don't know what exactly it is that I'm sorry for. He must though, because all at once, he stops.

Frozen, he stands a few stairs above me and I wonder what of me he can see in the light of my phone. Do I look that bad? Because this expression he wears now isn't one that I have ever seen. Normally, Gavriil looks so begrudgingly happy to see me. Hiding his smile behind his hands, or biting the insides of his cheeks. When I show up on his block, he wraps his arms around my lower back and eases his body against mine, every time.

Every time, but this one. Now, his cheeks are hollow and his skin is pale and his fire-colored hair is nearly silver in this light. It shoots up and away from his face in all directions. He's got on a white tee shirt and black sweatpants. He grimaces but doesn't speak.

"Gavriil?" I hiccup and Gavriil retreats from me half a step. The top half of his face disappears into pure darkness so that I can only see the severe line of his mouth. "I'm drunk," I say stupidly.

"*Suka blyad*, I see that," he barks. And those are the first words he says to me.

I try to laugh, but it comes out forced. "I shouldn't... shouldn't have gone out tonight. I didn't mean to. I...the drinks. I think they messed with my meds."

"Are you in pain?" Gavriil hisses.

I shake my head. "No. It's okay. Just a little sore still when I open my mouth like this." I make a stupid gesture with my mouth, expecting laughter but Gavriil doesn't say anything for a while.

Then, "Why you come here?"

I waver where I stand, but lick my lips and stretch my arm forward until it reaches the railing. Taking it in a tentative grip, I walk up a step and when he doesn't move, I take another. "Do you want me to leave?" My head swirls with chaos and confusion, but I'm where I want to be. But he doesn't want me back.

He doesn't answer, but reaches down and takes my cell phone from my hand when I finally get close enough. He uses the torch to inspect me from head to foot. I wince, and close my eyes against the invasion. Then he touches my forehead after a moment.

"Do you…were you injured?" He says.

"No. Just my head."

"You hit your head?"

"No, just a headache. From the booze."

"Then why your knees are bleeding? Your hands too."

"They are?" I glance down and sure enough, there are small beads of blood budding along the heel of each of my hands and below each kneecap. There's also a tear down the inside of my tights, one that disappears under the hem of my skirt.

My face sizzles and I rearrange my hair so that it covers most of my cheeks. "I fell."

"How much you have to drink?"

"Not that much," I say, but the more I try to sound like I'm not slurring, the worse it gets. "It was the meds." Do you like me? Am I pretty?

He says a few words in Russian. They all sound like curses. "Why you drink when you take medication? This is bad for you."

"He said it would be okay."

"He?" And his voice is three octaves lower.

I shudder outside while inside, my confidence slides down to my toes. Nowhere to be found. "I mean, I thought it would be okay."

He snorts, but doesn't speak.

I lick my lips and swallow hard. My mouth is ash. Has it ever been so dry? "Can I come inside?"

Gavriil nods, but only after a moment and the disappointment in my chest drops like an anchor to the soles of my feet. I struggle forward and in his room, I don't know where to sit. I hug my opposite arms and watch as he locks the door up after him.

"I fucked up," I tell him, chewing on the insides of my cheeks. "I didn't think so I let the Uber…the Uber dropped me off in front of this place. I don't think anybody saw me, but I…I can't be sure." I try to stay present, to form coherent thoughts, but I'm so tired.

I hang my head, waiting for some sort of punishment – verbal, or otherwise. But Gavriil doesn't say anything and when I glance back to his face, his unchanging expression starts to freak me out. Fear. Is it…is it time for you now?

"Look Gavriil, I…" My lower lip trembles. "If you're pissed, I can…I can leave." Please don't make me leave. "I can also pay for you to stay in a motel somewhere far out of town if you're worried about security. I just…" I wanted to see you. How many times do I have to tell you that? "I just didn't think. I came because I..." I care. "But..." You're rejecting me. He's rejecting me. I'm being rejected. He's hotter than a fire's first spark and I'm the last girl in line. Right now the only girl. And that's why he slept with me so many, many glorious times. "But I'll go if you're mad, which you clearly are. I'm sorry I came in the first place."

I start forward, towards him, but his voice stops me before I reach either him or the door. "You think I am mad because of Uber?"

"If not Uber, then what?" I shake a little bit and turn towards him.

Gavriil's right hand twitches and he balls it into a fist. He looks lethal, but for some reason, the fear impulse I had dies. Gavriil wouldn't hurt me. He may not like me, but he wouldn't hurt me. Not like Cliff, who I've known for a long time...

He lifts his hand and I hold my breath as his fingers finally find my face. Delicately, they stroke the side of my jaw and I lean into the sensation, but he keeps his touch light and cold, a distance forming between us that has nothing to do with space. Then he holds up the little torn tag of my dress along my shoulder and his nostrils flare. His hand drops back to his side.

"Someone hurt you?"

"No. I..." It tore. How did it tear? I can't remember. "I ripped it in the bathroom. I'm not quite sure how."

He gives me that look that says he doesn't believe me. He never does. He's never wrong. "Who you go out with?"

"Just some girlfriends."

"Then why you smell like a man?"

"What?" Oh no. No no no no no. Why didn't I just tell him about Cliff from the beginning? That, I can actually answer. Because here, Cliff doesn't exist. Shouldn't. But he's everywhere. In my thoughts, muddling the smell of my perfume. His fingers are still inside of me, his kiss still glimmering on the corner of my mouth. Oh no. Does Gavriil think…

"You smell like cologne and your hair is flat in back, like after we lay together." He turns away from me and pulls a portable electric lantern out from his desk's right drawer. He switches it on and sets it on the floor so that it casts a freaky white light over everything. He uses it like an interrogation lamp and I feel interrogated by it. Why is he being like this? I just wanted to see him to leach his warmth but he's so cold.

I reach up and touch my hair as my voice fails me.

His eyes narrow and his spine is perfectly straight, bringing him to his tallest. He has to stare straight down the bridge of his nose to look at me and even though his voice is loud and cruel, I still find myself leaning towards it. "Who did you fuck tonight?"

Oh my lord. Have mercy please. "I didn't…I didn't with anyone. I swear." I lick my lips, tasting the truth for once.

"Do not lie to me now," he growls, voice louder than it should be. I can imagine that the pros at the far end of the block can hear us at this pitch, but now doesn't seem like a good time to remind him. His eyes say that he doesn't care. He doesn't care.

"I'm not lying." And I'm not weak. I won't let him see me cry, but the alcohol is wreaking havoc on my system. He doesn't care. The words ring in my skull. He doesn't care about me.

"You lie again."

"I didn't fuck anyone!"

"Who touch you then?"

Tell him about Clifford. Tell him you didn't want it, that you said no. But why does he deserve that? He went into this conversation with nothing but accusation. I'm a whore, is that it? Is his opinion of me really that low? "Why is that your first thought?"

Gavriil shoves his fingers through his hair and rubs his face. He pulls on the collar of his tee shirt and walks away from me. For the first time in my life, I don't want to be the one to speak first. There's a rattling in the back of my throat and a fire in my chest and a cold pressure in my teeth. I feel like I'm going to be sick and I know I need to leave but I'm mounted to the spot by absolutely nothing.

No thing but the one thing: There's nowhere else I'd rather be.

"Because you are selfish and you lie and you live another life. Why would you not fuck someone else and come to me?"

"Because I'm not a whore!" And I wouldn't do that to him. Because he's enough for me.

"Why you come here?" he roars, turning on me like I've said something to cut and wound him when all I did was stand up for myself against the one man who I thought saw more. Clifford was right. Clifford's always right. I'm wrong.

He punches his fingers through his hair again and a third time, looking like he'll rip it out by the root. "You don't know why you come? Why you come here again and again? You like to torture me, *da?*"

"I…" I falter, I still don't have an answer for him. My head swirls and the walls of the room swell and bend, like I'm seeing the universe in a fish eye lens. "What do you mean, torture you?"

"I mean torture me!" He turns and slams his fists down onto his desk with so much force I hear some bit of wood splinter. I jump, then jump again when his arms swipe the surface of the table, scattering all of his things. His computer hits the ground and when it slams shut the screen shatters and keys go flying.

Gavriil roars, "Just get out." His cornflower gaze has fire inside. They hate me, those eyes and I am seconds from unraveling.

"Why are you like this?" I shout back. My palms are clammy. I wonder how badly I reek of booze as my whole body breaks out into a cold sweat. "What is happening? I don't understand. I went out and I had a bad night and I came to see you? Isn't it obvious enough why? And why do you care who touches me? You don't care about me." Oh no. I should have stopped before, but now I'm talking and I'm still talking and Gavriil is right because I never shut up when I should. I wring out my hands and fight against the tears with everything I've got.

I blurt out, "All you care about is getting some ass while you're trapped here in solitary. I could be anyone. And when this is all over and done, you'll go back to the tall, blonde Russian models you dated before, leaving me with nothing but disappointment and memories…" I've said too much. I've nearly said those three enormous words, but it doesn't matter because I can't control my mouth and he isn't listening.

He points a finger at me threateningly and seethes between his teeth. "You know, maybe you are right. Maybe when this is done, I will go back to tall, Russian blonde because they know that when they are mine, they do not fuck other men. You are mine, Ify. *Mine.*"

"I'm not yours and I'm not anyone's property and I haven't fucked anyone but you for the past two months and you can have your blonde model because I don't want you either. You're such a...such a fucking ass hole!"

"You do not turn this on me to try to make me seem like bad guy..."

"You are a bad guy! You are *the* bad guy."

"So you think you are better than me? That is it? That is why it is okay for you to fuck another one?"

"Maybe I am better than you. I'm not in the mob and I'm not a murderer!"

"At least I am not selfish, lying whore!" He shouts so loud something in the bathroom falls and shatters. In this room, I collapse back, hitting the wall beside the front door as the whole world – my whole world – comes to a standstill. Gavriil is towering over me, standing too close to accommodate the canyon that now separates us. For a second our eyes meet. His gaze hollows.

"So this is what you really think?" I feel the tear that hits my cheek. He tracks it with big, hollow eyes. "Same as everybody else? That I'm a selfish, lying slut."

"You...you are...I..." Gavriil roars. He kicks the chair – the only chair he has – with his bare foot and it shoots across the room, clacking loudly against the chest of drawers I'd first come to investigate. "Get out!"

I wipe my cheeks feverishly. The tears make it even harder to see straight so when I glance over my shoulder for one last look at him, all I see is a blur. "Goodbye, Gavriil Popov."

I pound down the stairs and fly through the front door. I stumble two, three times. The heat I'd felt before, brought on by the anticipation of seeing him, is gone. I'm cold. Freezing. I regret everything, from going out to the club tonight, to meeting Cliff way back when in that jail cell, to the decision I made when I first put a pen to paper and decided to be an author. Everything that brought me here, to the doorstep of heartbreak, standing outside in the cold, knocking. Knocking…

My hand shakes, but it's still clutching my phone, and that's enough. I look around to find a street sign, my eyes so blurry I can barely make out the letters. Eventually, I manage to call an Uber. It cancels almost immediately, but the second accepts and is fourteen minutes away. My lower teeth chatter against the upper and I hug myself hard. I slump against a lamp post and squeeze my eyes shut tight, as if this way, I might erase memories and time.

I didn't think it was possible to feel this way – correction, I didn't think it was possible for me to feel this way. I suck in a breath, waver where I stand and wonder how it is possible for a single person to cleave through my chest with an axe made of words, obliterating everything in its path. I feel as if I am made from a million broken pieces, and the fine strands that had been holding them together are suddenly gone.

My phone buzzes with a text from Nikita, wondering where I've gone and if I'm okay. I let her know I'm fine and at home. Another lie. Gavriil's right about me. I'm just a stupid, ugly, lying, whore…

The distant sound of wood splintering draws my gaze up and over my shoulder. A breath shudders into my lungs as Gavriil, two blocks away from me now, emerges onto the street. He looks left, then right, then directly at me. "Ify!" He's running and I don't bother trying to get away. I'm so cold. I shiver and close my eyes and let the tears stream freely down my cheeks.

I force my lungs to inhale and my chin to lift. He may be four times my size, but I am determined to stand my ground against him. Gavriil doesn't speak. His hands run up and down the front of his tee shirt. The fabric catches in a breeze I don't feel. I'm too hot, too cold, too numb.

"I do not care," he says finally.

"I know that."

"*Nyet*, I mean…" He shakes his head and slaps a closed fist into his opened hand. "I do not care why you come to me. I do not care."

"What?"

"I care that you come. I care *only* that you come. You must…" His voice breaks and he clears his throat. His body pivots to face mine fully, but he continues to keep his eyes averted. "You must stay this night."

"No way." And this time my words also warble. "Are you insane? I know what you think about me now. Why would I do that to myself? And why would you want to spend the night with a stupid, lying slut? I thought I was just here to torture…"

"Because I am in love with you." He meets my gaze and his voice softens. It trembles too. "I love you. *Ya lyublyu tebya.* And I hate that you go out this night. I hate that your hair is flat in back and I hate that you lie to protect the man who touch you and hurt you. I want to take his life."

The viciousness of his voice is in contrast to his touch. He takes my left hand in between his two gently and kisses my palm, and his lips are warm and soft and a tremble rips through me. He whispers Russian against my skin and I want to know what he's saying, but I don't want to ask. I want to hold onto this moment and let all the rest slip away so that I'm crystalized here forever, time suspended.

Gavriil licks his lips and they glisten under the street lamps and their flickering glow. "I want you here because I am not angry with you. I am angry that I was not there tonight to protect you. You went out and you make bad decisions and if I had been there, you would not have rip in your tights. Were you…raped?" His voice catches.

He chokes and I see him holding his breath until I shake my head. "But man touch you there?" I nod. He glows ghost white. "Did you want it?"

I shake my head. "No. I only want you."

He closes his eyes and his hand clenches around my hand.

My chest shudders as I try to inhale. "Do you believe me?"

Gavriil's eyes open and he opens his mouth to speak…

"Are you Ifeoma?" I jump and look right. There's a car there, a black Toyota. I hadn't seen the Uber drive up.

It takes me a few tries to answer in the affirmative and when I shift towards it perfunctorily, Gavriil's hold on my left wrist tightens. I glance up into his eyes and they are dazzling and sure and afraid. I don't know how they can be so many things simultaneously.

"You will leave?" His breath is cool against the inside of my wrist, skin so light against mine.

I nod and say nothing. I don't have anything to say. My heart is thumping and my mind is too battered and beat. It's what I wanted, but I'm not used to it. I'm so used to lies and deceit I can no longer recognize love or loyalty or understand why he would give either to me.

Gavriil releases me and goes to the car's back door. He opens it and warm air clashes with the chill of the outside air that I am beginning to feel more acutely. "You will come tomorrow?" His voice is a question, so unsure.

But I don't know what to say. He hurt me. He didn't believe in me. Maybe he still doesn't. And what about what Cliff said? Gavriil said he'd go to the other girls. Maybe he just loves me because they're not here. I'm so confused. Too confused to stay or give him any other answer than no.

"Gavriil?" I slip into the backseat and roll down the window when he closes the back door.

"*Da?*"

My mind forms the word, no, but that's not what I say. Instead, I whisper, "I love you too. I'll come tomorrow."

His eyes, exploding with color, grow enormous and round. "I believe you," he says, but the Uber beneath me is already rolling and I'm left watching him through the back windshield staring after the car with his arms hanging limply at his sides. He's watching the car like he'd give anything to bring it back. His whole heart.

Gavriil

I'm having trouble focusing on what Anatoly is saying and it is what is most important. It is what I have been waiting for.

"Roman is here and he is demanding answers. The drugs, but more importantly, the deal with Jordan. He wants to know why Jordan is collecting so much of the profit and why half of our trucks are going to Jordan in the Ternary."

My voice is empty, hollow. I close my eyes. "I do not even know."

"None of us do. Erik is trading with the cartel with one hand and feeding Jordan with his other. Jordan has his own operations that we are not a part of. I do not even know who is backing him, but it isn't any of the regular players. I think he is in league with powerful men. Men as powerful as Roman and much, much more powerful than Erik."

The pain forking across my forehead like white lightening across a bitter sky grows more intense. I try massaging my temples, to no effect. Anatoly is still speaking though I wish he would stop. I have had enough for one day. One lifetime.

"We just need to be patient. Allow Roman a little more time to see the state of affairs his son has plunged the *Bratva* into. Give him a chance to realize that there are holes in Erik's lies. With the drugs. With the women. With the agreements he has with Jordan. I suspect he has even more going on with him than I know about and if he does then god is the only one who'll be able to help him when Roman finds out. And when his credibility is weakest, you will arrive with the drugs and cut the legs out from under Erik. Maybe out from under them both. Days maybe is all it will take. A few weeks at the worst."

Anatoly is pacing. It's driving me mad. My leg is bouncing on the ground, which shakes my whole body because I've got my elbows braced on my knees. Anatoly finally looks at me. "I will go with you to make contact with the brothers at the end of the week to negotiate with them the retrieval of the drugs."

"You do not need to come," I respond in Russian though Anatoly continues speaking in English.

"You'll need backup. We don't know what those men are capable of."

"I know them. I will be fine."

He lifts a thick black eyebrow and tightens the ponytail at the nape of his neck asking me a question without words.

"They take good care of my sister. That is all I need to know to know of their character."

Anatoly doesn't move. His nostrils flare and his long, hard face is suddenly bleak with bitterness. It oozes out of him in a way that is nearly palpable. "How do you know this?"

"Move on, Anatoly."

Anatoly snorts. "Don't tell me you've found yourself an informant in that little *schluha*."

"*Ti cho suka?*" I stand when Anatoly calls Ify a whore. Ironic since I called her the exact same thing not more than twelve hours ago. Who the fuck raised me that I speak to a woman like that? Let alone a woman I am in love with. One who, for all her lies, I believe when she tells me she loves me back.

Anatoly jerks, hand reaching instinctively for his gun. He bows his head subtly, but not as quickly as he should have for me to believe he's showing true contrition. "*Prosti.*"

"Don't you fucking dare bring Ify into this."

"Ify," he repeats.

"*Pashol nahui.*" But I'm not pissed at him. I'm pissed at myself. He wasn't meant to know anything about her and with that little information, I've given him everything he'll ever need to find her. "Forget about her. She has no place here."

Anatoly doesn't respond. He just watches me with an expression that's dangerously close to critical.

"What?" I snap.

He seems to consider speaking, then says, "You say she has no place here, but she's everywhere. Her perfume is all over your sheets. She has a toothbrush in your bathroom. There are a pair of her panties under your pillow and worst of all, she's in your thoughts. I'm trying to save your life and save the family, but you're with her someplace else."

"You are out of line, Anatoly."

"*Da.* But am I wrong?"

The answer is no, but I can't say that. He is one of my men. Loyal, and he looks up to me. I cannot display weakness even though I am weak. She said she would come today, but she has not yet. I did not sleep the night before – the night of our fight.

I kept replaying what I'd said to her and the way she'd looked, so drunk and unlike herself, so vulnerable with her disheveled hair and tired eyes. I hadn't been angry at all that she had been dropped off directly in front of the building but I had been angry about everything else.

She reeked of liquor and men's cologne and her tights had been torn and bunched just below the hem of her short dress. She'd been bleeding. Someone had touched her and caused her pain and she had lied to protect them and at the end of the night, it didn't matter because I care for her and I trust her – not to tell me the truth, but enough to know that she didn't lay with another even though I had wanted to believe she did. It would have made it easier to hate her.

I want to hate her because the alternative terrifies me. Perhaps it terrifies me most to know that it is already too late. I am in love with the crazy woman with the wild hair and the lying lips and the pussy so perfect I get hard every time I catch a whiff of lavender.

"Tell me about Roman. Where does he stay? Who does he see?"

Anatoly's dark and cunning eyes flick away from me. "He stays in South Shore at his estate abutting Erik's, but he spends most of his time in Elmer, trying to contain the damage."

"Damage?"

Anatoly grimaces. "Erik has started pulling women from the streets. American women with families who care when they go missing. People have started to talk and the good cops are onto us. Our contact in the bureau is running low on favors to give and is, at every opportunity, increasing his price. He even called this morning and what he asks for..." He makes a face then and when he looks at me it is with sadness in his eyes. "You would not approve to say the least."

"Monster," I snarl.

Anatoly nods and agrees with me. He returns to his pacing and as he walks, the lavender scent surrounding me is muddled by Anatoly's male smell – like some kind of foreign wood and spice too exotic to name. It is a smell I recognize, and one that should comfort me more than it does now. There is something wrong. I can sense it. Does Anatoly hide something from me? No, he would not. Anatoly knows that beneath everything else, a man's word is all he is.

"Dissent is fomenting. We are ready for a change in leadership." Anatoly looks at me with wide eyes, imploring.

I suck a breath deep into my stomach as I say the words I should have said the moment we put my father in the ground. Words that would have started a war then, but saved us from the war that is happening now.

"I am ready to take it. I will meet with Roman the week after next, after he's had time to see how mad his son has truly become, as you say. I will need you to find me an opening either when Erik is away and Roman is in Elmer or when Erik is in Elmer and Roman is at South Shore."

Anatoly sighs, and I can sense that it is a sigh of relief. "Done. I will make sure it happens as soon as possible. We don't have time to waste. The women don't either."

Anatoly's nose twitches and his left hand shakes. He wipes his palm off on his jeans and removes his M1911, but keeps the safety on. He does this sometimes when he's upset. He just holds it, as if it carries some sort of calming presence. I understand the need of a talisman well. I just wish that mine was not another person. Unlike a gun or any other object, another person can leave.

"You should see…" Anatoly starts. He doesn't continue. "If you came to Elmer and saw what I do every day, you'd never want to touch another woman again in your life. You'd never want to talk to me again either." Again, his hooded eyes sweep my face. They hold mine and I know that I could trust this man with anything.

I nod. "I'll see it soon enough, and I will end it. I will strike a bargain with Roman in exchange for the drugs and move back into a position of leadership. I will break the deal with Jordan and put an end to the sex trade. You will no longer have to do what it is you do."

"You think it will be that easy to resume your place in the family?"

Nyet. I do not. "We will have to see. If Roman is a smart man, then he will fold me back into the *Bratva* or risk losing the allegiance of those still loyal to me. You say they are not an insignificant amount."

"No. They are not. We need you." Anatoly exhales and pulls the band from his hair. "And once you do, and once all is settled, I want only one thing from you."

"Whatever is in my power, is yours to have."

"*Spasibo.*"

"What is it?"

He hesitates, then says softly, "I want to leave."

Sadness fills my chest like a hollow drum. Dully, my heart still beats. "You want to leave the family?"

"After everything I've seen, I'm done. My last mission will be to reinstate you and save the family. Save those women."

"You know there is only one way out of the family, Anatoly."

He nods. "You were supposed to die a dozen times, and here you are, still breathing. Maybe I can learn a thing or two from you."

I smile and go to the cupboard. I pull out a jug of vodka and take a long swig before handing it to him. He mimics the gesture and makes a face. To this I laugh. Anatoly has never been a vodka man. "You should never have left Russia."

"I know."

"You should have married Aiy Syene when you were seventeen."

He laughs in a loud guffaw that reminds me so much of him even though it isn't a sound I've heard in so long. It reminds me of Russia, of when we were boys, before Erik lost his mind, before I believed I was untouchable.

"*Dalbayob*," he laughs, wiping his mouth with the back of his hand before taking another swig from the handle. "I can't believe you remember her."

"Remember her? She had nine toes and beet-stained teeth and you thought you were in love with her."

Anatoly nods and looks off into the distance. "Yeah, that was until my dad showed me an issue of Sports Illustrated. He told me all women in America looked like that."

"And you left the next week. I remember that." I take the vodka when he offers. "You never did find that model."

He grunts, shakes his head and rubs his thumb over the smooth barrel of his grandfather's gun. But then his eyes grow distant enough to make me wonder what he sees.

"Anatoly?"

He jerks up, rubs his face, shakes his head. "No. I didn't find any women. Another tip I could pick up from you, I guess." He glances at my phone. I'm clutching it in a mirrored image of the way he holds his gun.

I sigh and indulge in staring at the screen for a moment. It's a relief not to have to constantly remind myself to look away. Scrolling back through my text messages, I confess, "She was supposed to come by today. She swore she would, but she has texted saying that she is sick. Begging to postpone to tomorrow."

"Begging sounds good."

He has no idea. I love the way she begs for me. "I don't know. She's upset with me. We got into a fight last night. I was jealous." Because she was out living her life, without me.

"You'll get your life back soon enough."

I laugh, but this sound is humorless – not at all like Anatoly's. "I'm not pissed she was out. I'm pissed I wasn't with her. All those other men," I hiss. "She came to me last night and it was clear that another man touched her and she did not want it. And Ify...she is so small and vulnerable and I wasn't there."

"Want me to find the man and kill him?"

I grin, more genuinely this time. "Maybe."

"You don't seem like yourself."

"I'm not. I want to be with her. Not just to protect her, but to simply be with her in public and to show the world that she belongs to me. I want to make her happy. I am in love with her." I glance up at him, well aware that he's giving me his most skeptical look. Grinning again, I ask, "You must think me weak."

"Never."

I laugh again. "You are the only one who I could never tell was lying."

"It's because I would never lie to you. You are my leader. My brother. You always have been."

"Always will be." I hold out my hand and he clasps it and I am able to forget the budding anxiety in my chest for a time as I recall what it was once like to be normal, to have friends, to desire a woman, and to go to sleep without the worry that I won't live to see morning.

Ify

I sit in the middle of my living room with my arms wrapped around my knees, scrolling through my and Gavriil's last texts. They're all terse and clipped and I know we need to hash out our last conversation – at least the bits of it I can remember – but I'm afraid. I'm so afraid. I'm shivering and cold and trying to do anything I can to avoid this conversation. Oh lordamercy. What am I going to say? I told him I loved him. I've never told anybody that before. The truth is hard. Lying comes easy.

Wincing, I toss my phone onto the fluffy white rug beneath me and hang my head in the darkness between my arms and legs. I try to meditate, but that reprieve doesn't last long because after a few minutes, the doorbell rings.

"Crap on a stick." My shoulders immediately flinch towards my ears as the front door swings open. "What in the frick are you doing here?"

Clifford's standing there wearing his uniform, his thumbs hooked into the belt loops. "Ify, please. I was on my way to work, but I had to stop by and talk to you."

I jerk up to standing, clomp towards the front door and try to shut it. But instead of slamming with satisfying resonance, it bounces off of the edge of Cliff's black boot and he takes a step into my house, coming close enough to make me panic. He looks the same, but everything else about him is different. I've never met this person before and he terrifies me.

"Cliff, I don't want to talk to you."

He smiles at me sheepishly in a way that I no longer trust. "You still call me Cliff."

"What do you want, *Clifford?*" I say with emphasis. "I really don't have time for this today."

"What are you busy with?" He wades past the stairs and into my living room in a lazy kind of stroll. He touches one of the stacks of papers on my nearly clean table. I'd been packing it up — all my files, everything. The last step that remains is just shredding them, or incinerating them. There can be no traces of this hunt that's almost gotten me killed.

And yet…it's still too compelling, because even though I might have decided to remove myself from the equation, Gavriil's still seeped in it somehow, leaving the little detective in me screaming with a desire to answer the question of who's hunting him.

"Move on, Cliff," I say when his gaze lingers a bit too long on the papers.

He holds up both hands and ducks his head, attempting to look apologetic. He doesn't come close. "Sorry. I thought you'd be around, laying low and trying to nurse that hangover."

"I'm done nursing. I have work to do."

"Really? I don't think I've ever seen your shit so organized. If I didn't know you any better, I'd say you were packing this project up."

"I am. I just happen to have other things brewing. I'm not a one trick pony. I have other stuff to work on." Like repairing a broken relationship.

"Well then that's a shame, because I've got a present for you that I thought you'd like."

Work to make Gavriil like me again? What did he know about that? "Like I said, Cliff, I don't have time to talk to you about stuff. Anything. Since that incident in the parking lot I realized how dangerous this town can be and I'm not interested in…"

Clifford rolls his eyes and rocks back on his heels. "Since when does Ify care about safety? You really have changed."

"I've always cared…"

"You carry a library card around as your best defense." Clifford laughs and the sound makes me frown because it's uncharacteristically malicious. "And I'm not saying that's a bad thing. I'm just saying you shouldn't lie about who you are. You'll want what I have to tell you, trust me."

I step on the tips of my left toes with my right and behind my back, twist my fingers together. "That's not who I am," I say quietly. But I'm not sure anymore. Who am I except a girl too chicken to go tell a boy that she's sorry?

"No?" He cocks an eyebrow and crosses his arms over his chest. The muscles of his arms bulge against the tight cuffs of his shirt. I wonder if he took his coat off before knocking on the door. Not knowing why he's not wearing a coat bugs me.

I shake my head. "No."

He breathes air out of the corner of his mouth and ruffles his blonde hair. It's greasy at the roots. "Then I guess I really don't know who you are anymore. I'll leave you to it."

He strides towards the door with his head high and a sudden bubbling fills my belly that I hate. I wish it would go away. I wish I wasn't scared to go to Gavriil. Wish I wasn't looking for an excuse not to say what it is that I need to say. Wish I was able to be meaner to Cliff right now. Wish I wasn't such a horny, selfish, curious... I wish I wasn't me.

"Wait." Shut up, shut up, shut up. You made Gavriil a promise. "Cliff, I said wait."

I jog to meet him because he's ignoring me. His hand is on the knob and the door is three inches open when I barrel into it, slamming it closed. I glare up at him. "Just tell me." Clifford grins and steps up close. His body is inches from mine and so much bigger. He reaches forward like he'll touch me and something shifts in his expression as he registers mine. His grin stretches even more and his eyes glitter with a promise I can't identify. He drops his arm.

"Remember when I told you about those two mystery trucks?" he says.

"What about them?"

He cocks his chin towards my desk. "Go on. You're going to want to write this down."

I lean left then, wanting to appear strong and keep my feet planted. That strength only lasts a second. Cliff's grin spreads to consume his bright pink cheeks and I'm humiliated. It doesn't stop me from gravitating towards my notebook though.

My hands touch the topmost paper in the stack. It's an old photograph of Alina Popov, one I clipped from a tabloid from about a year back. She'd been exiting an Eckhardt law building hand-in-hand with a boy three shades lighter skinned than I am. I'd done my due diligence though. He's a twenty-one year old junior at Eckhardt's main campus and a friend of hers who'd been sad to see her disappear, but not such a good friend that he'd thought about reporting it. According to his Facebook page, she was somewhere in Russia. I didn't blame him for his ignorance though when I saw the note posted to all of her social accounts. He couldn't have known that she'd already been taken by that point and that whoever was writing those messages was probably some sick Russian mafia mother fudger.

I lift the small black notebook off of my desk and snatch up the pen next to it. I click the top and the sound reverberates through the room, down to my bare feet and into my consciousness, which is still screaming at me to stop this madness.

"What is it and it better be good or you know there's no reason for you to be here today. I'm still pissed at you."

His smile doesn't fade. "Yeah, whatever. This is good so sit and listen." He comes to my side, too close for comfort and touches my neck.

I twitch and he pulls away. "What do you have, Clifford?"

His hand is frozen in the air. His glance switches between me and it before he tucks his hand into his pocket and says, "The trucks are headed to the same address: 322 Elmer Street and it just so happens to be the same address that yesterday, cameras picked up Alina Popov."

"What? No. That's not possible. You've got your facts out of order, Cliff..."

He just shrugs. "Why don't you ask your informant?"

"What would he know about it?"

"You told me you had him tagging Anatoly Zherdev. Well, we've spotted Anatoly in Elmer too over the past few months."

"There's no way! My informant…"

"When was the last time you talked to your informant?"

I don't answer. It had been a few days. Weeks, actually. "Recently enough."

"Recent meaning in the past two days? There has been a lot of activity there. Like the mobsters are getting ready for something, and the Popovs are in on it."

"Alina isn't with the mob…"

"How do you know?" He says, lifting a brow. "Are you sure?"

"I…" No. I'm not sure. I have no idea who that man was who was with her in the stairwell. He could have been Russian, but his accent didn't sound like it. And even if he wasn't, that doesn't mean much. A lot could have happened since then. Maybe she is with the Russians. I don't know…but I want to…and Clifford knows this.

Cliff steps right up next to the computer, body sliding between my hands and the keys. He slides his finger under my chin but withdraws more quickly this time than he had the last. "Have I ever lied to you?"

"No," I admit.

"Then why would I lie to you now when I want you to like me the most?" He grins and grows just red enough in the cheeks for me to believe him.

I purse my lips, feeling tense. "I just don't get it. Why wouldn't my informant tell me that, but more importantly, why are you only telling me this *now*? You knew I'd been following Anatoly. We talked about it for hours. And you know that my ultimate goal is to find Alina." Because Cliff, you weren't just my informant. You were my best friend. What happened? Who are you? Why did you touch me like that in the car? Why am I sitting here talking to you?

Cliff's expression falls. "I should have told you, but I didn't want you chasing the Popovs down to someplace that could be dangerous. You know I care about you, Ify."

I narrow my gaze even further. Something about all of this is off. Way, way too convenient. But at the same time, what if he's right? Cliff really hasn't ever lied to me before. And what if Alina really is there? I could take that to Gavriil and he'd be so happy. All of our problems would be over. We could focus on that and not on the fact that we confessed our feelings to each other. Facts are easier than feelings. Mystery is easier than love.

"And now that I've rejected you, you don't care about me anymore?" I whisper.

Clifford straightens up and edges off of my desk like I've just stabbed him with a pin. Anger flashes across his face that I don't understand, but then he covers it with a grin. He ruffles my crazy hair, which is pulled away from my face in an uncomfortable bun. "Let's just say I have extra incentive to make you happy now. And besides, I don't expect you to go down there by yourself. I'll take you."

"No, that's really not necessary." I stand and head to the bathroom. I need to get ready. "You know I like to sleuth alone."

"I know," Clifford says in a hushed tone. "Well, let me know when you want to hang out."

"Not anytime soon."

Clifford just smiles at me from the center of my living room and there's still that sparkle there that unsettles me. I wish I knew what it meant. "Whatever you say, Ify." He winks. "I'll see you very soon."

My bags are already packed, my coat on, when I hear the door open and close. I'm in the Ternary half an hour after that. "Come on Lenard," I mutter to myself, "you high bastard. Come on."

Not that I don't believe Clifford, but I need corroboration before I go on a wild goose chase. He may have few scruples, but he'd have nothing to gain in keeping information from me. Clifford, on the other hand, gets his info from the police. They've got nothing in the way of scruples and not a whole lot of motivation to do stuff right. It's likely they messed up somewhere along the way. Not to mention, Clifford's argument about wanting to keep me safe seems razor thin. He would have told me. Should have.

I keep a printout photo of Lenard with me and I show it to the junkies and homeless people I pass because the name Lenard isn't likely to mean a whole lot here. Plus, I don't want to flash my phone and end up getting it jacked. I've got my Nokia with me, so if I get my phone stolen I'll still be able to text Gavriil and let him know I'll be late. My face flushes and I finger the Nokia brick in my black jeans' back pocket.

He's going to be pissed...I should just go there now. Why am I so scared? Because emotions are scary. Dad said I'm allowed to be scared once, but I don't think he took emotions into account. I'm scared shitless now, and I'm scared all the time. I should just go to him now, and unless I can find Lenard in the next ten minutes, I tell myself, I will.

I turn the next corner and come upon a narrow street. It's empty except for some dumpsters, but I take the turn and delve deeper into the Ternary. I wonder if I should just come back and find Lenard tomorrow? After all, Elmer Street isn't going anywhere. I don't believe the mess about Alina. I could just wait to check it out until then. And Lenard isn't here. He must be someplace else. I know he sometimes hangs out by the docks. He loves the sea. And he would never go this deep into the...

"Lenard? Oh my frick, Lenard!" I nearly walk right past him. Even in broad daylight the smear of darkness against the concrete side of the building looks more like a pile of fabric and garbage than a person.

I go to the mass of cloth and grab the front of his jacket. I jerk him upright and push his hood back. Lord almighty, he reeks. Is he alive even? "Lenard, answer me, buddy." I slap his cheeks and my knees buckle as I absorb most of his weight.

After a second, he coughs onto my neck and even though the parched and broken skin of his lips tickles my shoulder through my thin, black jacket, I exhale, relieved. "Fudge in helium," I curse. "Thank you," I say to no one, and then to Lenard, "Lenard, can you hear me?"

He nods, and smiles very slightly. The smell that wafts from his mouth is enough to make bile rush up the back of my throat. "Lenard, I need to get you to a hospital. You know no ambulance is going to come this deep into the Ternary. Come on. Stand up and I'll take you to my car and get you some help. Come on, Lenard. Come on!"

Lenard doesn't move and when I manage to get my shoulder wedged under his armpit he actively resists. "Don't mess this up for me, Ify," he slurs. "I feel good. I never felt so good."

"Cheesum crepes, Lenard. How did you get so high? Where did you get the money?"

His head rolls back like it's tethered with string. "Not money. Drugs."

"Drugs?"

"A whole bunch of them." He reaches into his pocket and fishes out a brown envelope. The paper is nearly as dry as his hands when I take it from him. I consider running off with it, but I know it would kill him if I did that. It might kill him if I don't. I stare down at the paper packet and feel totally lost.

"Who gave this to you?"

He laughs up into the sky and his throat sounds torched, like it's been days since he's had any water. "I promised I wouldn't tell."

"Who, Lenard? Tell me."

"You're the detective. Why don't you detective..." He starts to slump over until I realize he's trying to stand. I help him. He starts away from me on the instant. "Why did you come here, Ify? Let me guess. You want to know about Elmer..."

How in the hullaballoo did he know that? "No. No," I lie. "No. Right now I just want to help you."

"You?" he slurs, voice choking on a laugh that shakes the entire frame of his body. My arms are too weak for this and I have to use my hip to help hold him up against the wall. He's about a foot shorter than Gavriil, but still six inches taller than I am. "You don't help people…If…Ify Smith just helps her…herself…"

"That's not true," I snap. "How can you say that?"

He laughs some more, then starts to cough and I cringe away from him. He grins again. "See? You don't want to do anything that hurts. You don't want to get your hands dirty. You just want a good story to tell."

"Lenard, I…"

"Get lost, Ify." He pushes on my shoulders and though he's weak, I'm evidently weaker because I stumble.

"Lenard, stop it."

"You stop it. Just go. Three two two Elmer. That's where Anatoly went. That's where you're supposed to be to go find Alina Popov. Not here."

"How are you…" Three twenty two. Anatoly and Alina. The exact details that Clifford said, and Clifford knows I have an informant, but he doesn't know who that informant is. What are the odds that one and not both of them are correct? "I'll go there, but you've got to come with me."

"Get away from me, Ify…" He slumps against the brick wall, his weathered coat bunched up around his ears, nearly concealing his face. His jaw is working up and down and his fists are clenching. He manages to open his eyes but they are totally jaundiced and red. He looks demonic. He looks already dead.

I plant my feet and let the wind crash into my right side. It tunnels between the buildings, smelling like a faraway rain. It doesn't rain often it town, but when it does it comes down hard and mean. I always hated the rain. "Lenard, I'm not going to…"

"Get away, Ify! I don't want you here," he screams. His voice is hoarse and harsh and when he advances towards me, a half drunk bottle of something clear drops from his back pocket. He kicks it when he steps forward and I don't back up because I don't think he's going to hurt me until he does.

He shoves my chest and when I fall, he falls with me. We come down hard, the scrapes on my palms reopening and singing with a sharp, but ephemeral heat. Lenard falls on my shins and quickly scrambles away from me. He shifts and shuffles against the opposite brick wall, moving straight through a patch of liquid. It gleams against the sidewalk and smells like piss. Maybe something worse.

Lenard doesn't notice and doesn't care. He kicks my feet with his, nailing my black Nike's as well as my shins and ankles. His cheeks are rubicund and there are tears in the wells below his eyes. "Just go, Ify. Elmer Street. Just be there. Don't be here. Leave me alone!"

I'm shaken and rattled and I struggle up to my feet. "Lenard..." But he doesn't let me speak.

"I hate you! I hate you, Ify. You come here and you... you...aughh," he screams. "Just leave, Ify. You leave and go to Elmer and don't come back again."

"You're going to die, Lenard," I say. "You're going to die and there's no reason to kill yourself. You're a great guy. You may hate me but I..."

Lenard scrambles as quickly as a user can over the concrete. With my brain mushy from the alcohol a day before, he's still quicker than I am. Plus, I'm stupid. I don't understand what he means to do with the bottle until he throws it at me. It clips my forehead and I spin around, fingers damming the sudden splurge of blood that eeks out over my forehead, draining into my right eye.

"Go, Ify, just go! You go away forever and leave me here. Let me die." He charges me and I scream, but he's only reaching for my fanny pack. We wrestle with it for a moment until the clasp eventually snaps and I stagger back, slipping and falling onto my ass on the concrete. Lenard's coming at me again, so I grab the leather pack and run.

I run all the way back to my car, rip open the door, get in. I grab a wad of tissues from the glove compartment box and press them to my right temple, then I switch on the ignition and shoot down the road. I don't think. My thoughts power down and I hallucinate road. I'm driving to Gavriil's. I'm done with this. I'm going to tell him that I fudged up – again – and that I went against his direct orders – again – not to go hunting. It's sad really because this time, I don't even know what I'm hunting for except for an excuse not to have to tell him the truth.

And as I drive I wonder, what was I ever even hunting for? A girl in a body bag in a building? Maybe Clifford was right all along. Maybe I am just hunting for death and a story. He knows me better than I know myself. Maybe he knows me even better than Gavriil does. Because when I pull over to the curb and flick on my right blinker, I glance up at the street sign. I've arrived at the three hundred block of Elmer. I turn off my car.

Looking at the tattered remains of my sleuthing gear in the passenger's seat next to me, I begin unpacking it. Slipping my ID into my front pocket, my money and my library card into my bra and my two phones into each pocket, I'm ready to go. My arms are sluggish and slow as the adrenaline crashes within me.

I fight not to cry. I don't get to cry over Lenard. But I want to. And I want to cry, not just over him but over Gavriil and Alina and everyone trapped in this crap town of prey and predators. I wonder which I am and think that maybe Lenard was right. Maybe I'm worse than both. A carrion crow. Nothing but a scavenger. A coward. A stupid, drunk whore. A liar. Gavriil asked me if I thought I was better than him, but that's far from the truth. The truth is that I'm not good enough.

The breeze is cold and crushes against my hair, pushing it into my vision, tasting of snow and silence. It's eerie how quiet the world is beneath the sheet of clouds overhead. Four large buildings are stacked on each corner of Elmer and Eighty-Fifth. Three are made of some crappy metal material that looks like corrugated tin, but the building kitty-corner to where I'm standing is brick and black. Rainwater run-off has stained the space below its eaves and beneath each of the exceedingly narrow and oddly spaced windows, making them look like crying eyes.

There's something unpleasant about that building and it only occurs to me as I stare at it longer that there aren't any cars passing on the streets. I move into the intersection and stare down each road. Nothing, nothing, nothing…one blue truck coming down the street towards me. Right now it's just a smear some half a dozen blocks away. I shudder, zip my coat up to the throat, bury my chin in the oversized collar and as I turn to inspect one of the brick buildings on the opposite corner, I notice something else.

There are small, spherical lenses mounted on the corners of each building near the intersection. "Are those...cameras?" I think out loud.

"Yes."

I flinch and spin, only to find two men standing by my car. "Oh, I..." I start. "Hello. I umm...I'm a tourist from out of town." What in the beluga whale? Where did they come from? Why do they look so...apathetic to see me, and to be here?

One of the men is standing in front of my front tire, the other is testing the door. They're both wearing the casual clothes of any guy in town, except for the gloves. Black leather. And the chains that glimmer beneath their open collars look expensive. They don't look like robbers.

"What are you doing?" I ask. The man by the tire says something to the man by the door in another language just as a clack of thunder ignites the sky above. Russian. The mafia. Are they *Bratva*? I'm hard pressed to think they could be anybody else. My pulse starts to thump like the thunder overhead.

"Get away from my car."

The blonde with the corduroy jacket cocks his head to the side. He says something else to the other one, who then speaks to me directly, in English this time. "You look surprised." His accent is heavy, like Gavriil's but less severe. "He said you will know..."

"Would know," corduroy jacket corrects. His accent is perfectly American.

The Russian flips his friend the bird. "Would know."

"Wh-what?" This whole scenario is so strange. I don't understand. "I don't understand."

Corduroy jacket slips his hand into his back pocket and pulls out a folded piece of paper. He shows it to his partner who squints at it for a while before flicking his gaze to me. "Are you Ifeoma Smith?"

"No," I reply.

The partner advances on me in a few quick steps. He reaches for my jacket and I don't think he'll grab me until he does. I shout at him to stop, but he's already got both hands in my pockets and he's much stronger than I am. Ignoring my phones, he shoves his fist into my pants and, finding my ID, shoves me back. I stagger, slipping and falling onto my ass on the concrete. While I amble to my feet, the two men look at my ID.

Corduroy jacket shakes his head sadly. "Ifeoma Smith. The man said you would know."

"Who said? Know what?"

"Why you're here. Why we're here. He said you were a smart girl and that you would understand why we have to take you." He blinks and shows me my ID. It glitters in the light and a stone sinks in my stomach. I didn't listen to Gavriil when he said not to do anymore sleuthing. I didn't listen to him when he told me not to carry my ID when hunting in the night. And now they've got it, and look like they have no intention of giving it back to me and all I've got are a couple phones, a little bit of cash and the library card still stuffed in my bra to defend myself with. How did they get it? How did they know?

"Take me?" I glance around. The ice in the air is more cutting than it had been before. The wind is heavy and on its chilling tentacles I can smell salt and shit. The docks are nearby, but we must be in a bit of a valley because I can't see them. Where are they? Where am I going? "Take me where?"

Corduroy jacket frowns. His partner shakes his head and advances towards me. He looks at me while I look at his hands. My feet back away from him steadily as a dull and distant ringing begins to sound, like church bells. I stumble up onto the opposite sidewalk. There are voices – male voices – and a shout – a woman's shout – from the building to my left. One of the warehouses, the metal menace stares down at me and I suddenly understand. Everything. And it all comes back to Clifford and Lenard and Gavriil and all the stupid, foolish lies I've told. Each and every one.

"No." My lips feel like rubber. So do my legs. The moisture in the air has become sleet and its touch against my face is like the cold, dead hand of a corpse.

"You can come with us quietly, or we'll have to give you a dose," corduroy jacket says. He withdraws a small syringe from his pocket. It flashes in the rapidly fading light and my mouth floods with saliva. I swallow hard and a taste lingers on my tongue: fear. This time, the kind my father spoke of. I'm not supposed to feel it now, but I've never been cornered like this.

That time they had me in the barn and I thought I was going to get burned, I knew that Clifford would come and find me. This time it's Clifford who set me up. He must be doing this to teach me a lesson, but he'll come for me after a few days and I'll scream at him and he'll apologize and tell me this was his version of a sick joke. But somehow, I don't think it'll be that easy.

"So what will it be? The easy way or the hard way?"

"Ha…" I lick my lips and swallow to moisten my throat. It's bone dry as I take another tentative step back. "Hard way. I'm not going without a fight."

He grins with one side of his mouth in a way that makes him look uncommonly handsome. It's a crap look for the villain. "You seem like a nice girl. I'm sorry it has to be this way." He looks like he means it, which makes the panic in my chest pulse with even more violence. "Are you ready?"

My lips tremble and my left leg shakes. I nod and take off down the street even though I know how this will end and so does he. His footfalls echo on the asphalt long enough after mine to let me know that he's given me a head start. Something cold and wet brushes at my cheeks. Tears or the snow? I'm not supposed to be crying. I'm not supposed to feel fear. But when his heavy arm circles my waist and a small, sharp pain tickles my neck just below my left ear, I scream. My body goes limp and a sickening, sinful euphoria sweeps me.

He cradles my legs and the back of my head while the world around me mutes itself and whispers, *"Printsessa, I'm sorry."*

Gavriil

Where is she? That's what I think. What I say into the phone instead is, "Yes. Mondays and Tuesdays seven to nineteen he is in Elmer. Saturdays he visits Jordan. Sundays he will attend church before returning to his estate at thirteen hundred. Wednesday to Friday, he is not stationary. So I will visit him on Saturday at his estate, where he is most comfortable. I have been there, Darya knows me, she will allow me to enter. She will tell Roman and I will wait for him in his study at his desk to assume the position of power and he will laugh and I will laugh because we will both know that I am not there because I have power but because I do not."

Anatoly curses. "Don't say that. You have power. If you didn't, the men wouldn't be galvanizing for you every day. You shouldn't meet him in his office. That will be what he expects. Instead, you need to meet him on the staircase. You'll be sitting there when he finds you. Don't tell Darya or any of the help that you're coming. You'll sneak in through the back entrance. I'll help you."

"Fine." I don't answer right away. My thoughts are somewhere else.

"Good." Anatoly pauses. "There's an echo. Am I on speakerphone?"

"Yes." Because I'm checking my texts. She was supposed to be here three hours ago. She is late and I have followed up once but my pride prevents me from doing so again. She should call. No matter how late she is going to be, she always calls. Maybe it's because of our fight. Maybe she's nervous to talk to me. That makes sense. She told me she loved me and I told her I loved her. Perhaps she has had some time to reflect. Perhaps she lied again… And if this is the case then she should be nervous, because I will not take anything but her love from now on.

It makes sense…but it doesn't at the same time, because I've never seen Ify nervous. She is never nervous. She is angry and petulant and disrespectful and disobedient and anarchistic and a liar, but nervous? Not Ify. And if she isn't nervous, then she's angry. She isn't coming.

"Why?" Anatoly says.

"Because I am locating the estate on my phone. Google Earth shows all the entrances."

He pauses before asking, "Are you ready?"

I nod and stare at the window across the room. It shines light onto the laptop I destroyed. Winter is ending. Summer will come soon and I will be free of this place and in my own home with Ify in my bed. She will clutter my space with her things and I will be irritated with her but not enough to stop her from taking up more and more of the closet and the dining room and the living room and the guest room she will use for her books and she will not cook though I will want her to and she will not clean either and she will spend nights out but when she does, she will spend them with me and we will dance and I will catch her when she stumbles and she will kiss me when I stumble and call a cab to take the both of us home because I will be just as vulnerable around her as she is around me.

"*Da*," I tell him in Russian. It has been two days without Ify and English seems a distant memory. Ify, not so much. I see her everywhere. I hear her voice. I replay the conversation we had…the things I said to her. What she wore. How she acted. As if she did not care. Maybe she does not. Maybe my fantasy is just that. A fantasy. "I am ready. I will strike this Sunday."

"No. Gavriil, have you been listening to me?" Anatoly lowers his pitch so that it is both deep and angry. "You will not strike this Sunday. We need more time. Last we spoke we agreed next week at the earliest. If you're eager, the following Sunday you can meet with Roman. We haven't even gotten the drugs yet from the brothers. This we will do the day after tomorrow, on Friday. And I need to coordinate with the men this side to make sure that Erik is out of town and I need to confirm that there's nowhere else Roman might be that day. It is a delicate situation. Not all of the men despise Erik and those that don't are wary of my intentions. They exclude me," he admits after a moment. "They think that I want control."

I know I am meant to feel surprise, but I don't care enough to be shocked. I'm still staring at my phone. "What are the numbers?" I say, closing my eyes and gripping my phone so firmly, I have to coach myself to relax before I shatter it. I destroyed my computer so it is the last technology I have left.

"What numbers?"

"For my leadership and Erik's?"

Anatoly pauses to think. "It's close. The men that want you, want you to lead the family. The rest want Roman. Erik is collateral. That's why, if you are able to strike a deal with him and return to leadership, you'll unite the factions."

"Factions," I whisper, massaging my eyelids. "When did it get like this?"

"It was bound to happen. Events were set in motion outside of our control. Starting when your father passed." Anatoly clears his throat. "I'm sorry," he whispers in the formal, as if he was not there at the funeral, as if he has just become aware of it.

"No need for apologies, Anatoly. You did not murder my father. My father was a bad man, just as I am. He made many enemies. I loved him, yes, but his death was inevitable." As is mine.

"Do not say such things," Anatoly rasps, curses on his lips lasting for many moments. I wonder if I have not said that last part out loud. "Don't think about death or your father when you go to meet up with Roman."

"I won't." I will think of Ify.

The last text I got from her was, "Be there in one hour. Just checking on something first." That was hours ago.

"So is the plan set? Hold tight, get yourself cleaned up. Saturday, we will go to the brother's house and next Sunday at dawn you'll pick up your car from the hiding place and go to the South Shore estate. Address is eleven thirty one. We'll go through the neighbor's backyard to reach the pool house and come in through that entrance. You'll need to time it so you arrive inside and on the stairs at eleven before Roman leaves church and I will need to leave far earlier than that to be back at Elmer. The men cannot suspect that I assisted you."

"Of course not. You will be back in Elmer well before then. You do not even need to come."

"You do not want me there?"

I groan, "Of course. You are my most loyal friend. I trust you and value your opinion, but I also care for your safety. As I know you would do nothing to jeopardize mine, I would not jeopardize yours."

There is a sigh on the other end of the line, one that fills me with guilt. Here he is thinking of family first and me as its patriarch while I sit staring petulantly at my phone, no better than a child. "It is good to hear, Gavriil."

Gavriil. Hearing my name on his tongue brings me out of my stupor. Not much, but some. "You are my brother, Anatoly. I love you as one."

"I..." He seems taken aback.

I choke back laughter. "It is alright, Anatoly. I know you." He is not a man of emotion because he does not lie, so with him, words are not necessary. He is truth. The only one I trust.

He laughs nervously and exhales, "Thank you."

"This is entirely your operation, Anatoly. That is how I know it will not fail." A lingering silence prevails, broken up by his attempts to speak. They are unnecessary. "Thank you, Anatoly."

"You know you are my brother, too."

"I know, Anatoly. And I promise..." I will push thoughts of Ify aside and focus on the task at hand. I close out of my text messages and click open Google Earth. "I will not fail you."

"I know," he answers. "You never do."

Ify

The urge to vomit wakes me and when I wake, I wake slow. "Oh cheese and crepes," I moan into the pillow beneath me. It's been overly starched and overly bleached and feels like sandpaper against my cheeks and eyelids and forehead. I'm lying face down, or something near it. I try to twist a little and some sensitivity returns in my neck. A second or two later, it's much easier to breathe.

I lay like that for a little while, tasting the dry, bleach-flavored air before I decide that I've lost my other limbs. My arms. Where are they? Gone maybe. I try to roll over, but I can't get onto my back. I wonder if the blonde in the corduroy jacket tied me down, but a second of wrestling against nothing and I understand that it's just my arms pinned beneath me. I angle my left hip down into the mattress and manage to wriggle my right hand free. I use that hand to roll myself onto my side and on my side, I fall onto my back.

I'm too close to the wall, so I end up crushing my shoulder, but to move away from the wall would require a full body effort so I just lay there with my head cocked back and groan. "Fliiiip." I draw out the word while my stomach gurgles angrily. The room is spinning slightly, or maybe it's just out of focus. Hard to tell.

"Am I dead?" I ask the wall beside me. Glancing my eyes open, I see it and see that it's grey. Clean, grey concrete that ends in a low, grey ceiling. The corners are all thin black lines and when I manage to cast my gaze three-sixty, I spot a single window covered by a heavy metal grate. The world is black behind it.

"You're not dead."

I look up, clutch my stomach, and after a few seconds manage to sit up. I grin shakily. "Thank the lord almighty. I don't think I've ever been so glad to see anyone in my life."

Anatoly Zherdev is standing just inside the small grey box with me with his hands down at his sides. He's holding his gun, and strokes it lovingly in an absent way. "You know me," he says, more than questions. He cocks a black eyebrow.

I nod and fall back against the wall, placing one elbow on the metal frame of the headboard to keep myself upright. It's hard. Almost as hard as remaining conscious. "You're Anatoly Zherdev. You've been helping Gavriil."

"He tell you that?" He speaks in a perfectly American accent, one that's familiar.

I shake my head. "You were there at that place the same day I was. Gavriil tried to keep me from seeing you, but your voice is familiar." Plus I had a guy tailing you for weeks – not that I need to tell Anatoly that.

He nods and tucks his gun into his back pocket. Coming towards me, he tucks a strand of inky black hair behind his ear. It's fallen from his low pony tail and is the same color as his eyes: intense. Open and glaring and framed by inky black lashes, I have no idea what he could be thinking. Nothing like Gavriil, he's a wall.

"You're smart. Too smart to have ended up here."

I smirk, "I guess not."

He doesn't smile back. "I guess not."

"So where am I?"

"Nowhere a woman should be. Did you tell Gavriil you were coming here?"

I shake my head. "No."

"What was the last thing you said to him?"

I think for a moment, then remember. "That I'd be at his place in an hour." Guilt. Grief. Regret.

"Can I see?" Anatoly holds out his hand and I rifle through my coat's front pocket, withdrawing my Nokia brick. My and Gavriil's last correspondence flashes across the dim screen making me feel even more nauseous.

Gavriil: "I need to see you."

Me: "I'm so sorry, I feel so sick. Tomorrow?"

Gavriil: "Tomorrow."

Gavriil: "You coming today?"

Me: "On my way. Be there at two."

Me: "Frick. I need ten more minutes."

Gavriil: "Do not lie to me Ify. Do you come today or no?"

Me: "Be there in an hour."

Gavriil: "Ify, where are you?"

Gavriil: "Ify, you lie to me."

Gavriil: "You do not want to see me you tell me. You do not lie to me. Now tell me, where are you?"

The last three messages from him are new. The most recent of them came in at seven forty five. I glance at my phone's clock. It's now five to eleven. I'm nine hours late. My bottom lip trembles and I feel tears in my mouth though they haven't yet reached my eyes. "I need to text him back. He's probably so P-Oed." P-Oed is what I say, but what I'm thinking is worried. He told me he loved me and I blew him off.

I hit the reply button, but Anatoly gently slides his hand against the back of the phone. "Wait," he says, "can I see?"

"Sure." I nod.

He scrolls through our conversation with his black eyebrows bunched. "Is this the only device you have on you with his number on it?"

I shake my head and somehow manage to wriggle my other cell out of my back pocket. I hand it over too.

"This everything?"

"Yeah." Anatoly stands there thoughtfully for a second before slipping both of my phones into the inside jacket pocket of his beat up black leather coat. "What are you doing?"

His hands pause though the stoicism of his expression does not falter. "You can't keep these on you."

"Why not?"

"If one of the other men happen to find Gavriil's number they'll turn it over to Erik. If Erik makes contact with Gavriil it will be over. You don't want that do you?"

"Wh…what? Want what?"

"Gavriil to die."

"What? No! Lordamercy, no. Why…"

"Because you have Gavriil's number. If Erik calls Gavriil and tells him where he found this number, what do you think will happen?" He tilts his head to the side and speaks to me in a quiet, calm way that makes my heart start to beat harder.

I push my feet under me so that I'm tucked into a tiny ball. My shoes are gone. I wonder if that nice blonde man who attacked me took them. Staring at the coat pocket where Anatoly just put my phones, an uneasy realization begins to tickle the conscious part of my brain. A bright, hollow ball starts to burn a path up my esophagus. I swallow it.

Anatoly takes a half step towards me. "And you know what will happen if you tell anyone that you know, Gavriil, right?" I do know, but I don't want to say it. I don't need to. Anatoly must see the knowing shining in my eyes because he gives me a small, sympathetic nod. "You love him don't you?"

An involuntary gasp shuffles into my mouth. I nearly choke on it. "Yes," I say, reaching up to rub my face. "I do."

"And he loves you. Your being here puts him at risk because if he knew where you were, he'd stop at nothing to get to you." His gaze slides sideways and he licks his lips. They're full and dark red, pretty and gentle. But there's a tightening in my gut riding alongside the nausea that tells me not to trust them. "And I can't risk that. All of the others that are in this building with you – the women prisoners and the men imprisoned by Erik – need him. He cannot know you are here."

My lower lip trembles and heat flashes across my face. "They need him or you do?"

Anatoly's expression doesn't change. It's flat and desolate, even as he starts to walk backwards towards the door.

"Wait. Where are you going?" I shuffle to the edge of the cot and carefully place one foot, and then the other, on the cold concrete floor. "Anatoly, wait. You're still going to help me out of here, right? Anatoly. Anatoly!" I slam into the other side of the door just as he closes it between us. I can see his face hovering through the metal bars guarding the murky, milky white glass panel, like storm clouds brewing. It turns Anatoly's bronzed face into that of a ghost's.

Anatoly meets my gaze. He has no trouble doing it. "Your situation is beyond help, Ifeoma Smith. I am sorry for you," he says, but we both know he's not.

"No, no, no, no, no. Anatoly. Anatoly!"

"Remember what I said." His voice is muted through the door but I have no trouble understanding him. "You tell them about Gavriil, or he finds out you're here, you'll have killed him yourself."

I slam my fist on the metal. It's cold and impenetrable. Just like his expression, which doesn't change at all. And then he leaves. There one minute, and the next, I'm staring at another grey, concrete wall on the other side of a short corridor from where I stand. Alone.

I'm going to die in here. I'm going to die in here or *worse*. What had Clifford said? The Russians are running women? They wouldn't take an American woman off the streets would they? How the hell should I know? What has Clifford done?

A scream builds up inside of me and I release it all at once. Standing in the middle of the room, I scream and shove my fingers into the thicket of my hair and there is a wetness on my face that I refuse to acknowledge because I'm crying and I did this to myself by taking advantage of Lenard and by lying to Gavriil, the man I love.

I think of my friends and my parents. Mom and dad, what would they say if they could see me here? Because dad always said, you're only allowed to feel fear once. And now, I am consumed and slaughtered by it. There is nothing else. Not even hope.

Gavriil

I stare down at the text message on my phone without feeling. It has been four days and I've texted her thirty times at each of her numbers. I've called her four dozen times at least. She hasn't answered, her phone has gone straight to voice mail, and now after all of this waiting and worrying, I finally get this:

"Gavriil. I'm sorry I haven't made contact but I've been spending the past few days thinking about things. About us. I know you care about me. I care about you too. But our last fight really showed me how different we are. We live in different worlds and I need to be with someone who is a part of mine. I hope you understand." That is all.

I try calling her back over the next hour, but she does not pick up. I text instead, asking her why she lied to me, why she is doing this, to which she responds simply, "I'm sorry, Gavriil. Please don't contact me anymore."

Tossing my phone onto my mattress, I stand up from my bed and glare down at the sheets as if they have committed some mortal offense against me. In a sense, they have. They smell like her still. Just one week ago, she was here, body fit against mine and I was holding her and kissing her too large lips and fondling her too large ass and slipping inside of her tight heat, bringing our most tender parts together and I don't mean her pussy or my cock.

I thought I was falling in love with her, but I had already fallen deep into the cavity of her heart and now that she sends me these messages, with such bland callousness, I wonder if she ever had even an ounce of love for me at all. She told me she loved me, but it was lies. All fucking lies. Ify. Ifeoma Roberta Smith. The author, the seductress, the liar. I never thought her lies would go this far.

The room around me dissolves to ash and when I resurface from this haze, the few things I once had are gone. The table has been reduced to splinters, and so has the chair accompanying it. My dresser drawer vomits clothing. All of the drawers have been torn apart and the frame, dismantled. Clothes lie in disarray across the weathered floor panels. The bed is overturned.

I tore apart the sheets and the mattress and now piles of fabric sit scattered among the feathers of the pillow she brought me and that she was always so bad at sharing. But I never minded. I gave it to her, like I gave her every other little piece of me. She has them all and she has destroyed them. To what has she reduced me?

My hands shake as I remove the panels from the windows and look out onto the street, finding again the one young prostitute standing on the corner. I think about inviting her up, telling her who I am and letting the streets come find me. It's what my mind, but not my body, wants. Because my body wants the pussy made for my cock. My body wants to feel her submission beneath it as she lets me do whatever it is I want. She. The only she. The power I feel...the power I felt. I now realize it is nothing compared to the power she had and continues to wield. I thought she was mine, but I was wrong. I have been hers from the start.

I am meant to go to the brothers today. I am meant to go to Roman in ten days. Ten days and I will suffocate in this hell hole. It was once a sanctuary where nothing else existed but her body and mine as we worshipped each other in the only rituals I have ever known. Those rituals are gone now, my temple incinerated. God is dead. I have to get out now. Fuck Ify. Fuck the brothers. Fuck Roman. I have to find her.

I take my coat from the floor and go to the door. My hand is on the knob when I regain just a few of my senses. If I leave to go to her – when I leave – it is over. There is no coming back and there is a chance that I will not survive the evening. More importantly, if I go where I intend, I put her at risk and I hate that this is what stays my hand, more than anything. I want to tear her apart and the thought of dying myself in order to do it is fine, but the thought of being the cause of her injury or death is unbearable.

I inhale through my mouth and exhale through my nose. I drop my hand from the doorknob and flex it before moving back into the room. I need a plan, a shower, and a gun. Sifting through the mess, I find my Makarovs. I make sure they are both loaded and take a seat beneath the window against the wall. Nerves and tremors fire through my body in alternating waves of ice and heat. What I should do is call Anatoly. He would be best positioned to give me details on Erik's movement tomorrow, but he'd also be best positioned to convince me out of my plan. My need. He'd tell me to go to the brothers and to sit and wait, but I'm not leaving this room unless it is to go to Ify. And to get to her safely, I'll need to go to Roman first.

Fuck the drugs. Fuck the plan. Fuck Anatoly's reason. I do not wish to hear it or his judgment so I text Ivan instead even though Anatoly is not sure he can be trusted. That risk does not matter to me as much as the result. When. Where. I stare at the small face of the screen without thinking of anything but the time it will take for him to respond. Then I wait as the flakes of my sanity dissolve into the lavender scented air.

Ify

Sitting up on the bed, I stare down at the food on the tray and think to myself, what's the point? I'm going to die here anyways.

I've got strips of the one sheet that covers the bed tied around my hands to stem the bleeding in my palms. I think I might have broken something in my left hand, because my pinky finger moves funny now. From the banging. It hasn't helped. In fact, it's had no effect at all except for destroying my hands, draining my energy and weakening my resolve.

I think of Gavriil. I try not to think of Gavriil. What would he say if he could see me now? Ify, why did you do this? Ify, why didn't you listen to me? Ify, why can't I trust you? Ify, I can't love you when you treat me so poorly. Ify, you treat everyone so poorly. Because you're Ifeoma Smith and you are a liar and a thief who doesn't care for anybody. Ify, you deserve this.

The thought makes me smile. And then I start to laugh. I start to laugh so hard that my whole body rocks. Tears come to my eyes and I flop back onto the bed and stare up at the blank grey ceiling and I know that this is what madness looks like. I'm lightheaded and there's not an ounce of strength left in my body. I'm dying. Or maybe I just want to.

A low thump wakes me some time later. Maybe seconds. Maybe eternities. The tears are dry on my face and there is still a smile stretched between my cheeks that is hollow and desperate. Then there's that thump. I don't begin to understand it until I hear it again, twice more. Thump thump. It's dull and coming from the wall to my right. I lift my hand and touch it and feel the vibrations coming through the dry concrete when the thumping continues.

"Hello?" I cough, choking on a painful knot of spittle lodged in the back of my throat. More hysteria begging for release. "Hello!"

"Stop it," a muted voice answers and the sound of it shocks me so much, I sit up and push away from the wall so suddenly I fall off the other side fo the cot. I land on my left hand and cry out in pain, curling around the injury as needles shoot through my palm to my wrist.

"Fuck," I curse. I never curse. My mom always hated it so somewhere along the way, I replaced or razed all curse words in my vocabulary. I back up until I knock into the bucket they placed in the corner. They replace it every day which is about all I have to be grateful for. Then again, I stopped trying to force-feed myself the various multicolored chunks of food a long time ago. I haven't pooped in two days.

"Who...who's there?" I say again and my voice is weak. I massage the thin bones in my throat and finally do what I haven't done in a while: I reach for a bottle of water on the edge of my cot, crack the lid and drink. The relief is immediate and so abrupt, my head spins.

"Shut up."

The sound is coming from under the cot, so I flatten onto my stomach and when I don't see any sort of boogeyman lurking in the shadows, start to crawl towards it. "Are you in the next cell?"

The female voice doesn't answer. I crawl closer until I'm entirely under the bed, fingers fumbling to try to find cracks in the wall. My chipped nails finally nick something and when I press, concrete comes off beneath my nails like powder. I scratch further.

"You're wasting your time." The voice is louder now – right up against the other side of the apparently flimsy barrier between us. I jump back so quickly, I bang my head on the metal tines crisscrossing below the cot. The underside of the bed is a mess of rusted coils and flaking paint. Luckily, my hair is large enough to stop me from concussing myself.

My fingers drift instinctively to where Lenard cut me with the bottle. I wonder what his involvement is in all of this. Did Clifford pay him to lie to me? Was Clifford the one to give him the drugs? I feel grief and pity more than betrayal. I helped keep Lenard an addict.

According to the rules of karma, it makes sense that his addiction would be the trap I fell into. So no, I don't blame Lenard at all. And if I ever get out of here, I vow that I'll find him and find some way to help him. Because I'm not that old Ifeoma. Not anymore. Because that Ifeoma is a magnet of death. And this Ifeoma won't be…if she ever gets free. Which she won't.

"Who are you?" I whisper.

She doesn't answer me. Instead she repeats, "You're wasting your time. The wall isn't weak enough on your side. If it was, I'd have dug my way through a long time ago."

"Dug?" I say, feeling stupid.

"Yes. Now stop digging before you get yourself caught and take me down with you. I can't afford any mistakes. Not today."

"What is today?"

"Today, I escape."

Surprise. "Really?" I say, trying desperately not to feel hope.

"Yes. But I can't do anything for you. I can't help you."

And in a swift instance, that non-hope, or pre-hope, is squashed like a bug against a window. I curl onto my side and use my arm as a pillow. I speak into the discolored bit of wall knowing that this cruel woman on the other side of it is my only lifeline.

"How are you going to escape?"

She sighs, like she'd rather not keep talking to me but knows already that I won't shut up. And I won't. Not when I'm this crazed and starved for human contact. "When they first brought me here they kept me in the basement," she says. "Near the foundation, the metal siding becomes cinderblocks and I managed to pry a few loose and get out once but one of the ass holes guarding us caught me. I didn't tell them how I got out and because I put the blocks back, they never found the opening."

"They brought me up here but they didn't know that the room had a weakness. Bad plastering in here. Weak enough I've been able to tunnel my way through the insulation to the outer wall. The fiberglass cuts, but I can take it. I can take it." The way she repeats the words sounds like she's convincing herself more than me.

I feel heat and cold at her words. Despite her hope, my terror renews itself like a phoenix. "How long have you been here?"

"Four months and a day."

I cover my head with my arms as tension begins coiling in my muscles. "Were you raped?"

"No. I'm a special case," she sneers.

"What does that mean?"

"They keep me here and bring potential bidders around to see me. Apparently, there's been some kind of bidding war between an old emir and a wealthy Texan. I don't know."

I bite down on my fist. I'm going to die here. I'm going to scream. "What happens to the girls who aren't special?"

"They're bought and sold in a couple days. I'm surprised you've been here as long as you have."

"Maybe I'm special too," I whisper, "I think I was bought by someone."

"You know who bought you?"

"Yes," my voice is a breathy wheeze. My eyelids flutter. The world feels so dark.

"Who?"

"My best friend."

She doesn't answer right away. "That's fucked. Sorry," she answers, but she doesn't sound it. Why would she? I'm not the first girl in this position she's met before.

"Where do they take the other girls?"

"I met a girl once who had been sold back. She told me they took her to a cartel brothel, but that the brothel was raided. The security there managed to make it out with most of the girls though and they brought them back here. She was only here for a day."

"What was her name?" I hate her apathy. I hate her. I hate her so much because I need her. She's all I have.

"I don't know."

"Why don't you know?"

She doesn't answer and that says enough. Furious and afraid and recklessly determined, I reach for what's in my bra. The last things in my possession. I withdraw my library card and the cash I have on me and despite her warning, manage to push both through a slit in the plaster.

"Can you reach it?"

"Reach what?"

"Through the wall. I'm giving you something. Take it with you when you escape. Find my parents. Let them know I'm still alive. Tell them where I am and that it was Cliff who got me."

"I can't do that."

"I have money too. Take it. You'll need it when you escape."

She waits a long time before eventually, I hear scraping on the other side of the wall. "A little to the left. There's a crack in the concrete. You'd never fit through but I can see... yeah...there." And then it's gone. I hear her snort on the other side of the wall. "No wonder."

"What?"

"No wonder your best friend wants you. You're pretty."

My stomach clenches. The compliment is one wreathed in torture so I don't respond to it. Instead. I croak, "What's your name?" She doesn't answer, so I repeat louder and more forcefully, "My name is Ify. Ifeoma Smith. What is your name?"

I don't think she'll answer until finally she says, "Candy Yin."

"Where are you from, Candy?" My voice is shaky. There are tears on my cheeks. I clap a hand over my mouth to stop myself from screaming. My whole body is shaking. I'm so cold. I'm going to die here. And I deserve it.

"Tucson. Arizona."

"Hi Candy from Tucson, Arizona. It's nice to meet you."

She snorts. "No it isn't. If you weren't meeting me, you wouldn't be here."

Laughter bursts out of my mouth. I try to cage it. "Sorry," I apologize.

"Whatever. At least it's not that insane way you were laughing before."

I laugh again and there's a panic in my chest that threatens to unravel me. Stay strong, I tell myself, stay strong for Candy. "How old are you, Candy?"

"Twenty-two."

Just a kid, almost ten years younger than me. "When's your birthday?"

She doesn't answer.

"Candy?"

She still doesn't answer, and then I hear the muted sound of someone else's voice. A male voice. It's one I recognize and it says, "Stop it now before you attract attention."

"The only person whose attention I ever attract is yours," Candy snaps. "Besides. I wasn't talking to anyone." The confidence with which she speaks is inspiring.

There's a pause before Anatoly answers. I wonder if he can tell if she's lying because I can't. She must be a good liar if she's lasted as long as this. "You're going to get yourself killed."

"What do you care?"

"Do you want to die?"

"Maybe I do."

"That, I know is a lie. You're a fighter. Keep fighting. Just stop talking," Anatoly snaps and his voice is dark, but more volatile than I'd heard it last. Like his wicked composure is finally cracking. It makes me afraid to learn what lies beneath the wall of that exterior. A fear this girl does not share.

She would make my dad proud. Because maybe she has no fear moment. And then I have a worse thought: maybe every moment for her is a fear moment. Maybe fear is just her constant. And maybe it will be mine too for the rest of my life. I have felt nothing but fear since they brought me here.

She spits, "You disgust me."

The sound of footsteps grow louder. I wonder if he's going to hurt her. I want to cry out, but what would that do? "I don't give a shit what you think about me. Just stop talking. I have to go somewhere and if one of the other men hears you and decides to teach you a lesson, I won't be here to stop him."

"Why do you care?" She repeats, even more acerbically.

"You think I enjoy seeing you injured?"

"Yes."

"Even after what happened?"

She hesitates, but only for a split second. "Don't think that changed anything. You might have done one decent thing once, but it doesn't redeem you. You're still a monster."

Anatoly doesn't answer her and for a moment, I think maybe he's left the room. Then his voice chimes even louder, so close I feel like I can feel the chords pulsing through the plaster wall. "You know nothing. Everything I do is to try to help...the people here."

The assertion makes me want to puke. I scream, "He's lying!"

There's a sudden violent thumping on the wall. "Don't speak to her," Anatoly shouts. "Don't you dare speak to her!"

Candy fires back, "Why not? She your next victim?"

Anatoly doesn't respond.

"Monster."

Anatoly shouts. A door slams. And then I hear his feet just outside of my door. I scramble out from under the bed in time to see his face pressing against the glass. He slaps his palm against it. "Don't speak to her. You brought this on yourself. If you had abandoned your hunt, you wouldn't be here now. Don't take her down with you."

He's right. That's why it hurts. I push back onto the cot and bare my teeth. I want to eat him whole. I want to kill him just as his words kill me. But there is nothing to say. He's on the outside of the glass and I'm trapped behind it and this woman on the other side of the wall has managed to survive for four months without me here. I can't stand the thought of being her downfall.

He points another threatening finger at me. "Leave her the fuck alone," he seethes. Then he disappears.

A few moments pass before light, malicious laughter floats through the thick, concrete wall. "Well, Ifeoma Smith. It was nice knowing you."

"What?"

"I'm leaving, now."

"*What?*"

"I said I'm leaving now. That was my cue."

"Wait, wait, wait, wait," I say, placing both hands flat against the wall and rising up onto my knees. Like I'll somehow surge through the wall and into her cell so I can disappear with her. So she can hold me. I don't want to be alone. I want Gavriil. I want him more than anything, but at the same time I don't. Because so long as he isn't here, he's safe.

"You're leaving? Just like that? I thought…" I don't know what I thought and don't finish my sentence.

"Yep." I hear some scraping. The sound of metal on concrete. Then there's a thump and a grunt. When she next speaks she sounds much closer to me. "I was waiting for Anatoly to come by. He's always coming to check on me. I needed him out of the building before making my escape, which I am doing…" She grunts and there's a banging in the wall so loud it tosses me back onto my butt on the cot. "Right now. Sorry I couldn't stick around."

"Oh fudge," I whisper under my breath.

Evidently, she can hear it because she laughs. It's full of anger and sadness. "I'm going to try to cover the hole as best I can. I don't know if it will work, but your best bet in not getting sold to your ass wipe friend will be trying to get switched into this room. Of course, Anatoly would probably know something was up, so make sure you do it when he's not around and move fast when you do."

Her voice is fading now and the scratching in the wall is becoming more distant. "When you crawl down through the insulation, make sure you follow the path that I took. Otherwise, you'll just get lost. The loose blocks are on the ground floor. About twenty feet down and ten feet to the right if you're facing the street. But try not to get lost. You get… you'll be…"

"I…I can't hear you! Candy, wait! Will you go find my parents? Will you tell them I'm still alive? Candy? Candy!"

"Ify…" That's all I hear her say. The last thing. I don't move though, hoping to hear something else. Her laughter, telling me that this is all some great big joke. Worse, I wait for the sound of Anatoly shouting as he drags her back. I expect it. Because she's been here for four months and I've only been here for four days and it feels like four months so what will it feel like when I've been here for as long as she has? Four years? An eternity? Will I even remember my life before captivity? Probably not. It already feels distant. Ifeoma? Who was she? She wrote books about stuff. She hunted out terrible stories. She sought out tragedy – reveled in it. She deserved this.

But there's nothing. There's nothing but a distant wail – two of them – one clearly from a truck, another human. I don't know how long I sit there listening to the sounds of human suffering. Eventually though, someone comes by and shoves a tray through the slot at the bottom of the door. I don't touch it. I don't move. I lie down. I don't remember falling asleep but I wake to the sound of rattling.

Blinking my eyes open, the harsh fluorescents are still bearing down on me. My head hurts. I need to drink water, but right now there's the beautiful man in the doorway staring at me. He's wearing a frown.

"Are you ready, *printsessa?*" He says quietly.

"Wh…what?" I blink and sit up slowly. I unfurl my legs from beneath me and start to back away, towards the head of the bed – the little good that will do me. There's no way out of this cell block. I need to get transferred to Candy's room, but I don't know how. Candy left and though my envy is a force in and of itself, the better part of me – the part that Lenard said didn't exist, the decent Ify – hopes to all that's good that she made it out.

Another man shifts into view. He is heavier around the middle, with a low brow and perpetual scowl on his face. I glance down at his hands. He's holding a syringe and a swatch of blue fabric. It looks like the same starched fabric of a police uniform, like the outfit I wore for Gavriil. The one Clifford convinced me to buy because he's a sick puppy and he's always had it out for me and I'm stupid and never noticed.

I thought he was my friend. My best friend. I'm betrayed. Betrayal. Just like I betrayed the man I'm in love with when I told him I'd stop doing all this stupid, dangerous shit, and I'd come to him to be in his arms in an hour. An hour. I would laugh at the thought if I weren't so flipping terrified.

I don't say anything as the two men come into the room and that's when I see a third man standing just outside of the door. His blonde hair is neatly combed and his fawn, near hazel eyes are bright. His ruddy cheeks are a lighter red than his mouth, which he licks when he sees me. There is remorse in his gaze, but only fleetingly when that gaze catches mine.

Then he turns his attention towards the blocky man and hands him a medium-sized rolling suitcase. The same one he used on that trip we took with Nikita, Jason, and Susie to Orlando last year. I'd made fun of him because he'd taken someone else's suitcase by mistake. It had been my idea to tie the bright pink band around the handle so he wouldn't forget which bag was his ever again. It's still there and somehow that, more than anything, stuns and numbs me.

"She'll fit in here. Change her first though," Clifford says. "I want her in my clothes."

"You bastard," I sob, and the tears in my eyes blur the room that has become my world. "You bastard! How could you do this to me? We were friends!"

"We were never friends," he says, "you're a fucking moron if you think we were. I've wanted you for years and now I own you so shut up."

The sound I make is something like a scream. The big guy is coming towards me and when the fabric in his hand unfurls, I see a police uniform. One with Clifford's name printed on the breast. He hands it, along with what looks like a white tee shirt and pair of lace panties, to the beautiful blonde, who looks down at the items with disgust.

"Please...*bajalsta*," I beg.

He shakes his head and meets my gaze with a sadness that feels final. Like death. "It is done, *printsessa*. Calm yourself."

Gavriil

I am showered, shaved, dressed and seated behind the wheel of the 2001 Toyota Corolla that had been parked in the ruins of the building at the end of the next block. More trash and rubble had collapsed onto it, so it took me longer than I had wanted to clear a path to the street. It is ten am now. I should already be in Elmer, either dead or with a promise from Roman that I will be safe until I bring him the drugs. I am confident he will accept these terms. Fairly confident. Somewhat confident. Confident enough to leave.

My phone buzzes in my pocket. Not for the first time that morning. Anatoly is likely at the Chinese shop by now, wondering where I am and how my meeting with the brothers went. He does not know about this new plan and is likely panicking. It is not kind that I have left him out, but had I told him the truth, he would have fought me knowing my true intention and I would have killed him because now that Ivan has answered me and I have my window to go to Roman in Elmer, there is nothing but that keeping me from her. I need to go to her. Need. More than I need to eat. More than I need to breathe. The only question remains whether, when I see her, will I wring her throat or grovel at her feet?

The engine rumbles to life as the jalopy passes beneath the once-yellow awning of the Chinese restaurant that had housed me these nine weeks. I left everything behind except for my laptop and a pair of Ify's panties. The pale blue pair she wore the first time she came to me. The laptop I keep in the trunk of the car while the panties I shamefully keep in my pocket.

I drive myself out of the projects and pass through town. Seventh Street bars and cafés are as bustling, as ever, and I surreptitiously peek at the sidewalks, wondering and hoping that I may see my sister trolling them as she so often did when she was out with her friends, driving me mad with a little light drinking. Men are hungry creatures and I worried for her safety. I still worry, thinking about the monster who keeps and protects and cages her just as I worry for Ify. Ify...who abandoned me.

My right blinker is on though I know that is not the way I should be going. That is the way to Ify's home, to her townhouse on Ninth Street. My heart burns there at the present moment, but my mind forces my muscles to focus and bend in another direction. I wonder how my arms do not tear off at the wrists as I switch my blinker to left instead, steeling my resolution. I growl as I drive away from the city and head towards the docks.

The sky hangs low over my vehicle and is grey and white in patches, yet bright all the same. The kind of sky that is too bright not to squint, and too dark to wear sunglasses. The sky is pain.

Elmer is quiet. I avoid the central road and take the narrow back streets instead. I find an alley three blocks from the warehouse where Roman is said to be, and though I'm want to trust Ivan, I park. I make sure that the exits are accessible in front of and behind me, knowing that this will only be useful should I make it out of the warehouse alive. I don't bother calculating my odds.

The air is cool and tastes of snow, cold enough that I pull my down-filled jacket tighter around me and lift the hood, hiding my fire colored hair. Alina always said I should be lucky that I didn't get Timur's orange locks. His was the brightest and, coupled with his shorter height, made him look like my kid sometimes instead of my little brother. A little brother I failed.

I circle the building block, passing the only building here made of brick and approaching one of the grey structures that sit like tin tortoise shells on the other side of the road. Ivan and Evgeny stand outside smoking. Evgeny's cigarette falls from his lips when he sees me. Even Ivan, who is expecting me, watches me with large eyes full of disbelief. Did he think I wouldn't show up? I told him I would. What sort of man does he think these many weeks have made me? Because a liar is something I have never been and still, am not.

"Gavriil," Evgeny gasps. His darker skin makes the whites of his eyes stand out all the whiter. "What are you doing here?" He asks me in English. He lives in the motherland. It is not often that I see him in America and his accent is evidence of it.

"Where is Roman?" I respond in Russian.

Evgeny glances to the left and right. He comes to me and takes my forearm. "I am pleased to see you," he rasps in the mother tongue we share. He steps away from me quickly and his gaze pans to Ivan's, who continues to stand there as if stunned. "I know that Ivan feels the same way. So do most of the other men."

My heart clenches in my chest. The tension in my muscles is equally severe. I move like a stiff mechanism, one in need of oil, and nod at him. "I need to see Roman."

"This way," Ivan answers finally, ashing his cigarette beneath his boot. He steps to my right side while Evgeny assumes the position to my left. Flanking me, they lead me into the brick building. It looks like a home, this building, and used to be a refuge for my brothers after a long day's work. A living area passes on the left, a dining area on the right big enough to serve fifty, as it often did. It is empty now and there is lingering dust settled over it as if it has not been used in months.

Up the stairs and to the right, we stand in the open doorway of Roman's office. The space doubles as living quarters and in the rooms behind the door at the far end of the space, I know that there are several others. Offices mostly, one with a fold-away bed in it. I have slept in that bed many times after long nights of work, and even longer nights of celebration. My brothers would come upstairs to drink and they would bring women to take all our minds off of work and I would pass out on that folded mattress with a woman under each arm and not a care in the world.

Now there is only one woman, but the man in the chair with the power to release me to hunt her freely is not the man I seek. Momentary panic consumes me and my first thought is how quickly I can get to Ify and remove her from this city. I need her to be safe. My own life is forfeit. If Roman is not here, that must mean that he is with Erik and that they are already aligned against me. I batter that panic back as I finally register the man seated in Roman's place. He is one of mine. A man I've known from infancy and one who I doubt would ever betray me. But I can't be sure. Much has changed.

"He's not here," Valery says. He sits at Roman's desk pouring over papers. He has two laptops propped open and I can see the grids of a spreadsheet reflected in the wide lenses of his glasses. His mouth is drawn in a severe line except for when he looks up. He double takes and then grins and then marshals that grin into something that is stark, once again.

Straightening to his full height, he comes around the edge of the desk with his shoulders rolled back. He looks like a man again, rather than the smear hunched over the desk that he had been, dissolving into the shadows.

"Gavriil. I…" He clears his throat into a meaty fist and switches from Russian to English, so that our lips will not easily be read in view of the cameras for it is certain that Erik will watch all these tapes back. A thousand times over. He likely already knows I am here. How much time do I have? Minutes? If there are enough men on my side, maybe an hour? I don't count on it, or them.

"I did not expect to see you here." I hear what he does not say: I did not expect to see you alive.

"I am here," I say, English coming to me ungainly because it has been so many days since I have spoken it. Again, the spear that is Ify in thought and breath skewers me. "I came to speak with Roman."

"Are you sure you should be here?" He drops his tone to its quietest decibel. "Erik hunts for you still."

"I do not seek Erik. I seek Roman."

Valery gives me a slight bow. "Apologies, boss," he whispers, then more loudly in Russian states, "You'll need to see Roman right away. He has set up his office in the building across Eighty-Fifth. I will show you the way."

The group flanking me grows as Valery joins Ivan and Evgeny in my wake. We walk down the stairs and through the brick carcass of a house that had felt so much like a second home to me less than a year ago, and out beneath the angry sky.

Entering the open portion of the warehouse, I am shocked to find it, in large part, empty. Elmer has always been a center of commerce for the family, but it is not as I remember it. So much has changed. The building that was once teeming with the voices of my brothers in arms – their laughter, open discussions over beers, calm, cool decision-making when required – is now silent. The few men milling past us keep their eyes on their feet or on the large crates they carry. Likely full of weapons or cash. *O gospodi*, how I hope it's weapons or cash...

Heads are down, hands are settled absently on the triggers of holstered weapons. Though I know these faces, I do not know this fear. Brothers frightened of their own kin. What has Erik done?

The sound of our footsteps carry and echo and, at the sound, some of these downturned faces glance up. Spying me out of the corners of their eyes, a few give small signs – a wink, a clandestine smile, a nod. Some that signal to me, I do not know well, and frown. I did not expect this type of reception or to be needed by so many, so desperate as to show outward signs of mutiny. In part, I suppose I had hoped that Anatoly's words were his own and that he did not speak on behalf of the family. I hoped wrong.

Valery holds a door open for me and we pass into a narrow hall with high ceilings that do nothing to cage — but rather seem to strengthen — the sounds of suffering. Sobs and howls of pain ricochet through my bones, affecting me in ways I wish they did not. I had wanted to be objective about this, but seeing the cells covered in smeared glass and hearing the pleas of the women – and some men – trapped behind them, my stomach turns. I inhale shallowly through my nose, and exhale hard.

This is a cruel manipulation of the legacy my father left. His legacy was not for good – none of us work in the realm of good, we are all shadow men and women – but this? What Erik has created? This is evil in its purest form.

I round the corner and at the intersection of this hallway and another, a scene is unfolding. One that I initially see, and register, but cannot understand. My mind is incapable of linking together the pieces of this cruel puzzle and for a moment, my steps stall and I trip over nothing but air. Am I hallucinating? Am I asleep? Is this a nightmare?

There is a man in the hallway. Light brown hair and pale skin, with a boy's face. I recognize him from photos I have seen online. Photos of and with Ify. I would pour over her photos, hating and resenting him and all the other boys she would appear with in her other life – her real life. Not the shadow life she carried on with me. But this one was the one I hated the most.

Clifford Walsh, pig in blue, and though she refused to see it, deeply in love with her. I had scheduled his death in my mind a thousand times over. Slicing his stomach from sternum to groin, pulling out his intestines, wrapping them around his throat and strangling him with them. This is the start I had mapped out long before this moment that brings him before me now. But not the end. My imagination had yet to arrive at a perfect, quixotic finality. That was for another time. A time long from now. A time when my life is no longer a risk to the women I love. A time when Ify can lay safely in my bed, cradled in my arms.

This is not part of the plan. What is this dead man with the face of a child doing here? In a blue coat and jeans, he is shouting down into an open suitcase on the floor. There are limbs protruding from it. Thin, delicate limbs the color of rich cherry wood.

I can see a halo of thick hair buoyantly floating above the edge of the suitcase and a quiet voice sobbing, "Please, Cliff. Don't…" I'd have recognized that voice anywhere. Singing songs of suffering in a chorus in the dark.

The bottom of my stomach drops out and a hollow wind carries away its contents, and whistles through my thoughts. I hear nothing. I see nothing, anymore. My feet. My hand. My head. They all throb with the same pulse. I can hear one of the men behind me saying my name, and asking me what is wrong. The man called Clifford looks at me and meets my gaze with faint recognition, even though he should know me well. He is in love with my woman, and I am the one that will piss on his corpse.

"Would you fucking help me?" Clifford shouts to two men I had not noticed behind him.

A large man who I recognize and have always despised – Yefim – edges towards the suitcase. Yefim will die as well. The third man, Konstantin – one of my own – grabs Yefim's arm.

The two men bicker, drawing Clifford's attention and giving Ify enough time to sit up. She glances around, as if lost, but does not see me. She does not seem to see anything. Her hands are weak as they reach for the floor, seemingly unable to find it. She looks so lost, and she must be, because there is no other reason I can think of that she would be here.

I start forward, wading deeper into my nightmare, at too rapid a pace. The men behind me are confused and shouting and the men ahead of me are looking my way. Everywhere there is confusion, but soon there will be blood, because Ify is in pain and I will kill every single man in this hallway and in the *Bratva* to ensure she never feels anything but my hands on her body, my lips on her skin, and my cock inside of her ever again.

Something tackles me from the side as I reach the intersection, just a few feet from her and the men holding her. I smell his scent, that rich spice, and hear his voice in my ear. "You do this now and she dies."

I recognize his voice and the babbling of my thoughts recedes to low, muted thunder. Blinking, my body stills as he says the only words he could have said to stall me. I glance at his face. The thunder is coming for me.

I growl, "Anatoly."

He blinks and his expression is guarded and stiff and so very lonely. "*Brat*," he says, as questions fire through my mind. How is she here? How long has she been here? Did Anatoly know? Why would he not have told me?

There is no chance he did not know of her presence here. He knew her face. He knew her name. He knew what she was to me. I glance down at the suitcase and Ify's hazy, unseeing eyes blink up at me rapidly. There are tears on her cheeks and there is no elasticity left in my arms. My hands are shaking so I push them into the pockets of my pants. Anatoly tries to pry my attention away from her, but he can't.

"Do not do this. She does not even love you," he says.

My eyes narrow. My chest implodes and then explodes in alternating bursts of frost and heat. He is right. And it changes nothing.

My foot surges forward another half an inch, but Anatoly's grip on my arm tightens. He speaks low, directly into my ear so that only I can hear while the gazes of all our men — mine and Erik's and this fucking pig — close in on us in stunned silence.

"She texted you, didn't she? I saw her phone. She told you she didn't love you. I would have told you, but I thought things between you were over."

She did. She did say it. And my heart hurts. The soreness in my chest is like a raw gash whose stitching was not clipped, but wrenched out of the wound. Blood and gore seeps out over everything even as my rage towards Anatoly plateaus. It does not excuse what he has done, but it helps explain it. A man who is not capable of love, as Anatoly isn't, would not understand that her hatred towards me does not impact the love I feel for her.

I glance down at her again. There are bloodied bandages wrapped around both of her palms. Her legs are bare despite the temperature and I am gutted by the sight of her smooth ass disappearing into a pair of lace panties. They match the color of the outer shirt she wears, which belongs to a uniform. A police uniform. One with Clifford's name stitched onto the breast. The man in love with my woman has marked her as his and is now trying to carry her away.

"Who the fuck are you?" The corpse roars, his voice breaking. His cheeks are flushed. His anger is only surface though, while mine runs bone deep. "Get the fuck out of here. I'm busy."

I meet his gaze — the blonde child who will die by my hand in the next moments — and start towards him. Anatoly grunts, "Don't..."

But then I hear it, the tenderest little voice whispering, "Run." I glance down at Ify in the suitcase and see her hooded gaze blink up at me as tears fall from the corners of her eyes. She mouths my name without saying anything at all and follows it with a choked, "Run."

She's telling me to run even though she's in a suitcase in a puddle of blue fabric and limbs. She's been doped. Her hands are bloodied, as if recently wounded, but there's a cut on her forehead that wasn't there the last time I saw her. It's totally healed, just a scar now. My stomach turns and I hallucinate hell. How long has she been in here? How many fights? How much abuse? How many raped her?

My whole body bucks and I hold onto Anatoly's shoulder as I bring his face to my mouth and growl against his skin, "She does not leave this place without me."

Anatoly looks like he will argue, but then bites his front teeth together. His eyes flash towards the girl on the floor and they are full of hate. "Go," he tells me, "See Roman. Finish it. She will be here when you return."

I draw away from him and glance down at Ify once more. Before her, I drop into a crouch. My hand reaches towards her and I am terrified to touch her, because if I do that will mean that she is really here.

The middle finger of my right hand strokes the scar on her forehead. Light brown and almost imperceptible, it winds from her temple back into her hair, which is as full as I have ever seen it. I grab a fistful of it and her head falls back on a sob. She can't keep it up.

"So small and weak, and three grown men still feed her drugs to tame her? She must have incredible weapons I cannot see." And I know she does.

"Fuck you! Get away from her. She's mine," Clifford roars, and though all here should know my face well, I wonder if he is truly not blind to the sight of me. Rather, he is consumed as I am consumed, his gaze locking onto my hand on Ify's arm. He reaches for her and I do not have the strength to let him touch her and my free hand reacts before I can stop it. I push the heel of my hand up into his nose, breaking it.

He howls up into the ceiling and tries to stem the flow of blood with both hands. "Do you know who I am?" Blood dribbles into his mouth, distorting his speech. "You fucking ass hole! You sonofabitch. Let go of her!"

My mind flashes. I picture prying off his fingernails with a razor blade, one at a time. The fantasy fades quickly and I return to hell, my present reality. Ify has a hold of my hand. I look down at her, though I know this is a risk because it weakens me even more than I thought it would. My lips part. My core frosts over. I am not the man I was, but so much less. Nothing. Or at least I will be, if I am not certain that she will make it out of here alive and unharmed. I need to be careful. I need to be calm.

Pulling away from her carefully, I stand. "This pig has disrespected me," I say, and my voice is not my own. It is poorly contained heartbreak and violence and bloodlust and slaughter. "The woman remains here until I conclude my business with Roman. Our agreement will include the woman for such disrespect," I lie, for perhaps the first time and it is for Ify, the one who lies to me. "She is mine this moment forward." And I lie again, because she has been mine from the start. From before I knew of her existence, she has been in my bones.

Clifford surges towards me and I nearly despise Konstantin in that moment for restraining the boy. I want him to come to me. I want to slide my thumbs beneath the skin of his cheeks and peel his face free of the bone. I want to swallow his lungs.

Yefim speaks. "You cannot. She has been promised by Erik…"

I cut him off and picture Erik's beautiful blood glistening on my hands. "Do you take orders from Roman or Erik?"

Yefim backs down. His lips curl up into a sneer. "Roman."

"So who do you think will give me permission to take the girl? I have a deal for Roman he will not refuse. Take me to him," I say, and my words are final. "Unless you challenge me?"

My hand moves to my Makarov buried deep in my coat. Yefim's does the same. The air in the corridor does not breathe. There is no room for that. There is only waiting. Ivan looks terrified. Konstantin looks wary. Valery appears angry. Evgeny looks surprised. His is the only expression I recognize. I would likely wonder the same – how things degenerated so rapidly over a woman in a suitcase – if I were in his place.

Nobody breathes. Nobody moves. Life and death comes down to this moment. If my brothers turn their backs on me here, I will side against them. I will not stomach Ify taken from me. Not from here. Not from anywhere. But certainly not with *him*.

"Somebody kill him!" Clifford screams.

Yefim groans and lifts his gun, pointing the barrel at my chest. Valery, Ivan, Evgeny and Konstantin all shout.

"No!" Ify screams.

"Stop." Anatoly says, stepping directly in front of my body. I could give a fuck that he presents a shield for me. What I want is a shield for Ify. A fortress surrounded by a moat and guarded by an army. "This woman will remain here until Gavriil concludes his business with Roman."

Yefim's face twitches, but he does not disagree. Anatoly outranks him and all of the other men gathered here. Right now, he even outranks me. Clifford shouts and thrashes against Evgeny's grasp. "You fucker! Who do you think you are? I'm Erik's right hand. He needs me. I've been the one doctoring all the records about the shipments. He owes me this!"

"Take me to Roman," I tell Ivan.

Ivan blinks, unsure of what has passed between me and the woman. His gaze is glued to her in a way that I do not like, but he says nothing. Only nods. "Follow me."

It takes every ounce of will to turn from Ify then. I meet her gaze as I do, but only briefly and in that instant, a renewed rush of tears flow down her cheeks. I abandon her. She utters a tortured gasp that echoes in the hall as I force my feet to take one step and then another and then the next.

I am hardly conscious by the time we reach a grey door. My thoughts are long behind me, in a suitcase on the floor, in the bowels of this horrible, tortured building. Ivan knocks and I pass over the threshold. I see a man with silver hair and wrinkled hands seated at a desk and it takes me far, far too long to remember who he is or why I am here.

What if they have disobeyed my instructions? What if they released my woman to the police officer? What if Anatoly allowed it? Something tortures my thoughts. Anatoly is my brother, but he knew she was here. Even if he had seen her phone and the messages between us, he would have seen that I was desperate for her. He would have told me, wouldn't he? He is my brother. And he would never, ever lie to me.

"Gavriil," Roman says, gaze finally finding mine. I wonder what he sees because he looks surprised. I feel surprised. I should not be here. I should be wrapped around Ify, using my whole body to protect her. Because even if she does hate me, and wants nothing more to do with me and my shadow life, that does not stop me from loving her. Ruthlessly. With everything my bleak and brutal life has to offer.

"Roman."

He waves the men off as he stands and comes to bridge the distance between us. The door clicks shut at my back and I hold out my hand when he offers his own. His grip is firm and does not tremble. Warm and dry, yet softened by age, I remember these hands grabbing my sides and throwing me into the lake in Polonova. I cannot believe that this is the same man.

"It is good to see you, nephew."

"Uncle. I would say it is good to see you as well, but your son…"

Roman grins. He was not an attractive man, even in his youth, but his eyes carried a kindness that I remember from when I was younger. A kindness that, when Nikoli died, was snuffed. "My son has been doing good work to make the family millions," he says before I can finish.

"*Recover* millions," I counter.

Roman waits a moment, rubs his hand over his shaved, wrinkled cheeks and then smiles widely. His dark eyes sparkle and are nothing like Erik's electric blue. They are two different men, scarcely believed to be related. But they are. They must be. Because no sane man would defend the whims and will of a lunatic as Roman does Erik.

Roman's gaze studies mine for a moment longer, as if searching for another truth that he will not find for there is only the one. Ceding, he frowns. Stepping away from me, he removes his coat and tosses it onto the leather sofa against the far wall. There are no windows in here, but six small monitors sit behind the desk, facing the door. All display rotating black-and-white images of the four-block radius that is Elmer. I try not to be distracted by them, searching for the one I want.

"From what I understand, things have not been easy for you."

I clench my teeth and step up to the other side of the wide, oak desk when he takes a seat behind it. Knuckle-down on the table, I watch the monitors in my peripheral vision. I still do not see her. "No. Your son has taken out a personal vendetta against me. You cannot be surprised at my timing here today."

"No. And I am well aware that you have allies within these walls that made this timing possible. That is why you are here now. If there were not so many who still admired you, I'd have shot you down at the door."

I don't care. Fuck this. Fuck him. I need to get Ify out of here now. Growling, I can't keep the contempt and hatred and bitterness and fear from my tone. "I did not come to hear your threats. I came to make a trade."

"You dare come into my house and speak to me this way? I could have you shot down now." He darkens, leaning back in his seat. He crosses one ankle over the other knee, and steeples his fingers. "You make such threats when you have nothing to offer. I thought you were smarter than this."

I was. But love ruined me. "I do not mean to speak out of turn, uncle, but you and I both know what I have to offer."

His expression falters. His eyebrows crinkle. "You have nothing."

"You do not know?" A small dose of shock breaks through the fever working its way across my skin.

Roman's smile dips. "There is nothing I do not know about this family and my empire."

"Then you know where to find the cartel's missing heroin?"

Something passes behind Roman's black gaze. Something that will work in my favor. "What do you know?"

"What everyone knows. Who has thirty eight pounds of the cartel's heroin."

"You have my heroin."

"You and I both know I don't. But my sister does."

Roman barks out laughter and when he slaps his hand onto the table, his ring clacks loudly against the wood. "Alina is dead…"

It is my turn to laugh, and the sound is not my own but someone else's who is malicious and cutting and wicked. There are ripples of fire spasming across my skin. I am not here. I am nothing but a terror made flesh as I recall Timur's blood spatter on Alina's screaming face so many months ago.

"You know nothing about this family. Erik misleads you."

"You dare…"

"I did not come here to debate the madness of your son," I say loudly, voice rising over his. "I come to offer you thirteen million in drugs in exchange for my life back, and Alina's. I don't want any more threats to her life or mine."

Roman's mouth moves towards his nose in an expression of disgust, but he holds my gaze evenly, as if in a challenge I do not back away from. Finally, he exhales, "You never were a liar."

"I hate liars." Except for one, one who can lie to me for the rest of her life if she wants so long as she remains alive.

"I know."

Another small pause, and then Roman does something that shocks me: he bows his head and rubs his eyes with his thumb and pointer finger while the tension in his shoulders dissolves. "You were always like a son to me. I do not know how the situation got so far."

"You do know," I whisper.

Roman looks up and he does not look like the leader of the Russian mafia, but like an old man who has led a sorry life. For a brief instant, I pity him. And then I remember that he has Ify and countless other women trapped here and for that act alone deserves nothing from me. Nothing.

"You have seventy-two hours to retrieve my drugs and bring them here. If you can do that – and I am not sure I believe you can – then I will remove the hit on your life Erik has ordered."

The enormous pressure in my chest releases. I have carried it for so long it has become a part of me, but now that it is gone, in its place is only a sickening sensation. One that urges me to run as fast as my legs can carry me to scoop up the woman on the floor and be free of this place. I am so close. We are so close. All of us.

"And Alina's," I say.

"And Alina's." He sighs again. "But I cannot allow you back into the family."

He looks sorry. It is a tragic thing. And for a moment, I feel sorry. But then I remember why I am here today as opposed to any other. Perhaps, once out of the family, I can one day hope to be the man I believe Ify deserves. Even with that thought, a cavity opens up in my chest as I nod.

"Yes."

"You were a good nephew," he says as I straighten.

"You were a good uncle," I reply, "Once."

He nods and looks away, down at the papers on his desk. Spreadsheets and numbers that have run away from him. I pity the man who struggles to recover for his son, particularly this son. The madman. "You may go now."

"I will need amnesty over the next seventy-two hours."

"Done."

Bile turns in my stomach as I take two steps towards the door. The casual way I turn, I hope does not appear rehearsed because I have been planning this moment in my mind from the moment I stepped into the room. "And there is one other thing I'd like from you."

"You ask for much," Roman scoffs, "What is it?"

"The black woman you've promised to the cop. I'd like her."

"To do what with?"

"Fuck."

Roman shakes his head. "Captivity has changed you."

He has no idea just how much it has. "I haven't fucked any woman in months and the pig disrespected me."

"That I can believe. He is a child. I do not know why Erik ever hired him. His clumsy bumbling is what led the men to pull the girl in off of the streets last week."

"Last week?" Last week. Last week. The words repeat themselves in my mind endlessly.

Last week. But how can that be possible, if the text I received from her — the one that was a sledgehammer to the chest — was sent two days ago? Did they forget to search her? Did she have her phone the whole time? Right, because if she had her phone, she'd be preoccupied with breaking up with me, and not worried at all about saving herself. That sounds like Ify. That sounds like a sane, normal human...

Nyet.

So if she had her phone stripped from her and Anatoly saw the text that shattered my soul to pieces, then...there is one other possibility. Only one. That someone else — someone who is *not* Ify — sent the message that broke my heart.

Anatoly. *Moy brat.*

Betrayal. Anatoly took her phone, sent me the SMS, and then kept her here with no intention of letting me know and every intention of letting the pig take her. He knew her. He knew who she was. He knows who she is to me. But something greater than his love of me pushed him to this point. He wanted out of the *Bratva*. Is that it? Could it be so simple? I thought he would die for me, as I would have for him, but instead he put my soul, heart and sanity into a blender just so he could retire.

"Gavriil?"

I blink. "Yes."

"Did you hear what I said?"

"No. Apologies. He dragged her in...a week ago?"

Roman rolls his eyes. "Yes. Apparently the pig – to use your vernacular – led her here for Konstantin and Evgeny to trap six days ago or so. As if I didn't have enough to deal with. When I heard that Erik had okayed the order, I was livid. Do you know who she is?"

Dangerous. My whole life. I shake my head because the words stuffed in my mouth are rabid and reproachable. I want Anatoly. I want his life, as I want Clifford's and Erik's — with equal violence.

"She's an author — a famous author — to whom this kid, Officer Walsh, had been feeding information. She knows too much and is far too known. She has a family for fuck's sake. And probably a husband who is out looking for her this very moment." No, but she will, and it will be me. Because as soon as I get her out of here, kill the three men on my list, and she's well and we're far, far from this sick town of murder, I'm going to put a ring on her finger and fuck her until she can't walk or stand. Because if she didn't send that message, then the last thing she said to me that I can be sure of, is that she loves me.

Roman shakes his head, his voice dismissive. As if we're speaking about a staff meeting gone awry. "So when you've finished with her, you'll have to kill her. Or hand her over to the pig. Make sure the body can't be found."

"Fine," I say, though what I think is, over my dead body. Or his.

Roman watches me with one eyebrow cocked. "You truly are different." The corners of his mouth turn down. "I did not think it would be Erik who ruined you. I am sorry for that. But this small gift is a courtesy to your dead father and his wife. I cannot give you more than this."

"I understand." My heart starts to race. I'm so close to the exit now. "Is that all?"

"Yes." His rich Russian accent is pitched in a question and as I reach the door, he calls for me to stop. "Why did you wait so long to come see me? I have been in town for over a week now. When you did not show up the first day, I assumed you would have come to trap me in my own home." He chuckles sadly. "Actually kept me on my toes. But this? This feels unprepared. What changed? How did you know I wouldn't kill you today?"

"I didn't, but I couldn't stay in hiding any longer." My heart is pounding. Anatoly betrayed me. Clifford betrayed Ify. I have Ify's love.

He grunts. "You are a lucky man."

"It doesn't feel that way," I lie again. So many lies in so few moments. Because I do feel lucky. I'm still alive and I have seventy-two hours to solve the crisis that Erik and a fumbled bag of drugs has put me in. Seventy-two hours to build a fortress around the woman I love. She'll be in my arms in just a few minutes. I turn again, and again, Roman calls my name.

"Gavriil?"

"Yes, Roman?"

"If you do not secure the drugs, you had best run somewhere far away."

"Of course."

Ify

I see everything like I'm watching the world through smoke. I dreamed of Gavriil. He was here, talking to Anatoly. I told him to run. Did he? I hope. I hope he's safe. I hope somebody gives me more of this drug so that I can die as it takes me away on a pleasure wave. I'm so numb. Please, I beg to everyone and no one, please let me die before Clifford gets me alone. Please.

There's shouting again and I try my hardest to pick my head up and focus on what's going on. There's red hair. And then there's red blood. Gavriil is beating up Anatoly just a few paces away from where I'm standing. Men are clustered around him, like they're trying to pry him off.

In the confusion, Clifford comes towards me. He licks his lips and his hands are smooth and soft as they close in around my shoulders and try to shut the suitcase over me. I cry out and that seems to draw the attention of the other men, or maybe just the one that matters. Because Gavriil is suddenly soaring over the top of the open suitcase and slamming Clifford against the wall. His fist is already red but it gets even redder as it slams against Clifford's face again and again and again and again and again…

Clifford isn't moving. I feel my lips curl up into a smile. I try to get out of the suitcase again, but I can't move. The other men who haven't felt Gavriil's wrath are just standing around, looking stunned. They're trying to help Anatoly, and the one blocky, cruel one is holding a gun. He points it at Gavriil and I choke, trying to warn him, but I can't get the words out.

On the ground, I hear Anatoly say something in Russian. The blocky one lowers his weapon, but Gavriil's still got Clifford on the ground and he's kicking his stomach and stomping on his groin and when he flips Clifford's body over and kneels on his back I watch as he lifts Cliff's head. The whole thing happens in slow motion.

Cliff's gaze meets mine. His light eyes are so panicked, so confused. I'd be confused if I were him too. Because he paid attention just enough to figure out how to trap me, but not where it counted. I all but told him that I was seeing someone and that someone wasn't one who lived in the daylight with us, but who lived in the shadows. And men like that don't take it lightly when someone fudges with their women.

I watch and smile at Cliff as Gavriil's heavy hands mold around his neck. He lifts and then jerks so quickly to the right that I lose track of it. But when he drops Cliff's head and it bounces on the concrete with a thunk, I know Clifford's dead, and I'm happy about it. Maybe tomorrow, I'll remember Gavriil murdered and will be sickened by it, but when they drugged me I didn't think there would be a tomorrow, so for now, this is alright.

Shocked faces stare around at one another and the air in the hall that tastes like chalk in my mouth, feels charged in ways it didn't before. Gavriil stands and meets each man's gaze. He looks like he'll return to Anatoly, but instead reacts towards me when I cough.

"Gavriil?" The word is mine, but it's so weak. Did he hear me? He must have because his whole body jerks like he's been stunned with a gun.

He turns to me, drops to one knee and with his bloody hands, lifts me carefully. Holding me against his chest, he starts racing down the long halls. His hands are shaking. He smells like bergamot, a rich, Earl Grey tea. And then suddenly there's a blinding light. I squint and blink and I hear Gavriil saying my name again and again. Finally, a little darkness passes overhead and I can see Gavriil shading my eyes with his hand. I grin up at the brutal, white sky while his watery blue eyes stare down at me.

"*Ya lubya tebya*, Gavrill," I say.

He kisses my mouth so hard it hurts me, but I don't dare push him away or pull back — even if I could. Because I need this. I never thought I'd taste him again, this rich tapestry of trees and flame, like a forest fire.

He pulls back and then we're somewhere else. In a car? I don't have the strength to look around and know for sure. All I do know is that Gavriil keeps me tight against his body while his hands work around me, navigating something else. The vehicle rumbles beneath me and we take off, going somewhere. I don't care where so long as it's with him.

"I shouldn't have gone hunting," I hear myself say. My voice is a scratchy, muted thing.

Gavriil laughs wildly. His chest shudders so hard and there's water on his face. I reach my hand to touch it, but every sensation is distant. It's too hard to concentrate. "*Nyet*, you should not."

"I shouldn't have taken my ID."

"*Nyet*, you should not."

"I should have gone to you right away."

Gavriil nods once, lips tight. The car is moving fast, or maybe it's just my thoughts and the sensation of Gavriil's heart beating through his shirt. So fast, too fast. Like a train about to jump its tracks and then tear itself apart.

"*Da.*"

"I shouldn't have believed the things Clifford said to me."

Gavriil winces violently, like he's just been stabbed. Suddenly he's pulling over and the car is slowing down. He grabs the sides of my face and kisses me with such intensity, I can barely breathe through the onslaught. I could imagine no better way to suffocate to death.

When we surface a minute or years later, Gavriil is staring very deeply into my eyes, demanding and commanding all of my concentration. "He will not ever touch you again. No man will touch you again but me."

I wonder if I smile, because I mean to. "*Khorosho*," I say, one of the Russian words my eighth grade teacher taught me. She was from Moscow and she baked the most wonderful bread around Christmas time. I can smell it here, and now, in Gavriil's tight hold. It smells like home. Like a better life. One where murder and lies cannot touch us.

Gavriil's mouth crashes again onto mine and I feel his erection swell beneath me. It makes me want to laugh. Even now, at a time like this, I can still want him and he can still want me. I reach for it with both hands and try to free him of his pants, but my hands are slow and soupy and clumsy.

"Ify…"

"I need you," I answer him weakly, "Please, Gavriil, I thought I was going to die. Help me live."

Gavriil doesn't need more invitation. He rips me out of Cliff's clothes, and though he yanks his shirt off over his head, he doesn't bother with his pants. He just reaches between us roughly, rolls the seat back, pulls his hard dick out of his boxers and lowers me onto it. The invasion is intense and I moan while pleasure from the drugs competes with what he's offering. And it's a much better offering.

Gavriil curses in a long stream. He moans. One of his hands leaves the steering wheel and cups the back of my neck. He forces me to kiss him and as his hot breath mingles with mine, he brushes my tears with his thumb. We don't use a condom and I don't care. I just need to feel him everywhere. He's grunting and I'm gasping. Things start to get hazy. He lifts me up and climbs awkwardly over the center console to the back seat where he lowers me down and licks me until the orgasm comes. It takes me away, I don't feel after that. Just watch as he tucks his dick away and zips his pants back up.

"But you…" I try.

He shakes his head, gathers me back to his chest and kisses my forehead and every inch of my face. "This is for you. When you are better, it can be for me."

I smile, but reality has already started to elude me. I just want to stay here, with him, but the drugs they gave me were strong and I'm not holding on. "Thank you for coming for me."

He pulls his shirt over my head and for a second the shaking is so bad, I think he's started the car, but it's just him.

He's shaking down to the bone. "I would come for you sooner if I had known. *Prosti menya*, Ify. I did not know."

"You shouldn't have come…"

"Do not ever say that. You are not realizing…do not realize what it does to me knowing you were kept there for those many days. I received texts from your phone saying you hated me. You broke my heart. I couldn't move."

"How could you ever think that I hated you?" I sigh, consciousness fleeing from me rapidly now, "*Ya lyublyu tebya.* I've loved you since the beginning."

He snaps up a fistful of my hair, wrenches my head back and punishes me with his kiss. His tongue penetrates my mouth and I am lost to the sensation. I am crying again when I resurface. "*Ya znayu, chto.* I know, I know now. And I will never forget it again."

His lips are warm and soft as they touch every spot on my face and neck and ears. He pulls one earlobe into his mouth and then the other. Like a spider-monkey, I do my best to coil my arms around his sides and press my face into his bare chest. I taste one of his nipples, flicking my tongue over it and Gavriil moans viciously.

"I want you all to myself, but we cannot linger here, Ify. We must go some place safe."

"Nowhere is safe."

"There is one place."

I shake my head, incapable of believing him, as I hide in the safety of his darkness. "*Nyet.*"

"There is."

"Where?"

He kisses my forehead and lets his lips linger there. Through his jeans, his legs are warm against my bare thighs and I can feel his hardened dick bulging against my ass. I want it inside of me. I want him to fuck me a thousand more times, until the wretched nightmare I've been in these past days is long behind me and nothing more than a distant pain, a healed scar.

"Yes. We will go there now."

"Where?" I repeat, tongue lathing his pec. He shivers as I nibble on his arm.

"The place you have been searching for these many months." He pauses, inhales, and when he exhales it's to sweep my hair away from my face and look deeply into my eyes. "Where you will be protected. It is guarded by friends."

"Friends?"

"*Druz'ya*. They are the men you seek. The brothers with the last name Cleary who own Seventh Street and much of town. One of them gave you that black eye. He is the protector of my sister."

My mouth goes dry as answers to questions I've had for months pour from his lips. "Alina Popov?"

"*Da*. She is with them."

Part VIII
The Princess

Alina

He comes to me and wraps his large hands around either side of my face, dragging me up to meet his mouth. He kisses me. Hard. And my whole body sways like a blade of tall grass in a light wind. I remember what it had been like waking up that morning to his mouth on my breast, tongue flicking my nipple. I may be more confident, but so is he. And I did this. And I have not ever been more proud. He touches me now with more than reverence, but with ownership. As if he is starting to understand what I have known all along: he is worthy of me.

When he finally pulls back and brushes the rough pad of his thumb over my cheeks, I savor the scent of his breath. Like clean soap and mint and him, so fully. He kisses the tip of my nose and closes his eyes.

"I think I like cooking," he whispers.

I laugh so hard my head falls back. "We are not cooking, Aiden. You do not let me start."

I am in all black – the outfit I will wear when I break into Erik's house – but Aiden's left hand swims beneath the hem of my shirt to touch my stomach. I gasp.

"Cold?" He whispers against my neck.

Yes, but that is not why my pulse is fluttering. When I don't answer except to moan, he slides his hand below the belt of my cargo pants. They are lightweight and loose fitting, equipped with many places to store guns, knives, and grenades. I told him I would not need many, but he told me that it was always best to be prepared for any circumstance. He has made love to me twice already today in this outfit, and I know it is not because he finds it attractive. It reminds him of what I have set out to do, the plan that is taking form and the will that drives me to complete it.

We sat down yesterday as a family, all seven of us except for Charlie, and we mapped out the whens the wheres and the hows. We agreed that it would happen tomorrow morning, when there are no shipments of cargo containers to and from Elmer, the Ternary and the docks.

Clifton drove by the estate two days ago. He rented a truck and posed in an electrical worker's uniform. He'd planted just one camera on the light post across the street from Erik's South Shore Estate. That's when we'd seen something a little surprising. Roman was in town already.

Not knowing how long he would stay, I pushed us to act fast. I wanted to go that day. Aiden pushed for the weekend, and I begrudgingly accepted. The only question was whether or not I'd be going alone. I told Aiden many times this was a solo mission, but he had never answered. In many ways I trust him, but not in this.

"*Moy boch*," I cry, torso pitching forward as Aiden slips two fingers deep inside of me. He is moving in the way I like, but not enough. He is holding back and I moan, frustrated while steam from the half cooked pelmeni simmering on the stove wafts up to greet my nose and wet my hairline. "Why you torture me?"

"Because you torture me." He speeds up. I am almost there. Heat and need fill me.

"Aiden!"

"Are you going to let me come into the house with you or are you going to kill Erik yourself?"

"*Nyet*, Aiden, you know…know…know…I must go… alone." I gasp on every third breath.

Aiden is merciless as he begins to withdraw from me entirely. His chest moves away from my back and I grab his arm, to keep him grounded. My eyes open and I look at him over my shoulder. His face is not smirking as I thought it might be. He is so serious. He is afraid. I am too.

"Aiden," I whisper, and this time I turn to him and throw my arms around his shoulders. He canters back and hits the island where I've still got homemade dough rolled out across a cutting board. He plants a fist directly in the center of it and when he withdraws, I can see the shape of his knuckles.

His mouth is on my neck and my fingers are pulling hard on his hair. He is moaning, and we are ripping at each other's clothing even though we are in the kitchen and in plain view if anyone walks in. There is more than desire fueling us now. A thing that tastes bitter in the back of my mouth.

I don't know how tomorrow will go. I don't know if I will live. What happens when I see Erik? Will I see Nikoli's eyes bulging from his head and the bloody hole in the center of Timur's forehead? How will I be able to act when those visions plague me?

I should just let Aiden come with me. He will be my strength. I will still kill – it is my responsibility – and I will put my body before his in case of any attack. But what happens when I fall? When the first bullet hits me, where will the second bullet go? I can't let him die for me.

"Aiden…" His pants are unzipped and he has a condom on. I wrench down my pants and bare my back to him. "I want you now."

He doesn't give in right away. Instead of penetrating me in one brutal stroke in the way he knows I like, he drops to his knees. Then he does something he never has before. He bites my ass cheek. I squeal as he licks the bite clean and then edges down towards my pussy. He has kissed me there, but never from behind. His mouth eats my pussy and I collapse forward onto my elbows as he devours me, one lick at a time.

He slides his tongue inside of me and kisses my clit. I am dripping all over his chin and nose and face and when I orgasm, I can see sticky clear liquid drip down his neck. He stands up with a grin on his face and it only occurs to me that I can't stand when I feel his arm hook around my waist to keep me upright. He bends over me and bites down on my shoulder, entering me in one thrust. I groan.

"Jesus Christ," I hear a voice say from the doorway, but they are smart enough not to enter. Because even if they came in and went about their business, there is no way I would stop the train Aiden has dragged me onto now.

"Fuck me," he growls into my ear. His arms are wrapped entirely around me. He kisses me behind the ear. I do not know how long we are in the kitchen, only that my pelmeni dumplings have entirely disintegrated by the time that we finish.

I am on the floor, straddling his hips when he comes. His eyes close and he has my hands wrapped in his. He brings the right to his mouth and is kissing my palm as he moans. His body tenses and tightens, his thighs straightening beneath me, hardening to bone. I love watching him orgasm. It makes me feel like I am princess of the world. Like I could conquer anything. Even, like I can sneak into my cousin's house like a bandit and slit his throat. For Timur. For Gavriil. Even for Nikoli and for all the women that have been bought and sold.

"Alina, I love you," he grunts as consciousness returns to him and I lower myself onto his chest. It moves like a wave beneath me, and I ride the crests and troughs. He kisses my forehead and I smile.

"I love you too, Aiden. *Ya lyublyu tebya.*"

"I love when you speak Russian," he says after a pause.

I giggle. "I know." He kisses me again and I can feel his cock hardening beneath the grip of my fingers when all at once, someone in the house shouts loud enough to be heard by all.

"We've got company!" The voice is Knox's and Aiden jumps to his feet. He's got a knife in his hand, held in a light grip by his shoulder, as if he's just about to throw it. Meanwhile, I'm still lying on the ground, looking up at him. Slow. Scared. Panicked.

And then it hits me: I have the confidence, but I don't have the skill. When I go for Erik, I won't come back. Aiden knows this. And maybe that's why he has used every spare moment he has to make love to me, knowing that he won't get another chance.

Feet pound down the hallway, and I hear, but don't see past the island in the center of the kitchen as someone comes into the room. "Get some clothes on, *puta.*" Mer calls, "Shitty black Toyota Corolla 2001 model just pulled past the gate and is heading down the driveway. Cameras couldn't catch a picture of the driver. Car's too small to be packing any serious fighting power, but we're moving Sara and Brant into the back of the house. Dixon's gonna stay with them just in case."

"Suicide bomber?" Aiden says, as if that would be the obvious next option. On the ground, I gasp. Aiden flinches at the sound, but doesn't look at me. He keeps his gaze trained on the door, as if waiting for any number of formidable and terrible things to come through it.

"Seems unlikely, but nobody's willing to take that risk."

Suddenly Clifton's voice joins the chorus. "Where's Alina?" There's a certain fear in his tone.

"She's here. With me." Aiden's voice is as flat and opaque as a brick while I feel like I just got hit over the head by one.

"Hi, Clifton," I say, though my throat is hoarse. I feel flushed as I struggle to put back on my clothes. Aiden is still standing there completely naked, dick half erect, as if that's not strange at all.

"Oh. Well. Umm. You guys should get dressed quickly."

"Would go a lot quicker if you'd get the hell out of here," Aiden mutters.

Clifton grumbles something unintelligible and I hear the sound of heavy feet moving quickly over the floor. Aiden and I dress in silence. When I've got my pants back on, Aiden withdraws a gun from on top of a high cabinet in the kitchen. He hands it to me and produces another. I shouldn't be surprised as we fix the weapons to the belts on our hips, but I still gawk. How many weapons does he keep hidden?

We charge into the living room, but Aiden presses me flat against the wall. He points at the windows and carefully, we move towards the foyer, remaining clear of them. When we get to the stairs, he points for me to go up. I shake my head.

"Go," he barks. His eyebrows are drawn and so is his weapon.

"*Nyet*, Aiden."

"Alina. *Poslushay menya.*"

"*Nyet*," I say again.

He looks like he'll say more, but then doesn't. Knox, Mer and Clifton occupy the foyer in front of us, each equally concerned to remain out of line of fire of any of the windows or the door. Aiden's eyebrows are drawn and his mouth is flat. "I'm going to open the door, and you're not fucking coming."

I feel my lips clench and pull back into a snarl. "Where you go, I go. Your life is not less valuable than mine."

"It is to me."

I don't speak. I don't know what to say. But rather than argue the point further, Clifton cuts in, "All four of you, get back. I'm going out." He chambers the round of the gun in his hand and moves towards the front door. And in a little small moment, my heart breaks and swells. He loves his brother, all of them, and all of us. How does he not have one hundred women, each of whom he cares for equally?

I want to stop him when he heads to the front door, prepared to face off whoever might be there first. I love Aiden too much to stop the man who looks so much like him. And I hate myself, because loving Aiden more means in this moment, that I love everyone else here less.

We're silent in the foyer, all watching with bated breath as Clifton eases down onto his haunches and cracks the front door open. He has a monitor drawn up on his cell phone and is watching the car, but it's only as he opens the door that something changes in his expression. He grins – practically beams – and stands back up on his feet.

"Alina. It's for you," he says, and there is true happiness in his tone.

I move forward, but Aiden holds me back by the elbow. Could have probably predicted that, but Clifton is looking at both of us as if whatever in the driveway is no more harmful to us than a pizza delivery man. "No fucking chance."

Clifton holds up one hand. The other he uses to shove the gun into the back of his shorts. "It's a friendly. Alina, it's your brother."

"Gavriil?" My voice shakes. My mind is a blank slate. I can't breathe.

Clifton laughs and throws open the front door. Cold wind billows into the space. It's bright out today, but in the center of the driveway stands a man I recognize. One with the wild red hair I inherited, even if his is a lighter red and mine is dark like cherries. He stands beside his car wearing only unbuttoned pants and no shirt, red coating his arms up to the elbows.

"Gavriil!" I scream.

"Jesus, Clifton," Aiden barks. He tries to put his body in front of mine, but I don't let him. I duck under his grasp, spinning out of it cleanly in a move he taught me but that I only master for the first time now. I hurtle out of the house, sneakered feet hitting the front step silently. Gavriil comes out from behind the opened car door just in time to catch me as I launch myself at him.

Our bodies come together and I scream my relief into his shoulder. I rasp a whole string of Russian words, which he does not answer except to say, "*Ya skuchayu po tebe,* Alina." I missed you.

"You do not know how I missed you," I tell him in my poor English, "You are dead."

He releases a low laugh that reminds me of much better times, even though judging by the newfound hardness of his muscular body and the blood on his wrists, these times have not been so good to him. And then I feel harrowing guilt. What has he suffered while I have found bliss?

"Are you okay? What did Erik do to you?" I choke.

He lowers me to the ground without answering and when I draw away, I see that his blue gaze is trained on something over my shoulder. I turn and look to see Aiden there, and I don't understand when Gavriil sidesteps me and advances on him. I try saying his name several times, but he does not stop. He continues until Aiden's eyes widen in surprise. He looks to me now for assistance, but he does not block when Gavriil levels a punch to his jaw.

"Gavriil!" I run up to him and stop him from hitting Aiden again, though it does not look like he means to.

Instead his narrow pupils have fallen to me now and widen ever so slightly. He glances down at my clothes then, and it is his turn to show momentary surprise. "You are different," he says to me in English, before asking me in Russian what this man is to me, the doctor with no name.

I feel myself flush, but try to remain strong. "He is my boyfriend now." I glance at Aiden and nothing shocks me more than the ferocious smile that lights up his face, which now sports a drop of blood just above his left eyebrow.

I have never seen him look so pure. He looks like no one I have ever seen. As if, for his entire life, he has seen no hardship. Only light and beauty. A surge of heat and wetness floods the space between my legs.

My brother's eyes widen even more and I fear what it is that he registers on my face. "Very different," he says, but there does not seem to be judgment in his tone, only something else. Something softer that reeks of understanding. He glances back to Aiden.

"You don't get to hit him." I thump his shoulder lightly with my fist. "I do not even know why you do."

He shakes his head and breathes out of the corner of his mouth, looks back at the car and as he speaks, returns to it. "That I do not kill him is only a courtesy to you."

"He is my boyfriend. And I am adult," I say, rounding on him while wind whips across my face. It is cold and I am only in a thin black shirt that does little against the ice in the air. "I can bed who I like."

Gavriil twitches at that, but shakes his head again. He smiles with just one corner of his mouth. "He deserves you for what he has done to protect you. And if you love him, I would not ever stand in your way. But for what he did to the woman I love, I would hit him again, a thousand times."

"Woman...you...love?" I don't understand and repeat the words in Russian.

"*Lyubit*," he says, and this time, he speaks with a blistering finality as he lifts a small body from the backseat of his car. He carries a woman against his chest as if there has never been anything more precious in his life, in the world. She has full, black hair that I would recognize anywhere and I gasp.

"The assassin," Aiden rasps, and I hear his voice much closer now, seconds before his heat comes against my spine. He holds the edges of my arms, as if prepared to push me out of the way or shield me.

"*Da*," Gavriil says, looking down at the sleeping woman with the big hair and the beautiful black skin. He kisses her forehead before looking up at me. "You tried to kill her. And Alina, you saved her life, and mine by consequence. She is everything to me. And I need your help to save her once again. To save us all."

"Tell me," Aiden says, because I can't speak. My mouth is filled with shock.

"I have met with Roman. And we have a deal."

Aiden

I watch the man who shares a bloodline with Alina as he lowers the tiny assassin onto my bed. I'd been spending nights in Alina's room anyways, but hadn't officially moved out. Or in. This just makes it official, I guess. New sheets on the bed. No more tape on the light switch. It's Gavriil and Ify's room now.

And somehow this house that I'd never loved — and that Dixon fought hard to keep just to ourselves — feels like a home. Finally. A home full of vagabond wayward criminals and killers. And I feel…something in my chest for each and every one. Even this new one. Because loving Alina has taught me something — any woman can be another man's Alina.

Ify Smith. She's an author who's been investigating the Popov family for a while now, and that's all Gavriil has spared the time to tell us. And while I still remember the fear and panic she'd caused me when she'd hunted Alina in that parking lot, it doesn't matter because there's no making a move towards her now. She's under Gavriil's protection. And it's clear that he's under her spell.

I can tell he's bound to her irrevocably in the way he looks down at her as he draws the covers up to her chest. Family. She's his family. The word comes to mind. I glance at Alina to my left.

She's standing in the doorway, biting on the skin around her nails. I take her hand in mind and wrap my arm around her shoulders, pulling her into my side. She shoots me a small worried smile. I doubt she's ever seen her brother like this before. And I bet at least a little part of her feels threatened that he's found a woman. Even just an hour ago, that thought might have made me smile. Back before Roman was dragged into the picture.

Gavriil stands and asks Sara if she'll be okay. She's on the other side of the bed fiddling with an IV that feeds into Ify's arm. She nods and smiles at Ify, strokes her forehead and pushes the wilderness of hair back from Ify's face. I gather that she's sleeping because she doesn't stir. Sara grabs her box of magic and starts to walk towards us, out of the room. She gestures for Gavriil to follow.

He hesitates at first, then looks back at Ify. Before joining us out in the hallway, I watch him go again to all of the windows, including the ones in the bathroom, to make sure they're locked. They are and he should know because this is the third time he's checked.

"So. She will be fine?" He rubs his face as he closes the door to a crack. His fingers still twitch for that sliver of darkness, as if he's able to feel her magic so long as the door isn't shut, barring him out.

Sara nods. "Of course. You say she was forcibly injected with heroin?"

Fuck. That's news to me. I feel Alina jump in her skin and hold her closer to me. What I would do if it were Alina in that bed with that diagnosis, I don't know. Burn the whole fucking world to the ground.

"*Da*," he answers first in Russian, then in English. His accent is as thick as Alina's. He swallows and his cheeks are hollow. He's white as a goddamn sheet. "She was given drugs but I do not know of how many. What if it is too much?"

"If it was too much, you'd know by now. She was responsive and awake until you put her to bed. That's a good sign. If we were looking at an OD, Ify wouldn't have been able to speak, at least not with any sort of coherence, and would have probably passed out. Her nails and lips would have also turned blue, which they didn't. I will say that the weak pulse was not a good sign," Sara starts.

Gavriil tenses. His jaw locks. His blue eyes look fucking wild. I know he'd never in a million fucking years hurt her, but I still pull Alina away from him. Sara says quickly, "But she reacted really well to the heat compress I placed on her chest. Well enough for me to know that the quantity used to sedate her wasn't enough to do any real damage. Whoever injected her most definitely wanted her alive."

Gavriil rubs his face roughly and grunts Russian words I don't know. Alina does though, and looks shocked by them, which leads me to believe they're something more serious than the average curse.

In English, I hear him grumble, "The one who hurt her, will not hurt her again. Or any other."

"She's fine, Gavriil. She'll be fine. You need to look after yourself." Sara places a hand on his arm gently. He looks at her and collapses back against the wall. The bags beneath his eyes are purple, like bruises even darker than the shiner he branded me with. I'd have done much worse had the roles been reversed.

Dropping his head back on the wall, Gavriil licks his lips and nods. "I need vodka."

Alina says something to him in Russian and he nods, leaving Sara and I to follow them down the hall to the kitchen. The rest of the family's there waiting. Faces are tense, Dixon's especially. We need to know what's going on and what level of shit we're in.

Gavriil sighs, and Alina quickly clears a place for him at the foot of the table, opposite Dixon. She grabs vodka, pours glasses, and rifles through the fridge for as many leftovers as she possibly can. I help her heat them up even though she has to instruct me. I'm no good at food. A microwave is about the most I can manage. Together, we manage to get people fed. We eat in silence, Alina seated next to her brother, me seated next to her, Dixon at the table's head, both our families close in around us. It's a long time before the moment breaks.

"Thank you," Gavriil says at last. He leans back in his seat and ruffles his deep red hair. "I know that I ask much of you."

Alina speaks to him in Russian. Gavriil nods patiently and reaches for her hand. I start, utterly fucking confused because I'm not used to people touching her and I don't like people touching her. But this is her brother. He raises an eyebrow at me as he brings her hand to his mouth and kisses her fingers.

"*Moya sestra* has chosen you," he says to me, "but do not mistake your place in our family."

"Gavriil," Alina hisses. More Russian that I don't understand. But Gavriil looks only at me.

I answer. "*Ya ponimayu.*" I understand. I do. "But for me, she comes first. There's clearly another that comes first now for you, so if you did something to save her that puts Alina in danger, I will do whatever I have to."

Gavriil's face collapses and he rubs his forehead. Alina tenses. She whispers to Gavriil and with what looks like great pain, he nods in the end. "*Da.* I have fallen in love with Ifeoma. She is mine."

Alina's jaw drops. Red rises in her cheeks. I grunt, and the sound is almost a laugh. "How, Gavriil? You were not in hiding? You were out and you did not come for me because of this woman?" Her pitch is rising. I take her hand. She squeezes my fingers near to the point of pain.

Gavriil raises both hands. He looks at his sister sternly and rasps something under his breath in Russian, before saying in English. "I was hiding for almost three months. Ifeoma found me. She had done research and had information on Anatoly."

"He was helping you?"

Gavriil's face turns a bloody and brutal red. He clenches a fist and slams it on the table. "You are to have no contact with Anatoly. He is traitor."

"He sold you out?" This time Dixon speaks. He looks confused and I echo that feeling. "We were monitoring him and from what we could tell, he was monitoring the other Russians. Checking on the bank, in particular, but never going in. We thought he might have been a good ally when it came down to it."

"Do not speak his name," Gavriil roars. He yanks on his hair and upends the bottle of vodka into his glass. He drinks half a tumbler's worth. "I do not speak of him. I speak now of Ify. She found me, and she helped me. She kept me alive while I thought I was dead. She has much information on the workings of the *Bratva* and when she wakes, she can answer your questions."

"Where will you be?" Dixon says.

"I will be negotiating for our lives."

Alina lifts up in her chair. I get the feeling she'd turn over the table if given the chance. "What do you mean, Gavriil? Negotiating with who? For what?"

"I met with Roman."

"You...what?" She gasps. "You went to the building in Elmer? With Erik there? You could have died."

"I had no choice."

"Was it Ifeoma? You almost died for her?"

Gavriil slams his fist again. "And what would you do for Aiden in my same place?"

Alina suddenly quiets and the flush in her cheeks level while I'm sure grow inverse in my own. The thought that Alina would put her life in any danger whatsoever for me makes my teeth ache.

I whisper, "You will never be in that position. Nothing bad will ever happen to you." I slide my hand over the back of Alina's chair. She looks at me and calm returns to her. She settles and turns again to Gavriil and lets him explain what will happen to us, uninterrupted.

The group breaks up an hour later, and everyone returns to their rooms. There is a plan in place. I'm not happy with it, but it requires me being apart from Alina only for an hour max, so I'll live. Tomorrow at dawn, we prepare. Four of us go to the bank. Clifton, Dixon, Knox and I. Mer, Sara, Alina, and Ify will wait at home. Were the ladies happy about the decision? Not a chance. But they're outvoted and outmatched because the rest of us men know that at home, they'll be safe.

The box is in Dixon's name so he'll go into the bank with me as backup. Clifton will drive the car. Knox will wait at the entrance. We'll drive to an abandoned lot where we'll meet Gavriil. He'll take the drugs from there. Alone.

We'll make the handover on the outskirts of Elmer where we'll leave him. Any closer and it puts us all at risk. He'll give up the drugs to Erik and Roman and head straight to the airport. On his call, Alina and I will meet him there with Ify. The four of us will take a flight to Europe. Call it an extended holiday or exile. In either case, we'll settle in somewhere new. Our tickets are booked for Italy.

Gavriil's connections would make visas possible with very little effort. It's a blessing I've even got a passport. And we'll live there with our new families. The...*my*...brothers and Mer and Sara and Brant will come visit in the summer.

By nightfall tomorrow, we'll all be separated and for some reason when I think of Clifton, my true brother by blood, I feel a heaviness in my chest, like a rock sinking through syrup. I push through. This is what I have to do to be with Alina and keep her safe. So it's a sacrifice I will make. The brothers will still be together. Charlie will one day come back into the fold. They'll forget about me as they make families. And maybe... even one day...I swallow tacks as sweat breaks out over my entire body...I glance at Alina...maybe one day we'll even have a family of our own. A beautiful girl who is one hundred percent Alina, one hundred percent warrior princess, for me to protect and love. Who, just like her mother, will speak English with a terrible accent and heal me whole.

Gavriil

The end is near. I can feel it in my chest, muddying my lungs. I feel sick. Ify did not understand why I had to leave her. She wanted to come. *Dalbayob.* She wanted to come after what she went through. I cannot believe she'd want to come. And she raised hell when I'd refused her and locked her in her room. Even Alina had been shocked to see Ify shouting at me in the way she did. No one shouts at me. My position in the *Bratva* prevents it. But Ify has no fear – of me or the *Bratva* – so she shouts at me regardless.

The corner of my mouth jerks up as I drive down the road alone and pull into the parking lot near the Ternary. There are many homeless here and I feel rage again when I think that Ify would come to these dangerous places by herself. She is tough, but vulnerable. Still so small. Impetuous and emotional, she wants to fight. She wants revenge and does not realize that she will get it, but that it will be by my hand.

I shake my head and turn off the car. Large brick buildings surround the parking lot. In one of them, I can see people wrapped in blankets watching me through broken windows. Their eyes are unseeing. So many drugs populate the Ternary, this nightmare wasteland. It is what one would need to survive the winter's cold. Drugs my brothers — my own fighting men — forced onto my woman. My skin prickles with rage as I remember their faces. Anatoly's flashes in my thoughts. He will meet his end.

The sound of rumbling jerks my attention to the large black vehicle crawling into the lot. I had not expected them to be on time, yet here they are, ten minutes before eight. Perhaps this will work after all.

I step out of my car. The air is warmer today than it had been yesterday morning. I cannot believe that's all it's been since I killed a pig, pulled Ify's beautiful body out of a suitcase and struck the deal that will save all our lives with Roman. I had wanted her this morning. To be with her and to have her close to me. But she had been too angry, too scared, too languid and slow, still stunted by the drugs they fed her. There was no time, but I will make time once we are free of this. I will make all the time in the world. Days of nothing but our bodies, holding her close. Keeping her safe. Bringing her pleasure. Maybe on the beach. Italy will still be beautiful this time of year.

"*Bratya*," I say when their leader approaches — the one who put me in the hospital. His drunken punch had not caught me off guard so much as the pipe had that harpooned my shoulder. It had taken weeks to heal and by then I'd already been shot, beaten, and tortured.

The other three are behind him, Alina's new lover among them. The doctor with no name. I still cannot believe it is to him that she has finally given her heart. And at the same time, I hate to admit, that I cannot imagine any better man. He has not only kept her safe, but he has in his own way, kept her happy. I had not seen Alina so happy as yesterday, in a long time.

Dixon smiles as he approaches. He holds the key. It is the brother Knox that has the duffel bag affixed to his wrist. I have no need for keys and locks though. My drive to Elmer will be direct. There is nowhere left for me to go.

"End it for us, brother," Dixon says, his voice chased away by the wind that howls through the empty space. It smells of human piss, and sounds of grief and loneliness.

"I will." I nod at him once, then meet each man's gaze evenly. Dixon's black eyes, Knox's emerald, Clifton's grey eyes that match his brother's. "Aiden. I see you at airport in four hours, yes?"

"*Da, vy budete,*" he confirms.

I smile. His Russian is not insignificant. More than that, I like how he tries for her. "*Khorosho.* Then I see you on the other side."

Dixon nods. Knox lifts the bag and I take its weight, the canvas rough against my palm. It has all been for this. So much madness over so little. Drugs to make the world sick, and the few dollars we get for them. The *Bratva* is madness. But it is my family. And madness is all I have ever known. Until now. Until Ify. Because we will be away from this soon, the madness of this town behind us in just a few hours.

I say goodbye to the brothers that I will not see at the airport and we all return to our vehicles. They drive out of the lot and turn right. I follow them until the asphalt and then turn in the other direction. I keep the radio off, enjoying the silence. I know I will not see much of it from now on. The thought makes me smile. I now have Ify's voice in my ears and she has both of them. I hear her even when she does not speak. She is my thoughts now. She is so much to me. Four more hours. A plane ride later. I already hallucinate her body in a bikini on that Italian beach as the district of Elmer begins and the buildings of the *Bratva* loom closer.

Four buildings. Three corrugated steel. One brick. But the cameras watching me enter the district begin far, far earlier. Already they will know I am here. And that is fine. All I need is to get to Roman. Once this fucking bag is in his hands, then it's over…it's over.

A distant shout distracts me, but the buildings I pass appear empty from the outside even though I know that they are not. The shouting grows in volume and I slow my car at the intersection where the four main buildings of Elmer crystalize in view.

"Gavriil!" My head jerks left. The voice is one I recognize, though it fills me with anger and shame. The traitor, whose name I will not speak. I told the bastard what I'd do to him next that I saw him, yet here is, rushing down an alley between two warehouses to meet me.

He slams a palm onto the window and his face is an angry mess of what I made it, all crusted crimson, sallow welts and plum-colored abrasions. His tanned complexion carries the scars of battles lost – more than just against me – because his eyes are bloodshot around the irises and ringed in black bags. His cheeks are hollow and his skin is whitewashed and chapped.

Whatever demons he has been slaying here in Elmer these past weeks and months seem to have caught up to him. They are ripping him apart now, and I am vindicated by this. Then I hear his words.

"Gavriil, *moy brat,* you must leave." His breath fogs up the glass and the urge to kill him grips me when he calls me brother.

"*Ismennik,*" I roar. Traitor.

I accelerate, leaving him behind in my rearview – he will not distract me from this task. I park in the same alley I did the last time, and when I step into the intersection, the traitor is nowhere to be found.

There are no men on the street today at all, though there are still screams. As I pass by the steel warehouse on the left where Ify had been trapped, one woman wails and a male voice shouts for help. I ignore them both and do what the *Bratva* has taught me to do. Care only for my own and myself.

Rage propelling me, I head inside. The smell of dust greets me, and of death, but I push past them and raze away thoughts of Anatoly. He is a madman who cannot be trusted. My brother. I would have died on the cross for him once, only to realize that he had my heart in a box and was fully intent on incinerating it.

I hesitate, feeling regret that I did not take the time to kill him as I move past the empty warehouse. Entirely empty? This is strange. Perhaps I should go back. No, no I chose the correct course. The correct course is Ify. It always has been.

I hold her face in my mind as I pass down one narrow hall to the next, finally reaching the stairs to Roman's office. My feet land hard on each step. Thunk. Thunk. Thunk. It is the only sound and as my rage parts, I recognize the silence. The presence of such an emptiness presses in on me. Why has no one come to escort me?

My hand hesitates as I reach the office door. I am already this far. Perhaps Valery is here, if Roman is not. I do not trust Valery — I do not trust anyone — but I can be sure that Valery would take me to wherever Roman may be.

I knock.

The door is not closed all the way and swings inward before me. The small breeze it creates wafts the pungent scent of pennies towards me. My mouth slackens and dries. The traitor had tried to warn me, but because of his treachery, it was moot. I would have fallen into this trap a thousand times over because never in a million years would I have expected to find Roman face down on the carpet in a pool of his own blood, or his son grinning at me from behind his desk.

"Erik," I say to the smiling madman seated in Roman's armchair, holding an antique Nagant M1895. It was Roman's, and Roman always said he had wanted to pass the gun down onto Nikoli. "What have you done?"

"What I should have done a long time ago." He tilts his head to the side and I look past him to the monitors. Most are smashed, the books on the shelves spilled out onto the floor, a filing cabinet overturned, and the right side of Erik's face — the one bearing a scar — is spattered in blood and swollen in places. He did not go quietly.

The smell of smoke pulls my attention left and when I push the door open a little farther, I see two bodies facedown on the floor and Yefim standing against the wall smoking a cigarette. He does not look at me. He stares straight forward at a point faraway.

My gaze returns to Erik. "You killed your own father."

"It runs in the family."

"Your father would never have touched his own. Blood meant something to him and now, his blood is on your hands…"

Erik roars with the laughter of one who is insane. The laughter shakes his whole body. It shakes me down to my core. My fingers around the bag's plastic handle loosen. What does it matter? This was never about the drugs. This was only ever about one thing: power.

"Your father was killed by my father. It's the only reason Roman let me live after he found out I killed Nikoli. He was worried I would tell. So if I inherited anything from my father, it's my capacity to kill brothers and do what I have to to take care of myself. To take hold of the throne by any means fucking necessary. Anyone who stands in my way falls. Everyone. Including you, dear cousin."

My mind roars. Darkness clouds all thought and all reason. "You killed your brother? Roman killed his?" My father and brother and now me. All dead by the hands of our kin. And here, we call ourselves *Bratva*. The word means nothing. What I told Anatoly those many months ago holds true. We are not *sem'ya*. Not family. Not brothers. We are *mafiozi*.

He lifts an eyebrow. With his soft face, it is impossible to believe. "Alina was there. She saw everything. You didn't know that either?"

I know nothing, because I thought I had understood madness before, but this is another level of sin. I firm my grip on the duffel bag, until the edges of the plastic handle bite into me. I hold onto that pain because it is all that I have left as Erik reduces my understanding of the world to pieces.

"Erik, stop this."

His blue eyes glitter menacingly, and the scar on the side of his face glimmers pink, shimmering when he moves, like water. Like Lake Opa. Was he a killer already then? Where I saw love, did he see only disappointment?

"Gavriil," he whispers, "I haven't even begun."

I take a step forward. He lifts his gun. But then another hard cutting sensation cracks my skull from behind, just before he pulls the trigger. I feel hot blood cascade down the back of my neck. The bag falls from my grip onto the floor with a thud. And then there is nothing.

I fall to my knees and as my cheek hits the hard, carpeted floor, I see Roman's blank brown stare shining back at me, like two jewels in the night.

Aiden

The drop went well. It damn near feels like a celebration in the car as we head out of the parking lot and drive away from the Ternary, leaving Gavriil to make the drop in Elmer. That sick, tragic fucking place. If I'd thought for a second Alina was in a place like that, I'd have torn this whole town down. As it stands now, I understand well the stressed hope I'd seen shining on Gavriil's face. He's so close to closure. We all are.

Clifton is looking at me. We're together in the backseat and he's smiling. "What?" I say.

He shakes his head and holds up a hand. "Nothing. Nothing at all."

I want to know, and feel the urge to beat it out of him. It's strangely easy to repress. The radio is on. Some pop song is playing. It's shit, but Knox is still humming absently along with it. Dixon is looking down at his phone. Sometimes I wonder if he doesn't have cameras installed in Sara and Brant's room, just so he can watch them playing. He's a sick puppy, though no more desperate than Knox or I.

We've all fallen, and fallen hard for our women. Charlie's too wounded and before that, was never interested. Which makes me wonder about Clifton. He could pull any woman he wanted and yet, he's still alone. I wonder if it's because he's spent so much time looking after the rest of us. Looking after me... I frown.

"What is it?" Clifton says.

"I..." How do I tell him? *Just tell me*, Alina would say, but what she's really saying is don't bullshit. Be brave. I clear my throat, "You're a good brother."

Clifton's eyes widen and in the front seat, Knox stops humming. The moment is tense, but Clifton's grin cuts through it. He beams. "Thanks, I..." But then his gaze pans past me. It widens. His mouth slackens, but he doesn't speak.

"Clifton?" I ask him in the moment of silence that follows.

The rest happens in an instant.

My whole body jerks violently. The seatbelt sears across my chest and lap and I know it'll leave abrasions, but that's only if I live. I know we've been hit, but I never heard the car coming. We're spinning. The sound of metal bending against metal fills the space between my ears. My eyes are shut, but I feel when the car is hit again, this time near the front and from the other direction. We tip, Clifton's side going down first so that I hang suspended.

I can't see but my hands are in my pockets and I've got the safeties off my Rugers. I point, but there's nothing there but blackness colliding with my thoughts. Everything spins. The tension in my shoulders is weak, but I try to firm up as I think of Alina. Where are you, baby? I want to know that she's alright. The second surprising thought that hits me? I hope my brothers are too.

"Fuck!" Dixon curses. But there's no time to respond. Glass shatters and there are hands on my body. I look up into eyes whose faces are hidden by masks. I point my gun at the first of them and blow off the top of his head without hesitation. Blood rains. But then there's the bat. It hits me hard in the arms and then the chest, then the head. Each time, I feel my grip on reality slip. Dixon was behind the wheel but he's not anymore. Knox is passed out, his head limp against the window. I look at Clifton.

"Aiden!" He shouts. Then there's the shock. I fight through it, but it comes again. Electricity firing through me at several thousand volts and I can't jump back. Stark pain, which otherwise wouldn't be a problem, but it comes again and again. I aim up, but at this angle, there's a chance I could hit one of my brothers and I won't risk that. Instead, I let them taze the shit out of me and eventually, drag my body out of the car by the arms.

Everything smells like metal and rich, sweet gasoline. My feet hit the ground and I'm dizzy, but I can still stand. I throw a punch. It finds purchase. A jaw I think. A man goes down. Another one's holding a gun. I tackle him and my arms light up in fire as the concrete rips the skin off of them.

I hold the guy down with ease, but before I can rip his tongue out through his throat there are hands on me. At least eight. They yank my arms behind my back and I feel handcuffs come around my wrists and more around my feet. There's thick smoke that stings my nostrils and my lungs on each inhale. People are screaming. Men that look like cops are marking a perimeter behind yellow tape. Either the cops are in on this, or they're lookalikes. Either theory equally as likely given the ones that hunt us.

A white van looms into view. The back doors are flung open wide with abandon. Head first, they throw me into the van beside Dixon, who's already been bound. He's passed out now too. I hit the floor with a bang, my head bouncing off of hard metal.

It smells like fresh paint. A little like human waste. We're not the first bodies to have been on this floor before. I feel a warm, heavy object thrown in behind me and when I blink my eyes open and struggle to focus through the film that's suddenly claimed my eyesight, I see my own reflection in Clifton's face.

"I got a call off before they got me. Told the girls to get to the airport," he says, body heaving with each word. His eyelids are drooping. I wonder how many times they tagged him because he's got the sharp purple blood bruises of electrical shocks staining most of his neck and arms.

I nod and am grateful. The girls will get out. Alina will live. She'll start over. She'll have a good, long life. And when all is said and done, she'll meet me when she's an old woman in the next life and I'll be waiting. I think of Marguerite. The one woman who told me I wasn't going to hell. I never believed her, but as my head clunks against the tin bed of the truck I'm in and the lights go out, I hope to fucking god she's right. I need to see Alina again. I don't care how many lifetimes I have to wait. I'd swallow eternity for just one chance to touch her, and the promise that she'll live in Italy, happy and safe.

Ify

We stand around the kitchen table. Me, Alina, Mer and Sara. There's a cell phone lying face up between us.

"Play the message again," Sara says, voice shaky.

Mer presses play. Clifton's voice fires into the line. Laced with panic and fever, I've heard this message before, but his tone sends my adrenaline into overdrive. Every time.

"Get out of the city. All of you. Go to the airport. Buy tickets. You know where we keep the extra cash. Combination to the safe is five, eighty three, forty six, thirty four. Do not, I repeat, do not come looking for us."

In the background there's gunfire. Scrabbling sounds lead me to believe he's dropped his phone. Crunch, crunch, crunch. Bang. Thud. A man's roar. Several other men speaking, their accents distinctly Russian. Eventually, after some time, I hear the faint slamming of a car door and the squealing of tires on pavement.

Mer pauses the recording. "It's all white noise after that."

Sara stands to my left. She's got her and Dixon's little kid, Brant, on her hip. Little yellow-boned boy looks just like the both of them. Damned cute too. He shouldn't have to be here for this. Maybe none of them should, except me. I got myself into this mess and I'd do it again a thousand times over just, at the end of the day, to say I knew Gavriil. He's the best thing that's ever happened to me. But where is he?

Knuckle down on the table, Mer's head drops for a moment between her shoulders. When she straightens, the wiry muscles in her arms stand out like steel. "So. Needless to say, I will not be catching a flight at four pm to Italy."

Alina grunts out a laugh. Even that brutish sound on her is attractive. She's fine as hell and I'm reminded of the first time I saw her in person. She saved my life. I owe her the skin on my back and the pulse in my wrist.

"*Nyet*," she says. Her mane of red hair moves around her when she shakes her head, like every strand on her head is alive. She exhales against her fingers in patchy breaths. "I do not either."

"Where you go I go," I say. She shoots me a confused look and I just shrug like it's nothing, even though my pulse thuds like a set of cymbals in a high school marching band, gone deranged. Where is her brother?

Sara nods and hoists Brant higher on her hip. "Ify's right. Wherever you ladies go, I'm going too."

"Fuck you, Sara," Mer sneers dismissively. Her tongue clacks against the backs of her teeth. "You're not coming."

Sara makes a face. "What I do is not up to you. I'm going to save my man's life."

"Sara," Mer barks. The sound is as loud as it is vicious. Brant on Sara's hip looks around wildly. He can sense something is wrong and his usual happy countenance is marred when he looks up at his mama's stricken face.

"I'm sorry, but I can't have you coming. If you die, Brant has nothing and I'm not sending that beautiful boy to a foster home. Besides. When we get Dixon out of there, do you have any idea what that man would do to me if I let you come? He's already put a hit out on me once."

"What?" Sara says. She shields Brant's face as if he might learn too much. The thought makes me smile a little bit. At least, until Sara asks the million dollar question. "Hit by who?"

Mer doesn't answer, but her gaze betrays her. She flashes a look to Alina quickly, then glances down at the phone again when Alina's face falls. "Never mind. The answer is you're not coming."

"But I..."

"I need you to do something else," I say, pitching my voice over Sara's. Everyone looks at me. I'm the newest member of the crew, I guess, but I've got something to say. I always do. "The brothers got jumped, sure. And we can be darned sure that they've been taken to Elmer if it was the Russian's jumping them. If they're even still alive."

Alina's brown face pales and she crosses her fingers over her chest. I keep going. "But what we don't know is if Gavriil made it out of Elmer. Maybe this is an unrelated attack. Maybe this is punishment for helping Gavriil. From what Alina told me, sounds like Erik is likely to be pretty frigging POed that Gavriil is making deals with Roman behind his back. Maybe this has nothing to do with Gavriil. Maybe the handover went as planned and Gavriil is already on his way to the airport." Please dear lord. Please...

"I can be helpful in Elmer. I've been there before, so I need to go. But Gavriil isn't answering his phone and hasn't called. So I need you to go to the airport and just make sure that he's not there waiting for me. For us."

Sara bounces her baby on her hip. She frowns around at us all. Creases worry her pretty face between the eyebrows and around her mouth. "You know he's not at the airport."

Yes. I do. Because if he were anywhere where he could get to me, he would. "Actually, it hadn't really occurred to me," I lie. When I woke up this morning with a headache from hell and heroin lingering in my veins, I promised myself I wouldn't lie again. I guess I lied again then too.

"You're probably right, Sara," Mer says, "but that's beside the point. Each of us…" She points at Alina, then me, then her own self. "…have been imprisoned in some kind of way by these fuckers. We know what we're getting into."

"I have too," Sara answers, but her resolution is softening as the baby grabs a handful of her hair.

Alina cuts in. "Ify makes good point. Please. Gavriil is my brother. If he does not see one of us at airport and we do not answer our phones, he will go to Elmer and may be killed."

Mer interjects, "Or at the very least, make things much, much worse. It's a good idea by Ify."

We wait. Then Sara whispers, "Why wouldn't we answer our phones?"

Mer just looks at her. She doesn't need to say it out loud, because I'm thinking it too. None of us that go to Elmer will make it out alive.

I spare Mer the grief of having to answer. "So will you go?"

Sara closes her eyes and massages them. Brant sticks his hand up and paws at her face. She looks at him and she sees the same thing we do. She's got her hands bound by the shackles of love.

"We'll bring him back to you," Alina says, a promise in her voice that makes me wonder if she really believes what she says. "I promise."

"Sh…" Sara starts, like she's about to curse. She shakes her head and shakes out her hair. It's greasy at the roots. I can tell this whole thing is going to age her at least ten years. Luckily the rest of us have melanin in abundant supply so we should be gorgeous when Sara comes to our funerals and stares into our open caskets…

Cynicism aside, I'm still relieved when Sara mutters weakly, "Fine. I'll go. But what's the plan? What are y'all going to do?"

We all look to Mer, and for a moment her eyes flare. She's a soldier, not a strategist. Alina's a princess. Sara's a saint and a doctor. But me? I'm a spy. I'm an author. I've already written our story and its every possible outcome and yeah, in most of them we die but…not in all of them.

"I have a plan. It's a little risky." I look to Alina when I say that. "But I've been into one of those buildings in Elmer. I was held in one of those cells and I met someone who escaped. She left an opening, a way in. And I'm the only one in the world besides her who knows where it is."

Alina says, "But you do not know if this is the building where the brothers are kept. There are four principle buildings in Elmer."

"And there are cameras. We'll need to get around them," Mer fires back.

I nod. "That's why we'll need two things. A distraction, to give us time to root out where the boys are, and someone on the inside to keep all eyes on that distraction. Alina, you have Anatoly's number right?"

She nods. "*Da*. He was like family. But Gavriil says not to trust him." Was. Past tense. Because the traitor fudged me over big time. I'm not thrilled about relying on him again, but I can trust at least that Anatoly will want to keep Gavriil safe if he's been taken, and keep Alina safe if he hasn't been.

"We don't have a choice. Anatoly will be our inside man."

"How do you know he won't betray us," Mer says.

"Because he wouldn't betray Gavriil. Not again."

Mer nods. "And the distraction?"

Alina sighs, "It's me."

"What?" Sara.

"I will be distraction."

I make a face. "Sorry, babe."

"No you are not, you liar." She rolls her eyes, but pulls her hair back from her face. She quickly throws it up into a ponytail and leans forward onto the table. "Promise me one thing. When I am distraction, you will find the brothers before Erik begins his torture."

Mer covers her smile with her hand. Then she breaks. She laughs and the sound is so foreign and weird it makes me laugh too. Alina and Sara don't quite manage a laugh, but both are smiling. I guess that's what certain death does to you.

"Sure thing, *puta*. But he's not going to torture you. You're going to kill him and I know how."

Alina lifts an eyebrow. "They will search me."

"They won't find anything on you. Not if I have anything to say about it. I'll show you."

"So then it's settled," I huff.

But Mer shakes her head. "There's one other secret weapon we haven't thought of yet."

"What's that?" I ask her.

She lifts her phone. "I just need to make a call."

Charlie

My Porsche squeals as I pull up to the sidewalk and jerk on the brake. I'd been on my way to the airport to say bye to Aiden, Alina, Alina's brother and his girlfriend. The fucking bastards wouldn't tell me why they were leaving — said it was better that way — but fuck them and fuck everything. Because I got a call a few minutes ago from Mer. One that changed everything.

If they'd told me then that I might not be going to the airport but actually into battle, I certainly wouldn't have brought my damn dog along and I wouldn't be stopping now if I hadn't already been so close to townhouse row. I don't have time for this shit, but the thought of me dying and leaving Checkers to die of starvation in the car doesn't sit right with me, so I grab him and throw open my car door. We're doing this.

The little pup barks. He can sense something's up. In the past weeks, he's gotten pretty good at reading me. The first night I brought him home, he'd been standing over me barking when I woke up with the same damn night terrors. He'd curled up at the foot of the bed and it felt good to pat him until my heart settled. And it did. Faster than usual too.

That happened a few times until one night, just three days ago the weirdest damn thing happened. I slept and I dreamed — no nightmares, but an actual dream that felt as real as

Checker's soft fur against my arms now as I run with him into the vet clinic.

There's a young woman behind the desk, blonde and real pretty like but I don't give her a second glance, not even as she tries to stop me from clearing the front counter and heading straight into the back.

"Sir. Sir! You have to sign in. Mrs. Monroe is with someone right now!"

"Shut up," I bark at her and while she scoffs in disbelief and horror, I charge into the first room. Empty. I let the door bang open and shut as I make my way into the second room, but only find her behind door number three.

Her brown eyes are round as quarters when she looks up and sees me. Her pink lips purse and my cock twitches in my jeans. No time for that shit now. But my body can't help it. It remembers the dream.

It had started the same as the other one. In bed, tied down, unable to move, a woman's snatch wrapped around my cock and squeezing so hard it damn near hurt. I'd tried to shout, but the words were all trapped somewhere in my chest. The woman's breasts loomed into view and they were huge — bigger than they had been in past dreams — and I cringed as I tried desperately to look away from them before the slicing began, but some invisible force held my face steady.

So I stared and waited as fear choked my throat and turned my whole body to ice. I'd stared as the taste of chicory flooded my mouth and fire in the form of tears welled in the pools of my eyes.

Why don't you take a picture, the woman said, *it'll last longer.*

My gaze had snapped up to the woman's face then and in the background I heard barking. Her tits floated just below her chin and were decorated by tight nipples colored in electric pink. She lowered one to my mouth and I sucked, tasting the sweat and vanilla on her skin. The smell of pumpkin pie swirled around me and I fell into the brown of her gaze as she started laughing that ridiculous, giddy laughter that had been floating through my mind all that day.

While she crushed my face with her tits and I lapped at every inch of her soft, padded breasts, she'd bent over and kissed my forehead — or more accurately, the scar winding its way across it. I'd woken up at the same time the pressure of her pussy tightened around my cock only to find myself dry humping a pillow, my cum spread in a thick paste across it.

Checkers was sleeping soundly at the foot of the bed and when I checked the clock it was nearly eight am. I'd never slept in so late or so long — not since my new half-life began — and I damn sure hadn't gotten off, not even by myself.

I'd laughed. I'd laughed so hard my whole body shook and I forgot the pain of my face or the scar on my heart. It had been short, and fake, but even dream Molly had given me something I hadn't had in months: hope.

Here in the now, I watch her cheeks redden rapidly and my dick turns into a full fledged hard on. I approach the table, where one little cat sits, and place Checkers down next to it. "I need you to watch my dog," I say quickly. "I was coming for a checkup anyways."

"Isn't...I'm with someone..." She points to the elderly woman I hadn't even noticed sitting on the bench seat against the wall.

I incline my head at her. "Ma'am," I say. Then I turn back to Molly. "So will you watch him? It's important."

"I…I mean, okay."

"Good." I leave Checkers there and head back out of the door before my body tells me to do something reckless, like fuck Molly in front of the old lady because this is likely the last time I'll get the chance to fuck her, or anyone. I make my way back through the lobby and am back out in the crisp wind when I hear the door open and clang shut behind me.

"Hey, when will you be back?"

"Later tonight. Latest, tomorrow morning." Or never again, and this will be the last chance I get to taste a woman. And not just a woman, right? The one who, in the dead of night amidst so many destroyed corpses, brought me back among the living.

"Oh. Okay. Well good luck with whatever you're doing." Molly calls out after me and my thoughts go wild. I'm too amped. I press my eyes shut tight. Just get in your car. Get in your car. Then she says. "Is that your Porsche?"

My lips twitch. How the hell can she make me smile at a time like this? "Told you I wasn't homeless."

"I just…it's purple. Isn't that a little flashy?"

"Midnight purple baby. My colors run wild." My hand is on the car door. It's cold to the touch. I glance up and she's standing just on the other side of it. What's she still doing here talking to me?

Her eyebrows crinkle. Her nose turns pink in the cold. She's only got a lab coat on over a thin, baggy shirt, one that tries desperately to hide some of her curves and, like every other shirt ever created, fails the job. "Really? Doesn't really seem like you."

"You don't know me." Except she does. She knows this new Charlie better than anyone in the world. Outside of the call Mer gave me ten minutes ago — the one that changed the course of my day and will probably change the course of my death — Molly is the only person I've spoken more than ten words to in the past three months.

Her gaze rips away from mine. "I guess not," she says, and she sounds so damn disappointed.

"Goddammit. Get your ass over here."

"Excuse me?"

"You heard me. Come here, now."

Her face burns an even brighter cherry and I wonder if she's afraid or curious or something else entirely as she silently obeys my request. In the open door of the car, I grab her by the front of that ugly shirt and I drag her up against my chest. I might not be able to fuck her — not that a married woman with a stick up her ass like she has would ever let me — but I can give her back something she didn't even know she gave me.

I press my twisted lips to her forehead, just where she kissed me in the dream. I let the smell of her — like Christmas and Thanksgiving made a baby and this is her, right here — overwhelm me. Her tits press against my chest, her hands lightly hold onto my arms. Her fingers shake a little. I don't expect a reaction like this and don't have the time to think about it. I wish I did, just like I wish I could hold onto this moment longer, but I can't and I don't and I won't.

I hold her away from me and am already in the car by the time she blinks her eyes open. So slow, she looks like I got her drunk. That pleases me to no end and my insides warm and as I rev my engine and take off with a wink, I hope to hell I'll see her again, at least once more.

The world rushes past. There's a gun in my glove compartment and I reach for it now. I reach the girls at their house — my old house — twenty minutes later that feels closer to twenty seconds. Molly is on my mind. And so is Checkers. I'm gonna miss that little mutt.

I honk twice and the sound blares across the driveway. The front door opens and Mer rushes out, accompanied closely by a black chick I've never met. "Thanks for coming," Mer says when she throws open the backseat and unloads a duffel bag into it. She strains under its weight and when the items inside of it clatter around noisily, I know she's brought the whole damn arsenal with her.

"You look like a couple of killers," I say, because they do. Both women have braids that tie their hair back away from their faces. All black everything are the outfits they've chosen.

Mer nods once, her lips tight. "Thanks for coming, brother."

"They're my brothers, too. I'd die for them." I nod at her once. "And for you."

"Good," the black girl says brightly as she slides into the backseat next to all of the guns. "Because you're about to." She smells like lavender and holds her hand out to me. "My name's Ifeoma Smith. Don't call me Ifeoma though. I prefer Ify. I'm Gavriil's person."

"Well shit," I answer, taking her tiny hand in my much larger fist. I notice that she doesn't stare at my scar and it irks me. Does she not see it? Instead she keeps talking.

"Alright, I can guide you to where we're going. You'll need to take the highway north. Seven stops past the Ternary, you'll take exit 21A like you're going to the ports. I went to the ports once with my dad when I was a kid. He was doing some research on a crime taking place down there and now that I think about it, I wonder if it wasn't actually related to some *Bratva* nonsense because it totally involved some shipping containers and I remember thinking, even then, that there was something fishy about the books. I bet they doctored them. I should call my dad and ask him if he ever solved that case…"

"What the fuck is going on?" I shout. This little chick won't shut up.

Mer rolls her eyes. "Just drive." She takes a breath and I reach over and knead her shoulder.

"You know you don't have to do this. Knox'll be pissed at you for going back and confronting any of the Russians after what you went through."

"What did you go through?" Ify pipes up.

Mer glances back at her, but her eyes are bright and nothing but determination and resilience fills them. She takes a gun out of the sling she wears around her shoulders, and chambers the round. Clack clack. The sound fills my stomach with heat and dread.

"Rape and torture," she says flatly. "Not something I want for my man, or any of them. Let's drive."

I do as she says and take off down the street going ninety. "Where's Sara and Alina? They going to be safe at the house?"

"Alina's gone ahead. Sara's heading to the airport to make sure Gavriil and none of the brothers got away and showed up there. We're not optimistic, but Ify's right, it's a good base to cover."

She goes back to checking the weapons she wears and setting some aside for me — one of them, Aiden's favorite Steton pistol machine gun — while Ify says, "Alina should already be in Elmer by now."

"The fuck? Why'd she go ahead?"

Mer cocks her head back, and a few stray strands of her short bangs slip free of the braid she wears to bind them. Her fists are wrapped. She's prepared to go to war and die fighting. If Valhalla's a real place, I'm sure it's got a seat with her name carved into it. I just hope she doesn't have to take it. Not today. Not for decades more. What I hope for this crazy bitch is a boring death in her sleep, utterly without theatrics and that the lords of Valhalla forget all about her.

"Ask her, she's leading this operation."

"Ify?"

"Damn straight. *Puta's* got a plan."

"Is it gonna get us killed?" I ask, angling the rearview so that I can see her.

She tilts her head to the side and glances out of the window, seriously giving it some thought in a way that might have made me laugh if I wasn't seriously setting myself and my sisters up for the slaughter.

"It's our best option. Or at least, the best one we could think of with the time and resources at hand. I've already written the end of this book in my head, and I'd say *probably* not. We've got a shot, at least…"

"It's a good plan," Mer says flatly.

I rev the engine and take the freeway fast, gliding between cars as we race to meet the last people I want to see — the ones that butchered me. "Fanfuckingtastic."

Alina

This is not a bad plan from the little writer. We have known her only one day, and yet it is from her that we take our orders. Which is why I now stand in the bleeding heart of Elmer shouting Erik's name.

"Erik, you coward! Where are you?" I speak in Russian as I walk down the center of the street. I am near the intersection of Elmer now, where Ify told me that our men will be found in one of the four adjacent buildings. She has a way into the steel one, but according to Anatoly, that is not where they are being kept. But with Ify's plan, and if she is right, and if it works as it is intended, then more lives than just our mens' will be saved today. Or we will be responsible for dozens and dozens of deaths.

The steel building Ify spoke of passes on my left. It is frightening, towering over me like a slave ship docked at the harbor. Moans waft from it on the wings of a wind that pushes and pulls my hair and clothes in many different directions. Like it also tries to escape this place of pain. These building are pain – especially the steel – and this is the one that Mer and Ify will break into first.

In order to give them the time to approach, all cameras must first be pointed my way. Anatoly has said he will make sure of it. I do not trust the man in anything except for his love of my brother and in this moment, that is enough. It will have to be.

"Erik!" My voice is loud, full of an authority I have never heard before. In my brothers yes, but never in myself.

But I am not princess anymore.

A shifting in the shadows pulls my attention to the right where I see the first of the men lurking in the doorways of the buildings around me. I cannot imagine their surprise, and I hear a few voices speak my name. I hear others tell me to run.

"Why do you all hide like rats?" I shout as two men step onto the road from beneath the awning of a warehouse entrance. "Are you ashamed? You should be. I know that you have helped Erik kidnap four innocent men and my brother, Gavriil. I know that you helped him torture my brothers and kill Timur. Do you also know that he killed his own brother? He killed Nikoli," I shout the truth loud enough for all to hear.

"I was there. A child. He threatened the lives of my family so I never spoke of it, but I was there to witness as Erik suffocated Nikoli to death and moved his body into that car. It was no suicide. Erik is a murderer."

Konstantin watches me from the intersection. His face is ashen and haunted. "Alina…"

"Alina," a second voice barks. Over his shoulder, I see one of the men who helped kidnap me and my brother approach.

"Yefim," I growl.

He smiles at me, baring all of his teeth. Shoving Konstantin behind him, the sound of his boots against the asphalt carries as he comes to meet me. "This is a surprise.

Last time I saw you, you were being transported like luggage. I see you're doing much better now." He tilts his head to the side. "For now. But not for much longer."

"You are a madman to follow Erik like this. Do you not know what he is?"

"I know he is the leader of the *Bratva*. So I do what he says."

I balk, "And what does Roman say about this?"

"Roman says nothing anymore. He died this morning."

The timing is not lost on me. Erik wants nothing but the world burned to ash beneath his feet. It makes sense that all deals honored would be broken with him holding both the matches and the gasoline.

"What did he do?" A gust of wind hits me, pushing the words back into my mouth.

This day reminds me of a Spring day in Moscow. The minarets of our church would still be topped in frozen snow, but the birds would be out on the boughs of sun-drenched trees, singing their songs of the summer to come. Summers where our family would meet with Erik's and we would go to the lakes. I let Erik convince me that Nikoli's death was an accident. It's what I'd wanted to believe, but I know better and now I pay the price.

Yefim reaches out and touches a strand of my hair, then tucks it behind my ear. I bite the inside of my cheek until it bleeds. It is all I can do to remain fixed, and not jerk away from him.

"He has assumed leadership after your brother killed Roman," he says, but there is a lie in his eyes and a truth that falters.

"What did *you* do?"

He breaks the line of my gaze. "It doesn't matter what I did. Erik will want to speak with you."

I wrench my arm out of his grasp and when he reaches for me again, I stand my ground in a way that makes him hesitate. He looks so suddenly unsure. "I am Alina Popov, heiress to the *Russkiy mafiozi* and you do not touch me without my permission. Now tell me how Roman died. What lies did Erik feed to you?"

Fear. Shame. Regret. And then violence. It appears like a blood cast sunrise in his pale face. "There were no lies. Your brother killed Roman. I saw it myself."

I want to tear out Yefim's teeth and stab needles through his eye sockets. He was always a dumb brute but this level of stupidity and blind loyalty to a madman is nothing I could have imagined. "You know that's not true. Why would Gavriil kill the man who would give us our lives back?"

"What if that man was the one to kill your father? Do you not think Gavriil would be capable of murder then?"

Derr'mo. This can't be happening. They are all murderers, the lot of them, and for a second, I do not know whether or not Yefim is telling the truth, or if the truth even matters. If Roman killed our father, then he has a right to die and Gavriil has a right to kill him. It is the *mafiozi* way. This never ending death cycle.

"Where is Gavriil?" I say, narrowing my eyes.

The haunted look in Yefim's eyes clears, and he returns again to the confused imbecile I remember. He grins at me and steps in so close I can smell the cigarettes on his breath. "Do I need to check for weapons first?"

"Do what you must." I straighten and hold out my arms, prepared for this.

His hands slide meaningfully over my breasts, behind, and crotch, but he does not linger anywhere else and he does not find the blade tucked into the lining of my jeans as Mer knew he wouldn't.

It's a thin blade. I'd have to be right on someone to get in a clean shot or it will not penetrate. Mer says not to take chances. Not to make mistakes. Because being smart is better than being brave. So as much as I long to slit Yefim's throat, I let him touch me as he likes, and then I let him lead the way.

My heartbeat picks up speed and is thrumming like a machine gun in my veins as I climb the concrete steps to the brick building. Inside, I can feel the strain bleeding through the light wallpaper, and in the dust that lines the dining room table we stalk past.

There are six men sitting in a room on a sofa. Their heads are close together and they look up and, seeing me, their eyes widen. Three of them stand. One of them starts towards Yefim, but he barks an order to the rest to stand down. Still, they might have revolted had I said something. I can feel it — their desire to disobey, to protect me, to end the chaos a little boy who should never have been made leader started — but I give my head a little shake and try to communicate to them with only my eyes. They must wait. They will get their chance, just as I will, but it will not be now. Soon. But not yet.

Yefim barks another order and slowly, the men ease back in their seats while I head towards the stairs, their eyes watching me. I know most of them by face and many of them by name and a few of them, I know their deepest hopes and fears.

I know that Sasha had his heart crushed by a Russian ballet dancer when we still lived in the motherland. I was there when Zeinolla had his first tooth pulled, and when Kristoff jumped from the roof of the house when Nikoli dared him to – he broke both of his legs. I know Vlad's mother, and am close with Erol's sister. I meet their gazes now, each of them in turn, and they watch me with either anger or sadness. Only one, Gregor, looks away.

The blade flexes against my outer thigh as I turn right at the top of the stairs and enter a small study. It reeks of age and carries with it the dark, ancient scent of blood. My heart leaps into my throat and I pray it does not belong to one of the brothers.

"Alina." Erik leans back in an old armchair and grins at me and I have never seen him look so pleased, or with such madness in his eyes. Not even then, the day he killed his brother or the day he killed mine.

"Erik."

"You honor me."

"I come to pay my respects."

He laughs. "*Derr'mo,* you have changed."

"Death changes the living. You should know better than most."

"I have had my fair share of loss, this is true, sweet cousin." He speaks to me in English, so I answer in English, and I wonder if he is even Russian anymore. Where is his honor? Or has that also gone with his sanity? Because when he stands, I see his shirt buttons are off by one and there are stains on his lapel. The same dark stains are crusted beneath his fingernails.

"Such excellent timing. Alina, please let me introduce you to Jordan Monroe." He holds out his hand and I turn, surprised to see a tall, well-dressed man standing in the doorway behind me. Yefim turns as well and though he watches the stranger warily, he steps out of the way, pulling me with him.

Erik and the man shake hands and when the man removes an alcohol wipe from his inside jacket pocket, I find the entire orchestra even more unsettling and odd. I was born into this family — this closed family — and I have never seen this man before in my life and I have never seen anyone treat a member of the *Brava* with such brazen disrespect. There is a power exchange here that I do not like. Who is this Jordan? Or rather — what? Because in this moment, all I sense is danger and a threat.

"Jordan, this is Alina Popov, my cousin back from the dead."

"I recognize her. The model." The man's perpetual scowl lands on me. Then he tilts his head. "Is she for sale?"

I tense. Erik beams. "She will be soon."

"She'll do well at auction," Jordan says as he finishes wiping off his hands. He tosses the napkin into the bin by the front door. Even Yefim scowls, though Erik does not seem to understand the slight against him.

"You're not asking for yourself?" Erik asks with one eyebrow cocked. The scar slithering across the side of his face flashes when he tilts his head to the right.

"You know I don't like colored girls." His voice is flat and without emotion. There is nothing to this man. He is soulless.

Erik laughs. "Of course. Bruises don't show up as well. But I think we'll manage to make some show up on this one." Erik touches my cheek. I wince away from him and pivot so I can keep an eye on all three men watching me at once.

"Erik," I say firmly, "I want to make a deal."

"A deal? Well good thing my lawyer is here then." He cackles.

I glance at Jordan and when I speak, I speak to both of them because I am suddenly very aware of the fact that Erik does not have the power here he thinks he has. "My life for Aiden and Gavriil's. I come with you willingly. I will let you sell me to whatever man you like, to do whatever they like to me. I will be willing. I will not fight. I will not resist. I do not ever try to escape."

"But I want my revenge, dear sweet cousin. Gavriil did kill my father, after all." His eyes twinkle. So blue. So full of madness. "And I've worked so hard to get him to this point. Don't you remember, Alina? Even when we were children he's just been hungry for all that I have. He's coveted it — everything of mine — and threatened to take it all away from me. I won't be safe until he's dead."

He continues, "Timur and my father didn't see the threat. That's why I did what I did. I had to. Don't you see why, little cousin? Your brother is the crazy one. Everything I've ever done has just been to protect myself from him. So your pretty face means absolutely nothing to me without his corpse to shit in. He's mine."

I hiss and think of challenging him, but then I cede. This charade does not matter so long as Erik ends the night bleeding. "Fine. Then you give me Aiden alone. A trade one-to-one."

My pulse tap tap taps away, nervous. I just need to stall long enough to get the signal. The one that should send this entire building into chaos. In chaos I will find my opening. I just need the signal…and proof of life. Because if they're dead already then this has all been for nothing. Revenge doesn't interest me. What interests me are the living members of my family — the last one left — the man who has my heart, and his brothers beside him. They are all my family now, much more than the *Bratva* ever was. These are men and women who know honor. Who would run through fire for one another, for me. As I would them. As I do now…

Erik leans on his desk and I notice that his arms tremble beneath his weight, as if his skinny elbows and his weak wrists are the only things keeping him standing. I wonder how many nights his paranoia has kept him from sleep.

"So quick to turn on your kin for your lover?" He laughs and shakes his head, as if there has never been anything to amuse him more than this. "And as for the rest, you're fine with me killing them?"

This must mean that they're alive. I hope. *Moy boch, bajalsta.* "I know I cannot save them all," I rasp through gritted teeth, "so I do what I can."

"Oh dear, sweet cousin of mine…"

Erik laughs, but Jordan cuts him off. That surprises me. Erik is leader of the *Bratva* but so far this lawyer has only treated him like a child. "This is a good offer. It would increase her value considerably. Buyers like their participants submissive, but the drugs lessen the experience."

Drugs? Was this why Ify came to us with drugs in her poor, small body? Disgusting. My arms tense beneath my shoulders and my fingers twitch towards the knife concealed against my leg.

Erik frowns. "You think it's a good deal?"

The lawyer nods. His jaw is a hard block of granite and his mouth is unkind. It frowns down at me, for he is also a tall man. Well built, like the brothers are, and like my brothers are. Difficult to take down. "Certainly. The deaths of these other men earn me nothing. One compliant, submissive female – and a celebrity? She could earn us more than the sum of women that have passed through these walls in a single auction."

"How much?" Erik frowns harder and squints his eyes like he's having trouble keeping up with the conversation. His fingers gripping the table's edge are clenching convulsively and his jaw…it occurs to me for the first time that Erik might be high. *Slava bogu…* I cannot believe it, and yet this is good. This will be to my advantage. The only challenge will be the other men. Yefim will cave when Erik dies, this is sure, but this lawyer frightens me with his calm, clean diplomacy as he discusses torture and imprisonment.

Jordan paces in a slow circle around me. He speaks as he walks. "Three million if she's drugged. Fifteen if she isn't."

"Fifteen for one woman?"

"Release the man she wants," Jordan says, cutting Erik off, "and I'll take her from here."

"I only go with you on my own without fighting once I have proof of life. I want to see him released."

Nervousness rises in my bones as I wait for Erik's answer. He watches me and then the lawyer, then grins all at once. "Good. It'll give me a chance to tell Gavriil just what our good friend Jordan has in store for you. Right this way, Alina."

As he turns, I catch him pop a pill into his mouth. He bites down hard, then bends his head back and cracks his neck a dozen times. The gesture screams insanity as he produces a set of jangly keys and uses them to open the door at the far end of the office.

I walk into the room. Destroyed furniture has been pushed back against the four walls. Two men kneel bound and gagged — one to my right, the other to my left. Dixon and Knox, respectively. I exhale my breath. They're alive. *Spasiba, moy boch, spasiba…*

Knox's eyes flare when they see me while Dixon's narrow. Somehow I know exactly what both men are thinking. Knox is shit scared because he knows that Mer is here somewhere, and Dixon's going to skin me alive if Sara and Brant are anywhere but on a plane to Italy.

We pass through the room and arrive at the next door. While Erik unlocks it, I lick my lips and glance behind me at Jordan. If he were not here, then there may be something I could say to warn them of what will happen next, but this one sees everything, so I clip my words and hope that this will appear unrehearsed, and convincing.

"I am sorry that I could not save you. Just know that your family is safe." I look into Dixon's eyes and Knox flinches, but doesn't react more than this. Dixon settles. He exhales deeply through his nose and nods at me once.

"*Ya tak vinovat*," I tell them because it's all that's left to say. I'm so sorry. And I am. I'm so sorry that this is my life and that this is my kin and that this is the situation we are all trapped in.

We pass into the next room and Erik closes — but does not lock — the door behind him. I make a note of this. The following room is much bigger and has both Clifton and Aiden in it. My heart squeezes in my chest as my gaze locks with Clifton's first and then rips across the room to where his twin kneels, bound and gagged like the rest. He's safe. He's okay. They both are.

I have to mentally beat the smile from my face even as Aiden roars against his gag and thrashes violently against his bindings. It does not matter though, because I thought he'd be dead. God has taken so much from me, but Aiden is still here, blood spattered yes, bruised and beaten and covered in what look like blood bruises or burns and he is livid, yes, but through his torn shirt, I can still see the chain on which my grandfather's cross thumps against his chest. It still catches the light.

Erik laughs and runs his fingers through his hair several times in quick succession. He licks his lips. They appear dry and papery. "This one must like you a whole lot. I'm guessing, it's the one you want released." It, he says, not even he.

"*Da*," I answer, clenching my knees and my fists. "It is."

"Get her out of here. We don't need to inspire this man to come hunting for her," Jordan says beside me, bored again, though an edge has creeped into his voice. His eyes scan

Aiden's face and the blood on Aiden's chest and arms – or maybe not the blood, but the chains. They might be steel, but Jordan looks uncomfortable. His fingers flex and I see them flex towards the lapel of his suit jacket. *Blyad*. He must be armed.

"Can I just give him a kiss goodbye?" My voice breaks, unintentionally but I'm glad it does. It fuels the authenticity of my request.

"No," Jordan says behind me. "Move on."

Erik shrugs, but I frown. "I thought *you* were leader of the *Bratva*, Erik. Or did you sell it to this lawyer? An American?" I sneer.

Erik rounds on me and when the lawyer tries to speak, Erik speaks over him. "I *am* leader of the *Bratva*, like I should have been all along."

"And I'm asking *you*," I say, "not this disgusting American."

Erik's gaze flashes to the man just behind me. His pink cheeks flare brighter pink. "Yes. Jordan can wait."

Jordan's cold eyes bore into me, and I can still feel them pressing into the back of my head as I pass Erik to reach Aiden, chained to the wall on the left. I drop to my knees in front of him and grab either sides of his face, removing the gag from between his lips. I wipe them with my thumbs, tracing every harsh line and plane of his jaw and cheek bones with my fingers and my memories. This could be the last look at him I get.

His eyes are huge. Grey and worried, like cloudy skies. Full of barely restrained violence. He is a storm. And he is mine. "I love you," I tell him in English and as I speak, I use the opportunity to push the needle under my tongue against the inside of my right cheek.

His shoulders sag just a little and he looks like I've gutted him, a punishment much worse than anything Erik could have doled out. "*Ya lyublyu tebya*," he rasps. "Why did you do this? Why did you come here?"

"To make trade. I want you to live."

Aiden sucks in air through his teeth. "You know I can't fucking live without you. I'm going to come for you…"

I silence him with a kiss, pressing my mouth against his not only because I need to taste him but because I want him to take the needle in my mouth and free himself and help me kill every last one of Erik's evil men.

My tongue maneuvers around the blunt end of the needle, lifting it from its place against my gums. The sharp end has been covered with a piece of plastic so it doesn't spear me when I rotate it around and shove it into Aiden's mouth. But the other side is still sharp enough to scratch and cut. I wonder, when I kiss him twice more, if he can taste the blood.

"I'll see you on the other side, Aiden," I whisper, and take in his scent for what I hope will not be the last time. Simple clean soap, fabric softener, metal. His warmth gets to me, like it does every time. I love him so much. I never knew how a love like this could be possible without breaking a person apart because that is just what will happen to me if he dies.

"Forget about me." I stand and move away from him. He jerks against the chains, his eyes so great and gobbling and in them I see something I have only seen a few times in our training. A trust and determination that I can do this, and that we can do this and that he will take my lead.

Erik holds the next door open and his bright red cheeks still burn. Jordan is frowning and watching me and Aiden as if he's trying to determine what just happened. Aiden doesn't answer. The needle probably prevents it. He just tightens his lips and shakes his head and that's the last thing I see of him, before I turn away.

I walk into the next room and see Gavriil bound like the rest. He shouts curses through his gag when he sees me. Erik approaches him, throwing a fist but only because Gavriil can't fight back. I wince when I hear the crack of Erik's knuckles against Gavriil's cheek. His eye is already swollen and I can tell that Erik's been beating on him for some time. He's got blood all over him and his right leg is bent at a funny angle. *Blyad.* If he can't walk…I don't know how this will work. His hands are bound in his lap and his head swivels when he looks up at me, like it's hard for him to focus.

"How long do you torture him?" I say on a weak breath.

"Torture?" Erik's voice rises. "You think this is torture? I haven't even started yet. Gavriil will suffer before this is through. He will suffer for everything he has done to me, and everything he has made me do."

"He has done nothing to you, and yet he has already suffered much for it…"

"Gavriil has always had everything I've ever wanted!"

"So that's what this is about?" I scoff, advancing while Gavriil rises up onto his one good knee. "The boy who coveted the other? This has been about Gavriil this whole time?"

Gavriil shakes his head, like he's trying to warn me, but I switch my body between his and Erik's. I won't let any more harm come to him while I'm here and my fingers flex towards the metal tucked into the seam of my jeans. Ify called it a sgian-dubh. Mer called it a shank. I wish it was a gun. It would be so easy in this moment just to bury a bullet right between Erik's too blue, too lying, too crazy eyes. Just like Aiden and Mer taught me.

Spit comes out on Erik's breath when he speaks. "You don't know shit. You've never had to sacrifice. You don't know shit about what I've done to get to where I am now. I'm the head of the damn Mafia. What are you but a spoiled little princess?"

I narrow my gaze. "*Da*, but at least I am no traitor and no coward."

Erik charges across the small room towards me and I don't back away even though that is my body's first impulse. It's second impulse is to pull out my shank, but it's too conspicuous standing here in the center of the room. I'll have to move quickly and discreetly if I want a chance to use it. I need to be on the ground. I need Erik to come at me in the one position Aiden told me never to be in with a man.

"You bitch!" Erik hovers over me, smelling like lime and sweat.

I rise to meet him and I am nearly as tall as he is so we meet eye-to-eye, our noses nearly pressed together. In Russian, I shout back, "You're just a child. A nobody. So easily overlooked in the presence of giants, like my brother and yours, that you had to kill them!"

"Shut up." Erik pulls back far enough to hit me and though I could have blocked the strike, I don't. I let it take me to the ground.

I hear a terrible ripping scream from the other room. Aiden. He's going to break both his arms if he does not wait for the right time to uncuff himself. I know he suffers thinking I am hurt so I roll onto my back and shout loud enough to be heard from the other room, "Aiden, I am alright. This man hits like small boy."

The door cracks loudly, sounding like a bolt of lightning as Jordan snaps it shut, boxing Yefim and the sounds of Aiden's seething out. Meanwhile, Erik screams and throws himself on top of me. Gavriil is fighting his manacles, but Erik is no more dangerous than that fat man in the truck, and I am not even the same princess I was then. I don't need my brother to save me.

Erik punches me in the stomach and I roll onto my side. My fingers flip open the patch of jean, ready to slide into the slit, and pull the blade free. But not yet. Soon. Seconds. I count them.

Erik shoves me onto my back and fists my hair in his hand, tilting my face back. "How would you like to die?"

"You don't have the guts," I spit in Russian again, "That's why you killed Nikoli when he was sick and Timur when he was tied. You knew you couldn't match them when they were strong because you are so pathetic and weak."

He punches me in the stomach hard enough to knock the wind out of me and I can hear thunder in the other room. "No, Aiden, not yet," I wheeze in Russian, frustrated at my lack of breath because I do not know if he can hear me. I don't need Aiden running in here when I'm exactly where I want to be and Jordan could so easily gun him down.

"Erik, this is foolishness. You will reduce her purchase price if you damage her. Fifty-five percent of all profits from the women that pass through these doors is mine. That was our arrangement for access to my distribution. Now come. Be done with this and give her to me so I can sell her."

The lawyer is speaking, but Erik does not hear him. He is white hot rage and little else as he hits me again. The pain is stifling. My head spins and it takes me too long to reorient myself. When I do, I hear feet pounding. Mr. Monroe goes to the door leading into Aiden and Clifton's room and opens it. Passing Aiden, he crosses the full length of the room to the door leading to Dixon and Knox. He opens that too.

Though I can't see past Erik's form, pulling and tearing and pinching and punching, I recognize Yefim's voice as he shouts, "The product is escaping."

The signal. Finally. Even as Erik hits me again, I am relieved and exhale contentedly.

"What?" I hear Jordan say.

"We need Erik to call all the men to Elmer *now*."

"Erik!" Jordan shouts, but Erik is gone. His full attention is on me, our hands grappling with one another. Jordan curses, then says, "You don't need Erik. The product is *mine*. Retrieve it or I'll have your fucking head."

Yefim is a stubborn brute and if it had been another man, Jordan might have gotten his way. Instead, Yefim roars back, "You are not *Russkiy mafiozi*. You do not give orders here. Erik!"

But Erik is fisting and ripping at my clothes and his eyes are frantic and his hands are around my throat and he's got tears in his eyes. He's a dead man, dying, and I need to move now if I'm going to help him along.

"Erik," I whisper. I hold him back with my left forearm pressed against his throat. With my right, I finger the opened pocket on the side of my jeans. My body is angled away from the open doorway where Jordan and Yefim stand shouting at one another. Now. Not soon, not then, but now. Now is my moment.

Erik's eyes shoot to mine and are full of bloody veins, capillaries exploding like fireworks. "It's going to be alright," I tell him, and I've never meant truer words in my life. I pull the blade free, fisting its hard edge in my palm.

"Yes, it is." He nods at me and his spit drips down onto my cheeks. "Because I'm going to kill you and your brother and then there will be no one left to take this away from me."

I release my left arm and he falls forward. His hands find my throat, but before his slick sweaty fingers can squeeze, I free my knee from under his thigh and jerk it up to meet his solar plexus in a move I know well enough to execute in sleep. He grunts and gasps and manages to sit up enough to try to swing at me with his fist, but I block the punch with my left forearm and stare directly into his unseeing eyes as I grip the blade in my right hand and stab up.

I feel everything.

The moment is suspended in time. The sensation of the blade point meeting skin and then passing straight through it when I hit him in the side, too high to meet his kidneys, too low to meet his heart. There's no guarantee the wound will kill him so I rip the knife back and as wild, feverish tremors start to rocket down my arms, I stab him again, higher in the chest.

Erik looks down and I look up. I'm panting now. Sweat covers my whole body. *Derr'mo*, I'm doing it. I'm killing him. Panic and fear and sickness swell in me but I batter them all back because Erik's hand is coming for my throat again. I let out a yelp and buck my hips. I have done this to Aiden before and now I flip mine and Erik's bodies with ease.

Straddling his waist, I lift the blade up and I bring it down again and again and again. I hit his chest so many times. Blood flows over me. Everywhere. It's hot and scalds me and all I can think about is being in that black duffel bag while Timur's blood splatters against my face like hot rain.

A gunshot from the other room claims my attention and when I turn, I can see straight down the connected rooms, clear from one end now to the other. So I see Aiden throw himself across the floor at Yefim. I don't know where the bullet went, but I can be sure that I was the one he'd been aiming for. I can hear Yefim's Russian curse seconds before it's cut short.

From where I sit, I see the shuffling of bodies. Aiden switches on top of Yefim and in one fluid motion, lifts Yefim's head from the floor and snaps his neck. He moves so effortlessly. I wish I had his calm. Because right now there's a dead body under me and I can't move my arms. I killed him.

I killed my cousin.

Erik's wild blue eyes stare up at me, but there is no more madness. Only a tragic euphoria. I wonder what he sees. If the afterlife will be good to him. His torso is so hot between my legs. It smells of sulfur and butter and I want to get off of his body, but my knees are locked and my whole body shakes with uncaged energy. This shock is not part of the plan. I need to move. I need to save them… And that is the last thought I have before Gavriil roars.

I look at him, but he's looking past me at the doorway and when I follow the line of his gaze, I see Jordan, standing in the middle of the room all the way at the end of the hall. Where I'd come upon Erik sitting in a leather armchair. Back when he'd been alive and not the corpse beneath me.

I'd forgotten all about the lawyer, standing there watching me with that bored look. Did he wait for this moment? He could have stopped me before. With a gun in his hand, trained on my face, he could have shot me while I stabbed Erik, or is he glad that Erik is gone? Did I also do him this service? I imagine, yes.

Gavriil roars again against the tie gagging him, this time a word that sounds like Aiden's name. Aiden has his hands in Yefim's hair and he looks up at the sound, but he's too far to throw himself between me and Mr. Jordan Monroe when the devil in a suit levels the gun at my chest and pulls the trigger.

Boom.

Ify

The world is pure chaos. Candy, that brilliant little b, left the way she came in harder to find than I thought it would be and I pray to all the gods of this murder town that our extra time doesn't cost Alina, the brothers, or Gavriil any more than a few seconds of discomfort. Not a life. Please dear lords above, not a life.

We circle twice, but eventually we find the opening. Just a few loose cinderblocks built into the foundation before the warehouse siding turns to metal. Kicking them in, we slip between the metal outer wall and the concrete inner wall and shimmy up, using thick gloves to scale the fiberglass insulation. Candy was right. This shiz *cuts*.

Face full of scratches, I eventually find the room that neighbored mine, making me shudder and shiver all over. Bile rises to my throat and I try not to glance at the little crack in the wall behind me where I thought I might also have been able to escape. I close my eyes, take a few bile-laced breaths, and haul into the cell that had once belonged to Candy.

The girl in here now is Chinese and speaks no English. She doesn't even scream when she sees me. She just cowers in a corner, eyes wide and desolate. I wonder if she's sedated or broken or both but I don't take the time to ask. I can pick any lock in the world with the right tools and I brought them all.

Once I get that door open, it's just a matter of sneaking through the halls and unlocking doors, one at a time.

Mer has a different tactic. She's more hammer over needles, and that attracts a lot of attention. Luckily, we aren't alone. We've got Charlie. Mer hadn't wanted to call him, but it would have been unfair not to. These are his brothers too and he's got just as much to lose as the rest of us. He'd already been on his way to the airport, so had arrived at the house in just a few minutes, burning rubber as he rocked up in a Porsche — a purple one that was wicked cool — to land himself with us in this bloodbath together.

Three guys come tearing around the far corner at the sound of Mer's hammer. Panic jacks up my heart rate and I turn and see Charlie block the hallway with his body, lift his gun and fire three times. Each shot a kill shot.

He stands there for a minute. A full sixty seconds. I keep fiddling with the door in front of me and only hear Mer speak through the sounds of that deranged marching band stomping its way through my body, that adrenaline? panic? relief? "Ever killed anybody before, bro?"

"Nah," he answers after a beat. "You?"

"Yeah. First time when I was sixteen. In the pits."

"Fuck."

"Yeah. You need to be sick?"

He doesn't answer right away, then I hear him take a ragged breath. "No. I'm good. How's that door coming?"

The sound of a hammer echoes down the hall at the same time the door in front of me swings inward. Within minutes, a horde of girls with red-rimmed eyes and a few men with shrunken faces stand with us in the halls. Charlie has to carry a woman who couldn't get up on her own. Drugs, I think, but I didn't exactly stop to take her pulse. The smell of sweat and fever fills the space as we walk like a funeral procession towards the exit.

We open every room we find. Set every prisoner free. I want them free but I also need them to be. Because they're product, they're *safe*. And as such, they're the best chance we're going to get to rattle Erik and disperse the guards and draw them away from the brothers in the other building. They're a distraction yes, but in their value, they're also a shield.

A guard streaks around the corner and I close my eyes and breathe through the bile that fills my mouth when Mer charges for the guard and takes her hammer to his skull. The man's eyes…they're stunned as the gun he carries slips from his limp fingers and Mer wrenches her gun free, bits of brain matter and chunks of bone showering one of the victims standing just behind her. The girl wilts to the ground and Mer spins just in time to catch her before she collapses entirely.

"Come on. We need to move. There are more coming," Mer says evenly and I know then for sure what I've always suspected. Mer, is a fudging savage. "Move!"

The air is dry and my sneakers make shuffling sounds against the floor. All these people have so little clothes on, so I take off my jacket and the layers I've got on under it until I'm in just a tank-top, and I'm reminded of the last time I should have but didn't give up my coat to the pro standing on Gavriil's street corner. That old Ify was a selfish b.

Now, I pass my clothes around to those need them most. Charlie lifts his eyebrows at me when he sees what I've done and after a second's delay, does the same thing.

"Alright fuckers, this is it." Mer crouches low. Charlie lowers the woman he carries and the one hanging on my arm releases a sob. I try to tell her to be quiet, but it doesn't matter. We're at least forty people now and we're not quiet. We're a band of bleeding, broken survivors and we've been heard. It was inevitable, but knowing that doesn't dull or quiet my rabid heartbeat.

Frick on a cracker. Panic ensues. Some of the people run. Some ball up their fists, like they'll try to fight even though they have no weapons. A lot of people could die now and this was my stupid plan. Why do people listen to me? Oh cheesum crepes, can we really do this?

Mer and Charlie back against each wall. "Get down, *puta!*" Mer shouts and it takes me a second to realize she's talking to me.

"Everybody down!" I say as I throw myself onto the dusty concrete.

The guards come into the hall and are too stunned to react at first. And that gives Mer and Charlie all the time they need to gun them down. Six guys fall under the fire of automatic weaponry. Three more rush around the corner. Scattered lights twinkle across the pile of bodies left in the entry. My pulse is a cannon in my wrists. My bones are brittle and hard. I haven't seen dead bodies before…not like this. Only in nightmares. Only in my books and their fade-to-black epilogues.

My hand clutches my phone. I want to call Bob, but I know the risks. He called me yesterday, I'm guessing to talk to me about Clifford, but I don't have time right now for the dead. Only the living. Gavriil. With my arms draped over my head and the head of the woman beside me, I squeeze away thoughts of him because it's too hard. I switch up my prayers, and direct them to the gods of storytelling. Please let Gavriil have a happy ending. Lord knows my books never frigging do.

"Let's move," Mer barks.

I throw myself up onto my feet even though my whole body is in free fall. I follow the sight of Mer's braids as they whip around the corner of the last hall, and I keep going through a large empty warehouse room. I imagine most of the men died back there somewhere in that labyrinth of hallways. I do worry though that Alina has jumped the gun on the plan and might have attracted the rest. I lost count of the sixty-two men Anatoly said were somewhere in Elmer today. So few, it seems, to manage so much suffering.

I close my eyes, grip the woman clinging to me and plunge ahead. We reach a door and when Charlie gives the okay, I push the woman through it and turn to help the rest of the people out. They ward away the light with their hands and some of them gulp in air. Some of them burst into tears. Some of them scream, like vampires disintegrating in sunlight.

"No. Now's not the time. This might be the only chance you get to escape," I shout, "More are coming. You have to run. Run now! Run and don't stop running."

The people that can take my advice do. Some try to help others. Most are just out for themselves. I don't blame them. I can't. I've been in one of those cells. I remember Candy and what she did to save her own life. And my whole body clenches on the inside when I see the *Bratva* men emerge from the buildings on the other side of the street and, seeing the escapees, start after them.

"Ify!" Mer screeches. I turn away from the survivors running in the opposite direction and tear after her.

Feet slapping over the pavement. Behind me I hear screams. They're safe. That's what I tell myself. They're product so they're *safe*. They have to be. Please. Otherwise, this is my fault.

Of the four buildings on the street corners of Elmer, there is one made of brick. It almost looks like a home. Like someone loved it once. Now Anatoly stands on the front stoop and even though my stomach clenches at the sight of his bruised and battered face, I follow him into the building.

He smells of a rich, distant spice and his feet almost drown out the sound of his voice as they pound on the floorboards. "Gavriil is on the second floor with the brothers and Alina. Last I checked the monitors, they were all alive. Alina handed over the lock pick to Aiden. She's in the room now with Erik and her brother. It is up to her now. All has gone according to plan." Two stairs above me now, he sees me over the top of Charlie's head and I can feel the animosity he has towards me beaming from his gaze. But I also know that he won't try to hurt me. Not again. "There's only one we didn't account for. The lawyer, a man they call Jordan Monroe."

Boom.

I hear the gunshot, and my ears — which are already half-deaf from the bullets exploding around me for so many minutes or hours or days now — cock up towards the sound. There is a pause. A moment of total silence where not even our footfalls can be heard.

Boom.

A second gunshot blasts off and the roar that follows is an inhuman sound, agony being rippled through a rib cage. Skin peeled from flesh. The taste of corrosion and rot. Sickness, burning like the blackened bottom of a kettle left on the fire. Screaming. My stomach drops out and my knees collapse in unison.

From the step below me, Mer grabs the back of my neck and hauls me upright. She says something, but I don't know what it is. All I know is that pain ricochets through me because no matter who it is, it will be a loss. One on our side because Erik wouldn't cry like that if he lost someone close to him, and there's no one on this planet that would cry like that for him.

I try to run but my legs are honey. Molasses surrounds my thumping heart. Mer surges ahead of me and I can see the stagger to her step. Charlie and Anatoly are running too. I can feel my sweat. Underneath my arms. It freezes there and makes my whole body cold, which doesn't make any sense because I'm burning up, cheeks on fire, thoughts too. We round the corner and Mer and Charlie and Anatoly disappear into the first room. I try to see past their bodies. Who's dead? Who'd they get? Who is it? And then the very small, very evil part of me hopes and prays and wishes that it isn't Gavriil — that it's anyone but Gavriil.

I glance to the left and right. Dixon. Knox. They're chained up to the bare yellow walls of this place, but I don't see any bullet holes or any substantial amounts of blood on their skin or clothes. Charlie goes to Dixon while Mer drops to her knees in front of Knox, all business as the brothers are freed. I move forward after Anatoly like I'm in a dream.

There's a body in this room, one I recognize as one of my captors from before. I never knew his name though, and now his head is twisted on his neck in a way that's grotesque and makes the acid in my stomach rebel violently.

Breathing in deeply through my mouth, I switch my gaze past the corpse, to the threshold leading into the next room. There, Anatoly stands a little apart from the group that's clustered there. I see Aiden's back. His tee shirt is shredded and there are taser burns, blood bruises, abrasions, scratches and scars covering him. But his muscles seem to be heaving, not in pain, but in desperation. When he roars again, I feel unsettled, like the floor is suddenly at a tilt. Like this isn't reality anymore, but a blood soaked video game dream.

My heart flutters fleetingly when I hear the words exchanged between Knox and Mer behind me. They're reprimanding and full of a desperate, drenched love. One that I feel coursing through my veins when I see pale arms covered in blood, Aiden on his knees while another set of pale arms kneels on the other side of the body, across from him.

Alina. And if Aiden was screaming, and it's not Alina… then who…I take another step to the side, so I can see over Aiden's body. His cheeks are gleaming, like they've been sprinkled in glitter. Almost like…like he's been crying…like those are tears…how…if he's…words leave me, thoughts too. They all flit from my mind like a bird.

"Gods…" I whisper, knowing I'm now talking to the gods of this town. This forsaken, bleeding, fighting, lying, murdering, wretched, cheating, hunting town.

I move closer. Alina wipes her cheeks. Her pale, freckled brown arms are also covered in blood to the elbows. She's shaking violently, but she's pressing down on a cloth over his stomach. His stomach. His…Aiden's. And suddenly I don't understand. How can Aiden be kneeling here crying, if he's lying dead on the ground? And then it comes…No. Not Aiden. His mirror image.

Clifton lies on the ground and my heart burns for him. I clutch my chest. But then I remember, there had been *two* shots. What if the other one got Gavriil? Where is he?

I carefully edge into the next room, imagining it painfully empty, but when I blink Gavriil appears. On his knees, his hands are bound in metal shackles and he has a gag in his mouth that prevents him from speaking, but when he looks at me, his eyes widen. He surges against the bindings and I go to him, almost tripping over the dead body that lies sprawled across the floor of this room, and throw myself at his chest with every intent of burying myself inside of him and never climbing out.

I rip the gag away from him and my lips move over his and his move over me and I comb my fingers through his fire-colored hair and I hold him against me.

"I love you, Gavriil. Thank frick you're okay. Thank you. Thank you," I whisper, though I don't know who I'm thanking.

He's speaking too, words overlapping mine like little waves. Some in Russian before he says, "Ifeoma, you are idiot. You should not be here. You do not even have gun. What are you doing here? I love you, Ify. Are you hurt?"

His arms jerk against his restraints and I switch around his body to try to undo them, but I can't. My frustration and panic leaves me with fumbling fingers and I don't have time for this. Clifton doesn't have the time...

"Charlie," I shout, but a hand comes down over mine, not quite Charlie's honey brown color, but close.

"Anatoly," Gavriil growls. His eyes narrow to slits and I remember that the marks covering Anatoly's face belong to Gavriil's fists. "You *dare* to touch her."

Anatoly's jaw clenches. He does not meet Gavriil's gaze, but quickly refocuses on the lock in my hands. "Hold steady," he says, and when I steel my arms, he doesn't hesitate. He strikes the lock with Mer's hammer and the moment it falls apart, Gavriil surges up, one leg strangely bent. It makes me panic, and then my panic shoots up into my mouth, because it looks a lot like he wants to kill Anatoly.

I grab his arm and blurt out, "He helped us, Gavriil. And there are more important things. Life is more important."

I turn to go to Clifton, but the sight of the body on the floor shocks me. Erik. I've never seen him in person, so this is quite a first impression. His eyes are huge, pupils small and constricted but surrounded by an ocean of blue and a sea of red. So many burst blood vessels, so much rage. He's got a scar on the side of his face and his mouth is open wide. There's blood all over his chest and neck and face. How many times was he stabbed? I don't know. And I'm not going to count.

I wince as I brush the dead man's boot with my knee and quickly shiver away from it. I crouch down and crawl across the floor to where Aiden and Alina are pushing on Clifton's stomach. Alina has blood on her face below her eyes, and it gets thicker and more brilliant each time she wipes the tears away. It makes it look like her eyes are bleeding and it's beautiful in its own terrifying way.

The air in the room is charged and I want to help, but I don't know what to do. Gavriil moves me out of the way so I just sit back and watch as he assesses the situation. He barks an order, "Elevate his feet. Anatoly, go get Valery. You," he points to Charlie. "The vehicle you came in. Can it transport body safely?"

Charlie nods. "Yes, but Alina's is better. She came in a van."

"*Da.* Here." She reaches a bloody hand into her back pocket and tosses Charlie the keys.

"Get it now," Gavriil orders. "Bring it out front. A knife. Who has?"

Mer is kneeling at Clifton's feet with Knox's hand in her own while he props Clifton's heavy boots up on his knees. Wordlessly, she unhooks the hunting knife that hangs on her sling. She tosses it and I clench, but Gavriil easily plucks it from where it spirals through the air, hanging suspended as if by invisible threads.

Charlie and Anatoly leave while Gavriil returns to Erik's body. Crouching down, he says something to the corpse, runs his fingers through Erik's hair, and shakes his head softly.

Then without warning, he stabs the thick blade into Erik's neck. Blood sprays, slashing across his shirt. He removes the head.

I'm going to be sick. I'm going to be sick. I'm going to be sick. Bile rushes up my throat and I have no choice but to swallow it back as Gavriil stands, holding his cousin's disembodied head by the hair.

"Alina," Gavriil says, "come."

"She's not going anywhere," Aiden growls and there's anger and wrath and rage on his tone.

Alina says something to Gavriil in Russian. He considers, then nods. His gaze turns to me then. "I will unite them now. I will take over. And under my orders, my men will save your brother." He holds out his hand. "I am king of *Bratva*. I need my queen."

Frick on a nugget. "Me?"

His mouth is a razor sharp line. He nods. "It is not the life I wanted for you, but I cannot let you go."

"I…I don't want to go." Gavriil clenches. He looks furious, and also a little destroyed. That's when I realize what I've said. What he understood from it. "I didn't mean that. I meant is that I don't want to leave you. I go where you go."

"*Koroleva*," he replies, and there is a twitch at the corner of his lips and a renewed lightness in his tone, "come with me."

"Will he be okay?" I say before taking his hand.

Alina looks up at Gavriil when he doesn't answer. She says something else in Russian. He makes a face. His eyes are kind and that kindness makes my heart hang heavier in my chest. "He is strong. But gunshot to the stomach is difficult."

"Fuck," Aiden whispers to the body beneath him. His hands are pressed viciously over Alina's and his face is blood red even beneath the blood covering him. Clifton's blood. "You fucking ass hole. Why did you do this?"

Clifton coughs and I jump. I hadn't realized he was awake. I stare down at the top of his head. Matted blonde hair splayed in every direction. His eyes are closed and he's got a gunshot wound to the stomach and his face is drained of all color so that he looks almost grey, but he still smiles. Like this is just any other day.

Clifton croaks in a voice that's near inaudible, "Bastard was about to shoot you in the heart. Couldn't let that happen...you're my brother..."

"He was going to shoot *me*, Clifton," Alina whispers.

"Like I said...he was going to shoot my brother in the heart." He smiles.

I understand and feel tears well in my eyes that mirror those streaking down Alina and Aiden's faces. The kill shot might not have been aimed for Aiden, but it might as well have been.

Aiden curses under his breath. He removes one hand from Clifton's stomach and slides the other behind Alina's head. He drags her in so that their foreheads touch and together, they sit like this in a triangle of devotion. I edge quietly away, wanting to leave them in this moment. A moment that I can only describe as true love.

I look up at Gavriil and see my dark fingers twine with his pale ones. In his other hand he holds a head. He helps me to stand, and as I rise, that's how I – a middle class, black,

adopted author with a loud mouth and a lucky streak –
become queen of the *Russkyi mafiozi*.

Six weeks later...

Aiden

The doc is looking at me like she'd rather be anywhere else. Still she's tough. That's why she's still here. We've been through four docs already and she's the first woman, but she's also the first that'll meet my eyes for more than a few minutes at a time and that won't make passes at Alina.

"I've told you before, Mr. Cleary, your brother Clifton is in capable hands, but a gunshot wound to the stomach is one of the most difficult kinds to recover from. There was damage to the peritoneal cavity, the liver, the intestines, and spleen. Because of its proximity to the spine, and the fact that these were exploding rounds, we haven't been able to remove all of the bullet fragments yet. He's had one surgery and has recovered well, but he'll need at least two more."

She holds herself straight and firm. No shifting from side to side, no tapping her pen on her clipboard. She's got it tucked under her arm with her hands at her sides and hair tied back into a series of knots and twists so that I've got no idea whatsoever how much hair she's actually got back there. She's tough. And it fucking annoys me. Intimidating doctors is the only fun I have in the hospital these days.

"He's not going home anytime soon, so you might as well go home and have a rest and come back tomorrow and the next day and all the next days for the next four months," she huffs, sounding irritated.

"We have a doctor at the house."

"Yes, and I've met her and she's highly skilled and very competent according to my colleagues at Westfield. But you don't have a full surgery, surgeons on staff, or the facilities of Heart Oak. This is a private hospital, not Westfield. Another reason why you're able to stay overnight," she says, though she doesn't sound particularly happy with that fact.

Her eyes are black like her hair and give away nothing. Any way I look at her, I want to punch her lights out. And then wrestle her into a bear hug for being as good as she's been to Clifton. She's head of surgery or trauma or whatever they call it here, but she's been overseeing every bit of Clifton's care since she came on. Since I fired the last junior doc last week. And besides, Clifton's always been a caretaker. He's not used to having people take care of him.

I sigh and rub my face. "Fine."

"Good." She nods at me curtly, then turns and heads to Clifton's room – where she'd been headed anyway before I intercepted her. Nothing I can do but follow.

She opens the door and steps inside and I'm throttled into the past for half a heartbeat. Alina's curled up on a chair next to Clifton's bed. She's got her grandfather glasses on and a blanket spread over her lap, red this time. Makes her look like some sort of fire goddess.

The sensation that I'm looking at someone who's not from this world gets stronger when she flashes me a smile, and her bright red lips part around straight, white teeth. She's so fucking beautiful. And I can't believe the most beautiful woman in the world could be happy like this to see me.

"*Privet*," she says.

"*Privet*," I answer.

"*Kak tvoi dela?*"

I lean down and kiss her. "*Khorosho. Seychas.*"

She smiles up into my mouth. "Were you bother to Dr. Chadha?"

I just grunt and kiss her again. I still can't believe I get to kiss her like this. Whenever I want. Whenever she wants. All day and all night long.

"Answer the question," Clifton grumbles from bed. I stand up and glance down at him. My brother. My twin. I remember the first time I saw his face. He'd come with Marguerite to get me from that shit hole full of rapists and killers. By then I was one of the killers and had never touched a woman I didn't pay to and he'd just looked at me like that was okay. Like I was okay. I hadn't believed him then. But now I do. And I hope he sees in my face the same thing he tried to convey to me then. Because I know he'll be okay too.

"Aiden," Clifton barks, "you have anything to say to Dr. Chadha, you say it in front of me."

I frown. He actually sounds pissed. I've done a lot of crazy, fucked up, murderous shit in my life, but nothing has ever phased my brother like talking to his doctor seems to.

"What's your fucking deal?" I snort.

Alina doesn't seem to find the tension between us as problematic as I do. She laughs, "Just say *da*, Aiden, and sit down."

"*Da*," I say. And sit down.

She leans in and kisses my cheek. As her soft skin glances mine, her lips find my ear. "He likes her. You make him nervous when you speak to her alone. You do not like when other men speak to me alone, least of all the ones that are dangerous."

"*Da*," I damn near growl. Just the thought of it makes my teeth hurt.

"You are dangerous man. So be nice." Her teeth bite down just a little on my earlobe and my dick shoots up like a goddamn rocket in my pants. I quickly grab a corner of her blanket and try to cover it. She laughs again. She knows just what she does to me. She knows she's got me completely wrapped around her soft, slender fingers. I'd do anything for her. Anything she asked at all.

"Fine," I bark, loud enough Clifton can hear it. "Sorry if I bothered you, Dr. Chadha."

She glances over her shoulder at me from Clifton's other side. She's adjusting something in his IV and he's staring at her like she's the most fascinating thing he's ever come across. His fists are clenched in a weird way and his jaw is set in an expression that reminds me too much of me for my liking. He doesn't look like a carefree kid anymore. I'd say that's what being shot does to you, but I get the feeling that the gunshot in his stomach has very little to do with this new aggression he's developed in the past few days. No, the past week. Since Dr. Chadha took over. Alina thinks he likes her? But maybe it's just the opposite. I'll talk to him when she leaves about getting a new doc.

"No apologies needed. And I've told you all many times. Please call me Jiya." The woman says, a professional smile crossing her face before fading. She quickly turns back to the IV even though I get the impression that now she's just kind of fucking around with it.

Clifton doesn't seem to care though, or mind. His fist clenches harder around the blankets as he watches her back, like he's x-raying her insides. They're plush and fluffy — the blankets, I mean, not the insides, though in my experience, I guess you could describe them as plush too. The blankets, we bought new. Alina picked them out. Some great big thread count. Six hundred bucks or some shit. I'd have paid ten times that. Because I'd do anything for this bastard. My brother. My twin.

He saved my life when he threw himself in front of that bullet. That Jordan fucker had pointed his Glock straight at Alina and my whole life flashed before my eyes. I knew what would happen next. Had already calculated it. I couldn't reach the target in time, or the bullet's projection. So I'd be left short, he'd hit Alina in the chest, she'd die in my arms, I'd shoot my brains out next and that minute or two of suffering before I did would be enough because I couldn't live through more than that and I wouldn't want to.

I reach over and grab her hand. Rub her legs through the blanket. I just need to touch her. I want her on my lap and I pull her over the arm of her chair and mine. She squeals but lets me do what I want with her and I like that. I kiss her neck. I need her and quickly excuse us. I find a supply closet in the hall – one we've used before, and that everyone knows we've used, which is why I suspect there aren't very many supplies left in it. I yank down on her leggings and find only flesh.

I grunt. My fingers slide over that perfect moon ass. "Where are your panties?"

"I was getting tired of you ripping them," she says on a laugh.

I kiss her hard and unzip my pants and slide into her. Her laughter turns to a moan. It bellows out of her mouth and I catch it with my lips. I kiss her hard and pump into her harder and my fingers rub her clit until she shakes and trembles against me. She tries to be quiet but isn't, and neither am I. I grunt as my hips piston up, meeting the soft flesh of her ass. I feel two parts barbarian, one part animal as my seed explodes into her body. I want to get her pregnant. Dixon's announcement doesn't help. Seeing Sara's belly get bigger only makes me want the same thing, but we're not ready for that yet.

Alina's still got a career. She likes modeling, but she likes her new job more. She's working with me. With us. A non-profit that's helping victims of sexual trafficking, and the survivors. Gavriil and Ify are in on it too. Trying to stop this stupid fucking practice that's somehow still cranking away even without the mafia. Seems like the *Bratva* was only a small part of it. Operating under the auspices of this Jordan fuck, who's filthy imprint our town can't seem to shake, women are still coming into the city through the ports, finding their way into the Ternary and then…disappearing.

Alina was able to use her law degree to find a way to shut down one of the port operators responsible for bringing in women last week. We think the law suit will go into effect as early as next month.

I'm so fucking proud of her. It's because of her that I started another non-profit on the side. This one, to help foster kids. Well, my brothers do most of the work to get it up off the ground, but it was my idea. I don't know what the fuck I'm doing, but I know that there's capacity and money to be able to help produce fewer kids like me. They need it, because not all of them will have an Alina to save them.

My mouth finds hers in the dark as the world settles around us. Cum drips down her legs. She curses in Russian. "I need to clean."

I smear my cum over her thighs with my hands. "I like being on you. Knowing you're covered in me."

Her breathing becomes shallow again. Her head falls back against my shoulder and I reach around her body to cup her tits. They're the perfect size and fit into my hands like they were made to fill my palms. I guess they were. She was made for me.

"We will be late for engagement party," she says as I grow hard inside of her heat and slide further into her, until I'm buried there balls deep. Where I want to be for the rest of my life. The only heaven I'll ever know or need.

"Their baby's not coming for seven months. We've got time."

She laughs. I can make her laugh. That makes me feel like I've won the game of life that I'd lost so many times, so many years ago. "But party is tonight. If we are late, Gavriil and Ify will..." She sucks in a breath when I bite her throat. "Worry..." she releases.

"What do we have to worry about? Gavriil and Ify run the streets. We're safe." And it's true. Gavriil was able to unite the factions – or he just killed the dissidents. I didn't pay fucking attention so long as it didn't get close to Alina or my brothers.

"They will be waiting for us to leave hospital. We ride with them."

I curse. "They can fucking wait." They're here visiting one of Ify's friends. A guy called Leno or Leopard or something. I guess he used to be one of Ify's informants, but I don't know the details, only that Ify and Gavriil brought him in after he OD'ed six weeks ago and they've been visiting him in the rehab facility next door ever since.

He and Ify are coming tonight to celebrate with us and the brothers. They come every week. They've got a room in the house, and I can hear Ify chatting away at lightning speed through the door every time I walk past it. Alina and I joke that we know when they're fucking, because that's the only time there's quiet from their corner of the house. We joke. I can't believe we can joke. Just like I can't believe I can make her laugh.

I can't believe I can give her pleasure.

"They will...Gavriil will..."

I spear her hair with my fingers and tilt her head back just enough so I can crush my lips to her mouth. "Shh...we don't talk about them here. There is only this. Me. You. Now."

"Aiden," she breathes. Alina's body sags onto my arm as she starts to lose herself to the pressure of my hand on her body, twisting her nipples, flicking her clit, and my dick pumping mercilessly in and out of her. And she'll never know another pleasure but the one I give her.

I feel my eyes get hot. I'm a fucking sap these days. I just don't know how I got to find a family – a twin, four brothers, a nephew and a new niece or nephew on the way, and a woman to love – this late. It was worth the wait. I don't know what I did to deserve her. I think of words like penance and reward, but I know that's bullshit. We're just two desperate people in a closet who fell in love with each other.

"*Ya lyublyu tebya,*" I whisper in the dark as I pump into her so hard, her feet jolt up off of the ground.

"Aiden," she groans. Her moans grow louder. I use my cum as lube against her clit and in a few rough strokes, bring her to orgasm. Her body collapses as I keep pumping in and out of her, and in between her whimpered gasps, she says, "*Ya lyublyu tebya,* Aiden. Forever." And that's the only answer I'll ever need.

Also by Elizabeth
Population series

An interracial, post-apocalyptic romance set in the Pacific Northwest featuring tough heroines, dark, possessive Alphas, epic battles & steamy romance...

Lawlessness, violence and desperation are all that is left of the world following the coming of the Others. Abel exists only within the boundaries that her rules allow – rules that she created to keep her alive. But when her best friend's daughter is taken by the Others, she can't keep playing by the rule book.

Instead, she must begin a life defining journey that will test her survival techniques and bring all of her instincts into question. When she finds herself allied with one of the Others, Abel must confront foreign concepts like allegiance and desire and trust as he challenges her ability to find what she has always feared: hope.

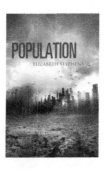 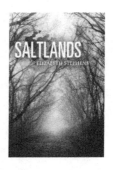

Purchase Population and Saltlands anywhere online books are sold, in Elliott Bay Bookstore or Park Postal-Leschi in Seattle.

Sign up to become an Advanced Reader for Elizabeth's upcoming novels, or read her short stories at www.booksbyelizabeth.com

Made in United States
North Haven, CT
09 July 2024

54573629R00275